TAKEOFF

EVELYN SOLA

Takeoff
Copyright © 2022 by Evelyn Sola
All rights reserved.
All rights reserved worldwide.

No part of this book may be reproduced, copied, or transmitted in any medium, whether electronic, internet, or otherwise, without the expressed permission of the author. This is a work of fiction. All characters, events, locations, and names occurring in this book are the product of the author's imagination or are the property of their respective owners and are used fictitiously. Any resemblances to actual events, locations, or persons (living or dead), are entirely coincidental and not intended by the author. All trademarks and trade names are used in a fictitious manner and are in no way endorsed by or an endorsement of their respective owners.
May contain sexual situations, violence, sensitive and offensive language, and mature topics.
Recommended for age 18 years and up.

Cover Design © Undercover Designs
Formatting: Lee Ching
Editing: Your Editing Lounge

Vickie

I am done with men.

I like my life the way it is. Calm, quiet and very private. I may be a brash New Yorker, but I keep a tight circle, and I prefer it that way.

Enter Colt Chastain, rising NBA star and magnetic single dad. He's set his sights on me and he's determined to change my mind. No way that's going to happen. Nope. Never. Did I mention he's tenacious? And hot? Very, very hot.

I told him he's the absolute last man I would ever be with. So, why does he think getting me into bed is a slam dunk?

I tried to resist. I really did. My efforts didn't work, and now I've found myself falling head over heels for him. Did I say quiet and private? I'll even accept the crazy public lifestyle.

Now, I can't picture my life without him and his adorable five-year-old son.

Colt

I live my life in the spotlight. Millions of fans, social media and press follow me everywhere. That's not my preference. That comes with the job.

On the inside, I'm a regular southern gentleman who can't fight my attraction to the tempting New Yorker who's caught my eye.

Victoria Taylor is everything I ever wanted. She's beautiful, sexy, confident and not afraid to put me in my place. She says she doesn't want me, but her eyes tell a different story. I'll stop at nothing to prove to her that we're really not that different after all.

To my readers. I couldn't do this without you.

ONE

Colt

"I HAD MY HEART IN MY THROAT THE ENTIRE FOURTH quarter. Why, I practically fainted three times." Mama, always the dramatic one. I let out a chuckle and continue listening to her voicemail. She's done this since my first year in the NBA. If she's not at the game, she'll leave voicemail messages throughout. Most of them praising me and anointing me as the best basketball player of all time, and a few criticizing my form or accusing me of hogging the ball. "But I knew. I just knew that my baby would win the game for his team. Son, I don't think I breathed for a full five minutes. When Law took the ball and scored that three-pointer, I thought that was it."

And on she goes, giving me a verbal replay of the last quarter. The one I just played. "But when he tried to fake you out, you showed him who's boss." Her enthusiasm is infectious, and I smile at myself in the mirror. Yeah, I sure did show them. I scored the last shot of the game. A three pointer that gave us the win by one. One measly point, but that's all you need to win. "Oh, your brother showed me how to use the Twitter. Make sure you follow me back. And

I can't wait to have you home this summer. Maybe you and Robin can finally connect, but if that doesn't happen, there's someone else I want to introduce you to." I end and delete the message after that. For someone who has chosen to remain single since my father died, she's doing everything she can to find me a mate. Once was enough, but I do go and follow her on Twitter.

When I step outside, the usual crowd is waiting for us. Some are family members of the team, but most are fangirls. Attractive women, dressed in their finest and hoping to go home with one of us. It's more prevalent at away games, but the single guys are never shy about finding a warm body to spend the night with, especially after a win.

"You coming, Chastey?" Wakowski, one of my younger teammates shouts from across the parking lot. He's with three women, two of them wrapped around each arm. The third is standing in front of him, trying to get his attention.

"No, you go ahead. And it's Chastain, not Chastey." Chastey Chastain is a nickname given to me by Wakowski because I don't sleep with everything female. One of the women, a pretty blonde, pouts.

"Okay, Chastey Chastain." A few of the guys guffaw at the joke, but I don't react. Truth is, I hate that name. And it's untrue.

When I first got into the league, I was with my fair share of women, until Kelsey came to New York and got pregnant with our son.

I shake my head, unwilling to let those thoughts take over. It's done. She died, and I keep her memory alive for the benefit of my son.

Who are you kidding? You do it for the benefit of everyone who thought your marriage was perfect.

I cross through the parking lot, all the while getting pats

on the back by Coach Walsh. His hands are like bricks on my shoulder. As a former professional basketball player, he stands at almost seven feet tall, but since he's been out of the league, he's been lifting weights. He doesn't look like any of the other coaches. He has long, dirty blonde hair that reaches his shoulders, and I know that underneath that custom-made suit, he's tatted all over.

"Ignore those fools and go home to your son," Coach Walsh says.

"Nice save, Chastain," someone yells just as my driver opens the door to my car. I sit back on the plush leather of my Mercedes. It's one of the few luxuries I allow myself. Expensive cars and luxurious homes for me and my son. And the best education that money can buy for Evan, so he won't have to depend on a sports scholarship like I did. When he grows up, he won't be responsible for taking care of his extended family.

It's a short ride from Madison Square Garden to my building in Central Park. I thank my driver and nod at my doorman on the way inside. He stands to the side, and I can tell he's holding his breath and waiting. I stop, chuckle, and pull the basketball out of my bag. Without asking, he hands me a sharpie. I scribble my signature and toss the ball in the air. He quickly grabs it and yells out a thank you.

My apartment is eerily quiet when I walk in. Marta, my son's nanny, turns off the telenovela when she notices me.

"Welcome home, Mr. Colt." Her Spanish accent is as thick as her waist and her glasses. "Good game tonight."

"Thanks, Marta," I say with a smile. I walk to the kitchen and grab a bottle of water while she puts on her shoes. She lives several floors down in a smaller unit I bought a few years ago.

I invest in real estate. That was the advice given to me

by a close friend. Buy during a buyer's market and hold on to it. Pass it down to your kids, but if you need to, you can always sell it. The only problem is there is never a buyer's market in Manhattan, but when your contract pays three hundred million over four years, you can afford whatever you want.

Marta lets herself out, and I peek inside Evan's bedroom. My five-year-old is in the middle of the bed in his racecar pajamas. The covers are off, and his butt is sticking up in the air like it did when he was a baby. I sit next to him and run a hand through his curly hair. That's the one thing he got from me. Other than that, he's his mother's spitting image. From his pale coloring to his dark eyes and his full lips. He stirs, and I put the blanket on him and tiptoe out of the room.

By the time I shower and eat the meal my chef prepared, I'm ready for bed and already feeling the effects of tonight's game. My legs are exhausted, and my shoulders are tight. Tomorrow's session with my personal trainer and masseuse can't come soon enough.

I step inside the master bedroom and imagine it's bigger than the small house I grew up in right outside of Birmingham, Alabama. My parents were working-class people, both working at a meat processing plant until my father died of a sudden heart attack when I was thirteen. Despite our lack of material things, we were a happy household. My older brother was a star athlete and made varsity on the basketball team when he was a sophomore. We were the type of family who ate together each night. Mama's always been a great cook. We'd go to church together on Sunday and had Bible study every Wednesday. Although we didn't have money for extras, we had everything we needed.

TAKEOFF

The night our daddy died was the beginning of the end of a lot of things, none of which I want to think of right now.

Tonight, I'll review the game and how I pulled out a win at the last second. I'll think about how a young boy from a small town has made good. I won't think about the bad side of that. I won't think about the loneliness and isolation that I've lived with for the last nine years.

No one ever thinks about that part of it. Everyone thinks fame and fortune only bring about the best. The best that money can buy. The best vacations. The best food. The best of everything, but you can't buy loyalty. You can't buy friends, and you can't pay family not to try and ruin your career before it begins. No amount of money can erase the pain caused by the ones you love the most. The ones you trusted.

"But everythin' has a season, Son." I can hear my mother's words. Her southern twang thickening with every excited breath. *"And you will know the truth, and the truth will set you free."*

Yeah, I'm free. Through no act of my own. Fate took my wife when she overdosed on heroin, setting me free from a marriage I never should have been in. Despite my issues with Kelsey, she loved our son. And she loved her daughter, too. The one she had by another man after I left Alabama.

I broke her heart when I left for college, and she tried to mend it in the arms of another. While she went and married before she turned twenty, having a child before she was barely old enough to drink, I spent my time as a single man sleeping with fangirls.

That was my only vice. I don't drink. I don't gamble. I don't even curse. The only difference between me and my teammates is that I was discreet, and they aren't. But when you have young men with more money than they can spend, they're going to indulge in a vice. Mine was sex. But that was then.

It only lasted until Kelsey broke up with her husband, and Mama told her where to find me. As discreet as I was back then, there were still rumors and innuendo. There were also a few photos, so as soon as Kelsey was free, Mama bought her a plane ticket to New York City and demanded I see her. She was familiar. I'd known her almost my entire life. She was my best friend when Daddy died, and her entire family supported us.

When she got to Manhattan, feelings resurfaced. It was like having a piece of home in New York City, which was like a different planet than my quiet, conservative hometown. Nothing was off-limits here. The city never shut down, and I had everything I could want at my fingertips. No twenty-year-old man who had hardly ever been anywhere could resist, and as much as celibacy was pushed on me growing up, I forgot all about that when I got here.

Kelsey got pregnant with Evan four months into our relationship, a long-distance one at that. We were married months later, and for a time, things were good. Until they weren't. I had no idea Kelsey had a drug problem until it was too late, but I got my son out of it, and for that, I don't regret our relationship. The reasons we shouldn't have married have nothing to do with her addiction. I just wish I knew sooner so I could have gotten her help.

Instead of sleeping like I should be, I watch the game again, taking mental notes on what I can improve on, but for now, I'll celebrate tonight's win. When I reach for the cold pillow next to me, I'm hit by a sudden bout of loneliness. The love you have for a child can do wondrous things, but it can't fill the deep void of emptiness inside. The kind that can only be fulfilled by another adult human being. The kind you can hold, kiss, and make love to on a night like tonight. The kind who would wait up for you to get home and jump in your arms when you walk through the door. The kind who will celebrate your wins and mourn your losses along with you. I never had that with Kelsey. Looking back, I was a means to an end. I was her ticket out of Alabama, and she seized it.

When Daddy died, Mama never dated when we were still living with her. She's still a beautiful woman, and back then, she got lots of offers. She still does, but she said her free time was only going to her sons, and she held firm. There was no string of men coming through our house. We continued to eat together each night, have Bible study every Wednesday, and church on Sunday. The only difference was that Daddy was no longer there. His chair sat empty at the head of the table, and Mama never disrespected his memory by offering that seat to another person.

I need to do the same for my son. He needs consistency, but more than that, he needs me. I'm reluctant to bring someone new into his life, especially after it went so horribly the one time I tried. But knowing that doesn't stop the loneliness from creeping in on me on a late night when half of my California king bed remains empty and cold.

TWO

Vickie

"Victoria, it's your mother. The one who gave birth to you. Remember her? I feel like I've been trying to get up with you for weeks. Can you please give your *mother* a call? The mother who gave you life. And you'll never guess who I bumped into the other day. Call me and I'll tell you all about it." The call ends, and I pout as I add Russian Red lipstick to my lips. Way to be subtle, Mother. Like I don't know the difference between her and my evil stepmother.

As if I need her to remind me that she's the woman who left her family, and my stepmother is the one who came in two years later and kept us all together. I know the difference. I lived it as a child, and I carry it with me every single day.

I delete her message and look at my reflection in the mirror, pleased with what I see. I add a little mascara to my smoky eye look. The rouge on my cheeks is subtle, so subtle it's barely noticeable. The brownness of my skin only enhances my red lips, making them look fuller.

My black skirt might be short, but my lacy red top is

ruched, hiding the slight bulge of my stomach. My goal, starting next week, is to get back into yoga and pull back on the carbs. But for tonight, I'll drink wine and eat whatever I want.

I pick up my phone, FaceTime my sister, and wait for her to accept my call. I laugh when I see flour on her face. She blows a breath upward, and her bangs bounce on her forehead.

"Hey. Just supervising the best sleepover in the history of the world." I hear giggles and the sounds of kids talking.

"I don't think anyone can outdo our evil stepmother when it comes to hosting the best sleepovers." I think back to my preteen years at home with my father and stepmom. She never said no to us having friends over, and she not only allowed sleepovers, but she planned them and entertained our friends. She'd help us prepare a menu, make elaborate appetizers and entrees, and let us stay up late into the night watching movies.

"Just watch me," Tara says. "And you look hot. Who's the guy?" Her boyfriend, a single father, stands behind her and waves. She turns and looks up adoringly at him. He bends down and kisses her.

"Hey! Enough of that, now." Tara looks back, not looking the least bit guilty about ignoring me to kiss her man. If I had a man as sexy as Ethan Bradford, I'd kiss him too. "I was calling to invite you two out to dinner with me and friends, but I see you have your hands full." They are both casually dressed, and my sister looks like she can use a hot shower to wash the flour away.

"No, you weren't. You're wearing your date lipstick." I stick my tongue out at her. She knows me well. The Russian Red only comes out when it's a hot date.

"You got me." When Ethan walks away, I lower my

voice and say, "Your mother has been calling me nonstop. Why?"

She shrugs. "*Our* mother," she reminds me. "She's trying to arrange a brunch or a spa date of some sort. She got me this afternoon just as I was leaving the office." I roll my eyes, but I know Mother won't stop until she gets what she wants. "She complained about not getting Alan on the phone too."

My twin brother Alan has been at a conference for the last few days. He's been too busy to take even my calls, and we always answer each other's calls. But I know when he talks to her, he'll agree to whatever she wants. Once he does, she will enlist him to convince me and Tara.

"What did you tell her?" I ask my sister.

"I told her I'd get back to her."

"I can't deal with this tonight. I need to be in midtown in an hour."

"Yeah, you look too fabulous to waste staying in." A small child calls her name, and my sister turns around. I lose her for a second, but when she returns, she's holding a little boy in her arms. Vincent, Ethan's son, waves and giggles. He's a sweet kid with spiky, dirty blonde hair and wire-rimmed glasses. Tara kisses his cheek, and he pretends to hate it, but he lets out a loud belly laugh. He wiggles, and she puts him down.

"Okay, lady. I'll let you get back to your evening. If you talk to your mother before I do, tell her I've been sick."

"Um, you know I can never keep my story straight when I lie, and don't dump her on me. She's *our* mother." We end the call, and I open my Uber app. One more dab of lipstick later, I grab my fitted black leather jacket, but just as I reach the door, my phone rings. I pull it out of my clutch. It's my mother. Having had enough of dodging her, I answer the phone.

"Mother," I say. I let out an exaggerated, rushed breath and hope she gets the hint.

"Is that my daughter? The one I carried with her twin brother? Do you know I gained over one hundred pounds with you two? After that, I said never again, but your father would have kept going if—"

One eye roll later, I decide to cut her off. "Mother, I've heard this a million times before. I'm on my way out the door. Can I call you tomorrow?" I have my hand on the doorknob, ready to walk out and get on with my night.

"I'll make it quick. Guess who I ran into?"

"No idea but hurry up and tell me before my Uber gets here." I put her on speaker and check the app. My car is still seven minutes away, but she doesn't need to know the details.

"He showed up at my job like a ghost. I almost fell over on my behind when I saw him. I thought I was seeing things." Never, ever one to get to the damn point.

"Uh-huh. Does this ghost of Christmas past have a name?" And why do I give a flying fuck is the better question, but she's going to drag this out until I end the call. "Don't you have friends to go out with tonight? You always do." I add that in for effect, but she doesn't react.

"Your ex-boyfriend, that's who. Doctor Gerald Prescott. And he's still tall, dark, and handsome." Now, that surprises me. That's the last thing I expected to hear from my mother's mouth, and it's a name I haven't thought about in a long time, but four years ago, he was a big part of my life. "Oh, Vickie, you should see him."

"Why did he come see you?" I ask her.

"Why do you think?" she whispers and giggles like an

excited schoolgirl. "Men don't get over the women in my family." I don't remind her how untrue that is. Dad got over her and moved on. She's the one who's never fully moved on from him, despite being the one who walked out of the marriage.

"Did he ask you out on a date?" I ask, pretending not to know what she means.

She lets out a long, exaggerated sigh. "Stop playing dumb. He's looking for you. Asked me for your phone number, but I told him I'd have to ask you first." I furrow my brows. What she's saying makes absolutely zero sense.

"Mother, I've had the same number since I got my first cell phone at twelve. Why would he need to track you down and ask you for it?"

"I made that same point, but he says he thought you had changed your number because he can't get in touch with you."

I let out a groan and wish I never bothered to pick up the phone. Four more minutes until my car gets here. Now that I think about it, I know why he can't get in touch with me.

"I remember now. I blocked him." It happened about a year after he left.

The relationship ended when he was accepted into a residency program, and I refused to go to Kentucky with him. I was a senior in college, and he was in his last year of medical school. He had spent a good chunk of his senior year traveling for residency interviews, and he found out he was accepted into Kentucky in the spring, the same week I was hired for my first job. After telling him I wouldn't be moving with him, he gave me an ultimatum. I called his bluff.

"Well, he's back and even more handsome than before."

"He had his one chance, Mother."

She scoffs. "He's a doctor, Vickie. And you both were so young. Maybe the separation was a good thing. You two are older and wiser now. So, where are you going tonight?"

Relieved by the change of subject, I give her the name of the midtown restaurant quickly followed by, "My car's pulling up. I'll call you later." Anxious to get off the phone, I tell her goodnight.

~

THE ICE CUBE IN HIS RED WINE SHOULD HAVE BEEN MY first clue, but like the lady that I am, I smile and pick up my own glass. It's a noisy Friday night at The Smith, a midtown restaurant.

My date, Draymond, a man who looks ten years older and fifty pounds heavier than his online dating profile picture, adjusts himself in the seat for the fiftieth time. He clears his throat, looks at my breasts, and licks his lips.

"You're a very attractive girl, Victoria." I cringe, but I force a smile if only to hear what he has to say next. I've always had strong intuition, and I have the feeling that there's a but coming. "But do you need all that makeup?" I don't answer. I stare and raise both eyebrows and wait. "Pretty girls don't need all that stuff." He waves his hand around as if that would erase all the 'stuff' he disapproves of.

"Woman."

"What?" He sips the wine, makes a face, and puts it down. He looks around the place, and I tell myself that if he asks for more ice, I will walk out of here right now.

"You called me a girl twice. I'm a woman. Haven't been a girl in a long time." His eyes return to my breasts, and he bites his bottom lip.

"Woman indeed." He says it so low that I barely hear it. He licks his lips and I resist the urge to gag. I pick up my wineglass and finish my drink before looking around the restaurant, packed with people having fun on a Friday night. I sigh in defeat. That won't be me tonight. At least not with this guy. "You know you don't have to do all of this for me." He gestures toward me.

"What do you mean by all of this?" I already know based on what he just said about my makeup, but I want to hear it from him.

"The makeup. The nail polish and the too tight shirt. I like my women simpler, more natural. There's a passage in Proverbs that says, 'Charm is deceitful, and beauty is vain, but a woman who fears the Lord is to be praised.'"

That was way more than I was expecting, but it always amazes me when scripture is quoted to control women. I flag the waiter and request another glass of wine. I'd take something stronger, but I need a clear head.

"But what if I like the makeup, nail polish, and too tight top? What if this," I gesture to myself the same way he just did a few minutes ago, "is about me and not anyone else?" Least of all you, you classless idiot. I bite my tongue. Unnecessary meanness is not one of my traits.

He leans back in his chair and one of the buttons on his shirt pops. I want to point out that I'm not the one in the tight shirt, but my wine arrives, and I focus on that. He sighs dramatically.

"Don't do that. Don't be one of those. You *women*," he emphasizes the word, probably because I just called him out on it, "you do all of this to get a man's attention and nobody can convince me otherwise. But that's okay, Victoria Taylor. You have my full attention." He pulls his body closer to the table. "And I do like what I see." He raises himself and tries to look down my shirt. Idiot. It's sexy, but it has a high neck and there's nothing to look down.

The waiter returns, and I order a bone-in ribeye and a side of potatoes. I'll pay for this in the morning when I meet my personal trainer for the first time in six months, but for tonight, I'll indulge, already thinking of the dessert I'm going to get to go. A nice slice of lemon cake with extra whipped cream.

"You know, if you're getting steak, you're going to have to put out." He masks the statement with a loud laugh, but I know he's serious.

"That's only for people who can't afford to pay their own way, Draymond." I give him my best fake smile, which he doesn't return. His eyes harden. "I don't have that problem." To prove my point, I call the waiter back and ask for separate checks.

"I was only joking," he says after the waiter walks away.

"I'm not."

"I see you're one of those." He sighs, almost as if he's disappointed in me.

"One of what?"

"Those independent types, but all you women do is use your pussy to try and manipulate and control." I lean against the table and look him in the eyes.

"I didn't realize my pussy was ever an option. Thanks for letting me know."

He picks up his wine and swirls it around, but he doesn't drink it.

"Not a fan of wine?" I ask, wanting to change the topic.

"No. And I don't like a woman who drinks. I can't stand to look at it." He glances at my glass and frowns. I put it to my mouth, tilt my head back, and down the remainder in one gulp. I dab the side of my mouth with my napkin.

"All done. You won't have to look at it anymore. Better?"

"This isn't working out."

"No, I don't suppose it is," I admit. I shake my head sadly, doing my best to act disappointed.

"Why did you bother if you weren't going to try?"

"Why did you? What part of me made you think it was okay to talk down to me? Or comment on how I look, and how I should change it. You quoted scripture as if that would move me."

"I'm out of here." He grabs his wallet and pulls out a wad of cash. "I'm sick of you New York bitches." He stands, and so do I. I call the waiter and tell him to pack my food to go and to bring it to me at the bar.

"You don't walk out on me, Draymond. You stand there and watch as I walk away from *you*." His nostrils flare as I point at his chest. I grab my clutch from the table and walk to the bar. I order a water and wait for my food.

A few minutes later, my water glass is empty, but my food still hasn't arrived. Someone takes the stool next to me at the bar, and I smell familiar cologne. I tap my fingernails on the counter, no longer in the mood to be around people. I have visions of eating in bed in nothing but a t-shirt while I catch up on brainless television. Maybe I'll get a heads up and start grading the essays from my freshmen.

"Victoria Taylor. Is that you?" I freeze at the sound of the voice. It can't be, but it dawns on me why my mother was so interested in where I was going tonight. I walked right into her trap. I should have known, but I hadn't thought of Jerry in so long, I was thrown off balance. Mother liked Jerry a lot back then. She was over the moon that I was dating a future doctor.

"Jerry." I look at his face. He looks the same. Clear brown skin with full lips. He looks like he just got a fresh haircut today because his lining is perfect. He's in a button-down shirt and jacket with jeans. Nothing about him has changed. "What a coincidence." I try to keep the sarcasm out of my voice.

He smiles. "Alone tonight?" He looks around as if he's expecting someone to appear out of nowhere. I didn't tell Mother I had a date, but I wonder if Jerry would still be here if I had.

"Just waiting for my dinner." I turn my body, giving him some of my back, hoping he'll take the hint and walk away just like he did before, but if he's seeking me out, he's not about to leave.

"You look good." I can feel his eyes on me.

From the corner of my eye, I see him staring at my bare legs. He was always a sucker for my legs.

"Thank you." I swing my legs underneath my chair and put my clutch on my lap to shield his view. While I'm at it, I consider all the ways I'm going to kill my mother when I get my hands on her. I'm angrier at myself for falling into her trap so easily.

"You always liked this place. This is where you introduced me to your mom."

"My memory works fine, Jerry." In truth, I had forgotten about that little detail, but knowing him, he's giving it more significance than he should.

"I've been trying to call you." I take a deep breath and turn to face him.

"For what possible reason?" I turn away, dismissing him before he can utter another word.

"I'm back in New York. Been back only a few weeks, and this city has always reminded me of you. I walked in here, and here you are. Must be fate." Yeah, because my mother set me up.

Thankfully a server comes to the counter and puts a large brown paper bag in front of me. She puts the check down, and Jerry grabs it before I can reach for my wallet. I take it from him and hand it back along with my credit card.

"I know you've seen my mother. Stop pretending this is a coincidence, fate, or whatever bullshit you want to call it."

"Let's have dinner together." He leans close, invading me with the scent of his familiar cologne.

I stand from my chair and take my bag. "I don't understand why you're here, and why you've been trying to call me." He stands too, towering over me. Mother was right, and I was wrong. He's changed quite a bit. He's filled out since the last I saw him. His shoulders are broader than I remember, but his smile is the same. It's the same one I went crazy for, but that was a long time ago. "Where is your fiancée?" I do my best to keep the sneer out of my voice.

He looks surprised by my question, and for a brief moment, he seems embarrassed.

"Yes, Jerry. I received the engagement announcement you so graciously sent me. Remember that?" It was a year to the date of our breakup. "The one with the picture of where you proposed." He clears his throat, and I can practically see the color rising from his neck to his face.

Jerry took her back to our old school, Duke University, and got on one knee right there in the Duke Gardens. The same place where he first told me he loved me. I always wondered if that was intentional. Did he do that because he planned on sending me his engagement announcement? Part of me still believes that.

"It didn't work out." I look at him up and down, offering no comment on his failed engagement. Unlike when I received the announcement, I feel nothing now. Not a twinge of jealousy, anger, or regret. "A lot has happened since I was last in New York. Let's have dinner together and catch up."

"I don't think so. We said all we had to say."

"I got one chance. That's what you told me when we got together."

"Right. That was before you called me a bitch and an ice queen because I didn't respond the way you wanted to your ultimatum to upend my life and move to Kentucky." He closes his eyes, but when he opens them, I see a flash of anger. It passes quickly. Jerry never liked to be challenged or questioned.

"We were young and foolish, V. We both said a lot of things we shouldn't have, but I've never stopped thinking about you." He runs his knuckles along my cheek, and I step back. "You can be an ice queen as long as I'm the one who makes you melt."

I push his hand off my face, put on my jacket, and walk away, hoping he doesn't follow me. Once I get outside, I open the Uber app and request a car. Unfortunately, luck isn't on my side tonight. Jerry follows me outside.

"Look, Vickie—"

"Stop. I'm not interested in going backwards. What did you add in the engagement announcement you sent? I think it was something along the lines of 'it's nice to be with someone who's not made of ice.'"

"That's not what I said, and you know it. We both said a lot of things back then. And I already told you that Janelle and I broke up."

My car pulls up, and I approach. "Have a good life, Jerry. You had your one chance."

He walks with me and holds the door open. "Call me." He hands me a business card. "My new number is on the back."

I don't respond. When he lets go of the door, I close it and look straight ahead. This is it. I'm giving up dating for the indefinite future.

∼

Darkness stretches out in my apartment like a blanket. I turn on the light, leave my heels by the door and walk to my kitchen. The quiet is interrupted by my loud hiccup. I grab a bottle of water from the fridge and do my best to erase the taste of the wine and that uncomfortable scene with Jerry. I place my food on the table and walk to my bedroom to change. I emerge from my room in a yellow, faded t-shirt. My stomach growls, begging for food. And because this isn't how I planned the evening, I still want to make it special. So, I light a candle, put my food on my deceased grandmother's fine China, place it on a tray, take it to my room, and devour my juicy bone-in ribeye. It's a couple of hours later that I eat the decadent lemon cake and lie back on the bed with a full belly. It's barely eleven o'clock on a Friday night, and I'm lonely in a cold bed.

My plan was to have a sexual walkabout this year. Just sex. No strings and no relationships, but I've learned there are always strings. And as much as I want to deny it to myself, I need a little bit more than just dinner and a drink before taking my clothes off for a man. I need a connection, and I haven't felt a spark with anyone in a long time.

I didn't feel anything for Jerry tonight. He's the first man I ever loved, and it took me a long time to get over him. I had started moving forward when I received his engagement announcement. It's as if he could sense I was getting over him and sent that announcement to fuck with me. His intentions were to hurt me, and he did, though he'll never know it. I set the engagement announcement on fire and never looked back.

My phone vibrates on the bed next to me, and I pick it up, expecting my brother or sister, only to be disappointed when I see an unknown number. Assuming it's spam, I let the phone go to voicemail, and a few seconds later, I'm alerted that I have a new message.

"V, it's Jerry. Despite how things ended between us, it was nice seeing you tonight. This is my new number. I'd love to take you out to dinner sometime and catch up. A lot has happened since I've been away, and I want to tell you all about it." He lets out a deep breath before he continues. "Sending you that engagement announcement was one of the stupidest things I've ever done. It's proof that I never got over you and that my engagement was doomed. Call me."

I won't, but I don't delete the message. Jerry was a lifetime ago. Back when I was young, but not dumb enough to give up what I wanted to follow a man to a place I didn't want to go to. My entire life is here, and I was not willing to give it up. At least not for Jerry.

THREE

Vickie

Six hours after my mother leaves a voicemail, I decide to listen to it. Whatever she wants, there's nothing I can do about it now, but I'm sure her phone calls are for fishing purposes. I never called to give her a piece of my mind about Jerry. She's probably been waiting to hear from me for the past seven days. Jerry's not worth the effort, and mother doesn't deserve to know the details after that stunt. Knowing Mother, it might have nothing to do with Jerry. You never know with her. It could be an impromptu invitation to do something in the city. That's how it always is. At best, she'll give me a couple of hours' heads up, at worst, she'll be outside my apartment asking to be let in.

For a busy Friday night, the bathroom at the 40/40 club is surprisingly quiet and empty. Just what I need as I slip into the last stall in the spacious bathroom and press the speaker button on my phone to listen to the voicemail.

"Hey, French fry." I cringe at the nickname. She has one for each of us, all based on the foods we loved most when we were kids. "I was hoping we could have dinner tonight. I can cook or we can go out. I talked to your sister earlier, but she has plans with Ethan. I'm going to book the three of us a spa day soon, four if I can convince your brother to come down for a weekend. I miss you guys. And I want to hear all about your night out last week. That quick conversation wasn't enough. Call me back. Love you."

I hit delete and only feel a twinge of guilt at not listening to it earlier.

Even though I didn't use the toilet, I flush before I walk out. As I'm at the sink washing my hands, Tamron, my good friend and fellow teacher stumbles inside.

"There you are. There are NBA stars here tonight." She raises both hands up, swings her hips then sticks her butt out and twerks.

"Hard pass, but you go ahead." I add lipstick and dab the corners of my eyes with concealer. "I do not see the appeal of athletes at all." I make a face like I taste something sour.

"Good. More for me to choose from. Stay away. You're looking too fine tonight for your own good." She approaches the sink and runs her fingers through her hair. I try not to roll my eyes. My dad would be over the moon if he were here, but I'm certain he's at home on this Friday night with my evil stepmother, living their best lives.

Dad got the best deal after he and my mother divorced. Well, after she left him and us.

"Why the hell are you staring off into space?" Tamron waves a hand in front of my face and snaps her fingers. "How do I look?" She spins around in her tight black faux leather pants and sparkly crop top.

"Fabulous."

"I'm going to see if I can get one of them to buy me a drink." She puts on burgundy lipstick and wiggles her brows at me through the mirror. "And then who knows what else?" She does a little shimmy with her shoulders.

"If a drink is all you want, I can buy it for you. No need to stroke some athlete's ego for an overpriced, watered-down cocktail."

Unlike me who grew up with a successful businessman father in a big house and attended nothing but elite private schools, Tamron grew up in a two-bedroom apartment in Queens with five younger siblings. She still helps them out financially, and she counts every penny she spends.

"I'll take you up on that later if I fail, and girl, I don't plan to fail tonight." She fluffs her curly hair and gestures for me to follow her. There are a group of women circling a crowd of tall men when we step out of the bathroom.

"Come with me," Tamron begs, but I shake my head and point in the opposite direction.

"I'm going to get two drinks. Come and find me and bring the rest of our friends with you." I walk away, disgusted at the site of women willing to embarrass themselves to get the attention of a man just because he's an athlete.

I don't get very far before I spot my sister and her boyfriend. Tara drops his hand when she sees me, and the two of us run to each other like we've been apart for years. You can tell we're related, but she looks more like our dad whereas I take after my mom. And even though Alan is my twin, he looks more like Tara. She's two years older than us, putting her at eleven when our mother left. The three Taylor siblings were always close. So close I don't think we've ever had a serious argument, but our mother leaving drove us closer together. We formed a bond that nobody can break.

After hugging her, I hug Ethan.

There are rules my sister and I have when it comes to dating, and she's broken every single one of them to be with Ethan Bradford. Rule one is that we don't date men with kids, and Ethan is a single father with a bitch of an ex-wife. Rule two is my rule, but celebrities and athletes are out. I don't need to be in a relationship with a man *and* his ego.

Ethan might not be a celebrity or athlete but being the CEO of the world's largest discount chain makes him famous. He bought out my father's business, which was not the least bit welcome by my sister who worked for our father at the time. Regardless, I liked him for her the minute my eyes landed on him. He was so different from the type of guys she's always dated, it was comical.

"Look at New York's power couple." I stand between them and twine my arms through theirs. "Ethan, your girlfriend's sister needs a drink."

Ethan talks to a bouncer, and he opens a VIP section for us. Once we're seated, he kisses my sister and walks to the bar.

"How the hell did you get VIP access? I called you to meet me here less than an hour ago." Tara looks at me, shrugs, and we both burst into laughter. "I get it. That's what happens when your man's a billionaire. You get all the good stuff."

"I'll try to remember you and my humble beginnings, dear sister."

A bartender approaches with two bottles of Cristal.

"Despite all the NBA players in here, your man's the real MVP." We clink our glasses, and I down mine. Before I can bother to put my glass down, our personal waiter refills it. "I love it here. If it's not VIP, it's not for me. That kind of rhymes. Should I put it on a t-shirt?"

My sister laughs at my antics, and I look for Tamron so

she can join us, but I can't see her through the thick crowd hanging by the athletes. I look around the room, and the friends I came with are all congregating near the NBA players, taking selfies.

"I can't stand women who throw themselves at athletes," I whisper to my sister. We clink our glasses again in agreement. "It's like you're dating two people. The guy and the giant chip on his shoulder. Oh, and let's not forget the fangirls. Those guys can't keep it in their pants for nothing."

"Well, let's not generalize. Don't lump them together like that. A lot of them are family men." While our server pours us another drink, another brings out platters of food. My eyes light up and my stomach growls at the platter of mini tacos placed in front of us. "You'll never believe who Ethan is good friends with." I stuff my mouth with a taco. I'm sure Ethan knows a lot of high-profile people.

"Oh my God, does Ethan treat you like this all the time?" I point to the food and the drinks. I already know the answer to that. He adores her, and she deserves it. "Of course, he does," I mutter. "As he should, or else. And why aren't you eating?"

"We just ate a huge meal. I'm stuffed and still buzzed from the wine. We had a different one with each course." But that doesn't stop Tara from finishing her drink.

"I can't believe I haven't told you about last Friday. You won't believe what Mother did and who I ran into." I put the word ran in air quotes before stuffing another taco in my mouth. "Damn, it's loud in here," I yell with my mouth still partially full.

"Oh, sounds juicy. Let me tell you this first. Like I was saying, since you watch basketball with Dad—" I tolerate basketball with our dad. I sit with him and look at my phone or grade papers while he watches. I do it because our evil stepmother refuses. And as many times as he's tried to teach me the basics, I have no idea what the rules of the game are. Most importantly, I do not care.

Ethan returns, and Tara stops speaking. He's not alone this time. Next to him is the tallest man I think I've ever seen. He must be close to seven feet tall. With my mouth full of taco, I crane my neck and stare into his face. After leaning down and kissing Tara's cheek, he looks down at me. He has dark brown eyes and a mop of dark, curly hair on his head. His eyes are framed with thick eyelashes, and his eyebrows are kind of bushy, but they make him approachable. Otherwise, he would be too perfect. Too handsome. His face has about a day's worth of stubble on it, and I didn't realize I like that look until just now.

He looks familiar, and as soon as I hear a group of women calling his name and snapping pictures, it clicks, and whatever interest I had in him vanishes. He stands tall, waves, and smiles at the fangirls. I don't think I've ever been this turned off in my life. As handsome as he is, I remind myself that I'm all about black love. I turn back to the tacos and shove another one in my mouth.

Tara jumps up and hugs him. Ethan playfully pulls her away and stands between them. The guy pretends to go around Ethan to hug Tara again, but Ethan blocks him. I wash down the taco and look around for Tamron so she can join us. Maybe this guy will enjoy getting his ego stroked by someone who actually gives a shit about athletes.

"Vickie," Ethan says, "this is my friend and neighbor, Colt." Colt's height isn't the most disarming thing about him. His smile is, and if I wasn't sitting, I would have fallen on my ass at the sight. His full pink lips hide perfect straight teeth, and the single dimple he has in his right cheek should be illegal. "Colt, this is Tara's sister, Vickie Taylor."

His eyes roam my body, paying special attention to my breasts in the tight corset top, which pushes them together, making them appear bigger than they are. The joke's on him. He doesn't stop at my breasts. His eyes travel south, slowly roaming my bare legs. I almost have the urge to pull down my skirt, but I don't bother. He's free to look, but he'd better not touch.

He extends a hand, and to show him I'm not affected by his face or his celebrity, I take it. I do my best to appear unfazed, but it's like a bolt of electricity has gone through me, and I'm grateful for the loud music that drowns the gasp of surprise that leaves my mouth. I try to pull my hand away from his, but he has other ideas. He lifts it and puts his full, soft lips on the back of my hand. Another gasp, and I feel my face flush, something that hasn't happened to me in years. When he loosens his grip, I pull my hand away and discreetly wipe his kiss on my skirt as if that would undo the jolt of lightning that's still surging through my body.

Needing to gain control of myself and the situation, I feign ignorance and say, "You look familiar. Do I know you? Are you an actor?"

His eyes light up at my question. He smiles deep enough for that dimple to make another appearance, and I eye his stubble up close. It's the kind that you want to run your tongue through.

"Forward for the Manhattan Mischiefs, Victoria. It's a pleasure to meet you." I almost combust at his words. His voice wasn't what I expected. I knew it would be deep, but I was not prepared for the baritone. I stand abruptly and move to the edge of the VIP section to look across the room for Tamron. I get no reprieve. He follows and stands next to me, invading my senses with the scent of his cologne.

"A forward for the Manhattan Mischiefs? What's that? Sounds like a lookout for a gang." His eyes light up with humor and the corners of his lips curl into a smile. "Are you in the mob or something?" He doesn't answer me right away. He signals for the server and orders a water with lime.

"Is that your subtle way of letting me know you don't watch basketball?"

"Basketball? Is that what you do?" I make a show of looking around the crowded club. There's a line of women and men looking and pointing at him. Two burly guys stand in their way. "You're in the wrong section." I point to the group of women trying to get noticed by him. "I think they're trying to get your attention."

"Vickie, Colt's son is Vincent's BFF," Tara says as she approaches. Vincent is Ethan's four-year-old son. My sister went from single to living with a single father and assuming the role of stepmom within months.

I look at her, and I purse my lips in disapproval. She smirks and I smirk back. Message received. I do a small eye roll, determined now more than ever to get away from this guy. Athlete and single father. No and no. Stick a fork in it, it's done. Tara shrugs. Traitor.

"What's this now?" Colt asks.

"What's what?" I ask him.

"That look between the two of you. It's like you were having a conversation with just your eyes. Like you can read each other's minds."

"We can," Tara tells him. "It's our superpower."

"And that look was about me, wasn't it?" Colt's deep baritone gets closer. He's standing so close, his body is practically touching mine.

"I bet according to you, everything is about you," I tell him. Tara giggles and promptly covers her mouth with her hands. Ethan leans down and whispers something in her ear. She nods at whatever he says, and they both look up and laugh.

"Why am I not surprised?" Ethan asks. "Let's go dance and leave these two alone." He puts his hand on the small of her back, leaving me alone with Colt.

"So," he says close to my ear. I pull out my phone to text Tamron to join me in the VIP. "Is that it? I'm dismissed?" I look up at him, raise an eyebrow and look back down at my phone.

"What on earth are you talking about?" I know exactly what he's talking about, but I refuse to admit it. I keep staring at my phone hoping he'll take the hint and leave. He doesn't.

"You learned something about me that made you dismiss me."

"Dismiss you as what, Cole?" I open my email and go through it. Mostly junk.

"Colt, darlin'." I pretend I don't hear him and continue to stare at my phone. He puts a huge palm over my screen. "Colt, darlin'," he repeats with more force.

"It's Victoria, never darling," I correct him. I move the phone, turn, and give him my back. He moves and stands next to me.

"Thank goodness I said darlin', not darling. So, what is it about me that turned you off?"

"I was never in danger of being turned on." I look at him up and down. He's well dressed in gray pants and a light blue shirt. His hair's a little long, but the curls make him look youthful. Yeah, this guy turns me on, but he'll never know it. If I was into white guys, he'd be my type. Tamron finally answers my text and tells me she's on her way. He inches closer, and I take a step away.

"Let's see what it could be." He purses his lips and pretends to be deep in thought. "Me bein' a basketball player was strike one. That was obvious from the way you pretended not to know who I am." I arch an eyebrow at his smug arrogance.

"As if I'm supposed to know who you are?"

"Everyone in this city knows who I am. I've brought you four championships."

"You alone? I might not understand the rules of the game, but I'm pretty sure it's a team effort. I guess it's good to know you take *all* the credit." I turn from him and head in the opposite direction. I don't make it two steps before he's standing in front of me, blocking my path.

"Don't try and distract me. Let's see. Where was I? I was still in the game despite bein' an athlete, but then your sister let it drop that I have a son. When you learned that you rolled your eyes, and I was out. Am I on the right track?"

"Not even close." Astute bastard. "Nothing about that exchange with my sister was about you. Check your enormous ego."

"I think someone is lyin'."

"What possible reason would I have to lie to you?" I let out an undignified snort. He takes a small step closer, and I'm forced to look up at him.

"You want to prove you're not interested." He leans down close to my ear, and I want to take a step back, but I won't give him the satisfaction of knowing how much he's affecting me. "That temptin' mouth of yours says one thing, but your body tells me something else." He stands straight and steps away, and I do my best to control my rapid breathing. Just the feel of his breath along the shell of my ear has sent my entire body on fire.

"Except I have nothing to prove, especially not to someone I've known for five minutes." I look around for my sister only to find her in the corner dancing with Ethan. "Enjoy your evening, Cole."

I take a step, but he stands in front of me, once again blocking my path. I arch an eyebrow and wait for him to move. Only he doesn't. All he does is smile that devilishly sexy smile.

"It's Colt, darlin', but you already knew that too. Everyone knows it."

"I told you, it's Victoria, not darlin'. And is that a southern twang I hear?"

He steps closer, crowding me a bit, but I refuse to step back.

"Alabama boy, born and bred. A true southern gentleman."

I cock my head to the side. "Alabama? You don't say." That's a definite hell no.

"Is that strike three? Do you have problems with Alabama boys too?"

"Not yet." If someone had dumped a bucket of ice water on me, it couldn't have done a better job of turning me off than this little revelation. I probably would have learned this if I paid any attention to those stupid basketball games I torture myself with just to spend time with my father.

"Good. In that case, do you want to dance? My daddy used to tell me to always ask a pretty lady to dance." He smiles, making him look playful and boyish. For a second, I imagine dragging him to a far corner of the club for a slow dance, but I think better of it. He's a friend of my sister's man, and I don't think Ethan is going anywhere anytime soon, if ever. He's an athlete and judging from the people taking pictures and videos of this interaction, he's a popular one. I like my quiet life, and I remind myself, when I'm ready for a relationship, I'm all about the black love.

"No, I don't." I try to step around him, but he continues to block me. "There are lots of pretty ladies for you to dance with."

"How about another drink?" he asks, ignoring my comment about finding someone else.

"I've had my fill, but I'm sure anyone of them would love to join you. Maybe you can order yourself another water with lime." I point to a group of ogling women a few feet away before giving the water in his hand the side eye.

"I'm not a drinker. Never have been." He looks down at me, particularly at my breasts, and licks those full lips of his. He inches closer, and I have no choice but to take a step back. Only, it's not just a step; it's a jump, and I resent the smug smile he gives me. "And I don't want any of them," he whispers before feasting his eyes on my cleavage. He inches closer. "I only want you, despite how judgmental you are."

"We always want what we can't have, don't we? I wonder why humans are wired that way. Huh? I guess we'll never know." I shrug and give him my back as I walk away.

He surprises me when he throws a casual arm around me. "Let's discuss. Though, that's not really a difficult question, darlin'," he exaggerates the word, "but I'll go with the most obvious answer. It's to fulfill a fantasy. Do you have any fantasies I can help you fulfill?" His accent gets thicker with each word. It's almost musical.

I stop walking and he stops too. I crane my neck to look up at him, and even in my five-inch heels, I feel like an ant next to him.

"Those are two separate questions, Cole. Let me break them down for you."

His eyes light up and he says, "Please do."

"Do I have any fantasies? Yes, lots. Can you help me fulfill any of them?" I look up at him and get on my tippy toes, cursing at the fact that he's so damn tall. I lower my voice and whisper, "Not a single one." I tap his shoulder and resume my walking, but he walks along with me. Not close enough to touch, but close enough for me to feel the heat emanating from his body.

"Vick, how the hell did you get in here?" I nod to the server to let Tamron in. Her mouth opens and her jaw almost hits the floor when she sees Colt. "Holy shit. Is that Colt Chastain?"

"It is. Cole, this is Tamron, and she's a huge fan. Tamron, do you want to dance with him?" Tamron doesn't utter a single word. She stands and stares at him with her mouth wide open. I take a step closer to him, making sure that our bodies don't touch. "Be a gentleman, Cole. Don't leave a pretty lady hangin', darlin'." I exaggerate a southern accent to get my point across and walk away, but I feel his eyes on me. As much as I pretend not to notice, I do. And as much as I don't want to be affected, I am.

FOUR

Colt

After introducing Tamron to my teammate Jarvis Jones, I escape. If fangirl had a face, it would be Tamron. I know her type. She wants to be with a professional athlete, and it doesn't matter which one. She was as happy to be on Jarvis's arm as she was when she wrapped herself around mine. I didn't want to be out tonight. I had to be dragged out by my teammates, and since my son is with his grandma, I had no excuse. Now, I'm glad I did. I never look to meet women at clubs, but tonight is a pleasant surprise.

Vickie was the first thing I noticed when I got here. All I saw was a nice ass and an incredible pair of legs. I recognized those legs the instant I walked into the VIP section. She was sitting on the chair like she was a queen on her throne. She has an air about her, as if she's above everything. I imagine those bare legs on my shoulders while I have my head between her legs, but it was her face that almost made me fall over.

Beautiful, smooth brown skin. She has high cheekbones and lips so full I know I can spend days kissing her. She has a cute little nose and big eyes, surrounded by thick and long eyelashes.

I look around the club and find Ethan dancing closely with Tara in the corner. When he finally looks up and catches my eye, I tilt my head and gesture for him to join me. He leaves Tara, and she runs to the ladies' room with Vickie, who makes a point not to look in my direction. I can't help but admire the way her tight skirt hugs her ass. That perfect, round ass. She's not a big woman, only a little taller than her sister, but her body is tight and lean, yet also soft and pliant. And those legs. I'm counting the days until I can run my hands freely over those legs.

I stare at her ass until she turns a corner and out of my sight. Jesus, the things I can do to that ass. Ethan's sharp elbow jab in the ribs brings me back to reality. I ignore his smirk and gesture for him to follow me back to the bar. I'm almost tempted to order a drink, but I get another water instead.

"How did you get a woman like Tara?" I ask him. "You lucky son of a buck."

The one attempt at a relationship I had after my wife died traumatized my son and left me jaded. That's one of the things Ethan and I bonded over. Both of us single fathers trying to raise our boys without their mothers and wading through a pool of women to find one who accepts that we're a package deal.

"What the hell is that supposed to mean?" He takes his drink from the bartender and downs it.

"I remember the last time you had a date," I remind him.

"Oh, shut up." He visibly cringes at the memory. "I don't consider that a date. And you better not say anything about that to Tara."

I let out a loud bark of laughter. "Relax. That was way before she came into your life. And what about that strawberry blonde I saw you eating with all those months ago?" I laugh at the angry glare he gives me.

"Obviously, I'm not into strawberry blondes. And it was business, and that was enough."

"Exactly my point. You were more anti-dating than me."

"Well, things changed when I met Tara."

I look around the club, and when I don't see Vickie, I lean closer to Ethan and say, "What's the deal with her sister?"

"Tough nut to crack, but nice. Loyal to a fault. All the Taylors are loyal like that."

"Put in a good word for me." He raises an eyebrow at me. "What?"

"All you have to do is step outside and women throw their panties at you. You don't need me to say anything for you." I down my water and request another.

"Usually, but she's different. I don't think she cares about me being an athlete. In fact, I think it annoys her."

"That sounds like Vickie."

"Is she with someone?"

"Don't think so, but even if she is, she doesn't strike me as the type who would invite him over for Sunday dinner."

"Ah," I say, raising an eyebrow. "The type to make you work for it. I should have known she doesn't have a man. He'd be crazy to let her out looking like that by herself." Ethan puts down his drink, sighs and shakes his head. "Did you see her legs? Jesus."

"Word of advice. Nobody *lets* the Taylor women do anything. Remember that. That southern gentleman thing that you do won't work on her."

I throw my head back and laugh. "You New Yorkers," I say with my best southern drawl. "I do declare, this is no act. You Yankees kill me."

"Yeah, good luck with that. And what happened to your —" he tilts his head until he finds the right word, "arrangement."

"That's over." After my attempt at a relationship imploded, I made a different arrangement with someone. It was purely physical and lasted less than two months. It became mechanical. Those early days when I was able to screw without an emotional connection are gone.

Ethan says something, but I don't hear any of it. Vickie and Tara return and walk back to the VIP section, and I follow those legs the entire way. A couple of guys follow, and Vickie waves them in. A set of twins approach, both tall, dark, and bald. They sit on either side of the women.

It's like Ethan has radar. He slowly turns around and sighs at the sight before him. I'd laugh if their presence didn't make my stomach turn. I wonder if the twins are more her type. It makes sense that a black girl from New York City wouldn't be interested in a white boy from Alabama.

"Every fucking time I turn around," he sighs. Ethan puts down his glass and leaves my side without another word. Once he approaches, he offers Tara his hand and escorts her out of VIP and into a secluded corner. He puts his forehead on hers and says something I can't hear. I look away, feeling like a voyeur during an intimate moment.

I never use my celebrity to get what I want. I pay my own way, and I follow the rules. Except now. Their reaction is exactly what I want when I step in. They both stand when I approach. Definitely two beta males. No way would I stand for another man, especially when I'm next to a beautiful woman. Victoria stands along with them, but unlike them, it's not because she's in awe of my presence. She crosses her arms and narrows her eyes at me.

Both guys hand me a napkin, which I'm happy to sign. We take a few selfies and I shake their hands.

"You see that room?" I point across the hall. "There are six of my teammates in there. I'm gonna send a text so you guys can get in. What are your names?" While they tell me their names, I send one of my teammates a text. The twins practically run away just like I wanted.

I turn back to Vickie and smile in victory. I take it a bit further and wink. She crosses her arms and looks into my face. It's fascinating to watch. She's doing her best to hide any emotions, but I can tell she's annoyed. It's in the way she blinks rapidly and the distinct rise and fall of her chest.

She tilts her head to the side as if she's just decided on what to say and says, "You should know something about me."

"Pretty soon, I'm going to know everything about you."

She ignores that statement. "What you just did, I don't find that cute or endearing. That's the first thing." She tilts her head up and points a finger in my face. I try hard to hold my laugh but fail. I recover quickly though and wipe the smile off my face, but the idea of this woman who barely reaches my chest trying to chastise me is the funniest thing that's happened to me in a long time.

"Fascinatin'." I do my best to pretend to be awed. "What's the second thang?"

"The second thing is, you're boring. Controlling wannabe alpha males bore me. Goodbye." She turns and walks away. I admire the curve of her ass and the swing of her hips before I catch up with her in two long strides. I walk past her, turn around, and block her path. She stops before she can collide with my chest.

"We didn't finish our conversation."

"I did." She does a fake pout and purses her lips together. Then something changes in her eyes. She inches closer to me and bites that plump bottom lip. "On second thought, I want to ask you something." She whispers the words and I feel a stirring in my pants. She gestures for me to lower down, and I do, putting my ear close to her lips. "Tell me something." Her words come out husky.

"I'll tell you anything you want to know, darlin'."

Her small hands glide across my pecs, slowly massaging me over my shirt. I flex underneath her hand. She whimpers.

"Have you ever—" She stops herself and looks around, almost as if she's too shy to ask.

"Have I ever what? You can ask me whatever you want."

"Have you ever had a five-inch stiletto lodged in one of your testicles?" All shyness gone from her voice, she shoves me away, and I practically fall on my butt.

I run ahead of her and block her path, make a face and wince. "Can't say that I have. I hope you're not into that kind of thing. I mean, I don't mind a little bit of pain, but—"

"Keep blocking me, and you'll find out."

I throw my head back and laugh while I try to imagine that. I'm positive I can lift her with one hand without exerting much energy. I'll have my hand wrapped around her wrist before she can take her shoe off.

"The last woman who threatened me was my mama," I tell her.

That statement doesn't impress her either. She makes a face and turns away to walk in the other direction, but I grab one of her wrists. She twists and turns to get it away from me, but I put my free hand in my pocket and wait. I even whistle a tune while she tries and fails to pull away.

"Don't tire yourself out."

"Let me go," she commands, and I drop her wrist.

"Come on, don't go. This is the most fun I've had in years." She gives me a look of disbelief, and I give her my best smile. She thinks I'm toying with her, but it's true.

I surprise her when I throw an arm across her shoulders. "Let me get you another drink." I flag the waiter down and ask him to bring her the same thing she just had. "Keep me company." I spin her around and take her in my arms. "See that? Perfect fit. Do you know what I think we should do?"

"I'm sure you'll tell me, Cole." To my surprise, she doesn't try to move away. Her lithe little body fits perfectly into mine, and despite the extreme height difference, it's not awkward.

"You should tell me all the things you find distasteful about me now, and I'll do the same with you. Let's just get it out of the way." Someone stands outside our section and snaps pictures of us. Vickie quickly hides her face in my chest, and as much as I like the feel of her against me, I don't like the reason she's doing it. I shake my head at the man taking pictures, but he doesn't move until security pulls him away.

"I don't think we have enough time. In the short time that I've known you, I found a lot of distasteful things about you. In fact, I can't think of a single good quality about you." She smiles into my face when she says that.

"I'll go first."

She jerks her head back as if she's surprised.

"What? You can't possibly be shocked that I would find something wrong with you."

"I am, as a matter of fact. How dare you, Cole?"

"You're withholdin'." She scoffs, but her face lights up. She appears even more beautiful in her unguarded state. I want to pat myself on the back for finally making her laugh.

"You're annoying," she retorts. "You can't take a hint."

"We're supposed to be taking turns. That's another thing I find distasteful about you. You can't seem to follow the rules, and as the primo athlete that I am, I can't abide by that." She's uncomfortable with my job, but it's what I do, and there's no point in pretending otherwise.

"Whose rules?" she asks. "Yours?"

"Mine?" I reluctantly pull my hands away from her and point to myself. I pull her back into me before she can run away. "Oh, you mean mine as in the patriarchy? Never. I don't make the rules, but I do play by them. So, that's another thing I find distasteful about you. You cheat at games."

She rolls her eyes and does a loud, fake yawn. "You don't know me well enough to make any of those statements."

"But I'm right."

"You're full of yourself," she tells me.

"You're a liar," I say back.

"There's no possible reason for me to lie to you. Ever."

"And you're a terrible actor."

"You like the sound of your own voice too much," she tells me.

"You live in a cloud of denial by pretending you don't want me."

"Oh, Cole," she says, looking into my eyes. "Delusional much?"

"And I could never be with you," I tease, pulling her

closer and we sway. We look totally ridiculous slow dancing to the fast song that's playing.

"Well, we finally agree on something. That's the one and only thing we have in common."

"I have about a million reasons why I could never be with you, but I can't imagine a single reason why you wouldn't want to be with me."

"Because women fall at your feet?"

"Every time I leave the house." Just as the words leave my mouth, a woman walks by and snaps a picture of me.

She sighs and the smile leaves her face. The playfulness is gone now. "Here are the facts, okay? I'm only going to say them once, so listen up." She looks up and gestures for me to lean down. When I do, she puts her lips so close to my earlobe that they almost touch. "One," she whispers, "I don't date athletes. Two, I don't date men with kids, especially the type of man who's at the club instead of at home with their child on a Friday night."

I put a hand to my heart and pretend to swoon. "Be still my heart." I exaggerate my southern accent as much as possible and channel Mama on a Sunday morning after she sees us dressed for church. "A woman who is protective of my son. I'm going to overlook how you're judging me without all the facts. Maybe now there are only half a million reasons why I can't be with you, darlin'. Keep going. You're knockin' down all my walls."

She stares and opens her mouth, but no words come out. She tilts her head to the side as if she's gathering her thoughts. I pat myself on the back for winning this round and striking her speechless, but my own smile is wiped from my face when she slides her hands up my chest and grabs my shirt with both hands. She pulls me down. She's about as strong as a fly, but I lean down if only to be closer to that mouth of hers.

"You think you're so charming, don't you?" My wide smile is the only answer I give her. "Those words stick to your tongue like honey."

"You're the only honey I want on my tongue right now."

She ignores my last statement and tightens her fists around my shirt. She pulls me down further. "Number three. Pay attention."

"I'm only human, Queen Victoria. How do you expect me to pay attention when you have your hands on me like that? And that perfect body of yours is so close to mine."

"Three. You're not equipped to ride this ride." And with that, she shoves my chest and lets me go. She walks away without another glance.

I watch her ass the entire time. A few other men do the same. She finds Tara and Ethan, and I go to the bar for a bottled water. By the time I catch up with them again, they're on their way out of the club. Not surprisingly, when I offer her a ride home, she turns me down and leaves with her sister and Ethan, but not before I put the bottle of water in her hand.

"I'll see you soon, Victoria Taylor." She puts her free palm in my face and walks away without a word. I watch her bare legs and wonder what her skin would feel like underneath my fingertips.

I text my driver and meet him outside a few minutes later. I don't bother saying goodbye to any of my teammates. They dragged me out tonight, and since Evan is spending the weekend with his maternal grandmother and half-sister, I decided to leave the empty apartment for a few hours. It's hard to believe that I live in a four thousand square foot Manhattan apartment overlooking Central Park. The house

I grew up in was less than half the size of where I now live. Mama still owns it. Paying off the mortgage was the first thing I did when I got my first paycheck. It sits empty, still fully furnished from when we all lived there. I make it a point to visit every time I go home. As sad as it was those first few years without Daddy, some of my best memories take place in that house. I don't think we'll ever part with it.

Mama struggled to keep me and my brother clothed and fed, and as two boys well over six feet tall, we were always hungry. She did the best she could, sacrificing time and money so me and Charlie could play sports. He wanted to play baseball, but she couldn't afford the equipment, so we both ended up playing basketball. Out of the two of us, he was the more gifted athlete. At least that was the case when we were both in high school. Until a decision he made took it all away from him. That was only the beginning of the rift between us.

By the time I get home, I'm tired and ready for bed. It's been three years since Kelsey died. Evan had just turned two the week before. All he has of his mother are pictures and stories told to him by his grandmother. All I have left is guilt. Guilt for not being in love with my wife. Guilt for thinking she got pregnant on purpose. Guilt for wanting out of the marriage. Guilt about talking to a lawyer behind her back because I did not want to lose custody of my son.

When Kelsey died a week after I left the lawyer's office, my entire world came to a standstill. My son's life would never be the same, and his sister, Mia, was taken away from him. Her father has custody, but she spends a lot of time with her grandmother and Kelsey's sister Robin. Unbeknownst to her father, I still support her through her grandmother. It was an arrangement we made soon after Kelsey died when I realized I'd be losing custody.

The house is lonely without Evan. All he's ever known is the two of us, other than a bad attempt at a relationship last year with a woman who was only interested in me. Since that relationship ended, Evan's gotten clingier, almost as if he's scared to have me out of his sight. Away games are stressful, but when I leave behind my crying son, it only heightens my anxiety. The only places he'll go without me are his grandmother's and Ethan's penthouse to spend time with Vincent. Since Tara's moved in, he's been spending more time there with his friend.

He talked about her for days after spending time upstairs. Though I had met her briefly before, I had to go and see for myself one night. My son was right. She genuinely loves spending time with Vincent, and by extension Evan. It's made me want to give him a home with a woman who loves him and wants to spend time with him, but that's almost impossible to find. It's akin to finding a needle in a haystack or a unicorn. The ones I come across tend to want me because of what I do, not because of who I am. With a young son, I don't have the time to weed out the good from the bad. I owe it to him and to myself not to make the same mistake twice.

I strip out of my clothes and drop in the middle of my empty bed before checking my phone. There's a text from Evan from several hours ago. He's sitting on the couch with his half-sister, both smiling into the camera.

FIVE

"Where did you say you are?" I toss the towel from around my waist and throw it in the corner of my bedroom.

"My future in-laws.'"

"In-laws? You popped the question already?" I barely have time to put my underwear on before Evan comes running into my bedroom. "Is the ring ready yet?"

"Daddy, I'm bored," Evan whines.

"Not yet. Long story. Her dad's a big fan of yours, and I—"

I cut him off with my laughter. "And you need me to get in good with your girl's daddy."

"She's a bit of a daddy's girl."

Evan climbs on my bed and jumps into the pile of clothes on the floor. I pick him up and throw him over my shoulder. He kicks his legs and giggles, squirming like a fish.

"Is her sister there?" I'm suddenly eager to do my friend this favor. I'd do it whether Victoria was part of the package or not, but I haven't been able to stop thinking about her since I saw her at the club almost a month ago. She's like a ghost. She's not on social media and Tara refused to give me her phone number.

"She's a bigger daddy's girl than Tara. Of course, she's here for her family's Memorial Day barbeque." I never would have pegged her for a daddy's girl, but I can certainly work with that, especially if he's a fan. That works in my favor.

"Text me the address. I'll be there." I end the call and toss my phone on the bed. I take Evan from my shoulder, spin him around the room and throw him on my bed.

"Let's get you dressed, Son. I'm taking you to see Vincent." He jumps off the bed, wearing nothing but his Spiderman underwear and a white t-shirt, and runs out of my bedroom.

"Come find me," he giggles. I sigh and prepare myself for a game of hide and seek. It shouldn't take long since he always hides in the same spot.

We are dressed and out of the house in under an hour. It's a good distraction from my day. After an early morning practice and workout session, I have the entire day to spend with Evan. It's just a bonus to have other adults around.

By the time we get to the Sugar Hill brownstone, Evan is practically bouncing on his heels, and when Ethan opens the door and tells my son where Vincent is, he runs in and disappears to the back of the house. I look around my friend, and even from the front door, I can hear her voice. She yells something and laughs. It's a loud, unguarded sound, and I want to hear it again. I've thought about her voice almost every day since I saw her.

"She's out back," Ethan says. "But that's not why I invited you here."

He gestures me inside, and I lower my head to step over

the threshold. "Yeah, yeah. I'm here so you can suck up to your almost father-in-law."

"And mothers-in-law. Two of them," he says, lowering his voice.

"Mr. Taylor has two wives? He's the real baller. I guess even billionaires suck up to their woman's family."

I look around the house. It's open with hardwood floors. I can see her growing up here. The walls are lined with family pictures, and I find Victoria. There's a picture of her in her high school cap and gown. She's smiling and totally unguarded and so different from the woman I met a month ago. That woman has her walls up a mile high.

"Here's some advice for you. You like Vickie? Get in good with her father and stepmom. It wouldn't hurt for you to befriend her twin brother either." He taps my shoulder and tells me to follow him. Ethan Bradford, nice guy, but commanding. I guess it's easy to be that way when you've always been sure of your place in this world. If being a CEO didn't work out for him, there are a million other things he could do, including doing nothing. He's so rich, he could do nothing for the rest of his life and still maintain his same lifestyle.

Basketball saved me, and it didn't hurt that I was good at it. If I didn't have that, I might still be stuck in my small town working at a meat processing plant like my mother did.

I follow Ethan to the kitchen, where he introduces me to Vickie's mother and their cousin Bernie.

"I see where your daughters get their beautiful eyes from." I kiss the back of her mother's hand, and she almost falls over. I do my best to exaggerate my southern accent, something I've found works well in certain situations. I do the same with Bernie, who is struck speechless. I wink at her and follow Ethan through the sliding glass door. This is where I find her. She's on the deck like a queen looking down on her kingdom. Her sunglasses are on top of her head with both hands on the deck rail. I follow Ethan down the stairs and into the yard, making sure to walk as close to her as possible without touching her. She jolts when I get close, and I claim a small victory.

Her father, a tall man likely in his late fifties, becomes awestruck when he sees me. Ethan introduces me to him and to Alan Taylor, Vickie's twin brother. He's tall and skinny, and he looks more like Tara than he does his own twin.

After asking them to join me in a friendly game, I take my shirt off. I normally would never do this, but she's still watching. As hard as our practices are, and as hard as my personal trainer makes me work, I'm suddenly grateful for it today. I'm lean, but I'm fit, and my abdominal muscles are proof that I can lift weights with the best of them.

I almost laugh when Alan copies me and takes off his own shirt.

"Alan, what the hell are you doing?" Victoria asks from her perch above us. Alan puffs out his chest and pounds it with his hand. He flexes his stomach muscles. "Cover that up. Nobody wants to see your bones."

"Women fight over this almost daily." He gestures at his body, and she rolls her eyes. "I had two fighting over me just this morning."

"Who? Our mother and evil stepmother fighting over you again?"

"They're women, aren't they?" Alan asks.

When her dad returns, he hands me a basketball, which I start to bounce on the small patch of concrete in their yard.

"You," Victoria says, pointing at me. I make a show of looking around the yard before pointing at myself.

"Me?"

"Yes. You." She uses one of her index fingers to call me over. I take the few short steps and look up at her.

"It's Colt, darlin'."

She raises an eyebrow in disapproval at the endearment.

"If either one of them so much as breaks a nail, Cole." Her eyes narrow at me in warning. I give her a boyish grin, followed by a wink. When she scoffs, I blow her a kiss, and she takes a step back as if the kiss touched her.

"What happens if *I* break a nail?" I tease.

"Have one of your fangirls bring you a band aid."

I toss the basketball to Alan and walk closer to Victoria. She looks down at me, her face completely stoic. "Are you jealous, Queen Vee?"

"The name is Victoria. Ms. Taylor—"

"If I'm nasty?" I wiggle my eyebrows at her. "I can be." I drop my head and do a dramatic bow. "Whatever my queen wants. I am but a pawn in your—"

"Oh, will you stop with the dramatics? Enough already. There's no one to fawn over you here." Someone throws the ball, and it hits me in the middle of my back, but I don't move away. I look into her dark brown eyes and lick my lips. She breaks the stare first, huffs, crosses her arms, and walks away.

But she doesn't stay away for long. I start a game of two on one with her brother and father. Alan's a good player, and as tall as he is, a few inches over six feet, I still tower over him. He's a good defensive player, doing his best to block my moves and take the ball. If this was a regular game on the court with regular guys, he'd be competitive, but not with me. I might as well be playing with Evan and Vincent.

I dribble the ball away from him and do a free throw, and I score. I turn to Victoria, who has now put her sunglasses on, doing her best to pretend she's not looking at me.

We have an audience. Ethan's come out, as well as Victoria's mother. Her stepmother is taking a video of me playing her husband and stepson. Alan manages to get the ball and throws it to his father. We play until John Taylor falls on his ass and his wife calls an end to the game. His wife and daughters run over to him, and I put my shirt on.

Our eyes catch again, but Victoria turns and walks away, calling the boys to go inside to frost cupcakes. I don't think Evan's ever frosted cupcakes with anyone. His grandmother might dote on him, but she's not one to teach a young boy how to cook. I never thought he'd be interested in anything like that. We have a housekeeper and a cook, but clearly, he enjoys being in the kitchen.

I'd love for my mother to be closer, but as much as she loves New York City, she'd never move here permanently. She loves the south, and she feels she's still responsible for my older brother, even though he's a thirty-two-year-old man who has made his own choices in life.

"Why don't you join us for lunch, Colt?" John asks. "Stay as long as you want."

Remembering what Ethan told me, I say, "Thanks, JT." He beams at the nickname, and I offer him a fist bump. Someone puts a bottle of water in my hand, and I lean back in my seat. "So, we're hanging out this week, right? Remember, Bradford is paying, so we're getting the best stuff."

Ethan laughs, but it's true. Whatever he gets, it's always top shelf. From alcohol to food to clothes.

Minutes later, Victoria returns with the boys, who take seats across the table from me. Both have chocolate frosting on their face.

"Did any of the frosting make it on the cupcakes?" I wipe Evan's mouth with a napkin, then do the same to Vincent.

"Vickie let us eat one before lunch," Vincent confesses. "She's nice."

"She told us not to tell, big mouth," Evan says, looking up at the heavens as if Vincent exasperates him. I try hard not to laugh. I eat a clean diet, especially during the season, and I make sure Evan eats healthy too. A cupcake before lunch is a very rare treat for him.

"We already ate it. What's he gonna do?" Vincent shrugs.

After his mother died, I worried Evan's childhood would be filled with loss and loneliness, until I realized it was up to me not to let that happen. We were older, but Mama was left in the exact same situation after Daddy died suddenly.

The sliding door opens, and the rest of the family comes out, including Elizabeth, Ethan's sister, who arrived unannounced. Victoria and her stepmother bring out the food, and my stomach growls. The last time I had dinner that wasn't prepared by my chef was last Christmas when I took Evan to Alabama, and Mama cooked a feast. The food had been the highlight. My brother ruined the holiday, and Evan, Mama, and I went to Florida for a few days after Christmas to get away from the drama. That was the last time I talked to him.

As if she can sense my thoughts, my phone vibrates in my pocket followed by my mother's ringtone.

"Excuse me, Taylors." I stand and go through the sliding glass door. I turn around, and Victoria watches me with an expression on her face that I can't read. I wink at her, and she yanks her sunglasses from the top of her head, shielding her eyes. "Hold on, Mama," I say into the phone, but I don't take my eyes off Vickie. She's in a loose floral skirt that reaches her knees and a light pink tee. She has a wide belt at her waist, giving it a tapered look. Her outfit is complete with a pair of tanned sandals. She's dressed modestly and that's what makes it so sexy. When I lick my lips at her, she abruptly turns around and gives me her back.

"Colton?" I hear my mom's soft voice on the phone.

"Yes, ma'am," I say. The Yankee accent I've tried to perfect disappears whenever I talk to anyone back home.

"I woke up thinkin' about you this mornin'. Been prayin' for you hard, Son. The whole congregation and your brother too." I look up at the ceiling and roll my eyes. She must sense what I'm doing because she says, "It's true. He's changed. He's been busy with the new restaurant."

"Okay, Mama. How are you?" I know my attempt at changing the subject won't work. Mary Leigh Chastain has made it her life's mission to heal the rift between her two sons, but how can you heal a rift that you didn't cause? We both played high school basketball. He was set to go to the University of Alabama on a sports scholarship until a fractured femur took it away from him.

At the same time, my star was rising, and two years later, I was offered the same scholarship. Unlike my brother, I was able to attend and was drafted into the NBA two years later at the age of twenty.

"Counting the days until I see you. I'm sorry about not coming to any games recently, but I want to stay close to home." That's code for I need to stay home and make sure Charlie doesn't start drinking again. "I promise if you make it to the finals, I'll be there for all of your home games." She prattles on and on, and I listen with only half an ear. I look outside and Victoria is sitting across from my son, reaching over and cutting his steak for him. When she's done, she messes his curly hair. "Charlie wanted me to thank you."

No, he didn't.

"Why didn't he call me himself if he wanted to thank me?" I think one hundred thousand dollars to start his own restaurant is worthy of at least one phone call. I'd even settle for a text. But then again, maybe not. I wouldn't have taken his call and I wouldn't have replied to his text.

"And you're an investor, so that means you own part of the business too." Of course, Mama would ignore my question. "This will be good for him, Colty. I think he's going to finally be okay, and if you have any ideas—"

"I hope he'll be okay, and I don't have any ideas, Mama. I'm not in the restaurant business." I almost snap at her, but I rein in my temper. Mama is forever the optimist where my brother is concerned. "And I'm not looking to be part owner. I don't want anything, but if this fails, I have nothing left to give him. In fact, I didn't give him the money, I gave it to you. If you want to be part owner, go ahead, but leave me out of it."

She sighs, and I can see her now. Hands wringing and tears pooling in her eyes while she blinks them away. I bet she's shaking her head as if that would somehow erase the words I just spoke.

"He has not dealt with us according to our sins—" I stop her before she goes any further.

"Mama, I don't need you to quote scripture right now. Please, stop."

"I raised you in the church, and I don't accept you turning your back on it."

"I don't need your permission to turn my back on anythang. That's just the way it is. I'm a grown man capable of makin' my own decisions." I immediately regret my sharp tone, but I don't apologize.

"You can't turn your back on your brother. Jesus died for our sins. We all have sinned."

"I wrote a hundred-thousand-dollar check so he can start a business. I paid for three stints at rehab. He lives in the house I bought for you. He lives a great life and hasn't had a job in years. Why do you think that is?"

"Colt—"

"No, I'm tired of this. And what has he done? He hates me because of things I had no control over. I didn't cause his accident. I didn't tell him to get drunk, climb a tree, and fall out of it. I didn't take his basketball scholarship away from him, but he's tried to take mine away from me. He tried to—"

"He was not in his right mind when any of that happened. He was drinkin', and you know how that affects him. How it affects the men in our family." I count to ten. Then I stuff the anger down because that will do nothing but mess with my head. My professional life might be going great, but my personal life has been nothing but a giant cluster for the past six years. I'm finally in a good place, and Charlie Chastain is not going to ruin it.

"Of course. Nothin' is his fault ever. Look, Mama, I'm done talkin' about it. We are grown men now. You don't need to play mediator between us like you did when we were kids." I take a deep breath and change the subject. "I was thinkin' me and Evan can come back to Alabama with you for a couple of weeks." And I bought another house there for me and my son. Mama doesn't know that yet. No need to tell her I won't be staying with her and Charlie.

"That sounds great." I can hear the enthusiasm in her voice. "I want to spend some time with my grandson." The happiness is back in her voice, and I relax now that the conversation has veered to a friendlier topic, at least for now.

"Yeah, the little traitor says he wants to play baseball. Can you believe that?"

She lets out a carefree laugh. "You let my grandbaby play whatever he wants." The conversation turns to Evan and my plans for him this summer. She talks some more, and I look out the sliding glass door to find Victoria staring directly at me. Our eyes lock and she doesn't look away this time.

"You okay?" she mouths. I don't know what I was expecting, but it wasn't genuine concern from her. I smile, but I know the smile doesn't reach my eyes. I nod, and she looks away, dismissing me again. I finally end the call with Mama and join everyone on the deck.

"Are you hungry, Colt?" her mother, Alicia, asks several minutes later.

"Yes. Thank you, ma'am. I'm always famished after a conversation with my mama." I say it loud enough for Victoria to hear that I was talking to my mother and not a love interest.

She hands me a plate and tells me to go help myself. I give her a smile in gratitude.

"Dad, can I spend the night here with Vincent?" Evan runs to my side of the table and practically jumps on my lap. "Alan says he will play video games with us. He says he'll teach us calculus because women love men who know math."

"Oh, really?" Victoria says with a snicker. "Where's your woman at, Alan?"

"I'm more of a player," Alan says. "One woman can't

handle all of this." He stands, lifts his shirt and punches his stomach.

"Yeah, me too," Vincent says.

Alan reaches over and gives him a high five.

"Um, no. We're not teaching them this," Tara says. "Ethan, say something."

"He's four, baby. What do you want me to say? He has no idea what a player is." While Tara debates with her brother and Ethan, I glide my hand along Vickie's shoulders. She visibly shivers.

"My only white boy crush is Bradley Cooper," she whispers close to my ear.

The smell of her musky body spray hits my nose. I lean closer and inhale. She gasps but doesn't push me away. I rest my forehead on her shoulder and say, "In that case, it's time you upgrade to a man, Queen Vee." I rub my nose on a soft patch of skin, taking deep breaths of her scent. "It's our first holiday together. Happy Memorial Day, darlin'." I lean in and kiss her cheek. She bolts out of her chair and runs inside.

SIX

Vickie

VICKIE

I BARELY TAKE TWO SIPS FROM MY VERY FULL GLASS OF white wine when Mother, Tara, and my stepmother walk inside. I pour two more glasses of white and one red for my mother. Mother grabs me and pulls me aside, and I down my drink in anticipation. "French fry," she says. She looks over my shoulder as if to ensure total privacy. "Have you heard from Gerald?" She drops her gaze after the words leave her mouth.

I haven't thought about Gerald since that Friday night over a month ago.

"I'm sure you already know the answer to that since you're the one who told him where to find me," I whisper to her. I look around the kitchen, and Colt is looking at me from the other side of the glass door. I decide I'm going to ignore him too. I'm sick of men.

"I was only trying to help." She reaches up and runs a hand through my hair. "You both were so young when you broke up. What's wrong with a second chance?" I pull her hand from my hair and put it down. She shrugs and smiles, and I hate how her smile is just like mine. "You're my daughter. The child who is more like me than anyone. I know you're lonely. I just don't understand why you've built this wall around yourself."

She says the words tenderly, like a loving mother would, but they slice through me like a knife. Being like Alicia Taylor is not the compliment she thinks it is, and I take a small step back to try and regain my thoughts.

"Mother," I shake my head while I think of a response, "let's stay out of my love life, okay? What about you? Are you dating anyone these days?" Changing the subject back to her has always worked in the past. She's dated a bunch of men and was even married to one for a couple of years.

She gives me a playful look, and I brace myself for a long story, but she surprises me. "We're talking about Victoria." She puts her glass down and takes my hand. "French fry, my therapist says—" The sliding door opens and Colt and the boys walk in. Whatever mother was going to say dies on her tongue. Relieved, I pull my hand from hers. Colt walks by, making sure to rub against me while Evan pulls him down the hall.

Mother's eyes widen at the interaction. Say what you will about Mother, but she's astute. She's about the smartest woman I've ever met.

"Really, Vickie?" she whispers before letting out a soft giggle. "He's not exactly your type." She leans closer, bumping her shoulder with mine as if we're girlfriends exchanging secrets. "I never would have thought."

"Why not? Tara is with Ethan."

"Yes, but Ethan is from New York City. Colt is from Alabama." She whispers Alabama as if it's a curse. "Alabama," she whispers again.

"What are you saying, Mother? It's okay for a black woman to date a white man if he's from New York City?"

Not that I'm interested in Colt, but her dismissal grates on my last nerve. "There's nothing going on with us," I tell her. "He's just a shameless flirt." I don't bother telling Mother that Colt is only interested because I made it clear that I'm not.

"Oh, good because that would be a disaster." She lets out a shaky, fake little laugh. I look behind me and lock eyes with my sister. Knowing exactly what I need, she comes over and stands next to me.

"Tater tot, there you are," Mother says. "I was thinking you, me, and French fry can get in a good spa day. You know? The three of us like we used to do. Or four if Alan wants to come." I catch Tara's eyes and roll mine. I can tell from her stiff posture that she'd rather do anything else.

Alan might be my twin, but the three of us are so connected, we can tell what each other is thinking without having to utter a single word. My stepmother, Cheryl clears her throat. She gives me a subtle nod, urging me to agree.

"Like we used to do?" I ask. "When did we ever do that? I remember you trying to sell us on that fantasy last November. Remember that? When you bailed on Tara's birthday and decided to go to Barbados with friends instead?"

She sighs, and her shoulders slump. I stuff down the twinge of guilt that hits.

"I'm trying to make up for that. Tara and I talked. She's not even upset about it anymore. Why can't you let it go?" She huffs and picks up her wine.

"And what about Cheryl? You made it a point to exclude her."

"I just want to have a few hours with *my* children. Cheryl understands." She waves in Cheryl's direction.

"Of course, I do," Cheryl says. "It sounds fun."

"See? Come on. It will be fun, and I want to talk to you guys in private." She gives Cheryl the side eye. "I have some stuff I need to get off my chest." I nearly scoff at that. Whatever it is, I don't want to hear it. The last time she tried to get stuff off her chest, she blamed our father for the demise of their marriage and Cheryl for the rift between us. "And Ethan and I were just talking about it outside. He thinks it's a great idea."

"Well, as long as Ethan agrees," I sneer.

Tara elbows me in the ribs.

Ethan steps inside while typing something on his phone. He pulls Tara away from my mother and wraps an arm around her.

"I had Hunter book a spa for you guys. He'll email Tara the details. It's for up to six people, so have fun." Mother claps and hugs Ethan, while Tara rolls her eyes at me. "You get whatever you want." He pulls Tara to him and whispers something in her ear.

I pull my mother to the side and say, "Cheryl comes, or I don't." She pulls me to the other side of the room, away from anyone.

"I have no issues with Cheryl," she whispers. She has no issues with Cheryl now. Not since we've all made it clear that we won't allow her to disrespect our evil stepmother. "But I would like to spend some quality time alone with my children. I told you I have things I want to say."

"We're her children too. And whatever you have to say, we've heard it all before. I don't think we need to hear it again."

For a split second, I regret my words. She drops her head and her shoulders sag in defeat, but like always, she doesn't stay down for long. She stands straight and looks at me directly in the eyes.

"How long are you going to punish me, Victoria? For how long? Have you ever done anything wrong in your life? Have you ever thought for a second that I might have my own demons?" She huffs and walks away without giving me a chance to respond. Chastened, I look at my sister, but she's busy talking with Ethan and Elizabeth in the corner.

Colt returns and Evan runs outside to join Vincent and Alan in the backyard. Colt stands next to me, much too close.

"Queen Victoria," he whispers. "When can I take you out to dinner?"

"We've been through this."

"I don't give up." He puts one of his giant hands on the small of my back. A shiver goes through my body. He notices and smiles. "My queen, my liege," he whispers. For some reason, I laugh at that.

"If I'm Queen Victoria, then we can never be. She married her cousin." He puts a hand to his heart and pretends to be shocked.

"Stop tryin' to get me to the altar. See, I knew you wanted me." He snatches one of my hands and puts it to his chest. I want to pull it away, but I leave it and feel the strong reverberations of his heart. His smile disappears when we lock eyes, and as much as I know that I need to look away, I can't. The playful flirtatiousness is gone and in its place is a look I can't interpret. The intensity of his dark brown eyes is so hypnotizing that all other sounds in the room fade away, and I lose myself in his eyes. I don't know what he sees when he looks at me, but I've never let anyone in close enough to fully see me.

After a loud throat clearing, my mother nudges her way between us and announces, "I want to have my children over for dinner soon. I want to get to know my daughter's boyfriend and his adorable son. Vickie, you too. Bring Gerald." When I give her a death glare, she waves her hand and says, "Or I'll call him. I'm going to help you." She floats away and approaches Tara and Ethan. She wraps an arm around Ethan's to get his full attention.

"Who is Gerald?" Colt whispers in my ear. I look at him and stare, not bothering with an explanation. "I didn't realize it before, but I think I'm a very jealous man, my queen. At least where you're concerned. I think it would be better coming from you."

"What the hell are you talking about?" I walk away from him and pick up the bottle of wine.

"That I'm the one who'll be escortin' you to the dinner party."

"Oh, please," is all I say. I refill my empty glass of wine and finish it in one big swallow. A dinner party thrown by my mother is about the last thing I want to do. Judging by the look on Tara's face, she'd rather face an execution squad than make small talk and pretend that Alicia Taylor is mother of the year. I'm fairly certain there will be no dinner party, so it's moot.

"That sounds nice," Ethan says. "On behalf of me, Tara, and Vincent, we accept."

My mother laughs with glee at Ethan's attention. Alicia Taylor, the consummate hostess. It wouldn't hurt so much if she was always a shitty mother, but she wasn't. She was attentive, firm but loving. She took an interest in us, often taking us into the city for shows and museums. She has a great appreciation for the arts and instilled that in us from an early age. We were blindsided when we returned home that Wednesday only to find her gone. It was as if our entire life had been a lie. One moment the five of us were together and happy, and the next, our father was a single dad doing his best.

We didn't realize she had left until a few hours after we got home. The three of us liked to watch TV in our parents' bed before they got home from work. Alan would eat chips in there, which was absolutely forbidden. That day, he brought chips and fruit punch, and when he spilled the juice on the bed, I ran to the closet to get a fresh set of sheets. That's when I noticed all Mother's belongings were gone.

She never gave us an explanation. Not then and not now. From what I can tell, she never told our father why either. Nothing beyond being unhappy and wanting out. We could have understood if she didn't want out from us too. We barely saw her that first year. It was three months from the day she left until we saw her again for an awkward lunch at a neighborhood restaurant. I did my best trying to hide how excited I was about seeing her. I held my breath until I saw her standing at the restaurant. Dad hugged us goodbye and left, promising to only be a phone call away if we needed him.

I remember crying and asking her to come home, but she told us she couldn't, but would be better about seeing us. She took us shopping after lunch, and looking back, it was a cheap attempt at buying our affection to ease her guilt over her abandonment of us, but three kids who hadn't seen their mother in months ate it up. Alan cried when she dropped us off. He didn't want me or Tara to see him, but I did. He spent the rest of the day in his room with the door locked and refused to come down for dinner. That night, I curled into bed with my new stuffed animal and cried for hours.

It was another month until we saw her again. Dad was

juggling his business and raising us on his own. Tara thought it was now her responsibility to care for us, but that only brought the three of us closer. We were an impenetrable wall. The three of us promised to always be there for each other no matter what. We promised to never have secrets from each other, and we've kept those promises. We're each other's best friends.

While Mother schmoozes Ethan about a dinner party that will likely never happen, I tune her out and pour another glass of wine for my evil stepmother. I don't know how she did it, but she came in and loved three children who were not receptive to her. We went out of our way to shun her as best we could without our dad knowing, but she knew exactly what we were doing and never gave up on us. She's been our evil stepmother since I was eleven and Tara thirteen. She never had any kids of her own, and it wasn't until I was an adult that she confessed she couldn't. Her first marriage ended after her third miscarriage, but she still came in and loved us as if we are her own.

"Darling, I think I'm going to let you three have a nice day with mother."

"You're our mother, too. And you love a mani pedi and a hot stone massage more than anyone I know. You're coming." I give her a kiss on the forehead and rest my cheek on her shoulder.. "We'll share an Uber."

"Uber? I'll arrange cars for you," Ethan says. Mother giggles like a thirteen-year-old girl, but her smile dips when she sees me standing so close to Cheryl. "Tara's not allowed to ride in Ubers."

I look at my sister and wait for her to react.

"Excuse me? I'm allowed to do whatever I want, thank you very much."

He leans in to kiss her, but she pushes him away. Undeterred, he takes her hand and pulls her close.

"Everything except get in a car with a total stranger. That's why you have a driver." He gently slaps her ass.

"When you get yourself a man, you go all out, don't you, Tara?" I wink at my sister.

"Her taste has improved a lot since she met me," Ethan says.

While everyone laughs, Colt comes closer to me. "Queens don't ride Ubers either, darlin'."

As I think of a smart response, the boys and Alan come running inside the house. "Daddy, I want to stay. Alan says we can stay up late."

"He can stay," Tara says. "We'll be staying here tonight, so he's more than welcome to hang out. I'll take good care of him."

"Let me think about it," he says, and for some reason, it irritates me that he needs to think about it.

Evan huffs, but he runs behind Alan and Vincent, who leave to go play video games.

"Don't you trust us?" I whisper to him. He takes my wine glass from my hand, smells it and hands it back.

"Do you want a glass, or would you prefer something stronger?" I ask, hating myself for wanting to know anything more about him.

"Mama says alcohol is the devil's milk." I raise both eyebrows, taken aback by the statement.

"Is that what Mama says?" I put a hand to my forehead. "Well, I do declare. What does Colt say?"

"Oh, so you do know my name. Colt says he doesn't care for mind altering drugs of any kind."

"That confirms it. Colt is lame."

"Darlin', I don't need drugs to alter your mind or make

your body beg for more. What I have is one hundred percent natural, and yours for the taking if you want it." He grins, showing off his perfect white teeth and that one dimple. Add the curly mop of hair on his head and he looks practically boyish, and so handsome it should be illegal.

"I already had that today." His smug smile disappears, and just to twist the knife, I add, "And yesterday. And the day before."

"You're a terrible, terrible liar. But I won't punish you because of that. I've been saving myself for you since I first laid eyes on you."

"When Alan comes back here, can someone please remind him that he's a grown man?" Dad grumbles, coming in from the outside. "He was having a food fight with the boys outside until I told them to knock it off."

"Colt, honey, good luck telling Evan he can't spend the night," Cheryl says to him.

I leave everyone in the kitchen and step outside. Elizabeth, Ethan's sister is in the yard having a heated conversation over the phone when I start to clear the table. Whoever she's talking to must say the wrong thing because she walks past me and goes inside, calling her brother's name. Minutes later, Colt comes out and starts to help me. Usually after a family gathering, the three Taylor kids will clean up. That's the way it's always been, so when Colt comes out and starts to help, I almost drop a plate.

"You don't have to do that." I reach for the plate, but he pulls away. "You're our guest."

"I'm a gentleman, darlin'. And my mama raised me to always help a lady." I roll my eyes and turn back to the table.

"What makes you think I'm a lady?" I ask him. "That's rather presumptuous."

"Oh, I can tell. You might want to be otherwise, but that's who you are." He drops his plate and walks over to my side of the table. When I turn to face him, he puts both hands on the table, boxing me in. "But I do want you to do very unladylike things to me, only not with the stiletto. And because I know you'll find it excitin', I can forget about being a gentleman once I have you naked and in my bed." He runs his nose along the base of my neck. "What do you think about that?"

I can hear my heart beating fast. He's so close, all I have to do is turn my face a fraction and his lips would be on mine.

"I told you the other night that—" He turns and one of his hands cup my jaw. I almost combust in my parents' backyard.

"You told me what?" he whispers above my mouth. "What did you tell me, darlin'?"

I lick my lips while I gather my thoughts. "That you don't exactly fit my parameters." He chuckles and lets me go. I almost stumble back from the loss of his touch.

"Look at me. I'm almost seven feet tall. I don't fit any parameters. Never have." I reach for a plate, but he takes my wrist. "Why are you so skittish?" His free hand caresses the small of my back. It's been so long since I've let a man get this close that I don't know how to react. This closeness is more than just physical. He's trying to get to parts of me that I've locked away. Parts that I won't ever let anyone get close to.

He puts a finger underneath my chin, and his touch is warm, like a shock to my system. He tilts my chin up, forcing me to look into his dark eyes before running his nose on my cheek, almost as if he's inhaling me and can't get enough of how I smell.

"Why don't I take you somewhere, hmm?" His large palm rubs my hip, kneading the soft flesh. Goosebumps spread across my body, and I feel the gentle thudding between my legs. "Have I told you you're beautiful?" His question is soft. "Easily the most beautiful sight I've ever seen. I thought so the second I saw you. Those pouty lips and those expressive eyes. You give it all away with your eyes. All I have to do is look at you."

If he wasn't holding me in his arms, I would have fallen over. I've been told that before by men, but never have I believed it as much as I do in this very moment.

"I'm sure you've been with your fair share, huh?" I shove at his chest, but he wraps his hands around my wrists. I'm not a big woman, but this is the first time in my life that I've felt tiny.

"Why would you assume that?" he asks.

"I might not watch basketball, but I know all about athletes and their limitless supply of women."

"I've been in the league nine years, was married for two, and have been a single parent for three. That doesn't leave much room for skirt chasin'."

"Skirt chasin'?" I say with a smile.

"Whorin'. Philanderin' or whatever you want to call it."

"It's not just that," I tell him. "I don't date men with kids."

"That's the biggest load of bull I've ever heard. The Taylors are a poster for the blended family. This week. You and me. Let me clear up some of your misconceptions about me."

"Colt, listen—" The words die in my throat at the sound of little feet approaching.

"Dad, Alan says—" Evan stops when he sees us. He turns his head and gives me a look like I just killed his puppy. He narrows his little eyes, walks over, grabs Colt's hand, and pulls on it. "Come play with us. Alan says he can whip your butt at video games." He stands between us and pushes his father away from me.

"He said what?" I giggle at Colt's fake outrage.

"Yeah, he said he's a video game champ and you're a video game chump."

Colt makes a show of pretending to be offended. He puts his head down and shakes it. Then he pounds his chest with a fist. "Did you tell him how many NBA championships my team's won since I joined?"

"I told him four. I told him you can beat anyone at anything." Evan raises his hand, and the two high-five each other. I cover my mouth to hide my laugh at the seriousness on Evan's face. "Come downstairs so you can beat him. Show him who the real MVP is." He takes his dad's hand and starts to pull him.

"I'll be right down."

Evan stops and stares at me. Unlike earlier, he offers me no smile. The friendly little boy who inhaled a cupcake in my parents' kitchen is gone. He's studying me as if he's trying to figure out the best way to get rid of me. I know that look. That's the same look the three of us gave Cheryl the first time we met her.

"Can you come now?" He drops Colt's hand, stands in front of him, and lifts both arms so his father can pick him up. Colt obliges and Evan rests his head on his father's shoulder. "Please. Vincent's daddy is already down there. He's terrible at video games. You have to come downstairs and show him what to do."

"Go ahead. I can clean up. Besides, you two are guests."

I can tell he wants to say more, but he walks inside with Evan in his arms. Tara comes out and starts to help.

"I see your sister-in-law's panties are still in a bunch," I say about Elizabeth. "Whoever she was talking to a few minutes ago got an earful."

"She's not my sister-in-law," Tara says.

"She will be. Will you say yes?" I ask her and grab the plate from her hand, staring into her face.

"Hell yeah." We both burst into laughter and fist bump. She leans closer and whispers, "But they just found out they have a younger brother. Their father kept it a secret."

SEVEN

Colt

"Hey, Colty. It's Charlie. I got your number from Mama." I put the phone on the counter, pull my shirt over my head, and toss it on the bathroom floor. I wait for him to tell me how he doesn't need my help, and he's going to pay me back with interest. "I want you to know that this is only a loan. I plan on paying you back every penny, plus interest." Sure, you are. Just like all the other money you've 'borrowed' from me over the years. "Anyway, thanks." The call ends without a goodbye, and I wonder why he even bothered to call. He never has before.

I hit end and call Ethan's phone.

He picks up and says, "He's fine. He's making milkshakes with Alan and Tara. Stop being a helicopter dad."

"Where's Vickie?" I ask him, wondering why she's not making milkshakes too.

"She's around here somewhere." We chat for a bit but he gets another call and we hang up.

I finally conceded and let Evan stay. He's not the most social, but he feels comfortable at the Taylor house. Besides,

I trust Ethan and Tara with my son. I trust them more than my own brother.

After a shower, I slide my naked body between the sheets. My phone vibrates. It's a picture of Evan and Vincent. They're both holding a fancy glass filled to the brim with a chocolate milkshake. There's whipped cream at the top, and they're both sporting mustaches. I send them back a thumb's up and decide to message another member of the Taylor household.

Me: It's Colt

The three dots indicating she's responding pop up immediately.

Queen Vee: I never gave you my number

She didn't. She left her phone on the kitchen counter, and before the screen locked, I called myself and saved her number.

Me: I have my ways. Come over.
Queen Vee: Can't. I've been recruited by my womb mate to help host the best sleepover there ever was.
Me: Maybe I shouldn't have left.
Queen Vee: I think you're too old for a sleepover.
Me: I guess we'll find out when I have a sleepover with you.
Queen Vee: Keep dreaming.

EIGHT

Vickie

"It's stupid, Ms. Taylor. Why would they kill themselves for each other? They've known each other two days."

This is the part of the job I love. When we go off script and the students delve into the material and tear it apart. While I think of the best way to respond, another chimes in and says, "No way I'm killing myself over some boy."

The ninth-grade English class cheers, and a couple of the girls reach over and high-five each other. "Boys ain't shit," someone shouts. The girls agree, the boys boo and I do my best to keep my expression neutral.

"That's not true love," a young girl from the back of the class shouts out. "Maybe because it's written by a man. Juliet was so unhappy at home that she grabbed onto Romeo as a way out. It's a shame that her only option was marriage, which we all know was also doomed. My aunt Rhonda's been married four times, and she still says men ain't shit." The class erupts, and I stifle my own laugh.

"Why are girls always popping that sexist ish? Romeo didn't have many options either," Desmond says. "Like boys had it so good. It's not like he could bide his time until he turned eighteen to get out. They were gangsta back then. And maybe Aunt Rhonda just has crap taste in men." Desmond stands and mimics dropping the mic. He runs around the room, high-fiving all the boys.

"Yeah, but—" someone says. I start to speak up, to keep this discussion from going off the rails. Normally, I love when we go off topic and have a good debate, but we have a unit test to prepare for and I want my students to do well.

"Hold on, guys." The talking stops at the same time the door to my classroom opens. I almost fall over when Colt Chastain steps inside. His head practically touches the ceiling.

All the kids go wild and jump out of their seats. They crowd around my desk and circle around Colt like he's the second coming of Christ.

"Holy shit!" someone yells out. Colt is handed notebooks, which he signs. Phones come out and pictures are snapped, and all I do is lean against the wall and watch as he disrupts my class. There's no way anyone will be able to concentrate on the rest of the lesson.

He makes himself comfortable and sits on my desk, flashing me a mischievous smile. "Romeo and Juliet," he says, picking up the book off my desk.

"I'll be your Juliet," someone yells. A couple of people sit on the desk next to him and start taking selfies. That's how the next twenty minutes go. Total chaos inside my classroom until the bell rings, and I force the kids out so they won't be late for their next class.

Once my classroom is empty, I close my door and look at my uninvited guest. He leans against the wall so smug that I fight with myself not to slap him. Good looking bastard.

"How did you get inside this school?" I ask him. They don't just let anyone in. "And how did you know where my room is?" It's a stupid question. The Manhattan Mischiefs have won four championship games in six years. They didn't win last year, but they made it to the playoffs and lost in the seventh game. Dad did nothing but talk about the loss for the next two weeks.

Colt Chastain is like royalty in the city. He can go anywhere and do anything. I'm sure doors and legs automatically open for him.

"I told Gary we're old friends." Gary is one of our security guards. He's an even bigger basketball fan than my father. I can imagine how he reacted to seeing Colt standing in front of him. "I told him I'd give you a signed ball for him."

"You disrupted my class. I was prepping my students for a test tomorrow."

Flustered to have him here, I turn my back and erase my whiteboard. My next and final class of the day starts in forty-five minutes, and we're studying Macbeth. It's been a week since he crashed our Memorial Day barbeque, and I've done everything to push him out of my mind. Which is hard since he texts every single day. I pretend not to hear his footsteps. Every time he takes a step, my heart pounds in my chest. Boom. Boom. Boom. He stands behind me, close but not touching. He doesn't utter another word, but I can hear his breathing. It's as if the room not only shrunk but has gotten one hundred degrees hotter. I erase until there isn't a single word left on the board. He stands behind me the entire time and I wonder if he's checking out my body.

Of course, he is.

I suddenly feel self-conscious in my fitted black slacks. I think I've recently put on a few pounds because they are snugger today than the last time I wore them. I push the thought away and convince myself they shrunk in the dryer.

But you get them dry cleaned.

Finally done, I put down the eraser and turn to face my surprise guest when all I want to do is leave this classroom and not return until he's gone. But I'm not going to let him or anyone else run me out. This is my turf.

"You interrupted my class," I repeat, still irritated by the intrusion.

"You didn't accept my follow request on IG," is all he says.

He sent that to me the day after he left my parents' house, and I've ignored it. I don't know how he found me since I don't use my full name. IG is the only social media I have, and I keep my account private. I checked his out. Nothing but pictures of him and his fans, practice videos, and workouts with his personal trainer. There are no pictures of his son. That can mean one of two things. He's a neglectful father or he's protecting his son from the media. After spending time with them, I reluctantly admit that it's the latter. As good as he looks in his jeans and plain black t-shirt, that's nothing compared to how he looks shirtless and sweaty from a grueling workout. There's one video where he was so sweaty that water ran down his forehead and into his eyes. He ran a hand through his curly hair, and it's the sexiest thing I've ever seen. I ran it back in slow motion several times.

"I'm not on there much."

"And you haven't returned any of my DMs." I walk away and stand behind the chair at my desk, putting some more space between us. "I need to know when the dinner party is."

"That's because we said all we had to say."

"Thought I'd come over here and take you out for an early dinner." He speaks as if he didn't hear my last words.

I make the mistake of craning my neck to look at him. Damn him for being so tall, especially when I'm in ballet flats. I pull out my chair but don't sit down. He closes the small space I managed to put between us and sits on top of my desk. The space is too small for someone his size. His long legs practically reach the wall that holds my whiteboard.

"I'm not into the whole celebrity thing. And I don't go out with athletes or people with kids. I made that clear the night at the club." I clear my throat and square my shoulders. "I'm not going to say it again." But I take a step closer to him. "And yet here you are, a single father, chasing after a woman who's made it clear she's not into the package deal thing. Evan deserves better." I give him my back and reach for a marker. He stands behind me, takes the marker from my hand, and traps me between his hard body and the whiteboard.

"That thing you just did right there," he says close to my ear. That thing where you defend my son and put me in my place. You have no idea how sexy that is." Those big hands end up on my shoulders, and he turns me around. "We have that in common. I don't date celebrities, athletes, or single fathers either." He smiles, showing off that single dimple. "Athlete is my job. Get to know Colt."

"Right. You're just a boy from Alabama."

"Man," he corrects me. When I stay quiet, he says, "Aah. I get it."

"What is it you think you get?" I ask, looking into his dark brown eyes. Just like the night we met, he has about a day's worth of stubble on his face. I want to touch it now as much as I did then. His dark curly hair gives him a boyish look, much younger than his twenty-nine years.

The Manhattan Mischiefs just renewed his contract, four years for three hundred million dollars, and that doesn't include endorsement deals. Every time I turned on the television this week, he was in a commercial. He's filthy fucking rich, but unlike some of his teammates, he's not flashy. In fact, a few of his teammates tease him and call him cheap Chastain.

"You New Yorkers." He does a bad New York accent, making it sound like New Yowkahs. "You guys think this city is the center of the universe and look down at everyone else. Especially a good ol' southern gentleman like yours truly."

"You mean New York isn't the center of the universe?" I shrug and say, "It should be."

"You don't deny it."

"Seems like you've already made up your mind. Who am I to contradict you? Believe what you want. No skin off my nose."

"I think you live to contradict everyone."

I gasp and pretend to be offended. "Wrong again."

"Again? So, it's not my southern heritage that offends you?"

I let out a loud laugh. "My dad is originally from Columbia, South Carolina. We visited there every summer when I was a kid. I love the south, so you could not be more wrong."

But there's still no way I would ever get involved with you.

"Oh, really?" He wipes his brow as if he's relieved. "Thank goodness, but just in case, you should know that I traced back my ancestry and I'm one percent Yankee." He puffs out his chest in pride as if that's supposed to be significant.

"Yankee?" He nods, doing his best to appear solemn. "Is that the word they used?"

"Let's go eat, and then I'll take you back to my place and show it to you."

"Show it to me?" I eye him up and down. "I have a pretty good idea of what *it* looks like, and I'm not interested. I'm not hungry," I tell him.

"Are we going to be one of those couples?" Bemused I take a step back to look at him. "You'll be the girl who says she's not hungry and then eat half of my food?"

That's exactly what I do to Alan all the time. He's so used to it that he orders two entrees whenever we go out.

"We won't be anything because we'll never be a couple." Especially to a widower because there's no way in hell I can compete with a dead wife. The circumstances behind her death are unknown. The theories range from cancer to a brain aneurysm to a drug overdose.

"I think your sister said the same thing to the man she currently lives with."

"I'm not my sister."

"And my kid is really cute."

He is, and he did everything to keep me away from his father, including sitting between us. He dragged his father away from me so they could go play video games in the basement with Alan. He even faked getting hurt so his father could get away from me and check up on him.

"He is," I agree. "No denying that. I love kids. Kids aren't the problem."

"You're giving me whiplash, Queen Vee, but okay. Don't date me. Eat with me instead. I don't want to date you either, remember?" His full pink lips turn into a frown.

"I found about a dozen other reasons why I won't date you."

"Eat and that's it? Why didn't you say so? I can always eat if all you're after is sharing a meal with me. You're buying, right?"

"I'd never let a lady pay."

"Right. A true southern gentleman."

"You say that as if it's a bad thing."

I'm not looking for a gentleman. I'm looking for a lover. One who sets my sheets on fire and then goes home after. One I don't hear from again until I'm ready for him to come back to my bed. One who has no expectations about being invited to my family celebrations. That's what I tell myself I want, but the reality is, I don't know how long I'll be able to handle such an arrangement.

This guy is probably about hand-holding and long walks on the beach during his annual family vacation with the kid who hates me. But now that I think about it, there are no pictures of his dead wife on his IG. There's never any mention of his personal life at all; only workout videos and pictures of him with fans.

He stands and corners me against the wall. He doesn't press his body into mine, but if I move away, I will have to rub against him, and he knows it. So, I do it. I rub against him, let the smell of his cologne invade my senses and feel his hard body against mine for just a fraction of time. He groans softly, and just to show him how unaffected I am, I go the other way and rub against him again.

"A few things you should know about me. As much as I love Tara, I'm not her. Don't assume I want the same things she does. I'm not looking for a relationship, especially not with a gentleman from *any* part of the country. I'm not a wallflower," I whisper. "I don't need gentleness, and I can pay my own way."

"Then I won't be gentle," he whispers so close to my ear that I get goosebumps. "But you should know that I'm all man, and a man pays for his lady."

"The man part is obvious." As if anyone would ever doubt that. He has testosterone written all over him. "Very obvious." His smile deepens at my words. "But I will never be your lady. I'll never be your anything."

It would be so tempting to be with him. I'd give him one night, maybe two. Nothing but dirty, nasty sex. The kind that leaves you breathless and aching in all the right places the next day. The kind that makes every inch of you sweat and leaves you slick between your legs. The kind that breaks your bed and ruins your sheets.

He's beautiful. Just the way I like them. Tall, lean, and hard all over. But I can tell he's not the type of man who will walk away. And the fact that he's friends with my sister's man complicates it. I'd run into him, and I don't like to run into the men I invite into my bed. They are there to serve a purpose, not to become a permanent part of my life. Besides, I'm all about the black love. I need to keep reminding myself of that.

"I'll remind you of this conversation when we celebrate your first anniversary."

"Normally, I find confidence attractive, but not on you. You should go. I need to prepare for my next class, and I'm sure your son will be home soon."

"He has a nanny," he says.

"But he needs his dad." I speak louder than I intend to, and I turn and give him my back while I gather my thoughts. I clear my throat and take a deep breath. Colt's relationship with his son is not my business, but it wouldn't be the first time I've had to put a neglectful parent in their place. It's something I do quite regularly in my line of work.

"Tell me how you really feel, Queen Vee. He has a swimming lesson—"

"Not my business." Deciding to shut this down before he says too much, I turn back to face him. "You should go."

My door bursts open. A group of teachers walk in and look around the room. Of course, word got out that he's here. I'm surprised it took them this long to barge in. The tension in the room lifts and Colt turns into the charismatic athlete that he is. In an instant, he smiles, turns, and signs whatever's put in front of him. Phones are taken out and selfies requested are granted.

I sigh, turn to my whiteboard, and write the questions I want to discuss for the next class as more people filter in and out of my room. I tune out the questions and laughter, but Colt's voice, just like him, carries and is impossible to ignore. I admit, he's charming. He's made every woman blush and every man feel important. It's something I noticed about him in his commercials. He has a presence that's far more than just his pretty face.

Once the bell rings, I turn to my full classroom and say, "Okay, everyone, make room for my students." I point to the door, and the teachers hurry out, likely to get to their own classrooms. I can only imagine the crowd if Colt doesn't leave before the final bell rings.

"I'll just stand in the back until class is over. You promised to eat with me." He walks to the back wall, leans against it, and crosses his arms.

"You'll only disrupt my class. Go wait outside." The words are barely out of my mouth when my door opens, and my students walk through. Word must have gotten out. It's pandemonium when they spot my uninvited guest. Any hopes I had of getting through this afternoon's lesson are gone. The kids are going wild. Cell phones they're not supposed to have come out. A few of them go live on social media.

Resigned, I sit at my desk and watch the scene in front of me. Five minutes. I'm going to give them five minutes before I take control of this. Colt signs autographs, takes selfies, and answers questions.

Once I've had enough, I clear my throat, but that doesn't get anyone's attention. I slam a desk drawer, and the class calms down, but barely.

"Class, come on. Settle down. We have a lesson to get through," I say above the talk.

"It's Colt Chastain, Ms. Taylor," a student yells out. "We don't care about Shakespeare right now."

I look over at Colt while he signs a student's notebook.

"Okay, guys. Let's give Ms. Taylor the room. I'll be in the back. We can hang out for a bit after class, but you do your work first." Everyone is in their seats within seconds, and I turn to today's lesson.

True to his word, he stands at the back, watching and listening to me the entire time while we discuss Macbeth. I do my best to put him out of my mind and focus on my students, but his eyes practically burn holes in the back of my head. Because of the disruption, the bell rings before I can get through what I had planned for today, and when the class ends, the students congregate around Colt. My door opens and other students and teachers walk in, crowding him for autographs and pictures.

"It's been fun, guys, but I have to go. Ms. Taylor promised to eat with me." The class cheers, and I plan all the different ways I'm going to kill him for making that public. I ignore him while I grab my things, and the crowd in my room thins out until the last person leaves.

"You ready?" he asks as if he didn't wreck my entire afternoon. He throws an arm across my shoulders. "You want me to carry that for you?" He takes my bag and slings it over his shoulder.

NINE

Colt

It takes us half an hour to finally walk out of the school, but I keep my arm around her the entire time. Her lips are pursed shut, and the smile she gives to the kids and her colleagues is fake. She hates the attention, and I get it. When I first got in the league, I hated it too. All I wanted to do was play, but everyone wants a piece of me every time I step outside the house. People in the city think they own you if you play for their team. By the time we finally exit the school, my driver has the door to my car opened and ready.

A large group follows us from the school, and I block Victoria with my body. The only place she has to go is inside my car, and she does just that. I'm sure it's to get away from the group, not so she can have a late lunch with me. She exhales loudly once she's situated inside the car and away from the crowd. I close the door, and she turns and glares at me. She snatches her seatbelt and snaps it on with more force than required. When I try to slide in the middle so I can be closer to her, she holds up her palm, telling me to stay put.

"Let's get a few things straight," she hisses. A piece of hair falls on her forehead, and she angrily swipes it away.

"Yes. Let's." The smile I give her only makes her angrier.

"First, you don't come to my place of work and disrupt it. How would you feel if I showed up at one of your games and made a scene? You screwed up my entire afternoon. Furthermore—"

"You want to come to my games?" I smile deeper. She huffs and turns away. I can hear her quietly counting to ten. "Why didn't you just say so? I will make arrangements—"

"No, I do not want to go to any of your games." She enunciates each word to get her point across. "I don't care for basketball. Do you know what else I don't care for?"

"I'm sure you're about to tell me."

"High handed men."

"High handed men are the worst. I agree with you on that." Her head snaps back and the look she's giving me would have made a weak man cry. "One time, when I was a boy, my—"

"And that." She points a long index finger at me. "I don't like that."

"My face?" I pat my cheeks. "I don't think there's anything I can do about this. I'm not getting plastic surgery for you, Queen. Anything else but that."

"Your attitude. I'm done." She turns away from me and leans forward. "Excuse me?" she says to my driver. "I'm Victoria Taylor. What's your name?"

"I'm Dante Rinoldi, ma'am."

"Dante, can you please pull over so I can get out?"

I catch Dante's eyes through the mirror and subtly shake my head no. He looks away and says, "Sorry, ma'am. Too dangerous to pull over here." I look out the window and curse at the lack of traffic on east 128th street, headed away from the high school. We come up to a red light, and she tries to open the door.

"Child safety locks," I say. "Evan would always try to open the door as a baby." She huffs, crosses her arms, and looks out the window. "These car manufacturers think of everything."

"You're really starting to piss me off, Chastain. Trust me. You don't want to do that."

"Consider me warned, but you did promise to eat with me."

Dante drives through the Harlem streets, and my guest seethes next to me.

"First off, I didn't promise. But you want to eat? Fine. Let's eat so I can tell you all the ways that you've pissed me off." She crosses her arms and stares out the window. She doesn't speak for the rest of the short ride. When Dante pulls in front of Melba's restaurant, he jumps out and opens the car door for her. She stomps past him and heads toward the restaurant. I run after her to hold the door open. That only makes her angrier.

"Southern gentleman," I remind her. We're greeted by the hostess and seated at a secluded table in the corner behind a plant. It's after the lunch rush and before dinner, so the place is pretty much empty. I pull her chair out before taking my own seat across from her.

She drinks her water and doesn't bother to pick up the menu. She seems to have calmed down from the car ride, and I do my best to hide my amusement. I've gotten so used to everyone falling at my feet, especially women, that I enjoy her obvious dislike of me. But there's more. Her eyes followed me everywhere I went when I was at her parents' house last week. I think she wants to hate me, but she can't. She wishes she could, though, which makes her angry.

"You want me to read the menu to you?" I ask, trying to get her attention.

"I already know what I want. I come here at least once a month."

The waitress arrives, a young woman who appears to be in her early to mid-twenties. She's a pretty black woman with big, brown eyes behind a thick pair of glasses.

"Vickie Taylor?" the waitress says.

Vickie's head snaps up, and she jumps out of her chair and takes the woman into a hug. They're about the same height, but there's something maternal about how Vickie holds her. She cups her cheeks and looks into her eyes.

"Tilly? You're all grown up," Vickie says. They hug like two people who haven't seen each other for years.

I clear my throat, doing my best to gain her attention. Finally, Vickie pulls away. "Tilly lived next door to us until she was twelve. Tara used to babysit her when she was younger."

Tilly blushes at the memory. Her thick round glasses have polka dots on the frame, and she has her hair in a tight bun, but all the female staff have the same hairstyle. They talk for a few minutes. Tilly recently moved back to New York.

"You moved back to the house? Dad didn't tell me."

"I've been back a week. I saw them once. I've been busy painting and unpacking. I'm only working here until I start my job in a couple of months."

A few people filter in and Vickie orders a French Martini and the jumbo shrimp. I stick to water and the pan seared sea bass.

Tilly walks away after promising to get together with

Vickie and Tara soon. A few guys approach when they see me, asking for pictures and autographs.

Vickie sits back in her chair, crosses her arms, and watches with a look of distaste on her face.

"Remember our first date when we told each other all the things we didn't like about each other?"

Her eyebrows shoot up to her forehead. "First date?" She does a fake laugh. "When did that happen?"

"Good point. This is our first official date."

"Do you always date women who are pissed off at you, Colt?"

"It's happened before."

Tilly returns with my water and Vickie's drink. She gulps down half of it in one sip and immediately orders another.

"How's your devil's milk?" I ask.

She eyes me, and I can see the steam practically pouring out of her ears.

"I'm an adult who enjoys a cocktail. I make zero apologies for that, and I don't see that changing ever." To prove her point, she finishes the drink and washes it down with her water.

"You're really beautiful." The compliment confuses her so much, it takes the wind out of her sails. She sits back and eyes me. "That's what I want to do today; the opposite of our first—" I think of the right word and say, "meeting."

When she just stares, I say, "You are beautiful. You have these really big, expressive eyes and full lips. Sometimes you pout after taking a sip of a cold drink. You sigh dramatically when your brother says something ridiculous, which is often. Your eyes soften whenever your father speaks, but they turn icy whenever your mother tries to join in the conversation, which I don't understand. Your mama is sweet, other than trying to convince you to get back with your ex. I'm sure once she knows about us, she'll forget all about him."

She stares some more, not offering a rebuttal. "Your turn to say something nice about me now. See? The opposite of our first meeting."

"You're a controlling jackass, and you don't know squat about me or my mama." She uses a southern drawl inflection when she says mama. Tilly brings her a fresh drink, but she sips it slower this time. She also puts a platter of crab cakes in front of us and tells us that it's on the house.

"I think you misunderstand the assignment, Ms. Taylor. That's really a shame considering your profession." I grab a fork, put a piece of crab cake on it, and offer it to her. She shakes her head and picks up her own fork. "You're supposed to say something nice about me."

"I can't think of a single thing." She looks up at the ceiling as if she's deep in thought. "Nope. Not a single thing."

"That hurts, my queen." I put a hand to my heart, and she rolls her eyes at me. Then something changes in her eyes, and she leans across the table. "Let's go back to that first assignment. You're high handed."

"I'm assertive and decisive."

"You try to hide your controlling ways behind your southern gentleman persona, but I can see right through you."

"I'd only control you in bed," I tease.

"You disregard my career. You have your driver kidnap me. And for what? I already gave you all the reasons why we can't be anything."

Our entrees are brought out, and I pierce a stalk of asparagus with my fork.

"Tell me again what those reasons are. My memory isn't what it used to be." And all her reasons are bull. It's been years since I've been this interested in a woman. It's been almost a decade of being able to have any woman I want, and I know this one wants me. "And try not to give me some bull crap reasons this time."

"Who says bull crap? God, you're boring, and just because you refuse to accept my answers does not mean they're bullshit." I wince at the expletive. Cursing was forbidden in my house growing up. Mama would get so outraged whenever one of us would cuss that Daddy would take out his belt. He never used it, of course, and a few times, he'd laugh while he'd chase me and Charlie.

She picks up a shrimp and bites it, and I wonder how her lips would feel wrapped around a certain member of my anatomy.

"You can be combative for absolutely no reason," I tell her with a smile.

"Okay, fine. Here they are again. I don't date men with kids. I don't date high handed men, and I don't date celebrities. That thing that you do to get your way, to sweet talk your way into a school and into my classroom, I don't find that endearing at all."

"So, it's not because you're not attracted to me. I knew it." I wink at her, and she groans in frustration. "I am very attracted to you, too, but I feel like you're holding back on me. Let's hear it because I want to get to the stuff you like about me."

"Your ego is not the least bit attractive, and neither is your dismissive attitude."

"That's another thing we have in common. *Your* dismissive attitude is quite off putting too. And when you curse. I don't like that at all." Her eyes widen at my last admission.

You'd think I just told her that I eat little children for breakfast.

"The way I talk fucking offends you?" I cringe. She stands and grabs her purse. "I'm going to get my bag out of your car, and then I'm going to take a cab home. This has been a huge fucking disappointment. And men who tell women how to talk? That's an absolute fuck no." I stand and approach her before she can take a step and hold both of her hands in mine. I look down at her, and she meets my eyes.

"Dante went to run a few errands. He won't be back for another hour."

"I need my bag. I have papers to grade tonight," she insists.

I pull out her chair and point for her to sit. "Come on. Sit. We're making good progress. I can learn to live with your cursin'. Just don't do it when you meet Mama, and drinkin' is a no-no too when she's around."

She calls Tilly over and orders a third drink.

"I won't be meeting Mama. You're not interested in me. You just refuse to understand why I'm not falling at your feet. You like to be worshipped, and I worship no man."

"Nope, that's not it. I met this pretty, smart woman, and I'm fascinated. I have the feeling you're holdin' back on me. Are you not interested in me because one of us isn't black?" I arch an eyebrow at her.

She starts to cough, and I reach over to pat her back. "That's not funny. And yes, I prefer to date black men. What's wrong with that?"

"It's limiting, not to mention unfair."

"Unfair? To whom?"

"To me, of course. Why would I care about anyone else? I'm a very jealous man, Victoria. I'm going to let you know that now."

"You are absolutely everything I loathe in a man. Controlling. Jealous. Preachy. Sanctimonious and staking claim to something that doesn't belong to you."

"I can work on those things. You want to know what else I am? Loyal."

"If I want loyalty, I'll get a dog."

I let out a loud belly laugh. It's so loud, the people from a few tables over look at me. "You're funny. I like that in a woman."

"Listen," she says as if she's searching for control. "It would never work. I'm not looking for a relationship right now."

TEN

Colt

She sits back and resumes eating. I study her from across the table as she dips a piece of shrimp in a creamy cloud of mashed potatoes. I keep a strict diet during the season and my sea bass is good, but I'd give anything to indulge in potatoes. She wipes the side of her mouth and takes another big bite. I love a woman who's not afraid to eat. The last person I dated barely ate, and I don't think I ever saw her without being fully made up and dressed. Vickie isn't wearing any now, and she hasn't tried to fix her hair once since I barged into her classroom. She's without a doubt the most beautiful woman on earth.

She was gorgeous the night I first saw her and the day I spent at her family's home. She's just as beautiful now. Maybe more so when she's completely unguarded. She figures she's already told me no, and I'll go away quietly, but there's something about her. Something that calls to me. Something beyond how she looks and how she feels in my arms.

"Well, I'm not going to enter into some scandalous affair with you, if that's what you're thinkin'." She looks up, surprised and a little confused by my words. "This," I say, gesturing at my body. "You can't just have this and walk away."

"What on earth are you talking about? Are you going to eat that?" She sticks her fork in my sea bass and takes a small piece. "Oh, that's good. Do you want some of mine?" She points at her shrimp, and I can't help myself. I take one, drag it through the mashed potatoes and stick it in my mouth. It's buttery and garlicky, just the way I like it.

"I bet you taste better." She finishes her third cocktail, and I brace myself for a fight. If she asks for a fourth drink, I'm going to object; accusations of me being controlling be damned.

"Of course, I taste better, though you'll never, ever know." I can see a little color in her cheeks. Those three drinks have definitely hit her bloodstream.

"I promise you, I will. Then the three of us will go out for breakfast the next morning."

"Three of us? You're into the group thing? I figured you for a square. No cussin'. No drinkin'. Borin'." She does a terrible southern accent. Tilly approaches and puts a pizza we didn't order on the table. In fact, pizza is not on the menu at all.

"The chef's planning a special menu for the weekend, and I remembered how much you like Hawaiian pizza." She takes our glasses and promises to return with water.

"You see this, darlin'?" I point at the pizza. "This right here seals the deal. There are only two types of people in this world. The type who loves pineapple on pizza, and the type who doesn't. We're on the same team." I pick up a slice and put it to her lips. Maybe it's because she's had three drinks, but she eats from me and moans. It smells so good, I eat two slices, knowing I'll pay for it at the gym tomorrow.

"You misunderstood what I said before." I revert to our previous topic that she mistakenly took for me suggesting we would have a threesome. We certainly will not.

"Misunderstood what? You know what? I don't care. Stop talking."

"You, me, and Evan are going out for breakfast in the mornin'. Unless you'd prefer we eat at home. Whatever you want. I'm flexible that way, but I'm not much of a cook, so you'll have to do it. I let the housekeeper and chef have the weekends off unless I'm havin' a party." She sighs and rolls her eyes, not offering me a rebuttal. Her dessert is brought out, and she eats the entire thing without offering me a bite. When Tilly delivers the check, Vickie pulls out a credit card to give to her, but I hand mine over first. Vickie offers no argument. A crowd of people walk in and see me. They approach, and I take pictures and sign autographs. While I stand between two older women, I watch from the corner of my eye as Vickie gets up from the table. I sign another autograph and run back in time to sign the check and leave a huge tip.

I catch up with her just as she's pulling her briefcase out of my car. Dante stands next to her, holding the door open. She pulls out her phone and opens the Uber app. I take the phone from her and gesture for her to get inside the car. A large crowd starts to approach, and I see the look of defeat on her face. She sighs and climbs inside the car. I only take a few pictures before I join her in the back seat.

"My phone, please." She holds out her hand, and I put it in her palm. "Dante, do you need my address?"

"Already have it, ma'am," Dante says.

She crosses her arms and looks out the window, doing her best to ignore me. I sit back while Dante drives us the short ride to her house. I have to get home after Evan's swim lesson, and we're supposed to host Vincent for a sleepover.

"Evan's spending the night at his maternal grandmother's tomorrow. I have a game on Sunday and will be away for five days after that."

She finally looks over at me. I can tell she's talking herself out of saying something. She opens and closes her mouth three times until she finally speaks.

"Does your mother look after Evan while you're gone?" Her tone is almost accusatory.

"Well, I have no family here." I raise both hands when she continues to stare at me. "I have a nanny who stays overnight when I'm away, but we FaceTime every night I'm gone."

She looks into my eyes until she finally nods, as if my words aren't acceptable, but will do for now. All too soon, we reach her building. It's three-stories, and according to Ethan, John Taylor gifted each of his kids with a condo when they graduated college. It turns out he owns property, both residential and commercial, throughout Harlem, refusing to sell when the neighborhood started to gentrify.

She thanks Dante for the ride, and I follow her inside to her door.

"I'll pick you up for breakfast tomorrow ," I tell her. This isn't the type of question you ask a woman like her.

"No, Colt. I don't like the publicity. You have a child who needs all your free time and attention, and you and I would be like oil and water. I drink, I cuss, I make my own decisions, and I have no intention of stopping any of those things."

She opens the door and I follow her inside. It's a very big apartment, likely having three bedrooms and two baths. The space is immaculate. There's not a thing out of place, and it's decorated in earth tones, but with splashes of color everywhere. There are fuzzy yellow throw pillows and blankets on her tan couch. The walls are lined with family photos, and there are fresh flowers in the living room. The kitchen has pristine white cabinets and marble countertops.

She puts her purse and bag down and turns to me.

"What about this?" I ask her.

She rifles through mail on the kitchen island, doing her best to ignore my presence. I stand as close to her without touching as possible and wait for her to face me.

"What about what?"

I take her by the elbow and spin her around, lower my face and take her lips with mine. Hers are soft, and she tastes as sweet as the peppermints she keeps in her purse. I wrap my arms around her waist and pull her closer. She's probably the shortest woman I've been with in years. My wife was six feet tall, and the last woman I dated was the same height.

I bend down, and she surprises me when she gets on her toes. Soft hands cradle the back of my neck. She tastes of alcohol, something I'm not used to, but it tastes delicious on her. I sweep her tongue with mine and she does the same.

She moans in my mouth and presses her body against mine. As quickly as the kiss started, it ends, and she takes several steps away. She stumbles, and I quickly approach and grab her hips to hold her steady.

"Okay, champion. You've proven your point. I have papers to grade, and your son needs you. I'm sure you have practice or whatever it is that you do to prepare for a game."

I step closer to her, but she walks away. I follow her to the fridge where she pulls out a bottle of water. "I usually eat whole wheat pasta with chicken breast and veggies, but I don't have a game tonight. You want to come home with me?" Her head snaps up, and her lips curl into a smile. She shakes her head and waves me away. "You can grade your papers there, and my chef will make you whatever you want."

She takes slow measured steps in my direction. I take an exaggerated step back and do my best to appear afraid when all I want to do is laugh. When there's just a sliver of space between us, she points a finger at my face.

"Do you just bring random women home? Do I need to remind you that you have a small child and that he doesn't need a turnstile of women—"

"Whoa!" I wrap her index finger in my much larger hand. "Every time you open your mouth, you make me like you more." I bring her hand to my lips and kiss it. "I do not do that. It's been a little over a year since I've tried to date anyone."

She puts her hands on her hips and continues to study me. "If I find out you're lying—" She doesn't finish her threat because her phone interrupts her, and she digs inside her purse for it. "Hey, Dad. Hold on a sec." She puts the phone down and approaches. "I'm going to talk to my dad, then I'm going to grade papers and do some writing. Thank you for the early bird dinner, but heaven help you if I find out you're not doing right by that boy." She walks past me and opens her front door.

"Okay, Queen Victoria. I'm going, but I'll see you soon." I kiss her cheek and walk out of her apartment.

ELEVEN

Vickie

I can still feel his lips on mine two full days later. He's texted, but I haven't replied. I haven't gone so far as to block him yet, but I will if the texts continue. Since he's in a series of away games, I don't have to worry about him showing up at my school again this week.

The events of the next few days are exactly why I know I made the right decision about not getting involved with Colt or someone famous. The buzz at school has yet to die down. It's all the staff and students can talk about. I'm bombarded with questions every time I step foot in the teacher's lounge, the hallway, or my classroom, but that doesn't even come close to the worst part. The worst part is the pictures that are floating on social media. Pictures of not just Colt, but of me. It took one day for my name to be revealed, and for my family's history to be written about. Not that the Taylors have anything to hide, but we do like our privacy.

Someone managed to get my yearbook picture from high school. There was talk about my job as a teacher and my connection to Ethan Bradford through my sister. All boring stuff, and I can't understand why anyone would care or find any of it interesting. The things I did find interesting were the little articles written about Colt. The things that add context to what he's already told me about himself. He's the younger of two boys, and his brother is two years older than he is. His father died when he was thirteen after suffering from a major heart attack. His brother, Charlie Chastain, was also a very gifted athlete and earned a basketball scholarship at the University of Alabama, but six weeks before he was supposed to move on campus, he was in an accident that shattered his right femur, and his plans of playing for a division one school were also shattered.

Two years later, Colt was offered that same opportunity and seized it before he was drafted into the NBA at the age of twenty. The articles about him and his late wife are where everything I've always assumed about him was confirmed. Kelsey Bennett Chastain had known him all her life. She has a daughter from a previous marriage, so there's a story there. The surprising part, though, is that they married a couple of months before she had Evan. There are no articles about them dating. They were married a little over two years when she died. There's speculation that the couple was having marital issues, and there's even talk that he only married her because she was pregnant. One article goes so far as to suggest that Colt was going to leave her and that her death was a suicide.

I spent hours looking at photos of them as a couple and as a family. Kelsey was a tall, long-legged brunette. In all her pictures, she was dressed in designer clothes and expensive shoes. I don't think she ever left the house without makeup. Her little girl, Mia, is her spitting image. In a few photos, they are dressed alike, but I don't see any pictures of a baby or toddler Evan. After spending hours searching the internet like a rabid fangirl, I shut down my computer and do my best to put Colt out of my mind. What I said is true. I have no interest in dating a celebrity who is also a single father. Beyond that, he's not interested in me. He's interested in the challenge, and I'm not trying to be anyone's conquest.

The rest of the week continues, and every night, I turn on the television to see how the home team is doing while on the road. I'd usually have it on in the background while I either work on my book or make plans for the summer. My summer plans are another reason why a relationship is not in the cards for me right now. I plan on spending a month in Atlanta, the hometown of one of my main characters.

"Family!" I slam my parents' front door and step inside. "Why don't I smell anything cooking?" The first floor is eerily quiet and dark for an early Friday evening in June. "Are we ordering out?" I yell from the bottom of the stairs but hear nothing back. "Your child needs food!"

I open the blinds and peek outside. The backyard is empty. I sigh, open the fridge, and pour myself a glass of wine. It's smooth, and after taking another gulp, I finally look at the bottle. A French rosé that I can barely pronounce. A quick glance in the fridge reveals two more bottles; then I remember that my sister and Ethan are still staying here. I finish my wine and refill my glass. I grab my phone to text my parents, when I hear footsteps coming down the stairs. There's a loud scream and male laughter.

"Get away, you ogre!" Tara comes running through the living room in a see-through silk nightgown that barely reaches mid-thigh. Ethan follows behind her in black boxer briefs and nothing else. He reaches for her when she gets to the couch, snatching one of her arms, turns her around, and lifts her off her feet. She wraps her legs around him and crashes her mouth on his.

Once the moaning starts, I let out a loud string of coughs, and he nearly drops her in their surprise. I arch an eyebrow while I sip my drink.

"Good evening," I say. Tara stands in front of him. I assume it's to block my view of his very broad chest. "Oh, girl, please. I like them dark," I remind my sister. I give them my back and rummage through the fridge. "Where's Dad and the evil one?"

"Ethan sent them to Tuscany for a week." I let out a loud whistle. When your man is a billionaire with his own plane, I guess that's nothing. I check my phone for the first time in hours. There's a text from Dad telling me they were surprised with the trip and would be gone for a week.

"Well, there goes my evening." I look at my sister and her boyfriend. She's wrapped in his arms, neither of them caring about their state of undress while he leans down and whispers something in her ear.

"Come to dinner with us," Tara tells me.

"Where's Vincent?"

"He's spending the night with my sister," Ethan says. I nod, finish my wine and grab my purse.

"In that case, I'm not about to crash your kid free evening. But I am having a dinner party next Saturday. I'm introducing Hunter and Cody, and I want you two to come." Ethan snorts and Tara swats his bare chest. Hunter is Ethan's personal assistant, and Cody is a teacher at my school.

"Hunter is a big enough pain in the ass. I don't want to hang with him outside of work," Ethan complains.

"We'll be there," Tara says for them both.

"I see who wears the pants in this relationship." I high-five Tara on the way out. "Neither one of you." Tara catches up to me, takes my elbow, and walks me to the door while Ethan runs up the stairs and out of sight.

"Are you going to watch Colt tonight?" She wraps her arm around mine.

"Where have your hands been?" I extricate myself from her, and she giggles but doesn't deny where her hands have been. "I'm telling Dad," I joke. We were never allowed friends of the opposite sex in the house unless an adult was present. "And that's a loaded question. Am I going to watch Colt's game? Hell no, but he's in so many commercials, I can't escape him whenever the TV is on. So, I'll probably have to put on some music tonight while I write."

"He's been asking about you."

"Come on. Are we back in high school? I'm all about black love and you know I'm not looking for a relationship right now. Especially with a person who can't take two steps without being stopped for an autograph." I cringe at the few things that were written about me. "And did you know he's from—" I lower my voice and say, "Alabama?"

"So?" Tara shrugs.

I wave her off. She's in love and won't see things from my point of view. People in love think the world is perfect and that everyone will find their soulmate too.

"He's a good guy," she says.

I wave her off. "Tara, he calls himself a southern gentleman who thinks alcohol is the devil's milk. That's code for boring control freak. And," I remind her, lowering my voice again, "Alabama. You know what that means."

"I don't know what that means. Enlighten me." I roll my eyes and shake my head at her.

"Come on. You know."

"Know what?"

I sigh in frustration. "Never mind. You're all in love, and your head's in the clouds."

"Yes, I am." She runs a hand through my hair. "I want you to be happy."

"I am happy. Weren't you happy before Ethan?"

"I was, and I'm not saying you need a relationship to be happy, but I don't want you to close yourself off either. At least be open to the idea. Let someone penetrate that wall."

I cackle at my sister. "Is that what Ethan was just doing to you? Penetrating your walls? Honestly, I'm not closed off to anything. I'm not available now, and Alabama boys need not apply." I gesture at my body. "Besides, I'm going to Atlanta for a month soon, and Colt is not the one. Trust me. Now, I'm going home. I'm going to order takeout and crack open my laptop. Enjoy your night. And I want you and Alan to come visit me for a few days in Atlanta. You can bring your family." I know she doesn't like to go far without Ethan and Vincent.

I give her a tight hug and walk out, taking the short walk to my apartment building. The wine in my fridge isn't as good as the stuff at my parents', but it will have to do.

I order Alexa to play soft music while I change into a pair of black yoga pants and a light blue t-shirt. By the time I turn on my laptop, my phone has dinged several times with incoming messages.

Colt: Will you be watching?

I groan and toss the phone on the couch, but I pick it up and respond to his text.

Me: Shouldn't you be practicing or eating whole wheat pasta?

Colt: So, you were listening. What are you doing?

I pick up my glass of wine, take a picture of it and send it to him.

Me: Having some devil's milk on a Friday evening. I might do some cussing later. Or is it cussin'?

Colt: As long as you don't do those things around Mama.

I text him an eye roll emoji and put my phone away. It rings. He's sent me a FaceTime request. Uncaring about the state of my naked face, I answer, making sure to take a sip of my drink just as I hit accept.

"How come you haven't responded to my texts all week?"

"Been busy. And I said it all when I saw you last."

"Did you? I don't remember. I miss you."

Shocked by the admission, I finish my drink and put my glass down. I wipe my mouth with my arm. "What do you miss?"

"A lot of things, but right now, I'm missing your soft lips the most. And the way you moaned when I kissed you."

"Oh, really?"

"Really. Tell me when I can see you. If you don't, I'll have to take matters into my own hands like I did before."

There's a knock on my door, and I drop the phone on the couch. It takes only a few seconds for me to get my Chinese food from the deliveryman. Colt is still on the phone when I get back.

"I'll be flying home tonight after the game. This is the last game in this series. We're getting that much closer to the Finals."

I stick my chopsticks in a container of chicken lo mein and nod, having no idea what series he's talking about. There's always an endless supply of games.

"Sounds awesome."

"I want you to come to my next home game."

"Aww, thanks, but I'm on a tight schedule. I have a book to finish, and no offense, but I find basketball incredibly boring, not to mention useless."

"No offense taken, darlin'." He smiles so wide, that dimple appears. "That's because you've never had someone to root for. Can I read your book?"

"You can buy it when it's published. Sure."

"Okay, forget it then. I don't miss you." He blows out a breath and pretends to be mad. He goes so far as to pout.

"One of the few things we have in common."

"Don't even think of kissin' me again."

"I didn't kiss you. *You* kissed *me,* and it was terrible." He flashes that sexy smile, the one that shows off that dimple.

"Your moans told a different story. I bet you wish you were kissin' on me right now." I give him a blank stare. Truth is, I do wish I was kissing on him now, not that I'll ever admit it. He looks so sexy with that curly dark hair, and those dark eyes make me want to drag him into my bedroom and climb him like the tree he is. "Darlin'," he says, breaking me out of my dirty thoughts. "I'm right here."

I clear my throat and put a hand on my warm cheek.

"Alright, I have to go now." I wave right before I end the call, cutting off whatever he was going to say next.

The phone rings again, but when I pick it up, it's not Colt. It's the same number that called me a few weeks ago. It's Jerry. I hit decline and put the phone on silent.

TWELVE

"Chastain!" Wakowski shouts. He throws a ball, and it hits me on the butt. I tell him to buzz off, but when I look back to the phone, the screen has turned black.

"What the heck, Wakowski?" I shove past him on my way to my locker. It's the seventh game, so we need to win to advance to the next series.

"Who was that? The only woman you talk to is your mama." I give him a hard stare, but he smiles and shrugs. He's been on this team for just a year now. Immature idiot. "Come to my hotel room after the game. There's going to be some serious partying." He does a shuffle and pretends to shoot a basketball. Every city, every hotel room, he has a different woman. Sometimes, he has more than one at a time.

"I'll pass," I tell him.

"Chaste Chastain." I hate that nickname. It's as if I'm supposed to be ashamed because I don't screw anything in a skirt. At least not anymore, but when I was screwing everything in a skirt, the team didn't know about it. "You into black women now?" I tense at the question, but I don't bother answering him. Am I into black women? I'm into one woman and she happens to be black. He wiggles his eyebrows at me. "She's cute. Let me have her if you're not interested." I look up at him, ready to pound his face through a wall.

"Yeah? Is that how it works? Just pass her off to you as if she has no say?" Vickie would rip his face off in seconds.

He gives me that cocky grin and ignores my question. "This," he gestures at his body, leaving both hands at his crotch, "is equal opportunity." He thrusts his hips twice then grinds, mimicking making slow love to a woman. "My dick is color blind. All it sees is pussy." He thrusts again and lets out a high giggle like an adolescent girl.

"One day, pussy is going to bring that idiot to his knees," Coach Walsh says after walking into the locker room.

"I'm not the one who gets on their knees, coach." He laughs like a raving lunatic as we're called out to the court.

Coach taps me on the shoulder, looking relaxed right before a big game. I guess he released the stress earlier in the gym. I've never seen someone bench press so much weight.

"You good coach?" I tap his shoulder. "That workout earlier..." I leave the sentence unfinished. All he does is nod. Coach is not one to ever talk about anything that's not related to his job.

We're away tonight, so as we're called out one by one, the crowd stays quiet. A couple of our players are booed, but that's not unexpected on a night like this. This game determines if we can proceed into the next series. There's a lot at stake, and I wish we were playing in New York and not on the other side of the country where I'm away from home, but more importantly, away from my son. The lights in the stadium dim as they announce the home team. The crowd goes wild. My heart rate picks up as I anticipate the next three hours. There's only one way this game can end, and it's with us winning and the Mischiefs moving to the conference finals.

Over three hours later, during overtime, Wakowski throws the final basket, winning us the game, and pushing us forward into the next round.

THIRTEEN

Vickie

Me: It's a success. Too bad I'm disowning both of you.

I barely have time to put my phone down and pour myself a glass of wine before it buzzes again. It's a rich, flavorful Zinfandel, sent by Ethan as an apology for not coming tonight. Not that it was necessary since they are all sick, but that won't stop me from indulging.

Tara: Trust me. You don't want any of this.

She sends a picture of her, Ethan, and Vincent in bed under a blanket. For three sick people, they sure look happy.

Alan: #notsorry for not being my twin's plus one at her own dinner party . Got too much street cred for that.

"You know I'm the one who ordered that and had it sent

to you, right?" Hunter, one of my guests, yells from across the room. He's Ethan's personal assistant, and when we first met, I promised to introduce him to my colleague, Cody.

I grab the bottle, walk over and fill their glasses. "Well done, Hunt." I put the bottle down to give him a high five. Cody drinks his in one gulp and lets out a loud giggle.

Dinner's over. We had the food I ordered, including dessert. We're currently on our second bottle of red. My guests have gotten cozier with each passing second. There's practically no room between them, and I give myself a mental high-five for my amazing matchmaking skills.

I dim the lights and return to the kitchen, busying myself with cleanup. I turn up the music to give them privacy, even though I have the feeling they will be leaving soon. I check my phone again, then remind myself that there's no game tonight. The Mischiefs won the last one, and according to my dad, they are going to the conference finals. If they win that series, they will move on to the NBA Finals, and hopefully bring another championship to the city of New York.

I was irritated two years ago when they won. The city was not only flooded with people, but with trash. Major streets were blocked off and the subway was packed with fans. And worse, my daytime TV lineup was interrupted for the stupid parade.

"You two want some more of this dessert?" I give the cupcakes the side-eye, knowing full well I will eat most of them if they don't.

"No, chica," Hunter says. "I'm watching my figure."

"Looks pretty good to me," Cody responds.

"Well, one of you take them home because—" My words are interrupted by a loud, determined knock. No one rang the bell, and for a split second, I think it's my mother bulldozing her way into my Friday night. Then, I think better of it. Mother wouldn't waste a Friday on one of her kids. She'd spend it with friends unless they bailed on her.

But she's been trying. You won't let her in.

The unknown guest knocks again, and I put down the plate and walk to the door. I look through the peephole but don't see anyone. Thinking it's one of the kids from across the hall playing a prank, I walk away, only to hear the knock again. I open the door to check the hallway, and Colt jumps in front of me from the side of the wall. I gasp and put a hand to my heart. He laughs, wraps his arms around me as if it's his right and pulls me into a hug. I hate to admit it, but he smells great. His body is a wall of muscle, and I want nothing more than to lean into it all night, but I pull myself away and make the horrible mistake of looking into his face. His hair is still a curly mess, and I reluctantly admit that I'm glad he didn't cut it. My fingers are dying to run through it and fix it, but I'm pretty sure it's untamable.

"Queen Victoria." He takes my hand and wraps it around one of his huge ones. I try to pull away, but it's no use. He puts our joined hands on his chest and says, "My Lady." He drops my hand and does an exaggerated and awkward bow. "I have come to conquer thy heart and thine lips."

He bows again, and he loses his balance, almost falling over. I cover my mouth with my hand to muffle my laugh.

"Shakespeare, my lady." When he gets to his full height, he gives me a salute.

"I've read all his work, and he never said anything like that."

"Are you going to let me in?" He cranes his neck to look inside my apartment before walking a few feet down the hall and returning with a bouquet of flowers. He pulls out a red rose and hands it to me. "For my lady."

I move aside and let him in. We walk past Hunter and Cody, who are now holding hands on my couch. They are so busy gazing at each other that neither of them is phased by the almost seven-foot-tall man in the house. He puts the flowers on my table and stares at me. Unable to look into his eyes for a second longer, I look away and say, "I'd offer you some wine, but Mama might not approve." He tilts his head to the side and waits for me to say more. "Devil's milk," I remind him.

"I'll tell Mama you remembered. She'll be pleased." He winks at me and looks around my kitchen. He takes my hand and pulls me into his body. "I've been thinking about this since the last time I saw you, even though you haven't texted me back in days." Soft music plays and he sways slowly with me in the kitchen, making me forget about my guests until one of them clears their throat.

"Vickie, thanks for dinner, but we're going to go. Hunter invited me for a drink at his place." My guests hug me and practically run out of the apartment.

"You sure know how to clear a room," I tell Colt. He looks around my place, running his hand on my counter. He even opens my fridge and looks inside. It's as if he's trying to learn as much about me as possible. "Do you want some dinner?" He walks behind me and puts his hands on my hips. He kisses the side of my neck, and I almost combust in my kitchen.

It's been months since I've enjoyed the touch of a man, and it wasn't that memorable the last time it happened. I lean into him and tilt my head to the side to give him better access. I tell myself that it's not the man that's causing the erratic beating of my heart or the dampening of my panties.

It's just a need for the human touch. I crave to be touched, and Colt has good hands. Strong, firm hands.

"Yeah, I want dinner. I'm starving." His hands come to my shoulders and slowly travel down my arms, almost making me shudder. I pull away, breaking the spell he's trying to cast on me. It would be too messy. He's friends with my sister. He's famous, and pictures are taken of him every time he leaves the house. He's a father to a small boy, and there's no part of me that wishes to date outside of my race. Relationships are messy enough. Why add complications when they can just as easily be avoided? But dinner with a man? I can do that.

I pull out the roasted chicken from inside the oven and put it on the table. And because I know he's on a strict eating regimen, I get the shaved Brussels sprouts and offer them to him. I offer to heat it for him, but he declines and proceeds to eat practically an entire chicken while I indulge in another glass of wine.

"How did you know I'd be home tonight?" I ask.

"Stopped by to see Ethan, and he mentioned feeling bad about canceling. Now, I feel bad that I wasn't invited."

"Couples only. And me, of course."

"Why of course? Because you don't do the couple thing?"

"At least for now. I'm taking a break from dating. I've decided I like my single life and have wasted enough time trying to find 'the one.' No such thing. I'm just going to live my life and enjoy every minute of it."

He shoves a huge piece of chicken breast in his mouth and chases it with half a bottle of water. "Sounds nice. You want to make God laugh? Make plans. That's what Mama always says."

"Why do you bring up your mother in every conversation?" I lean in my seat and add, "I must say, that's a huge red flag."

"Don't change the subject, Queen. Your plan was working until the plot twist." He uses his hands to scoop the vegetables and shove them in his mouth. "You should put that in your book," he says with his mouth full. "A big plot twist. You don't have to give me any credit. You're welcome."

"And what plot twist would that be?" I grab a napkin and hand it to him.

I have a feeling I know what he's going to say, and I'm proven right when he opens his mouth. "Me. Colt the bolt Chastain."

I can no longer resist the urge to laugh. I pull out the chair across from him and sit. "Cocky, aren't you?"

He wiggles his brows. "Very."

I lean forward and put both elbows on the table. "Where is your son, Cole?"

He surprises me when he takes hold of my hand. His touch is warm and a shock to my system. I do my best to appear unaffected, but when I try to pull my hand away, he holds on.

"I really, really love how you always make it a point to ask about him. For someone who doesn't like kids, you sure are thoughtful when it comes to mine."

"First off, what gives you the impression that I don't like kids? I love them. And I'm not being thoughtful. I'm judging you. Here you are on a Friday night, eating all my leftover food when I know for a fact you probably just got home from the west coast. Shouldn't you be spending time with him right now? You've been gone for days."

"Oh, darlin', I love it when you keep track of me." He lifts my hand and kisses it, surprising me yet again tonight.

"But he's spending the night with his maternal grandmother. I fly her in once a month so she can see him. Is that okay with you?"

I shrug. "No skin off my nose." I pull my hand away and stand up. My throat is suddenly dry, so I grab a bottle of water. I don't hear him move, but he's suddenly standing behind me, the heat of his body like a burning inferno.

"Stop pretendin'." He turns me around, and I crane my neck to look at him.

"I'm not pretending at anything."

He runs a hand through my hair, which I've had flattened earlier. Long fingers stroke my skull. "You're a bad liar, but I still like you."

"Everyone likes me."

"I bet they do. I'm leaving for Milwaukee on Sunday. I have meetin's and practice tomorrow." I wait and stare, doing my best to pretend like I don't understand what he's saying. "I won't be back this way until Wednesday for the remainder of this series, and when we win, we'll go to the finals." I look down and try to move away, but he holds onto me. "Let's have tonight, and when the season is over, we'll have the summer."

It would be so easy to give into that. Spend the night together, and the summer. Lose myself in this man and his bigger than life persona. I imagine how that would look. The three of us enjoying a carefree time at the beach or hiking in a foreign country. Then I remember I have my own plans, which I would not change for anybody, let alone with a man who's only interested because I told him no. There's also the added complication of his kid hating me.

"I won't be here for the summer. I'm spending most of it in Atlanta, then we have our annual family vacation. Dad and the evil one have a house in the Outer Banks."

"You know, I can travel. I do it pretty frequently."

"But you're not invited."

"Oh, darlin'. You underestimate me." He smiles and steps away. Just like he did the first time he came to my family home, he clears the table. He takes it a step further and loads the dishwasher too. Once everything is put back in order, he takes my hand and leads me to my couch. He takes the remote, but instead of turning on the television, he plays soft music.

"I thought you'd put on ESPN and watch the highlights from the game."

"See, that's what you get for making assumptions about me. I already have that on my phone. The only sport I watch for fun is football, and maybe baseball. Throw in a little hockey too. I don't hate soccer either. That's it, but for now, all I want is to sit here with you and talk." He lifts my hand to his lips and kisses it.

"So, you watch pretty much all the sports?" I roll my eyes. "Boring."

"I'm well rounded," he counters.

"You have women falling at your feet everywhere you go. Why me? Why the one who has made it clear she's not interested? You're wasting your time."

"You mean the women from my mama's church that she wants to fix me up with? Or Robin, my dead wife's sister?" I look into is face in surprise, certain that he's exaggerating.

"Oh, it's true. She wanted to take her sister's place. Full disclosure. I told her there wasn't a snowball's chance. Just so you know, I haven't dated much since my wife died."

I sit next to him on the couch, and his eyes land on my breasts. My sundress has spaghetti straps and shows off a good amount of cleavage. He reaches over and traces a finger along my collarbone. It's one simple gesture, but he's managed to ignite my entire body. The thin, thong panties I have on start to dampen. I move away from him, but he inches closer. He puts an arm around me and runs his nose along the side of my neck.

"One kiss," he whispers close to my ear. He kisses and licks the shell, almost making me combust. "One, and if you hate it, you tell me to leave." He turns my face to his, but I jump off the couch before our lips can touch.

"We've already kissed." I stand against the kitchen island with my back turned to him. I do everything to keep my breathing under control, but he hasn't only invaded my apartment. He's invaded me too. "I didn't care for it," I lie. I've thought about it nonstop since it happened.

I feel him against my back. He's pressing himself to me, pinning me to the island. Large hands grab my hips and firm lips return to the side of my neck. I tilt my head to give him full access. A wanton moan escapes my lips, and those hands leave my hips and travel forward, but he spins me around to face him.

He looks into my eyes and bites his full bottom lip.

"Your eyes give it all away every time, Queen. One kiss." I can hear the challenge in his voice. "Unless you're afraid you won't be able to stop."

"I'm not naïve enough to fall for that shameless attempt at reverse psychology."

"Hmm." His long nose inhales at the base of my neck. He slides his hands up my dress and glides his long fingers along my thighs. "Kiss me. Just once. I dare you." He lifts me off my feet, forcing me to look down at him. "Wrap those legs around me."

There's nothing I love more than wrapping my legs around a strong man while he holds me up. Gerald was the last man I did that with. "Wrap them around me. I know you want to." And I do. It's like coming home. We're a perfect fit, and it hits me that this man is dangerous.

He looks up but doesn't inch closer. He waits, and I admire those plump, full lips. I imagine putting my mouth on his and sucking that fat bottom lip into my mouth. And because it's been years since a man has held me like this, and because his brown eyes are like magnets, drawing me closer, I lean down. It's like an implosion of my senses. Everything gets scrambled, and I forget who I am, and who I'm with. One kiss. Just one kiss. That won't be enough. I'll need one night of kisses to purge him from my system. He smells so good, and feels so familiar that I close my eyes for a few seconds and just breathe him in. Right before I lower my mouth to his.

FOURTEEN

She offers no more resistance. At least for the moment, but I know that's subject to change on a whim. She feels so soft and warm in my arms that my body automatically reacts. I open my mouth to her, tasting her. It's been too long. I promise myself that we'll never go this long again without touching. It's been over a year since I've been with a woman. When things ended with Wendy, I decided I was going to focus on my son first, then my career. Everything else would take a back seat, especially dating. I didn't have a good track record there. My marriage was a disaster. Wendy only wanted me, not Evan. I thought there would be nothing else but the occasional one-night stand—until I laid my eyes on Victoria.

I wasn't looking for a relationship the night we met. And as pretty as she was when I first saw her, I wasn't looking for anything, but her disinterest and dismissal intrigued me. So, when she sighs and relaxes into me fully, I decide to pull the rug out from under her and say, "I like you."

The room goes deathly quiet. I expect her to speak right

away. I expect her to dismiss it. Roll her eyes and tell me that I'm only trying to get in her pants, but she doesn't. When she looks down at me, I see something I've never seen before from her. I see a little vulnerability, which she quickly erases in the blink of an eye. The unguarded expression disappears and the girl I met those first few times returns. "The feeling is definitely not mutual." Her tone is light, almost teasing. She runs her hands through my hair. I've never liked that before. Not until this very moment. "And stop it."

"Darlin', I can't stop nature." I know she can feel how much I want her. There's no hiding it, not that I would. I want her to know.

"Liking me. It won't end well for you."

I let out a laugh. "Really? What are you going to do about it? Beat me up? When you like someone, you can't just make it stop."

"Oh, please. Shut up." She kisses me. It's a kiss shared between two lovers. Like two lovers reuniting after time apart. It's a kiss full of carnal promises to come. I glide my hand down her body and cup her ass. There's not much there, but I give it a good squeeze with my large hands. The dress bunches at her waist, and I slide my hands underneath. Her ass is bare, and I pull her thong aside and trace my fingers along the crack of her ass. She moans in my mouth and deepens the kiss. Her fingers are now tangled in my hair, and I never want her to stop touching me. She reaches down and pulls my shirt up. I break the kiss only long enough for her to pull it over my head. Her hands caress and explore the naked skin on my back.

"Dammit, Colt," she moans. She's annoyed by this inferno between us, but it's the best thing that's happened to me since my son was born. I pin her against the wall in the kitchen and hold her with one hand. I remove her panties with the other, never once breaking the kiss. Her bare flesh presses against my stomach, coating me with her juices. I pull the neckline of her dress down, and when one of her breasts pops out, I take a brown nipple in my mouth.

"I always knew you'd taste good." I bite it, and she lets out a little shriek of surprise. I bite it again. She pulls my hair in retaliation. "I told you the first night we met, I like a little pain with my pleasure." She pulls again, and I take her in a savage kiss. I undo my belt and pull my pants down.

I spring free. Hands wrap around me, and I sigh at the sensation. It's been so long that I could combust and come in her hand, but I'd rather be inside of her.

"Fuck me," she orders. "Do it now before I die." Her hands find my butt. "God, you have a tight ass." She slaps it and digs her nails into my flesh. The stinging sensation makes me harder. I press into her. "Makes me want to bite it," she whispers. She takes my bottom lip between her teeth and bites down.

I make a mental note to give my personal trainer a raise.

I find her warm heat and sink two fingers inside.

"Oh, God, yes," she purrs in my ears. She starts to grind on my skin, likely looking for relief.

"You should know that this isn't—"

"Yeah. I get it. This isn't anything. One night, Colt, and it stays between us." She kisses me deep, sucking on my tongue and moaning into my mouth. "Now. Right now."

I don't think I can wait to take her into her bedroom. She grinds and I feel her clit on my stomach. I'm completely coated with her now. I inch her down, and she slides onto me, inch by inch. It takes all my willpower not to come instantly. I hold her against the wall and thrust into her.

"Oh, fuck," she groans. "That's way more than I was

expecting." I stop, giving her time to get used to my size. She's small, and I'm big and thick. "Don't stop. Fuck me." And I do. I ram into her, slamming her into the wall. She grinds onto me, screwing me back. She's wet and hot, and I fit inside of her just right. I forget everything and kiss her so deep, I don't know where I end and she begins. Those sharp fingernails dig into my ass, giving me just the right combination of pleasure and pain. She convulses, cursing into my mouth and biting my bottom lip as she comes. I'm so close, ready to let go inside of her tight, warm sheath, then I remember I didn't bother with a condom.

I pull out just in time to spurt on the floor. I grab myself and strings of cum hit her upper chest. She slides down my body, her wetness leaving streaks down my stomach and upper thighs. I kick my pants off, but I grab the pack of condoms from my pocket. I toss her over my shoulder and run to her bedroom. We fall on the bed, and I do my best not to crush her. With both of us naked, I rest between her spread legs and kiss those lips .

HOURS LATER, I SPOON HER, AND I FEEL HER BODY tense at the closeness. I push that feeling aside and plant a loud kiss on her shoulder. I push her hair out of the way and kiss her long neck. The moonlight gives the room a golden hue, and I sigh in contentment. I don't remember the last time I was so relaxed with a woman. Maybe I've never been. There have always been too many expectations of me to ever fully be relaxed. When I was in high school, it was the expectations of the professional league, and eventually, the money and celebrity that would yield. When I made it into the NBA, the women I met never wanted to get to know me. They wanted the athlete.

When Kelsey came into my life again, I held onto her. She was familiar. I'd known her since we were kids. I thought I understood her expectations of me, but that was all a lie too. Kelsey had changed, and not for the better, but I didn't figure that out until it was too late.

I've never been with someone who had their own career, their own money, and who has already made their own path in life. Those responsibilities have always fallen on me. Victoria doesn't want or need anything from me, and that's freeing.

I kiss the back of her neck and start to feel myself getting hard again. She sighs and slowly turns to face me. She looks well loved. Her cheeks are flushed, and the expression on her face is relaxed and happy. I glide a finger down her neck and down her sternum.

"My queen, my liege," I whisper in my fake British accent.

"I cast you away, peasant," she says back. Unlike me, her British accent is much better. "You're not worthy of being in the presence of royalty."

"I throw myself at the mercy of my queen." She giggles, and the sound is melodic. I pull her closer and kiss her soundly. "This is the best Friday night I've had in years."

"Well, you have the privilege of being amongst your queen." She laughs, and then her face changes. The laughter dies on her tongue and the cool relaxed look disappears. If I didn't know any better, I would have thought I had imagined it. She breaks my stare and clears her throat.

I put a finger to her chin and discover she has a cleft. I tilt her head up so she can look at me. "Where'd you go?"

She moves her head, and I drop my hand. Suddenly the

warmth in the room is replaced with a cold chill. "I have to get up early tomorrow. You should go." She rolls away and climbs out of the bed, leaving me confused. "Your curiosity was piqued, but now that you got what you wanted—" She doesn't finish her statement.

I stand and walk behind her. I rest both hands on her shoulders and slowly turn her around. She holds my stare briefly before looking away.

"Who hurt you?" I whisper.

She looks up at me in surprise, and I see a flash of softness, but it's gone in an instant.

"Stick to basketball, not psychoanalysis." She tries to pull away, but she weighs next to nothing, and I easily restrain her.

"You think I do this kind of thing all the time?"

"Don't you?"

"No," I say simply. "I don't. I'm here because I like you." I pull her into my body and wrap my arms around her. "You're short. Did anyone ever tell you that?" I ask to lighten the mood.

She snorts into my chest, and the heaviness dissipates. "Everyone is short next to you, Gumby, or do you prefer string bean? And for the record, I'm not short. I'm the tallest woman in my family." She puffs out her chest in pride at that declaration. I also notice she's pulled herself to her full height, which is not much.

"Gumby? String bean?" I step away. "Look at this Greek God before you, my queen. You might be royalty, but you're mortal. You're amongst a God." I strut around, doing my best to show off my muscles.

"Oh, milord. Forgive me. My mortal brain didn't realize it was amongst a god." I bow dramatically and kiss her hand.

"You know what I haven't done in a long time?"

"What's that?"

"Watch a movie with a girl I like." I think that takes her by surprise.

She blinks three times. "God, you're so boring. You want me to pop you some popcorn too?" But she laughs and goes into a walk-in closet. She returns in gray yoga pants and a matching crop top. Her bare feet hit the hardwood, and I admire her red nail polish. She straightens the bed and says, "Are you just going to stand there? I thought you wanted to watch a movie." She walks out of the room while I remain in all my naked glory. She returns seconds later and throws my clothes at me. I put on my boxer shorts and tee, but don't bother putting the jeans back on. Something tells me she would be mad about me leaving my jeans on her floor, so I leave them right where they are, her anger be damned.

I find her in the kitchen putting popcorn in the microwave. She points to the couch and says, "Gentleman's choice. I'm already cringing. I bet you're going to pick something boring. Maybe a documentary on the history and evolution of basketball." She dramatically cringes. I walk to her and kiss the top of her head.

"I said movie, not documentary."

She smirks and goes to her fridge.

"I'm going to make you a charcuterie board filled with vegetables and protein." I smile, happy at the sweet gesture. "Let's see if you can find something that won't put me to sleep in five minutes, but knowing what I know about you, I doubt it."

"A man can get used to this," I say while I dramatically drop myself on her couch.

"A smart man wouldn't."

"Who says I'm smart?"

"Good point. All you do is dribble a ball. That doesn't take much brainpower, I'm sure."

"Do you know how many times I've been hit on the head with a basketball? Too many to count. And where's my food? Hurry up, woman. I'm not here to watch a movie by myself." I pat the seat next to me, and she holds up her knife and starts to dramatically cut something on a cutting board. I flip through her channels and decide on a classic. A James Bond movie that me and my brother would watch with our dad.

She puts the board on the ottoman in front of me and gestures for me to eat. She goes and returns with water for us both.

"No more wine? Mama would be pleased," I tease.

She tenses and then bursts into laughter. "I don't worry about pleasing my own mama. I'm not worried about yours."

I put a hand to my heart, and she surprises me when she grabs a piece of cheese and puts it to my mouth. I let her feed me, and make sure to kiss her fingers.

"You should be worried about pleasing Mama. She's very protective of me." At least she is now after the Kelsey debacle. "She will want to vet you and make sure you're okay for her precious son."

She makes a gagging noise and goes so far as to stick her finger down her throat. "Victoria Renee Taylor does not get vetted by anyone. I'd tell your Mama where to stick it." She grabs a slice of cucumber and eats it while giving me a devious smile.

"So, you're saying you're okay with meeting her? Good, good." I pat her head, and she shoves my hand away.

"Absolutely not. I already know what she'll think of me, not that I'd care."

"Oh, and pray tell, Queen Vee. What would she think?"

I have a feeling I know what she's going to say, but I want to hear the words from her lips.

"She'll say, 'Colton, what are you doin' with that black girl?'" She does a high-pitched voice and an exaggerated southern accent. "Why I do declare, Son." Then she puts the back of her hand to her forehead and pretends to faint. "Go fetch me a mint julip."

I laugh so hard I hold my stomach. She punches my shoulder, but she laughs too. I sit up and pull her into my side. I kiss her temple, holding her close.

"She'd say, 'Colton, why that Victoria Taylor is as pretty as a picture and sweet as pie.'"

"We'll never meet, so I guess I'll never know."

"We'll see about that."

"Queen Vee only does what Queen Vee wants. Remember that."

"But Colton always gets his way. Remember *that*."

FIFTEEN

Vickie

We watch two James Bond movies, the same ones I've watched with my dad and Alan. After the second one ends, he picks me up and carries me to the bedroom. I was expecting him to put me down and leave, but he undresses and climbs into the bed next to me.

He pulls me close and kisses me senseless before removing my clothes. We take our time and make slow, sweet love to each other. He stares into my eyes the entire time, loving me with his body. I eventually close my eyes to escape his intensity.

Last night, he set my body and sheets on fire, but I refuse to let him get in my head. I reach over to his side of the bed. Well, it's technically my side, but he took it and I was too turned on to tell him otherwise. The pillow is cold against my hand. I sigh.

I should be relieved. I never bring men to my house because I want to be able to leave when I want. I should be glad that he left before I woke up, but there's a part of me that's disappointed. I shove that down, unwilling to let it come back to the surface. There are only four people on this earth who can disappoint me, and I know they never will. No one else gets a chance. No one else gets close, and that's just the way I like it. Last night was about sex and nothing else. It had been months since I've been intimate with a man, and there was a handsome man standing in front of me, wanting me. If I run into him, I'll be polite and distant. I've done it before with men I've slept with, and I can do it again.

I lay on my back and stretch. I roll out of bed, still naked, and walk to my closet for my robe. Once it's tied at my waist, I look at my reflection in the mirror.

My hair's a mess and in desperate need of a brush, but my cheeks are flushed, and my skin appears vibrant. As I start to walk out of my bedroom, I hear a commotion. I tiptoe to my door. I pull the top of my robe closer as if that would offer protection and look around my room for a weapon. There's nothing, and I'm kicking myself for my minimalistic lifestyle.

I'm jolted when I hear another noise. It sounds like a pot or pan hitting the floor. I slowly open my door and tiptoe down the hall. I open the guestroom and run to the closet, but the only weapon I can find is a small, yellow umbrella. I continue my trek down the hall and jolt at the sound of another crash. This one is so loud, I almost drop the umbrella. I peek around the corner, and spot Colt in his boxer shorts rummaging through my fridge. He pulls out a packet of bacon and throws several pieces on a hot skillet.

"Unless it's going to start raining in here, I don't think you'll need that umbrella." I stand a little dumbfounded at the sight. My immaculate kitchen is a mess. There are three skillets on the stovetop and a bowl on the counter. There are also eggshells and yolk on my pristine floor.

I cross my arms and stare at him for an explanation.

"Oh, stop it with that look. You couldn't scare a fly with that." He looks around the room and puts his hands on his hips. "Okay, so I can't cook. Well, I can make bacon and scrambled eggs, but that's all. I was trying to bring you breakfast in bed, but maybe I should have had something delivered." He lets out a breath and takes a seat as if he's already exhausted.

The skillet on the stove starts to smoke, and I walk over and turn the fire off. I slip on the egg yolk on the floor, but he grabs me, and I end up on his lap.

"What the hell, Chastain?" I reach for a paper towel to wipe the egg off my foot.

"I meant well. I promise." His arm tightens around me.

"Yes, and now my kitchen is a disaster."

"You feel good, do you know that?" He runs his nose along the side of my neck, reawakening my body. "The road to hell is paved with good intentions, I hear. Don't fret, my queen." He stands abruptly. He still has his arm around my waist, which is holding me up and keeping my feet from touching the ground. He walks me to the back of the house and into the master bathroom. He doesn't let me go until he puts me inside the shower. "In you go. I'll order us something while you wash up."

I take off my robe and hand it to him. I don't miss the way his eyes darken at the sight of my naked body. I gesture for him to leave, and he does. When he's gone, I step out, put on my shower, and step back in. Another reason why getting together with him is a bad idea. A black man would have known better. I shower quickly, and when I step out, it's to the sound of loud whistling. I know the song. Dad and the evil one play it all the time. It's an old Lionel Richie song called Easy.

By the time I'm dressed in a long maxi dress, the

whistling has stopped. I'm pleased to see my kitchen has returned to its pristine order, and Colt is wiping down the counter when I approach.

"So," he begins. He pulls out a chair for me and gestures for me to sit. "I need to leave soon. I have a session with my personal trainer, and I have practice and a team meeting. The first two games are tomorrow and Monday." He pours a mug of coffee and hands it to me. He goes back to the fridge and hands me a carton of half and half. "Sugar, sugar?" He laughs as if he told a joke.

I nod yes, and he goes to my pantry and returns with it.

"I see you've made yourself at home," I joke.

"Indeed." He pours himself his own coffee. "Now, back to what I was sayin'."

"Were you saying something?"

He opens his mouth to respond, but we're interrupted by a knock on the door. He jogs to answer it and returns seconds later holding a plastic bag. While he rummages through the bag, I get an alert on my phone. I glance at it, and it's an email I've been waiting for. I scan the first few sentences, then my shoulders sag in disappointment. I close my eyes and sigh. Then I toss the phone across the table.

"Bad news?" He approaches and rests a hand on my shoulder.

"Don't worry about it, nosy."

He scratches his head and stares down at me. "I'm worried." He cups my face. "My imagination is runnin' wild. I'm thinkin' you gave all your money to a Nigerian prince and now you need me to bail you out. I swear, Victoria—"

I roll my eyes and shove his hands away, but he takes both of mine in his. "Or someone is holdin' Alan for ransom. Is that it? Don't worry. I'll bust in there and—"

"Oh, will you stop! It's nothing like that."

"Then what, darlin'?" He cups my face again. "You can tell me. Let's see. What can it be?" He looks at the ceiling as if he's deep in thought. "You just found out the family dog you had as a kid didn't run away to a farm like your daddy told you." He sits and pulls me into an awkward hug. "I had the same thing happen to me. I don't want you to blame your daddy for this—"

"Oh, will you shut up? I applied to teach English in Mexico next year, and I wasn't chosen. Are you always so melodramatic?"

He sits across from me and puts a hand to his chest. He loudly exhales in relief. "I'm sorry, Queen, but the selfish part of me wants you here." He kisses both of my hands. "We still would have made it work, though." He returns to the bags, and I swear I hear him say under his breath, "My lady speaks Spanish."

He moves around my kitchen as if he lives here. He seems to know where I keep everything. "So, do you speak any other languages?" he asks while he pours me another cup of coffee.

"I'm fluent in French and Spanish."

"French? Ooh la la." He wiggles his eyebrows. "We'll stop off in Paris on our way to Madrid."

He puts a plate of food in front of me, kisses my temple, and sits. My stomach growls at the site of scrambled eggs, bacon, and potatoes.

"Thank you," I tell him with an appreciative smile. "I'm sure this is much better than whatever you were going to make." I decide to ignore everything he said about us traveling together.

"That's why I believe in specialization." He picks up his eggs with his hands and shoves the entire thing in his mouth. He bursts into laughter when he sees the disgust on my face. He wipes the side of his mouth with his fingers.

"You're gross," I tell him while I pick up a piece of bacon and put it to my mouth.

"So, my games? I'll have my assistant call you with all the arrangements. I'll send a car for you. And a few of my jerseys, of course." He sips his coffee while I stare at him, wide eyed. "What about the away games? I know it's the end of the school year, but if you can manage it, let Kendall know."

"Who the hell is Kendall?"

"Kendall is my assistant, and *he*," he emphasizes he, "will take care of everything." He sighs and takes my hand, causing me to drop my bacon. "I must say, that little bout of jealousy was unexpected, but not the least bit unappreciated."

I snort and pull my hand from his. "That wasn't jealousy. That was me wondering out loud why you're sitting here in *my* kitchen giving me orders. That's what that was." I poke his chest with my index finger to make my point.

"Your kitchen, your rules, yeah?"

I nod. "Fuck yeah."

He flinches but says, "Fine. Next time, you'll stay with me, and I'll be the one giving the orders while Myra cooks breakfast." He puts his fingers to my lips. "Myra is my fifty-five-year-old cook. No need to be jealous."

I swat his hand away and say, "Don't flatter yourself, and I don't want to go to your games. This," I say, gesturing between us, "is not a relationship."

"Are you trying to pressure me into a commitment, Victoria? I never took you for the manipulative type, but if a relationship is what you—"

I put a finger to his lips to silence him. He kisses my

finger and playfully bites it. While I gather my thoughts, he takes my plate of food and starts to eat it.

"I don't do relationships," I remind him.

"Right. Of course, not. But, you see, the thing is, I don't do random hookups, so I guess we're at an impasse."

Still using his hands, he breaks off some of my eggs and puts it to my mouth. It's too close. Too intimate, and I want to move my head away, but I open my mouth and take it. To tease him, I suck on his fingertips before letting him go.

"Yeah, I don't let random women suck on my fingers, regardless of how beautiful they are. It just so happens that I don't want to be in a relationship with you either."

I pretend to dramatically exhale and wipe my forehead in relief. "Well, then, conversation over." I grab my fork and reach into my plate, but he moves it out of the way to feed me.

"Right. I mean, why would I want to be tied down to a beautiful, sexy, smart woman like you? You only speak three languages." He leans close and says, "Do you have any idea how sexy that is? Wherever we go, I'm going to have the smartest woman on my arm. Everyone's going to be so jealous of me." He laughs to himself, and I do everything in my power to suppress my own amusement.

"We're not going anywhere together. I can do way better than you," I add. "When I am ready and willing to commit, that is."

He shrugs. "Undoubtedly, you can do better, but unfortunately for you, I'm what you're gettin'." He takes my hand and wraps both of his around it. He kisses it three times and stops. I look up and lock eyes with his. "I want you to come to my games, at least the home games for now."

"For now? Whoa. What you're suggesting sounds like a—"

"Relationship? You mean the thing that two adults have when they are into each other? Especially after a night of unbridled passion the likes of which neither one of them had ever experienced before?" He puts a hand to his heart. "Don't be dramatic."

"Who says I've never experienced it before? You think highly of yourself."

He picks up my hand again and brings it to his lips. The gentle touch of his lips on my skin causes something to stir in the pit of my stomach.

"Maybe I'm the one who's never had it before."

I watch as he eats the rest of my food. I sip my coffee and wait for him to look up at me. His hair is so big and messy, my fingers itch to try and tame it. He's still shirtless, and I take my time admiring his body. His skin is tanned and smooth. He has no blemishes, and unlike some of his teammates, he has no tattoos.

What are you doing, Victoria?

He clears his throat and I look up to find him staring at me.

"And not that I'm into you, but what are your reasons for not being into me again?" He stands and goes into my fridge. He pulls out a casserole dish containing a half chicken from last night. He sits down and rips the drumstick out and starts to eat. Disgusted, I look away.

"Many reasons, but we'll add your eating habits to the list."

"Right. A little bit of a caveman. So, what if I agree to use a knife and fork from now on? And I won't eat your food either."

I stare at him, pretending not to understand what he's saying. I arch an eyebrow and wait for him to say more.

"Nah," I finally say. "The way you eat is the least of it."

"Right. What else?"

"Things you can't fix." I stand and grab a vanilla yogurt from my fridge. I barely take a spoonful before he moves his chair next to me.

"You gonna share that with me?" I sigh, give him the yogurt and grab myself another.

"So, I'll have Kendall call you." He stands and offers me his hand. "I have to go, but I'll see you tomorrow." It's not a question. It's a statement of fact. He doesn't let go of my hand when he starts to walk back to my bedroom.

"I think we're having two different conversations here. No men with kids. No celebrities." He pulls on his jeans, covering his nicely shaped ass. The t-shirt goes on is body next, and I feel as if our little bubble is about to burst.

"And what else? No white guys from Alabama, right." I look down, neither agreeing nor disagreeing with him. "I can't help where I'm from, darlin', or my race. And I'm not a celebrity. I'm an athlete who's grateful for every fan. But, yeah, relationships suck." He grabs my wrist, pulls me into his arms, and holds me tight against his body. "We won't call it a relationship. Who needs titles? We're just two people who eat together, make love *only* with each other and share popcorn while we watch a movie on a Friday night. The fact that you were sprawled on top of me makes no difference." He takes both of my hands in his and brings them to his lips.

"Colt—"

"Just come to these two home games in a few days. I fly to L.A. tonight. If you can't come to the away games, come to the ones here. Not as my girlfriend or anythang."

"Girlfriend? Are you crazy?" I try to break free of him, but he pulls me closer.

He sighs as if I annoy him and says, "I said *not* as my

girlfriend. You just don't listen. No one will even know you're there for me. You'll just be a fan. My very own little good luck charm." He kisses my cheeks, my eyelids, and then my mouth. "That's it." He lets me go and raises both hands up. "If we lose, it will be on your head."

I huff and stare at the ceiling. "I hate basketball," I tell him while I stomp my feet.

"Other than it being my career, livelihood, and all I've known since I was a kid, I totally agree with you. Basketball is the worst. Football is where it's at." He looks around the bedroom for his belt. While he puts it on, he says, "And I know we're not a couple and we don't need to compromise, but I'll come to one girly thing of your choice. Like a doily making class or somethin'."

"A what?"

"A doily. Those white thingies." When I give him a blank stare he sighs loudly and says, "Mama will explain it better when you two meet."

"I think you've officially lost your mind."

"If you really want to punish me, drag me for a deep tissue massage. I'd be really mad about that." He slaps my ass and sits on the bed to pull on his sneakers. "Do you belong to a book club? You look like the type of woman who does."

"As a matter of fact, yes," I tell him.

"Drag me to one of those. If you really want to punish me, make me read anything by John Grisham. I hate those." He winks and kisses my cheek. "I know we're not in a relationship or anything, but if we were, we'd be kicking butt. We got this, darlin'."

"Am I supposed to come to this game by myself?" He looks up and smiles while he ties his shoes.

"Bring a friend. A *female* friend," he stresses. "Workout

the details with Kendall, but I have to go." He bows dramatically, and a piece of his hair falls on his forehead. "My queen, my liege. Until we meet again." He kisses me deeply and walks out of the bedroom and out of my apartment.

I drop myself on the bed and stare at the ceiling, wondering just what the hell I got myself into. Last night was supposed to be a night of fun and sex, the type of night I promised myself more of. The type of night where I indulge in carnal pleasure without the shackles of commitment, but I don't think Colt Chastain understands what casual sex is.

I reach over to my nightstand and grab my phone. There's already a text from Colt.

Colt: I'm not thinking about you.
Me: Aren't you driving?
Colt: Worrying about my safety is a girlfriend's job. Don't get ahead of yourself.
I send him an eye roll emoji.
Colt: I have a driver.
Me: Must be nice.
Colt: I'll get you your own. Just say the word.
Me: If I wanted a driver, I'd have one.

He doesn't text back right away, and I admit that it was nice having him here for the night. I call my sister, but her phone goes right to voicemail. I don't bother calling Alan. I know Saturday is the one day that he sleeps in, but I do send him a text, telling him to call me when he wakes up. I return to the kitchen to clean up, and I find a single red rose on my coffee table. It's not from the bouquet that he brought with him yesterday. This one is brand new, and I pick it up and put the soft petals to my nose.

Don't do this to yourself, Victoria. The last time you fell for a man, he left you.

I push the thought aside. That was years ago, and I'm not in any danger of falling head over heels for Colton Chastain. He's a good time for now. I won't get close to him, and I'll be the one who walks away in a couple of weeks. That's all I can give him. When the time comes, and I am ready for a relationship, whatever that might look like, it won't be with a celebrity athlete.

SIXTEEN

Colt

When I showed up at Victoria's house last night, I had no expectations. No, that's not true. I expected her to slam the door in my face, but she surprised me and invited me in with little resistance. Sleeping with her last night was a wish I thought I'd have to wait longer to fulfill, if ever. I'm not naïve enough to believe that what happened last night means we're any closer. In fact, I think she slept with me to get rid of me. I was an itch she wanted to scratch too, and she thought I'd walk away after that, freeing us both from whatever the hell this is. She could not have been more wrong.

I lean my head back and close my eyes while Dante pulls up to my building. I hop out when he opens the door for me.

"I'll see you in a few hours," I tell him. My apartment is eerily quiet when I get home, and I miss my son. I miss the mess and the noise. It's been the two of us and the nannies, and the house is extra lonely whenever his grandmother shows up for the weekend, but I believe it's important for him to spend time with her and with his sister.

I shower quickly, dress, and pack for the two nights I'll be spending in Los Angeles. My hope is to sweep this series so that I can spend some time with Evan before the Finals start. Next week is his last week of school, and afterwards, Mama will visit before we all fly back to Alabama. Victoria complicates things, though. Now, I need to figure out a way to get her to Alabama, and somehow, I believe that will be a fight. Maybe our first, but it's a fight I don't intend to lose.

I leave the suitcase in front of the door and walk out of the apartment to go a few floors down. I own another unit in this building, and this is where Evan's grandmother stays when she visits.

I knock on the door, and Isabel, Evan's grandmother, opens it. She doesn't smile, but she hasn't smiled since her daughter died. Part of her blames me for bringing her here, even though I didn't. She refuses to see that Kelsey's problems with drugs started way before she stepped foot in New York City. She gestures for me to come in.

Evan runs to me, and I pick him up. "Daddy! You want pancakes?" It's after eleven in the morning. He's usually almost ready for lunch now, but she lets him stay up late despite me telling her not to.

"Hi Colt." Mia, Evan's eight-year-old sister, walks over in a long nightgown. She hugs me tight, and I bend down to kiss the top of her head. "I've missed you."

"Me too, Mia. Me too." I put Evan down and follow them into the kitchen. Isabel makes me an omelet, even though I've told her I've already eaten. I eat it while the kids laugh and talk about the movie marathon they had last night.

"I wish I could go with you," Evan says.

"Me too," Mia agrees.

"You can come to one of the away games since you'll be

out of school next week. Mia, if your grandma agrees, you both can come too."

Isabel huffs and shrugs. She's a big woman, close to six feet with wide shoulders. She was once pretty, but hard living, and the death of her daughter has aged her.

"You two have fun and listen to your grandma. I have to go. I have practice and I'm flying out this afternoon. I'll see you in a few days." I kiss my son on the cheek, hug him tight, and leave the apartment.

Leaving him is always the hardest. It never gets easier. In fact, it gets harder because he needs me more as he gets older. I never set out to be a single father. I never set out to be a father at all. I didn't want the responsibility. I saw my parents struggle with us, and then I watched Mama try to do it all herself. I always wanted my life to be mine until Kelsey got pregnant. She claims it was an accident when it first happened, but during one of our fights, she admitted she did it on purpose.

By the time I get in a practice and have a session with one of the massage therapists, I'm ready for the flight west. We leave the stadium on a chartered bus that takes us to Teterboro Airport, an airport for private planes just twelve miles outside of Manhattan. I'm hungry and tired by the time we board, and when the smell of food hits my nose, my stomach growls.

"Move it along." I playfully shove Wakowski, who bumps into Hayden, a seven-foot power forward. He pushes Wakowski off him and he falls into me. We continue shoving him back and forth until he sits down and gives us both the finger.

Hayden runs a hand through his messy blonde hair and down his face.

"I bet Chastey finally got his dick wet. He's been in a

good mood all morning." I reach over and slap Wakowski in the back of the head.

"Watch your mouth, boy."

I pull out my phone and frown when I see no missed calls or texts from Vickie.

Me: I still don't miss you.

Wakowski tries to take my phone from me, but I turn and give him my back.

I put the phone in my pocket and say, "Grow up, Wakowski."

"What's this?" Jerome Peters, a small forward, asks. He takes the seat facing me. "Tasty Chastey got into some pussy?" He uses one of the many nicknames the team has given me. "No wonder he was smiling today. And I think it was a full moon last night."

"Shut up." I start to say more, but my phone buzzes in my pocket. Ignoring my teammates, I pull it out and smile when I see a text from her.

Queen Vee: You're wasting your time.
Me: I'm not. I said I DON'T miss you. Only people in relationships miss each other.
Queen Vee: Good because I don't miss you either.

"She's black," Wakowski announces.

"Who's black?" someone from the back of the plane asks.

"Peters," I announce. "And Ingalls, and Harris—"

Everyone boos me when I start to name all the black players on the team.

"Chastey's girl," Wakowski says. He gives me a playful grin, and I remind myself the idiot is only twenty-one years old but acts ten years younger.

"Yeah? Save some for the rest of us." Peters playfully punches me in the arm. "Is she cute? Introduce me."

I let out a loud bark of laughter. "You live with your mama, Peters. You can't even have girls spend the night." Everyone on the plane howls with laughter.

"She lives with *me*, asshole." Peters and I probably have the most in common on the team. He's from Tampa and grew up with two brothers and a single mother after his father died when he was seventeen. He takes care of his family, and his mother is extremely religious.

Me: Are you going to not miss me until you come to my game in four days? Not that I'm counting.
Queen Vee: I'm not wearing the jersey.

I can see her now, wearing my number seven in the gold and magenta jersey.

Me: Would you rather wear something else of mine? Like my scent.
Queen Vee: You're annoying. Stop texting me. I'm busy.
Me: What are you doing?
Queen Vee: What's with all the questions? We are not in a relationship, remember?

Me: As if I would ever be with a Yankee. But tell me what you're doing?
Queen Vee: Writing
Me: Writing what?
Queen Vee: My book, you dumb jock.

I send her a brain emoji followed by a smile.

Me: My queen is brilliant. I won't brag about you since we're not in a relationship.
Queen Vee: Please don't.
Me: Text something sexy to me in French.
Queen Vee: Nope
Me: I won't be thinking of you while I'm gone.
Queen Vee: That would be a waste of your time
Me: And I don't want you thinking of me
Queen Vee: Who is this? And don't tell me what to do.
Me: You know who it is, darlin'. You called my name about a dozen times this mornin'.

She sends a GIF of someone doing an eye roll. I shut off my phone in anticipation of takeoff and look up to see my teammates staring at me.

"Yeah, he definitely got fucked," Gilbert, another teammate shouts. Everyone cheers. Wakowski jumps up from his seat and dives on top of me while everyone catcalls. I manage to push his lanky body away.

"A gentleman doesn't kiss and tell," I announce to the plane.

SEVENTEEN

"I'm not going," I say to Tara for the millionth time. I have my phone on speaker while I look at my reflection in the mirror. My hair is curly tonight and my makeup is minimal, but my red lipstick sticks out like the hot sun on a desert island.

"And why is that?" she asks. She coughs a few times.

"Because I don't date athletes. I don't date. At least not at this moment. I'm focusing on these books and—"

"And you're allowed to have a life, sister."

I sigh. She's the wrong audience. I should have called my twin. He always agrees with me.

"I have a life. I have a great life." It's true. Working in the public school system was an eye-opener. This black girl who grew up in Harlem is privileged, pampered, and adored by her entire family. The things that some of my students experience daily only shed light on my privilege. Not only the love of a family but money and wealth. I left college without owing a dollar in student loans. My father gave me an apartment when I was twenty-two. I've traveled the world. There's nothing that I want that's not attainable. At least not anything that money can buy.

"You do, but also need—"

"Don't even say it." I cut her off before she can say the dreaded word. "I don't do that."

She lets out a loud snort. "Yeah, okay." I grab a pair of tweezers and pull out a few stray hairs in my eyebrows and curse myself for not getting them waxed earlier. But I came home right after school, wrote for a solid two hours and got ready for this. Now it's the middle of the week and I have to go to a basketball game. Which means I probably won't be home until after midnight. But it's the last week of school and there are no assignments to grade this week. I can afford to stay out late a few nights.

"It's just a game. I'll go tonight and that will be it. God, I hope Dad doesn't see me because I'm not ready to answer any of his questions."

"We'll all be at tomorrow's game. We're bringing dad. Evan's going with us too, so we can all sit together."

My heart drops at the mention of Evan and how he reacted when his father paid me a little bit of attention.

Um, nope. I'm not going tomorrow. This is a one and done. I don't even like basketball. And we're not a couple. We're just two people who enjoyed a night together.

I'M A CITY GIRL WHO HAS LIVED WITH TWO AVID SPORTS fans. Basketball is Dad and Alan's favorite sport, but they also watch football, baseball, soccer, and even hockey. You can walk into the Taylor household and find one of them watching a game. When they're together, they're loud, often cheering for the home team or cussing up a storm if they lose.

None of that has prepared me for the experience of Madison Square Garden. The entire stadium is full of people dressed in gold and magenta.

"Chica," Hunter whispers from behind me while I follow the usher to our seats, "this is center court. Holy shit, Cody is going to be jealous, but heaven help you if I get hit in the face with a ball." I ignore him and say another prayer that my dad doesn't see me. I know he's watching. We talked about it this morning over coffee, but I didn't mention going to the game.

"Magenta is my color though," Hunter says. We take our seats. "You don't look so bad yourself. Nice boobs." I look down and do a little shake for my friend. After fighting a war with myself, I put on the jersey, along with the matching Mischiefs cap. I pull it down, hoping it will shield me from any prying eyes.

Colt promised he would not acknowledge me. I'm just a fan watching the game. That's it. And even though I didn't want to be here, the excitement of the crowd and the enormity of the stadium has given me unexpected excitement.

"Will you calm down?" I put my hand on Hunter's thigh and wonder if I made the right choice in bringing him. Tamron would bring too much attention, my dad would ask too many questions, and Alan's not here. Tara is coming tomorrow and couldn't make it tonight.

"So, you and Colt doing the nasty or what? You're going to have to climb him like a tree with your short ass." Someone offers each of us a cup of beer, and I happily accept. Apparently, we get free food and snacks too. "And if you're not, start because I can get used to this." He sighs and leans back in his seat.

TAKEOFF

We take selfies with each other, and he posts on his social media. I relax slightly and tell myself that I'm going to enjoy tonight. I might not know how to follow the game, but I'm here with a friend, and I promised him a good time. The Mischiefs won one of the away games, tying the series. If they can win both games while on their home turf, that would mean they only need to win one more game to move on to the championship.

The stadium fills up, the lights dim, and they announce the opposing team. Hunter grabs my hand and squeezes when the Mischiefs are announced. When Colt comes out, the entire stadium stands and cheers. He won the last game in the last second by throwing up a three-pointer, giving them the win by one point. Hunter and I stand and cheer. All thoughts of not wanting to be here flee, and I give in to the enthusiasm of the crowd.

Colt waves, looks around, and I swear that his eyes lock with mine. He winks, and I wink back.

For the next hour, we watch and cheer each time the Mischiefs score. The exhilaration of the crowd is not like anything I ever could have imagined, and I ask myself why I've never been to a game before. When we lead by ten points after the first quarter, Hunter and I hug as if we just won a war. We turn around and high five the people around us. The lead doubles by the end of the second quarter, and the stadium goes wild, as do Hunter and I. We're in a tight hug, jumping in the aisle, so lost in the excitement that I don't see what's happening until it's too late.

The roar of the crowd triples, and the announcer loses his train of thought.

"Looks like Chastain isn't going into the locker room with the rest of his team like he should. Oh, wait! What's happening here?"

I look up in time to see him jump over two rows of seats. He gets to me and Hunter before I can register what he's doing. He grabs me by the front of the shirt and plants a hard kiss on my lips. It's over before it even begins. He lets me go, I stumble back, and Hunter catches me.

The crowd goes wild, and I see my shocked expression on the jumbotron. My mouth hangs open, and I can feel the heat creeping up my neck as I imagine the hundreds of ways I'm going to torture Colt Chastain until he dies.

I sit, stunned, and grab Hunter's hand.

"I'm going to kill him." The words are barely out of my mouth when I feel my phone vibrating in my purse. There are text messages from everyone I work with, my dad, brother, and sister. There's also one from Jerry. I sigh and shove the phone deep in my purse, unwilling to deal with this now. I pull the lid of my hat down, shielding my face, but Hunter pulls it off, pulls me closer, and whispers, "You're definitely doing the nasty. Don't hide, chica. He just outed you to the world. Be fabulous."

EIGHTEEN

Colt

We won with an eight-point lead. L.A. got their act together by the fourth quarter, but we were too pumped with the roar of the crowd. I was pretty much unstoppable, scoring a total of forty points.

A body crashes into me on the way to the shower. The locker room's energy is infectious. When Wakowski tries to jump on my back, I move out the way, put him in a headlock, and mess his hair.

"Chastey! Introduce me to your girl. Maybe she can give me a good luck kiss at the next game." I tighten my arm around his neck and toss him aside. Coach Walsh walks over and pats my shoulder in approval.

"Good job, Chastain. Maybe next time, save the kiss for after the game." He walks away and I walk into the shower.

Thirty minutes later, I take a few questions about the game from the press, but after three questions, the reporter turns to my personal life.

"Since your wife died, we've only seen you date one woman, and that ended over a year ago. Can you tell us what that kiss at halftime was about?" Talia, a very determined reporter, waits for my answer.

"She's someone I've started seein'."

"Yes, Victoria Taylor. A public-school teacher and daughter of John Taylor, founder of the now defunct Taylor Toys." Well, that didn't take long.

"Well, I guess you already have all the answers, Talia."

"Are you in a relationship with Victoria Taylor?" she asks.

"I wouldn't have kissed her if I wasn't, and that's all I'm willin' to say about my private life. I will, however, answer questions about the game."

Talia starts to ask a question, but a more abrasive reporter cuts her off and says, "How do you think your fans from back home will react to this relationship?"

Coach Walsh is beside me, and I feel his body tense.

"Questions about the game. Do you have one?" I look around and wait for someone else to raise their hand.

"You're from a small town outside of Birmingham," he insists.

"I know where I'm from. You have a question about the game?"

"Then what are you doing with a black woman?" All patience I had disappears.

I point a finger at him and say, "What's your point? And watch your mouth."

But he doesn't stop. He stands and starts to speak again, but Coach stands and says, "He said watch your mouth. Next question." He points to another reporter, a black man sitting in the front.

I take several more questions, each related to the game before I step away from the podium and Coach takes over with the reporters. I ignore my teammates while I walk to the exit. The adrenaline from the game has yet to die down, but I take a deep breath because I know what's waiting for me on the other side of the door.

My car is there, and Vickie is leaning against it with her arms crossed and eyes narrowed. I nod at Dante, who mouths good luck before getting inside the car. I hold the door open and gesture for her to get inside. She doesn't.

"I am so going to kill you," she whispers. She looks around, and when she makes sure no one is paying attention to us, she turns back to me and cracks her knuckles. I'd laugh if the look on her face wasn't so serious.

"Where's your friend?" I ask her, relieved that I don't see him.

"He took an Uber to his boyfriend's."

I sigh, cup her face, and kiss her. She relaxes for a fraction of a second and kisses me back. Right before she bites my lower lip.

"Mmhmm. Do that again." Like I did at the stadium, I grab her shirt and bring her closer. "I like my women feisty, and a little pain turns me on." She pushes me, but I take her hand and put it on the growing bulge in my pants, but she yanks it away as if burned.

"I told you I didn't want anyone to know. My dad saw that. He's been blowing up my phone for two hours, you thoughtless jerk."

I put both hands up in surrender. "I'm sorry, darlin'. I got so excited, and I looked up and saw you wearin' my jersey and forgot myself." I take her hand and put it to my chest. "I've done it with my Mama a million times. I just get so excited when someone I care about comes to my games."

She pulls her hand away and swats me several times.

"Don't compare me to your mama, you mama's boy." I put my hands up to shield myself from her hits and laugh when she only hits me harder. Well, as hard as someone her size can hit.

"Queen Vee, come on." I grab her wrists and pull her against my chest. "Nothing's changed. We're still not a couple."

She doesn't say a word. She stays pressed against me. I let go of one wrist and snake my free arm around her waist, holding her in place. God, I like how her soft body feels against mine. Even as she pants like a cornered animal, all I want to do is bend down and kiss her.

"I saw your post-game press conference or whatever it's called," she says. She flares her nostrils and her words come out in pants.

I drop her other wrist and scratch my head. "Press conference?" When she twists her mouth in disbelief, I pretend to finally remember. "Oh, right. Yeah, I'm contractually obligated to have those. Part of the job. They're always a blur. I never remember a word I said."

She shoves me away and I pretend to take a few steps back, but my laugh gives me away.

"Really? You don't remember a word you said?" I shake my head and do my best to look confused.

"I don't understand what you're mad at."

She pulls out her phone and replays my press conference from a few minutes ago. I put a hand to my mouth in shock.

"Oh. I see why that would make you mad." I point at the offending phone. "My goodness, I don't know what got into me. Must be the post-game endorphins. Now do you understand why I don't drink? I just can't be trusted."

"Thanks to your wandering lips, they know my name. This is what I told you I didn't want. You did the exact opposite of what we talked about the other night."

"Darlin', that definitely shouldn't have happened," I explain quickly. "But look at it from my side. Cameras and the adrenaline from the game. And that Yankee reporter was talkin' so darn fast, I could barely understand what she was sayin'." I make sure my southern twang gets thicker with each word. "I have no memory of utterin' those words, but I'll fix it at the next press conference. I'll tell them we're not datin', and that I don't think about you when I'm away. I won't tell them how much I'm looking forward to the off season so we can spend time together. Or how I want to take you to Alabama so you can meet my old high school coach. And forget about meetin' Mama. Those are things that couples do, and we're not a couple. What else do you want me to tell them?" I scratch my head and appear deep in thought. "Do you want me to tell them that we can't possibly be a couple because of your rules? What were they again? I've been hit in the head by so many basketballs, my memory ain't what it should be. I'll write it down next time, I promise."

"Will you shut up, Chastain?" She hisses. "So, I guess Mama raised a liar." I give her a blank stare. "You know what, just stop talking." I gesture locking my lips and throwing away the key. "This is not what we talked about, and I don't appreciate being set up. Goodbye, jerk." I take a step closer, but she puts a finger to my face and says, "I'm done with you."

"I'll tell the press that you would never consider being with me because I have a kid. Or because I'm from Alabama? How about how you don't date white men? You tell me what you want me to say, and I'll say it."

She stares at me, eyes wide and mouth hanging open. She jerks her head back. It's like she's trying to decide what to make of me. I reach for her hand, but she moves it away. I catch it and bring it to my lips.

"You're an asshole." This time the laugh I was trying to hold in slips out. "I don't want to be with you because you're a manipulative, thoughtless jerk. Don't say a word about me to anyone ever again. You've done enough damage."

I turn her hand over and kiss the middle of her palm. Her nostrils flare and she tries to muffle her groan with a sigh.

"But hear me out."

She snatches her hand from me, moves away, and crosses her arms. "I don't want to hear another word from you." I put a finger under her chin, but she wraps her hand around it and twists it. It doesn't hurt, even though I think that's her intention. I give her what she wants and let out an exaggerated pained yelp. She tries to bend it back, but I press against her palm. "Let's see how well you play with a broken finger, you liar." I pull my hand away and hold both hands up in surrender. "You set me up."

"Did I?" I reach for her hand again and quickly intertwine my fingers with hers. "I asked you to come to my game and wear my jersey, and you did. You let my driver pick you up, and you waited for me after the game."

"That's so I could tell you off for being a lying jerk to your face. We said we weren't dating." She whispers the last word as if it's a sordid secret.

She walks away, and I wonder if she knows where she's going. We're in the back of the stadium. It's just after midnight and dark outside. I count to ten, mainly to get my laughter under control.

"Dante, come and find us in ten minutes."

"You got it, boss."

I wasn't prepared for how fast Vickie walks. By the time I catch up with her, we're on an isolated and dark street behind the stadium. I try to get a firm grip on her elbow, but she yanks it away and starts to run.

I look to the heavens for patience before I start chasing her. It doesn't take long. She's turned a corner, taking us out of the desolate stretch of street, and she bumps into a burly man. A second man approaches, and the hairs on the back of my neck stand up. There's more light at this corner, but we're alone.

"Let me go," I hear her say, but the man is holding on tight.

"You ran into me, sweetheart," he says, and from the slur of his speech, I know he's drunk. He's not very tall, a couple of inches under six feet, but he's wide and husky. His friend is built the same way. He tightens his arm around her. "Good thing you did too because you feel good." He turns to his companion and says, "I'm gonna have her first, then you can have her."

Vickie lets out a string of expletives and tries to get out of his hold but can't.

"Hands off," I say as I approach. "She's with me."

"Get your fucking hands off me you piece of shit," Vickie says.

"You can have a go after my brother," the guy says. "Get in line." He starts to chuckle and looks at his brother. That's when my fist connects with his jaw. He lets go of Vickie and I push her behind me.

"Get out of here," I yell at her. The two guys come after me. It's not much of a fight. I punch the first one in the stomach, and he doubles over. When the brother approaches, I elbow him in the nose, and blood gushes out.

They both try to come at me at once, but I trip one and punch the other in the face hard, knocking him out.

"Your hand!" Vickie says from behind me.

"I told you to go!" I yell but she approaches.

The guy that fell on his face starts to stir. He turns on his back, and that's the biggest mistake he's made tonight. Vickie kicks him hard in the balls, and he lets out a noise like an animal whose just been shot. She kicks him again and says, "Think of this the next time you want to force yourself on a woman." She jumps on top of him and stomps him a few times. Then, she approaches the other and starts to kick him.

I see a set of headlights. Dante parks the car and jumps out. He quickly assesses the situation and pulls out the gun he keeps holstered to his side.

"Dante carries a gun?" Vickie asks. She runs behind me as if the gun is the scariest thing to happen to her tonight.

"Go, boss. I'll handle this." He pulls out his phone and texts something. "I'll call you once it's handled."

I lift Vickie off her feet, physically put her in the back seat of the car, and slam the door. I get in the driver's side and pull away from the curb.

"Why didn't you tell me that Dante carries a gun? I should have known I was around a firearm." I don't answer. I grew up with firearms. Daddy taught me and Charlie to shoot at an early age. We knew about gun safety by the time we went to kindergarten, but people in this city believe guns are dangerous. "Is he going to kill them?" I look in the rearview mirror. She's craning her neck to look behind her.

"Of course not. He used to be a cop. He's going to take care of them, but everything will be by the book." She sits back, closes her eyes, and exhales. She puts a hand to her chest and spends the entire drive to her house with her eyes closed.

It takes a couple of minutes to find a parking space. I'm not sure where I park is legal, but I don't care about any of that right now. They can tow the damn thing away. I step out and open Vickie's door for her, offer her my hand, and she takes it without a fight. She's still breathing hard by the time we step inside her apartment. She throws her purse on the couch and goes right for the freezer to pull out an ice pack.

I wince when she puts it to my chin. I don't remember getting hit on the chin, but now I can feel a stinging sensation there and above my right eye.

"I'm so sorry," she says. "I'm so sorry. I shouldn't have walked off like that. I can't even imagine what would have happened if you didn't follow me." I press a finger to her lips, lift her off her feet, and walk us to the couch.

"You have nothing to apologize for. It's not your fault. Promise you won't walk off alone again at night."

I expect her to fight me, but she surprises me. "I won't."

I cup her face and look into her eyes. She's still breathing erratically, and her eyes are unfocused. "Are you okay?"

She nods. "I'm fine. What about you? What about your hands? How are you supposed to play if you break a bone?" She grabs both my hands and turns them over. I have a couple of cuts on my knuckles, but nothing more. I flex my fingers and wave my hands around.

"They're fine. I've done worse in fights with my brother when we were teens. I know how to throw a punch. Don't worry about me." I caress her cheek and she audibly exhales. She jumps off my lap and returns with a first aid kit. She cleans my cuts with an alcohol swab and wraps them in a bandage. She cleans my face afterward. Once she's determined I'm okay, she rests her forehead on mine.

"Thank you for saving me, Colt. Thank you for being there when I needed you." I kiss her cheek.

"You don't have to thank me. I was exactly where I wanted to be. I'm exactly where I want to be now." She leans into me and cradles my face. "I admit, Queen Vee, as much as I love having your sexy little body pressed on top of mine, I miss my little firecracker. Since we're both okay, why don't we finish the fight we were havin' before you took off."

She cups my jaw and plants kisses all over my face then rests her forehead on mine again and says, "You're a big fat liar, and I want you out of my life." Then she bites my chin, making me jolt in surprise. "See yourself out." She jumps off my lap and points to the door, but I take her wrist and pull her back to me. I wrap my arms around her, securing her in place.

"You've told me, Queen Vee. Can I tell you something now?" The adrenaline from earlier starts to evaporate, and all I want is my Vickie back. The spitfire who wants nothing to do with romantic relationships.

She turns her gaze on me again and says, "Will it be the truth?"

"The absolute truth." I grasp her chin and turn her head so she can look at me. "I want you." She opens her mouth to speak, but I put my finger to her lips. "Not only in bed, and if you're honest with yourself, you'll admit that you want me too. Otherwise, you wouldn't be in my arms right now. I want you at all my games, in my jersey, and I want the world to know you're there for me." I put my nose on her shoulder and plant a soft kiss. "You want to know my wildest fantasy?"

I lift my head and look into her eyes.

"What is it?" Her voice is low, and the fear and anger from earlier is gone, replaced with mild curiosity.

"The other night when you made me snacks and cuddled with me on the couch?" She stares and waits for me to say more, but I remain quiet.

"What about it, Chastain? I don't have all night," she snaps.

"It was everything. Believe it or not, I've never had anyone other than Mama"—she sighs at the mention of my mother—"do that for me."

She snorts and looks away. "Liar. I'm sure your wife did that for you. And if that's your fantasy, you're boring. I don't do boring."

I take her chin and turn her toward me. "She didn't, and one day I'll tell you all about that, but not tonight. Tonight, I want to be home with you. I want to eat dinner with you, go to bed with you, and wake up with you. I just want to be boring with you." I cradle the back of her neck and kiss her forehead. Her body finally relaxes into mine. "I'm going to climb this wall that you've got around yourself." I kiss her forehead and rest mine against it.

"You better take your butt home to your son," she mutters, and I let out a loud laugh.

"You're perfect, do you know that? Absolutely perfect, and anyone who doesn't see that is blind. He's spending the night with his good friend Vincent. I talked with them both after the game. Is that okay with you?" I kiss her lips, and as much as I want to deepen it, I don't. The next move is up to her. She stares at me, and I pick up her hand.

"I suppose you're hungry?"

I exhale in relief and say, "Famished."

"Don't get used to me cooking for you. I'm not the type of woman who serves a man."

"I'll only require it after every home game. Have I told you that women who don't serve men are my favorite type?"

She hops off my lap and starts to rummage through her fridge. I admire her backside. She has my jersey tied at her waist and has her hair in a high ponytail, leaving her long neck exposed. She slams the fridge shut and approaches. I brace myself for what she's going to say next.

"You get one chance." She holds up her index finger. "And I don't know what this is." She gestures between us. "But I'm not labeling it." I nod in agreement, but she narrows her eyes at me and says, "I mean it. No labels."

"I hear what you're saying, Queen Vee." She rolls her eyes at the nickname. "But the thing is, I like labels. I'm a forward. I'm Evan's dad. I'm Mary Leigh's son." Another eye roll. "Labels help keep me organized, so as much as I don't want to, I'm going to embrace the label of Victoria Taylor's boyfriend." Her eyes nearly bug out of her head at that announcement. She shakes her head, and I nod yes.

"Boyfriend? Are you out of your god damn mind? You overstep." I stand and wrap my arms around her.

"I can see how one might come to that conclusion about me, but since I let it slip at the press conference, we're kind of stuck." She crosses her arms.

"Oh, really? We're stuck now? You said you'd take care of it at the next press conference."

"I did, but I've thought about it." I scratch my head and make a face like I just tasted something bitter. "Just think of the hit my reputation would take if we're not seen together." She sighs and walks away from me. "The world will think I'm some sort of philanderer and Mama would get mad. Not to mention—"

She puts a hand up, signaling for me to shut up. "I swear, if you mention your mama one more time, I'm going to hit you. Just shut up. Do you need to shower?" She opens the fridge and pulls out three Tupperware containers. "And I assume you're ready to eat now."

"More than ready." I surprise her when I wrap my arms around her from behind and kiss the side of her neck.

"I meant what I said. One chance."

"That's all I need."

"Screw it up, and that's it."

"My queen, my liege. I swear my fealty to you." I let her go so I can bow. She sighs and tells me to sit down. "Does that mean I have myself a girlfriend?"

She returns to the fridge and starts to rummage through it.

"I'm not labeling it, but you call it whatever you want."

"It's your own fault, you know."

She slams the fridge shut and says, "What is?"

"You." I point at her. "With that face and those sexy legs. Remember the night we met? I couldn't stop looking at you, and then you try to dress me down about my son. I'm a single father. That's like feeding a stray cat and expecting it to stay away. I was a goner within ten minutes of meeting you. You sealed your own fate."

NINETEEN

He's so smug, my hand aches to connect with his cheek, but he's so sexy sitting at my kitchen table. Despite the redness and bruising on his chin and eye, he's still the most handsome man I've ever been with. He's so tall, he sits sideways because his knees won't fit under the table.

I put fresh fruit, cheese, and a few crackers on a plate and put it in front of him. He snatches my wrist and yanks me onto his lap.

"Thanks, Queen Vee," he says right before he presses his lips to my cheek. I giggle at the nickname and relax in his lap. He feels good. Hard but comfortable, and when he wraps those arms around me, I want to stay in his embrace all night.

"You're welcome, jerk." The microwave pings, and I start to climb off his lap, but he tightens his hold.

"You smell good." He sticks his face in the crook of my neck and kisses my skin. "You feel even better. I already like being your boy—"

"If you know what's good for you, you won't finish that sentence." He lifts his head and gives me the same mischievous smile from earlier. A piece of his curly hair falls onto his forehead, and I swipe it out of the way.

"What can you do to me?" I make a fist at him, and he covers it with his large palm. He closes his hand around mine and squeezes it when I try to pull it away. "If I want to say that I like bein your boyfriend, I'm going to say it." He kisses my temple. "And you are going to like being my girlfriend." I look at him, give him my best stern look and shake my head. "Yeah, you will. I don't think you've ever been spoiled by a man, have you?"

I throw my head back and let out a big belly laugh. "Spoiled by a man? There's nothing a man can buy me that I can't buy myself. I don't need to be spoiled."

He puts his forehead on my shoulder, and I rest my chin on his head. He tightens his hold around my waist, and I relax fully into him.

"I'm not talking about buyin' you things, which I will do. I'm talking about calling you to make sure you're okay. Bringing you coffee in bed. Loving on you when you're sick. Cheering your victories and fixing your mistakes. Someone who just accepts you, warts and all. And I know I'm away a lot with my job, but even when I'm away, I'm going to be thinkin' about you and takin' care of you. All you have to do is let me."

He peppers my temple with kisses, and for an instant, I close my eyes and imagine what that would look like. I've kept myself closed off, even in relationships. There's a part of me that I don't let anyone have, and with Colt's long arms wrapped around me, I imagine what it would be like to let him be that man.

I thought it would be Jerry, but when it came time for me to fully commit, I couldn't do it. I told myself it was because I didn't want to leave New York or my family, but the truth was, I didn't think Jerry was worth it. There hasn't been anyone serious since him. I made sure of it. I wasn't looking for anything when I met Colt, but my stepmother says lightning strikes when you least expect it. That's how she met my dad. She backed into his new car in a parking lot, and she was bracing herself for a verbal beat down, but she fell in love instead.

Tonight, when he ran to protect me without a second thought for himself, it thawed something in me. He was so feral, so protective. He pushed me aside and told me to run, as if I would ever leave him to deal with those thugs alone. But the way he protected me is not something I will ever forget. Nor will I forget what he looked like taking those two guys on by himself.

"Will you let me be that person for you?" When I don't respond, he grasps my chin and holds my stare. "Will you let me in? It will be good, I promise. I've never had it either," he says.

"Never had what?"

"A lover who's also a friend. Someone who will take care of me like you're doing now. I'll be the happiest man on earth if all you do is eat with me after a game."

I run a hand through his curly hair.

"You're easy to please, then. You should demand much more than that." He stares up at me while I caress his scalp. "You're selling yourself short, champion."

"You're right. Tell me you're mine. Tell me you'll let me in. Tell me—"

"Jesus, are you always this damn dramatic? Okay, fine. Yes, but you better not—" The words are cut off when he kisses me. It's a gentle but deep and possessive kiss. I kiss him back, savoring the taste and feel of his tongue on mine.

"Colt," I say when we finally break the kiss. I rest my

forehead on his and relish in the feel of his hands caressing my back.

"Yes, Queen Vee."

"Why haven't you had those things before in a relationship? You had a wife." I think back to my dad and stepmother. They're not one for overt displays, but they hold hands when watching television. He puts an arm around her whenever they go out. Dad held Mother's hand too when they were married. I can't imagine the cold marriage that Colt has hinted at.

He runs his hands up and down my back, paying special attention to my lower back, right above my buttocks.

"It wasn't a good marriage. I'll tell you about it one day, but not now. Tonight, I want to have dinner with my girlfriend." I nod and kiss him one more time before getting up from his lap.

I'm still full from the snacks and drinks I had at the game, so I only prepare a plate for him. I slice the chicken and add the mixed veggies and a few potatoes.

He thanks me when I put it in front of him, and he pulls me back onto his lap. He offers me a piece of chicken, and the gesture is so unexpected, that I accept. He kisses the back of my neck, and a shiver runs down my spine.

"Are we sharin'? I think I like us using one plate." He offers me another bite but I shake my head.

"No, I'm full from all the food at the game."

"Good. I like knowing that I took care of you, just like you're taking care of me right now." He eats but he pulls me fully into his chest. For the first time in a long time, I relax against a man.

"You want some water?" I ask him a few minutes later.

"Thanks, darlin'. I'd love some." He releases his arm from around me, and I go to the fridge.

"Don't call me darlin'," I warn him.

"There's my girl," he says with a smirk. "You're right," he says right before he shoves a fork full of food into his mouth. "This is delicious by the way, dumplin'." I miss a step on the way back to the table. He reaches out with one of his long arms and takes the bottle of water from me.

"Dumplin' is worse than darlin'," I tell him. He grabs my wrist and pulls me back to his lap. I rest my head in the center of his chest.

"That's what Daddy would call Mama." He lets out a loud chuckle. "He'd say, 'honey dumplin', we gotta go. You're already the prettiest girl in all of Alabama.' Mama was always late for everythin'. Still is." He dropped his voice a few octaves when he quoted his father.

"Don't you ever call me honey dumplin'," I warn.

"I won't. You're my darlin', not my dumplin'."

I turn in his arms and lock eyes with him. His eyes are so brown, they're almost black.

"You always figure out a way to get what you want, don't you?" I ask him. He gives me that playful grin.

"Always, darlin'." He exaggerates the last word.

"Remember what I told you. You have one chance."

"That's all I need." I caress his chin. It's already turned red and imagine it will turn an ugly shade of blue by tomorrow. I leave him only to return with the ice pack. He hisses when I put it to his chin, wraps a hand around my wrist, and pulls the ice pack off.

"Do you know what I need right this second?" he asks. He pushes his now empty plate aside. I imagine him throwing me on the table and having his way with me.

"What do you need?" I can hear the huskiness in my own voice.

"It's wet, but warm. It's sweet like molasses. I want this,

darlin'." He cups my pussy over my jeans. "I'm ready for dessert. Put *this* on my face."

Without another word, he stands with me still in his arms and carries me to the bedroom. Once I have my jeans and jersey removed, he pulls down my black silk panties. My bra goes next. He cups my breasts before he bends his head to kiss them.

I let out a loud shriek when he picks me up and throws me on the bed. He jumps in right after me, gets on his back, and pulls me on top of him. His hand finds its way between my legs, spreading my pussy apart before sticking two fingers in.

"Hot and wet," he says against the side of my neck. He slowly takes his fingers out and puts them in his mouth. "And sweet. More, Queen. Put it on your man's face."

So, I do as my man asks. He holds my hips, and I hover above his face while he feasts on me. His tongue is magic. He teases my clit and my entrance. One of his hands finds its way between my ass cheeks. I tense, but he slaps my ass and says, "Relax, baby. It's okay." His tongue hits my clit right before he takes it between his teeth.

"Oh, Colt," I moan as I come on his face.

He flips us over, and I'm suddenly on my back with him on top of me. He traces his tongue on my neck and licks down to my breast. He takes that same stiff nipple into his mouth and sucks on it hard. My hand finds its way into his hair, and I sigh at the hotness of his mouth on my skin. It's been too long since I've enjoyed being with a man as much as I enjoy being with Colt. And it's too soon to admit this to him, but it's so much more than physical.

"I like being here with you. In your bed with your feminine sheets that smell like roses. And your soft, little body. I want to touch you all night." He runs his hand down my sides and cups one butt cheek. I lick my lips and wait for him to kiss me. He doesn't. He gives me that boyish smile. The one that's crooked despite his perfect features. I reach up and touch his straight nose, trace my finger down his cheek and across his full bottom lip.

"Kiss your man, darlin'." He holds his lips away from mine. He's so close, I smell myself on his breath, but he won't get close enough to kiss me. He holds my stare and waits. I know what he wants. By making the move to kiss him, I'd be confirming what we talked about in the kitchen. But when I feel how hard and strong he is on top of me. When I inhale his scent and feel his warm hand on my skin, I realize that I want this man. Even if it's not forever, I want this. I move just a fraction and graze my lips against his.

That's all it takes. He deepens the kiss and I know, in this moment, Colt Chastain has claimed me as his. His kiss is bruising, and he suddenly ends it and kisses his way down my body. Each kiss is like its own fire set on my skin. I twist and writhe underneath him. My pussy is so wet, so ready for him to slide inside.

"You taste good. Just like I knew you would." He slides a finger inside of me, and I almost combust. "You're drippin'." He adds another finger, pushing all the way inside of me. "I can't wait to get in this." He pulls out, leaving me empty and wanting more. He reaches over me and grabs one of the condoms he left on my lamp table.

He sheaths and positions himself between my legs, then slides inside of me slowly, filling me inch by inch. He grabs my hips and gives one last thrust, filling me completely.

"Colt," I moan. He pumps into me, filling me to the hilt and pulling out, driving me crazy with need. Sweat coats my back and drips between my breasts. He licks between the valley of my breasts while he squeezes one in his large palm.

Suddenly, he flips us over and I'm on top of him. All without breaking the connection between us. I plant both hands on his chest for balance and start to grind. Two large hands cup my ass, guiding me as I ride him. He thrusts deep inside of me, catching me off guard.

The orgasm takes me by surprise, ripping through me as I shudder on top of him, calling out his name. He's not far behind. I feel him pulsating inside of me. He grunts, and the sound of my name comes out muffled against my neck. His head falls back and bounces on the pillow. With him still inside of me, I put my head on his chest while I catch my breath.

He slides out of me and pulls off the condom. After he disposes it, he slides back in the bed, and I cuddle to his side. "That was amazin'. Thanks for tonight. Thanks for comin' to my game, for not killin' me after the press conference, for stickin' around to fight those guys with me even though I told you to go, and for takin' care of me tonight." His fingertips glide down my spine and goosebumps overtake me. "I have to make this count. I'm flying to L.A. right after tomorrow night's game."

"What's going to happen with Evan while you're gone?"

"He's staying with the nanny. Once the season is over, we go to Alabama and stay there a good chunk of the summer." Satisfied with his answer, I relax and resume my massage.

"Sounds nice," I say, unsure of how else to respond. "It's always good to go home again." Not that I've ever lived or would ever live anywhere other than New York City. As far as I'm concerned, it's the center of the universe and no place else on earth compares.

"Will you come to L.A.?"

"I can't. The last day of school is Friday, and I need to be there."

"Okay, but if we go to the seventh game, I want you to come. I want you there when we win. And I want you at all the games for the finals. Promise me."

"I promise." He smiles and tightens his hold around me.

"See, darlin'? We're already kicking butt in this relationship. Give your man another kiss before we go to sleep." When I don't make a move, he tickles my ribs, practically jolting me out of the bed. When I try to get away, he pulls me on top of him and covers my mouth with his.

TWENTY

Vickie

THE LAST FEW DAYS OF SCHOOL USUALLY HAVE ME dressing casually. The kids are ready for their break, and so am I. While I look through my closet for a pair of jeans and a shirt, Colt walks into the bedroom with nothing but a towel wrapped around his waist. His phone is to his ear, and I listen while he talks to his son.

"You bein' good?" He winks at me and blows me a kiss. He puts the phone on speaker and tosses it on the bed. Evan's childlike voice fills the room.

"The cook is making us chocolate chip pancakes." Colt whistles. "You never let me have chocolate for breakfast, Daddy."

"Maybe I should have them bring you back. I don't want you getting used to bein' spoiled." I close the closet to give them privacy while I dress, but seconds later, just as I have my jeans pulled up, he barges in and wraps his arms around me, pulling me into his chest.

"Good mornin', darlin'," he whispers in my ear. "I want nothing more than a repeat of last night. I can have you for breakfast."

Me too, but that's not a possibility since he's traveling tonight. It's been a couple of years since I've spent the night wrapped in a man's arms. I had forgotten the feeling of safety and comfort from sharing the human touch. I reach behind me and slide my hands into his hair.

"You're getting me wet." He spins me around to face him, and I tug his hair and slide my hands down his face. "They're not too bad," I say about his bruises. He has a red splotch on his chin and a small cut above his eye. Hopefully they won't become discolored. "How are your hands?" I grab them and flip them over. Other than a few minor cuts across his knuckles, he's fine.

"I'm fine, but I do like you fussin' over me." He sticks his hand in my pants and slides a finger inside of me. "And I like getting' you wet." I let out a moan and bite my bottom lip. As quickly as it appeared, his finger is gone, but I don't miss the smug grin on his lips.

A few minutes later, I step out of the closet. I stand in front of the long mirror as I adjust my clothes and wrap a long faux pearl necklace around my neck. I wrap it three times, making three rows with it. I turn around to find him sitting on the bed staring at me. My phone vibrates on the bed next to him, and Mother flashes across the screen. I pick it up and hit ignore.

"I'll make you coffee to go, but I can't join you. I usually stop off at home and have coffee with my dad and the evil one before work." I put on a pair of ballet flats, and after running a brush through my hair, I gesture for him to follow me.

He turns down the coffee but offers to drive me to my parents'. His driver is outside, holding the door open for us, and he gives us a curt nod before driving us to my parents'.

"Thanks, champion," I say to him once Dante pulls up

to the house. He opens the door for us, and Colt escorts me out. "I'll see you tonight."

"Open the door, darlin'. I want to say good mornin' to your family, and one day soon, you're going to tell me what issues you have with your mama." I want to tell him that's not likely to happen, but my dad swings the front door open. "What kind of a man would I be if I didn't greet your parents?"

"Colt! Come in." Colt gestures for me to go ahead of him, and he follows me inside. "Stay for breakfast," my dad tells him. "Vick, set the table."

"Good to see you too, Dad." He comes back, kisses my cheek, and turns back to Colt.

"So, what's this?" Dad gestures between me and Colt. "And how come you took Hunter to the game and not your old man." He pulls Colt into the kitchen and pours him a mug of coffee while Cheryl makes breakfast.

"Dad, Colt has practice."

"You can visit for a few minutes, can't you Colt?" Dad adds more coffee to Colt's mug.

"Nothing would delight me more, JT. In fact, I want to talk to you." The seriousness of Colt's tone puts me on alert. I turn around and narrow my eyes at him. "You too, Mrs. Taylor."

"Just call me Cheryl." The evil one is practically blushing at Colt.

"Well, JT, Cheryl, I'd like your permission to court your daughter." The plate I'm holding slips from my hand and lands on the table, and my mouth flies open. Thankfully, the plate does not break.

"Excuse me?" I take a threatening step toward Colt.

He takes an exaggerated step back. "Sir, ma'am, I care

about Victoria very much, and I want to make sure it's okay with you both that your daughter and I—"

"This is about to be the shortest rela—" I catch myself before I can complete the word. His eyes light up and he smirks.

"Say it," he whispers.

I clear my throat and say, "Whatever this is, Colton, is about to be over if you don't shut up right now."

Cheryl clears her throat, but I know it's to mask her laugh. Dad puts his mug to his mouth to cover his smile.

"Now, dumplin', calm down. I'm here to get your mama and daddy's blessin'." He turns away from me and looks at my dad. "Now full disclosure, she's already agreed, but I want to make sure it's okay with you." He snakes an arm around my waist, and I fight with all my might to get away, to no avail.

"We accept," Cheryl says.

I look at her with my mouth hanging open.

"Yes, calm down, dumplin'," my dad says. "Welcome to the family, Colt."

I elbow him in the ribs. He winces and pretends to be hurt.

"It's over," I tell him, but he lifts me off my feet and stares into my eyes, doing nothing to hide his amusement before spinning me around the kitchen.

"Kiss your man, darlin'," he says so that only I can hear. "Do it. I'll have no problems holding you like this until you do." He squeezes my waist, and I pretend to give in. I lean down and bite his upper lip.

"I told you I like a little bit of pain." He plants a loud kiss on my lips and puts me down.

"Now that that's settled," Dad says. "Where is Evan? You're both welcome here any time." Colt grins smugly, and

I mouth 'whatever.' He discreetly makes an indecent gesture with his tongue.

Breakfast is great, with Dad monopolizing Colt while I talk about plans for the last few days of school. Cheryl teaches at another high school and plans on retiring in a couple of years. Once breakfast is over, I start to clear the table, but to my surprise, Colt jumps in to help.

"Sit. You're our guest."

He leans in and rubs his nose against my cheek. "I'm part of the family now. You heard your daddy." He bites my face, and I let out a yelp of surprise. "That's for bitin' my lip earlier."

He removes the dishes from my hands and takes them to the kitchen sink where he rinses everything before putting it all in the dishwasher.

Once we're done, Dad drives Cheryl to work, and Colt insists on driving me to school. Just like he did when we arrived at my house, I turn to him before he can open the door.

"I'll see you tonight. You will not distract these kids today." He takes my hand in his and intertwines our fingers.

"What kind of man doesn't walk a lady inside? Especially when the lady in question is his."

"His lady? When did that happen?" I tease. "And I swear, I don't know what century you're from."

"Last night when I told you to kiss your man, and you kissed me. Face it, Queen Vee, you have yourself a boyfriend." He wraps an arm around me and pulls me close. "You're in a relationship. Labels, darlin'. We're labelin' everythin'." He gives me his playful grin, and that dimple makes an appearance. "Even your daddy approves of me, and you said you were givin' me one chance." He puts a fingertip underneath my chin and kisses my lips. "Let me walk you to class." The driver opens the door, and when we step outside, Colt intertwines his fingers with mine. "We would have done this if we went to the same high school."

I let out a soft chuckle. There are several people in the hallway, all staring and probably biding their time to approach. "I don't think so, Chastain. I was not the type of girl who held hands in high school." I was president of the science club. I worked on the school newspaper, and I worked on the yearbook committee. "And I wouldn't give a jock like you the time of day. And you probably wouldn't have noticed me anyway."

"Wrong. I would have noticed you." He cups my cheeks. "Have you seen you? Those perfect lips." He kisses me. "This short little body that somehow fits perfectly into mine. Those legs, and that smile." I do everything I can to suppress my smile, but I can't. It spreads across my face. "I swear my heart skips a beat every time you smile. I would have come after you, and if you had a boyfriend, I would have beaten him up." I stop abruptly and stare in this face. "Aah, my lady likes that. You want me to go beat up the principal? What about the gym teacher?" He makes a fist with his free hand. I shake my head and continue our walk inside, but Colt won't stop talking. "The result would have been the same as it is now. You would have been mine."

We approach my room, and he opens the door for me and gestures for me to go ahead of him. I wonder how long this gentleman act will last, but for now, I'll admit to myself that it's not so bad. We barely have time to close the door before it bursts open and about ten teachers and staff walk in. They circle around Colt like they're a pack of lions on a lonely antelope, but Colt doesn't flinch. He's in his element. I lean against the wall and watch him interact with everyone. He even takes the phone from a teacher who has her husband on FaceTime.

I sigh and turn to my whiteboard.

~

It's ostentatious. I squat down and use all my strength to lift the elaborate bouquet of flowers. It must weigh at least fifteen pounds. I pluck out the card once I put it on my kitchen island. I return to the door and bring in another box.

> Queen Vee,
>
> I don't miss you. I'm not thinking about you. I'm definitely not counting the hours until I can see you again. And I won't be looking for you in the crowd. And because I know you'd hate it, I won't have any caveman thoughts about you sitting in the stadium for hours on end watching a sport you hate because your man is playing. And I absolutely don't want you to wear what I left for you in your top dresser drawer. BTW, I need to revisit that drawer soon.
>
> Your champion

I turn to the other box, which is not quite as heavy as the flowers. This one is cold, and it takes me about five minutes to get it open. It's a tray of twenty chocolate covered strawberries.

> Queen Vee,
>
> I hope you enjoy these. Okay, I admit it. I was thinking of you. I got these in a moment of weakness, but

I like imagining you in bed eating these while thinking of me. I'll stop thinking about you now…..Done. I'm no longer thinking about you.

Your Champion

I'm not the type of girl who swoons. I'm not the type of girl who falls hard for a man. I'm not the girl who believes in happily ever after. People come into your life, and they walk out of it. And it hurts the most when it's the people you love. The ones you least expect to leave. I'm the pragmatic girl. The one who keeps men at a distance. The one who sets the terms in the relationships. I'm the one who walks away, but when I do, I don't leave collateral damage.

I drop the card and run to my bedroom. When I open the top drawer, on top of my underwear is a folded jersey. The colors are the same, but this one has more gold than magenta. I lay it on my bed, and without thinking I grab my phone and call him.

He picks up on the third ring.

"My queen, my liege." His voice is low and husky.

"Did I wake you up?" I ask, horrified. "I'm sorry. I should have realized you'd be resting before your—"

"You didn't wake me, darlin', but I'm glad you called. I don't miss you. I don't wish you were here with me."

"I don't miss you or want to be with you either. You snore. But I do want to thank you for the flowers, the strawberries, and the jersey."

"You're beautiful and well mannered." I bite my bottom lip.

Tara is the pretty one out of the two of us, but it feels good to hear it about me from Colt.

"Good manners aren't just for southern gentleman. Even Yankee parents try to instill them in their children."

"There's nothing gentlemanly about the things I want to do to you right now, Queen Vee. Or the things I want you to do to me. I want your juices on my tongue, baby. I want to eat you until you come on my face."

I drop myself on my bed and decide to play along. "Really? Well, there are a few things I want to do with you. More like I want to do them to you. One thing specifically."

"If it's what I'm thinking, I just might skip tonight's game."

"I won't let you do that, but just know that when I do get you alone again, you're going to explode."

"In your mouth, darlin'. I want to explode with those perfect lips wrapped around me. What are you wearin'?" His accent has thickened. "Take your clothes off."

I undo the button to my jeans and pull down the zipper when I hear a door open and close. "Daddy," a little voice says, "you're awake. I was watching the time and waiting."

I zip my pants back up, realizing that we've gone as far as we will right now.

"Yeah, I'm up, buddy. Come here."

"I'll see you tonight," I whisper.

"Hold on, Evan." I hear some muffled sounds and then he says to me, "I'm sending a car for you. Same as yesterday."

"Who's that? Is that Mr. Bradford?" Evan asks.

I hold my breath and wait to hear what he says to Evan. "No. Do you remember Ms. Vickie? She's Ms. Tara's sister."

He stays quiet for a while until I hear, "Oh, yeah. I like Ms. Tara better. Can you call her instead?" I don't hear anything else for almost a full minute.

"Sorry, dumplin'," he croons into the phone. My heart's still in my throat at the rejection, but I remind myself that Evan is a five-year-old little boy who's already lost his mother. He doesn't want to have to compete for his father's attention too.

"Who is dumplin'?" I do an exaggerated southern accent.

"Oh, sorry. We agreed I'd call you darlin'. Not dumplin'. I told you my memory is bad."

"We agreed on no such thing. You're full of it, champion."

"Your champion."

"You belong to the people of New York."

"I belong to you." My breath hitches in my throat, and I shake my head. "But darlin', as much as I don't want to, I have to get off the phone and get ready for tonight. Evan's waiting for me so we can have dinner, and—"

"Go. You don't ever need to explain yourself when it comes to your child. He should come first. Always."

The excitement of the game is the same as the night before. The difference is I have more company tonight. Since the boys are out of school, Tara and Ethan have brought Evan and Vincent to the game. Colt also sent tickets for my dad and stepmom, and we're all sitting center court, wearing matching jerseys, drinking beer, and eating the snacks that keep getting delivered.

Colt scores twenty-five points in the first half, and when he hits a three-point shot right as the buzzer rings, the entire place goes wild. The boys high-five each other and everyone around us. Just like he did the night before, Colt jumps through the crowd, kisses me then picks up the boys and tosses them in the air one by one.

I can feel the color on my cheeks, and Tara bumps her shoulder with mine.

"What?" I mouth.

"We'll talk later." More food arrives and she turns to the kids. Evan's smile drops when he looks at me. I smile, but he looks away. I let out a breath, defeated once again by a five-year-old boy who views me as competition.

"You boys want something to drink"? I ask.

"Soda!" Vincent yells.

"No soda," Ethan says.

"It's a special occasion," I tell Ethan.

"Yeah, Daddy! Please."

"Loosen up, Ethan. We're here to have fun." Tara flags down our server, and the boys tell them what they want. I give Vincent a fist bump, but when I offer one to Evan, he ignores me.

Tara notices, and I shrug.

"We'll be back," she announces and gestures for me to follow her. As soon as she stands, Ethan pulls her into his lap and plants a kiss on her. I follow her to a private bathroom I had no idea existed.

"The kid hates me," I say as soon as we're alone.

"Evan? He's a sweetheart. Since when does he hate you?"

"Since he figured out his father was interested in me as more than a friend." I tell her what happened the first time they came to the house, and how he said he likes Tara more than me. "But he's five and has lost his mother. His father is gone a lot for work. I don't blame him for not wanting to share him. Remember how we were with Dad?"

"He'll come around and see how amazing you are. Give him some time. So, the evil one called me and told me you and Colt are a couple."

I shrug and say, "Can anyone keep their mouths shut in this family? I'm not putting a label on it."

"You're at a basketball game two days in a row and wearing his jersey. Don't shrug at me."

"I told him I'm giving him one chance." I hold up my finger and say, "One. Singular. I refuse to label it."

"Uh-huh. Got it. You're not labeling it, but what about him?"

I inch closer to her and whisper, "He says he loves labels, and he's labeled himself my man." I put my man in air quotes. "And he calls me his Queen Vee." Tara puts her hands to her chest and lets out an undignified squeal.

"Queen Vee. I love it, and I know you." She points a finger at my face. "You're into him, or you wouldn't be here. I think Dad might be happier about it than you. He called me too and went on about you and Colt for a full fifteen minutes." She crosses her arms and stares me down.

"Is there no privacy in this family?" I lean closer and tell her about the flowers, strawberries, and the sweet notes.

"He's a nice guy. Great father. I think he was involved with someone after his wife died, and it didn't go well. I don't know the details, but I think she wanted him and not the kid, if you know what I mean."

"Then don't date a single father." I raise my voice louder than I should. "Single parents are package deals. That ticks me off." If I knew the bitch, I'd go find her and give her a piece of my mind. I tell myself it's because she dismissed Evan, not because I hate the idea that Colt was with another woman not too long ago. And this likely explains why Evan is so resistant to me and his father.

"Yeah, but he got rid of her as soon as he figured that out. That kid doesn't stand a chance against you."

TWENTY-ONE

Colt

It is with both relief and exhaustion that I board the private plane to fly to LA just after midnight, and after a quick bite, I sleep the entire six hours across the country. I wish we were playing against Boston or Philly instead of having to fly several hours every few days, but at least we won this game, giving us three wins to LA's one. If we can win tonight, we'll win this series and move on to the finals. I'm ready for another championship. It's barely four in the morning when we land. Everyone is grumpy and quiet, and when I get into my room in the hotel, I drop onto the bed on my back. I have a few hours to sleep before breakfast and practice.

As much as I need the rest, I need to make two phone calls. The first one is fast and easy. Ethan picks up and says the boys are still sleeping. Tara will bring Evan to my place to be with the nanny when they get up, but she's volunteered to keep him all day since she has the day off.

Once the call is over, Ethan texts me a picture of Evan sleeping soundly. I smile at his pink lips pressed against the pillow and the dark curls on his head that are identical to mine. Tara will have a hard time taming them when he wakes up. I miss my son. I hate being away from him so much, and I wish he still had his mother to make up for my absences. There's the guilty part of me that believes Kelsey would have fought dirty for custody, claiming she needed to be the custodial parent because of my work schedule. I'd rather deal with that so my son could have a mom, something he desperately wants.

He talks about his friends' moms constantly, and I think he's a little jealous that Vincent has his biological mom and Tara to take care of him.

When I make my next call, it rings four times before she finally answers my FaceTime request. She's wrapped in a green towel and has some gunk on her face.

"You have to give a girl some warning before you FaceTime her so early." She grins, and despite the green stuff on her face, she's still the most beautiful sight I've ever seen.

"You're supposed to eat guacamole, not wear it."

"This is going to help me look presentable after two late nights in a row, thanks to you, champion."

"I wish I could have spent the night with you again." She pouts her lips and slowly peels that green monstrosity off her face. "Welcome back, my queen."

"Hey." She looks into the phone, and I find myself relaxing for the first time in hours. I've gotten used to flying because I do it so much for work, but I'm never fully comfortable while I'm on an airplane. "You look tired."

"I'm exhausted." I run my hand through my hair. "Just wanted to check in before I crash."

"Check in?" What does that mean?"

"Yes, that's what people in relationships do. It means I'm letting you know that I arrived safely, and I'm checkin' to see how you're doin'. Am I gonna have to teach you everything?"

"I don't miss you," she says.

"You better not because I don't miss you either."

"Good. And you better win tomorrow so I won't have to go all the way to L.A. for your stupid game."

"Drop the towel."

"Excuse me?"

"You heard me. Drop the towel. I want to see those breasts." I expect her to argue with me, but she complies. The towel falls, and those perky breasts that I ache to put in my mouth stare back at me. Her nipples are hard, and I close my eyes and picture myself sucking one. I can practically smell her from here. "Bad idea. Now I'll never get to sleep."

"Show me," she orders. "Show me why you won't be able to go to sleep." I pull myself out of my sweatpants and drop the phone. I hear her moan. "Yeah, very bad idea. Put that thing away."

"I want to tell you something before we get off the phone. I know you leave for work soon, so I'll be quick."

"What is it?" I can tell she's stopped breathing while she waits for me to speak. "You've changed your mind about those labels?" She chuckles and lets out a dramatic breath of relief as she wipes her forehead. "Thank goodness. You were getting clingy."

"Not even close, Queen. Can you guess what the opposite of that is?

"No idea." She starts to wipe white gunk all over her face, and I watch, mesmerized until the white stuff is absorbed into her skin. "Get on with it. I have a life and a job to get to."

"I want you to spend some time in Alabama with me this summer. I spend about a month there, and I—"

"Colt—" she sighs.

"Queen Vee," I say back, using the same tone she just did. "Couples make plans, baby."

"I can't go to Alabama." She holds up the phone and says, "I already told you I'm going to be in Atlanta for a month. The main character in one of my books is from there, and I'm going for research. You can come visit me while you're in Alabama. See? Compromise. Perfect." She gives me her beautiful smile and waves a hand in front of the screen like she just solved one of life's mysteries. "You should get some rest. I'll call you after school."

She walks out of the bathroom, and I stare into her face until I hear the door to her bedroom open. "You look tired," she says again.

"I am, dumplin'." She gives me a blank stare. "Sorry. I meant to say darlin'. And Atlanta sounds nice. When are you going?"

"Mid-July."

"Perfect. Me too. We'll fly to Atlanta together, and we'll go to Alabama for a few days. It's only a couple of hours drive."

The line goes deathly quiet. She stares at me, and I look right back, neither of us speaking. She purses her lips and blinks several times.

"What?" I finally ask, breaking the silence.

"I don't know if I'm ready for Alabama."

"Oh, really? What specifically are you not ready for?"

She blows out a breath and runs a hand through her hair. She puts the phone down, and I get a view of her naked breasts. She pulls out a black bra and puts it on.

"Pity. I was enjoying the view."

"Okay, we can go to the coast, I guess. I do like the beach. Maybe Tara, Ethan, and Vincent can join us. That would be fun for the boys." After putting on a black shirt, she picks up the phone again.

"But I'm not from the coast. I want you to meet my—"

"I'm not ready for that," she says, interrupting me. "And I'm going to be late for my last day of school. Let's talk tonight."

It's my turn to let out a breath and run a hand over my face. I'm exhausted. I want to climb in that bed and sleep for the next eight hours straight. I miss my son, and if things go right in this series, I'm going to continue to miss him until the season ends. And despite how cagey she's acting, I miss my Queen Vee too.

"Let's try something new, darlin."

"Tonight because—"

"You have time. Let's try somethin' new. I was hopin' to do this in person, but I think it's time."

"What is it?" She looks up at the ceiling as if I exhaust her.

"No one knows this but about a week before Kelsey died, I saw a lawyer about divorcin' her. You're the only person I've told this to. She died from a drug overdose. My marriage wasn't happy for several reasons besides her drug problem, and since you're pressed for time, I'll have to wait to tell you more about that. I finally started seein' someone last year, but it didn't work out. What I'm tryin' to say is that I want to build somethin' with you. This isn't a fling, and I hate that you're treatin' it like that. I thought we had gotten past this the other night, but I guess I wasn't clear."

I think I've stunned her speechless. She swallows several times and runs her fingers through her hair.

"I don't understand why you're telling me this as I'm on my way out the door. I have work and—"

"It's the last flippin' day of school, Victoria. Stop hidin'. It's your turn. Confess somethin' to me." I can feel my voice rising and my accent getting more and more pronounced with each word, but she finally sighs and begins to talk.

"The last boyfriend I had was almost four years ago, and he left me because I would not move to Kentucky with him. He got into a medical residency there, and I didn't want to go, but I told him we could date long distance. He gave me an ultimatum, and when I called his bluff, he ended things. When it ended, he called me an ice queen bitch who would only bring misery to any man unlucky enough to meet her."

I close my eyes and exhale. "Your last boyfriend was an idiot. If we ever run into him, I'll beat his ass for you. Your current boyfriend would never resort to callin' you names. Forget him. Now, tell me why you don't want to meet my people." I can see the wheels spinning in her head. I have the feeling I know why and what she's going to say, but I need to hear the words from her mouth. "And no bull about how you don't do commitments or meet mamas, or whatever nonsense that's floatin' around in your head. You know what this is, Queen. You've always known."

"I'm who I am. I make no apologies for it. I would never want to be anyone other than Victoria Taylor, a black woman from New York City. If your family has any negative thoughts or viewpoints about that, there will be words. I will leave and never return. Do you get what I'm saying?" It's exactly what I thought.

"Yeah. You think I would bring you home to a bunch of racists, right? Like people in New York don't share those viewpoints too, but if that's what you're worried about, don't be. Trust me and come be with me. Mama is probably burstin' at the seams to ask about you, but she won't until the season is over. She knows how stressed I get."

"One chance. I'll give them one chance. Can we talk about the details tonight? I really need to get ready."

"Sure, darlin'. We'll iron it out tonight. Just talk to me next time. Don't make assumptions."

"That's fair."

"I still don't miss you."

"I don't miss you either."

"If you were here, I wouldn't kiss you."

"Me neither.

TWENTY-TWO

Vickie

THE LAST DAY OF SCHOOL WENT AT A SNAIL'S PACE. There was no work to be done. No lessons or papers to read, but the endless questions from colleagues and the kids about my relationship get old quick. Tamron barging into my classroom to shove her phone in my face didn't help my mood for the day. I barely got any sleep last night, and the conversation with Colt this morning left me feeling unsettled. I need a conversation with my siblings, not Tamron. My phone buzzes, and I pull it out of the back pocket of my jeans. It's another tweet with a picture of me from last night's game. This one is a close up of my face, and they've circled a pimple on the side of my cheek. The caption says, "The north's favorite southern boy can do better."

I shove the phone away and wonder why Tamron feels the need to send me this shit. This is the fourth one today, even after I told her I didn't want or need to see anymore.

The first thing she did this morning was show me a picture of me and Tara from last night's game. 'Are black men not good enough for these sisters?' I didn't bother to read more. I returned the phone to Tamron and told her that headline was complete shit.

Until now, every man I've ever been with was black, but no one talks about that. I check my watch and shove the rest of my belongings into a box. The building is mostly empty. The kids left hours ago, we had our last staff meeting, and we've said our goodbyes. I grab the box, check my classroom one last time, and walk out. There's no one in the hallway or the staircase as I walk down the three flights of stairs. I can see the front door, and I practically salivate at making my exit.

"Out already?" My footsteps stall, and Tamron approaches. "Colt sending you a fancy car?" I still, thinking I heard a twinge of hardness in her voice, but I shake my head and tell myself I'm being sensitive.

"I'm capable of getting myself home. Been getting around this city all my life," I tell her.

"Right. I'll text you later." I walk out and look into the sky, letting the sun warm my face. I call my sister before I pull up the Uber app.

"Where are your men?" I ask while I look around the penthouse. "Are you guys back here for good?"

"We're back," she says. "Ethan's at the office, and Vincent is out with Evan and their nannies. I'm returning work emails so follow me." I follow her down to the back of the first floor of the penthouse all the way to her spacious office. She takes her seat behind her desk, and I drop myself on the couch.

"Call our brother. I can't have this conversation twice," I moan.

"Sounds serious." Tara takes out her iPad to FaceTime Alan. He picks up on the second ring, and his face fills the screen.

"You look like crap," I tell him, looking over Tara's shoulder.

"Because I was up watching the game and celebrating. And you look worse than me." He gives us the middle finger. He drops himself down on his pillow and looks into his phone.

"Vickie has news," Tara whispers.

"Why didn't you start with that? By the way, why is our mother hounding me because Vickie won't call her back?"

"I've been busy, and this isn't about Mother. Listen." They both shut up while I tell them about me, Colt, and his plans for the summer. "It's too fast, right?" I ask them after I tell them everything.

"You're asking the wrong person," Tara says. She's known Ethan less than a year. They moved in together only two months after meeting. She's right. She's the wrong person to ask.

"Alan?" I ask my twin. He's smart and rational.

He shrugs and runs a hand over his head. "I haven't had a girlfriend in two years. If I don't get some soon, I might die, so I'm not the right person to ask either."

I take a paperclip and toss it at the iPad screen. "Not helpful."

"I like Colt, but you're going against all your rules. You have to ask yourself if he's worth it," Alan says. "He comes with a five-year-old, a career that takes him out of town a lot, fangirls, his public lifestyle, his—" Alan clears his throat. "Ahem, southern heritage. I'll be honest, twin. I don't think he's exactly your type."

That's Alan. Smart, rational, and direct when he's not being a goofball.

Tara puts a hand on mine and says, "Before you respond to that, let me say one thing. You like him, and don't you dare deny it. And sometimes people come into our lives that don't look like what we expect. It's okay. And I know Colt a little bit. He's sweet and a great dad. And he's managed to destabilize your wall." She nudges my shoulder. She knows I'm a sucker for a good dad, and Colt is that. He talks about his son constantly, and I know he feels guilty about leaving him to work. And he has the cutest picture of the two of them as his screensaver. They're both sticking their tongue out at the camera.

"What wall?" I shrug and pretend to be confused.

"Oh, please. We all have abandonment issues. We won't call it the wall. We can call it Mother, but this isn't about her. Not anymore. This is about you. You deserve love. You deserve companionship. And no, you don't need a relationship with a man to be complete, but take it from me, it's wonderful when you find it. I never thought that man would be Ethan. I never saw him coming, but when he came into my life, life got so much better."

I look around the fancy penthouse and wave my hands around. She nudges me with her shoulder.

"I guess that's not bad advice," Alan says to Tara. "But I have a date to get ready for." He wiggles his eyebrows at us. "This unwelcomed bout of celibacy is about to be over. You two know I'm a breast man." He raises a hand as if he's cupping something. "It's going to be like holding two cantaloupes. You know that's my favorite fruit."

"Don't make us vomit," Tara says.

Alan gives us the finger again and says, "Gotta go shave my balls," before he hangs up on us.

"He wants me to meet his mother," I whisper to Tara.

"I figured that when you said he wants you to go to Alabama. I know he's close to her. He put her on speakerphone one time when he was here. She was really sweet. And she's crazy about Colt." Tara lowers her voice and says, "I also know he has a tense relationship with his older brother, but I don't know why."

I lie on Tara's sofa and stare at the ceiling. After taking a deep breath, I throw my arm over my face. "I'm so fucking sleepy," I moan.

"That happens when your boyfriend is an NBA player who wants you at all his games." She sits at the end of the sofa and puts my legs across her lap.

"Ugh. Boyfriend. Blech." Tara starts to laugh, and so do I. "Fine. Okay. Boyfriend, but I hate the celebrity aspect of his life. There are pictures of my pimple on the internet. Someone took a picture of my ass and said Colt's not with me for my butt. Why do people even care?"

"Because people are assholes, and you're fabulous so they are all jealous. Come in the kitchen. I'll get us a snack." She stands, takes my hand and pulls me up.

"Speaking of." My phone buzzes and I pull it out of my pocket. I expect to see another text from Tamron, but it's our mother. "Yes, Mother," I say into the phone, exasperated and extremely tired.

"Oh, well I'm sorry to bother you, Victoria. Imagine my surprise when I saw my kids at a basketball game, and no one bothered to invite me. Am I still your mother or what?" I have her on speaker, and Tara rolls her eyes while she pulls something out of her fridge. She grabs a bottle of white wine and waves it in the air.

"Mother, we're still waiting on that spa day," I throw in. "What happened with that?" Tara hands me a wineglass, and I take a huge gulp. Mother starts to babble something about being sick, but I interrupt her. "Sorry, Mother. My Uber is here. I've got to go."

"Oh, stop lying. And I don't know about you and that Colt. I have nothing against him, but Gerald—"

"Mother, goodbye." I end the call.

It's not until after ten that my new driver drops me off at home. Colt sent me a text earlier with the driver's information, reminding me that I'd promised not to go off on my own anymore. Five minutes later, Cynthia, an amazon of a woman called and introduced herself. The snacks and drinks at Tara's turned into dinner once Ethan and Vincent got home. My eyes are heavy when I get to my front door, but I'll need a hot shower before I climb into bed. There's a tall plant waiting for me at my front door, and I pick it up, knowing exactly who it's from.

> Queen Vee,
> Our first plant together. This will be good practice. A bamboo palm for you to care for. Under no circumstances are you to think of me every time you look at it. I don't miss you.
> Your champion

Good practice for what? I shake my head. Colt is a puzzle. I drop my purse and box of school supplies on the floor, grab a bottle of water from the fridge, and walk into my bedroom. Just as I get my shirt off and tossed aside, I hear my phone ring. Mother flashes across my screen, and I hit decline, telling myself that I'll call her in the morning.

I'm too exhausted now to deal with any of her guilt trips and requests to get together.

By the time I shower and put on a clean pair of shorts and tee, I've missed three calls from Colt. It's almost eight on the west coast and almost eleven here. Before I get a chance to slide into bed and call him back, my phone vibrates again.

"You're not missing me, are you?" I ask.

"Nope. Just calling to make sure you're not missin' *me*. Better not be."

"I'm not. Haven't thought about you once all day."

He lets out a laugh and then yells something away from the phone. I hear a door open and close. "I'm going to FaceTime you." He ends the call, and seconds later, my phone vibrates with a FaceTime request.

"I had forgotten what you look like," I tell him. "You're still ugly."

He runs a hand over his face and says, "I beg to differ. I'm the handsomest man on earth."

"Don't you wish."

"That's what Mama always says."

"OMG. Enough with your mama." I make a face at him and roll my eyes. "Loser."

"You're the prettiest thing I've ever seen." I can feel myself blush at his words.

"Obviously." He stares at me as if he's trying to read my mind. Uncomfortable from that kind of scrutiny, I say, "You look tired."

"So do you, darlin'. I'm going to make sure we win tomorrow so I can have a few days off before the finals."

"You've got this, Chastain. You're going to win."

"Did you think about what we talked about this mornin'?" I put him on hold and drink my water. When I get back on the phone, he's smiling, and my heart rate picks up at the sight of his dimple.

"You need a haircut." He messes the mop of hair on his head and pulls it.

"You should see me after the season. I let it grow out over the summer. Mama hates it too. You two have so much in common."

"Time to cut the cord, Chastain. You're almost thirty. Yes, I've thought about what we talked about."

"And?"

"And I was being withholding. And I'll come to Alabama with you and meet whoever you want to introduce me to. I'll even smile and make polite conversation."

"And what about Sunday dinners?"

I raise my eyebrows and say, "You want to fly to Alabama for Sunday dinner with Mama each week? I'm down but only if there's wine."

"I'll get you some grape juice, but my point is, I want us to be in each other's lives. For family dinners."

"Well, you better be prepared to shovel the evil one's mac and cheese down your throat."

TWENTY-THREE

Colt

We lose the fifth game. Despite scoring thirty points and having ten assists, we lose by two points, and the team is deflated on the flight home. Everyone's quiet, but Coach Walsh gives us a pep talk and reminds us there are two games left, and we only need to win one. The next game is on our home turf, giving us the advantage. Not even the speech can ease my disappointment. I barely sleep on the flight home, and it's almost seven o'clock the next morning by the time the plane lands in New Jersey. My driver is waiting, and I climb into the back seat, not bothering to say goodbye to my teammates.

Myra is making breakfast by the time I get home an hour later. Evan comes running into my arms and I lift him off his feet and hold his little body against mine. I kiss his cheek, and he giggles before he wipes it.

"I missed my best buddy." He kicks his legs, and I put him down. He grabs my hand and pulls me into the kitchen. Myra places a plate filled with bacon and eggs in front of him.

TAKEOFF

After breakfast, Evan follows me into my bedroom. He climbs in the bed with me, and we watch last night's game while he gives me commentary on everything I did wrong. I send all the staff home, determined to spend the day with my son despite how tired I am. He must sense my fatigue though. After we watch the game, I put on his favorite cartoon. When I open my eyes a few hours later, he's sleeping soundly next to me, and I run a hand through his hair.

I roll out of bed, grab my phone, and walk into my bathroom. There are two missed calls from Queen Vee. My face is red and my chin, which normally has about one day's worth of hair growth, now has three. I run my hand over it and decide to leave it alone for now.

I return her call and she answers right away. She stares into the phone and inches closer, as if she's trying to study me.

"I called you twice." She leans the phone on something, and I see that she's at a desk with a laptop opened in front of her.

"Sorry, my queen. I fell asleep with Evan. I have to shower and be at practice in an hour."

Her eyes soften, and I think it's at the mention of my son. "Okay. I'll see you at tomorrow's game." She looks at the ceiling and exhales loudly. "Assuming you want me there." She puts both hands to her face and says, "God, I hate this relationship crap." She looks back at the screen, clearly frazzled and unsure of what to do next. The laugh bubbles in my throat and soon fills the large bathroom. Vickie starts to laugh too, and I've never seen her so unguarded. She leans back in her chair and covers her face with both hands while her body shakes with laughter.

"Have your driver bring you here in three hours. And pack a bag, darlin'."

"I will come, but I will not pack a bag. You have a child, so we have to set a good example." She purses her lips and nods once.

"Pack a bag."

TWENTY-FOUR

Vickie

He meets me outside. Right in front of his Central Park building, where hundreds of people are walking by at every moment. I barely have time to step out of the car before long arms wrap around me and lift me off my feet. His warm lips land on mine, and I give in to the kiss. I yank the Mischiefs cap off his head and ruffle his hair. He lifts me higher, and I wrap my legs around him. He spins us around and walks to his building, where a doorman holds the door open for us. He carries me into the elevator and kisses me senseless the instant the doors close behind us. I slide down his body, and he snakes an arm around my waist.

I lean my head against him, and because he's so tall, it ends up right under his armpit.

"You smell good," I tell him.

"I showered for you. I didn't miss you, though." The elevator dings, and we step out. His apartment is open and spacious. We walk down a narrow hallway until we get to his living room. It's decorated in neutral browns with splashes of yellow. There are toys and stuffed animals everywhere.

There's a middle-aged woman in an apron and chef's hat pulling something out of the oven. She looks up and smiles at me. She's a short woman with a round belly. Her dark skin has neither a blemish nor a wrinkle. I offer her my hand, and she wraps her warm one around mine.

"Myra, this is Victoria Taylor. Queen Vee, this is my chef, Myra. If you want anything special, just let her know."

"Welcome, Ms. Taylor," Myra says with a slight Caribbean accent.

"Vickie, please." She nods and returns to the stove. I'm not sure what she's cooking, but it smells good

"Let me show you around." Colt takes my hand and gives me a tour of his apartment. It's got to be at least forty-five hundred square feet. It's about half the size of Ethan and Tara's place, but it overlooks Central Park. I look out one of the large bay windows and see a crowd of people down below. The apartment is beautiful, with modern appliances, but is warm and inviting. There are pictures of Evan throughout.

We enter his workout room, and I see a quote. 'Definitions belong to the definers, not the defined...'

"Toni Morrison?" I ask, clearly impressed.

"What? I'm just a dumb jock." There's a framed photograph on the wall. It's a picture of Colt and an older man. I trace my finger along it, and he watches me.

"Who's this? Your uncle or somebody?"

He puts a hand to his chest and drops himself on his workout bench. He pants as if he's wounded. I cross my arms and look down at him.

"My uncle? Queen Vee, I'm hurt. Do I have to educate you on everythang? That man is Nick Saban."

"Am I supposed to know who the hell that is?"

He stands and runs a hand over his face in disappointment.

"Only the best college football coach in the history of the world. I'm going to introduce you to him when you come to Alabama. If you think I'm a god, wait until you meet him."

"Whatever. I'm rethinking this Alabama trip if you're going to subject me to football. I can barely stand the sport you play."

He snakes an arm around my waist and says, "Oh, baby, it's too late for you to rethink anything."

While he shows me around the rest of his workout room, I hear little feet run against the hardwood floor.

"Dad, Myra says I can't have a cookie yet. Can you tell her to give me one? It's not fair—" He stops at the door, and the words die in his throat when he sees me. He looks at me and then at his father. My stomach sinks when his little shoulders sag and he stares at the floor.

"Evan, you remember Vickie, right?" Colt reaches for him, lifts him up, and spins him around before putting him back down.

"Hi, Evan." I offer him a big smile and take a step closer. He runs to the other side of his father and wraps his arms around one of Colt's long legs. I stop my approach and drop my hand.

"Hi." He gives me a one hand wave. There's no enthusiasm in his voice. I know kids. I've worked with kids for years. This one wants me gone. "I'm gonna go watch TV." He looks at me as if I kicked his puppy and runs out of the room.

Colt scratches his head and says, "Sorry. He's usually friendlier than that."

"Maybe I should go. You just got back, and he probably wants all your attention, which I can understand." I drop myself down on his weight bench. "He's a little boy who has already lost his mother in the worst way. We didn't think this through." I stand and walk out the door, but he catches up to me and grabs my wrist before I can get too far.

"You're right. I didn't think it through. That's on me, not you, but you're already here and he's seen you. I'm not going to keep you hidden from him, and I'm allowed to have a relationship and a life. He's a good kid. Give him some time, okay?" He wraps his arms around me and rests his forehead on mine. He's right. Evan's a great kid. He's smart and funny. He even has a little protective streak in him. I've seen him look out for Vincent, even though he's only ten months older. He has a maturity that most kids his age don't have, but he's been dealt a bad hand in his short life.

"He's a great kid," I tell him. "I won't go. At least not yet, but if he doesn't want me here, I'll leave. He comes before everything."

He plants a soft kiss on my forehead. "Stop that. You're not going to make me like you. Don't even try it." He takes my hand in his, and we walk back to the kitchen together.

Myra pulls three plates from the cabinet, but Evan only takes two.

"You forgot this one, baby." Myra, who has a noticeable limp, walks to the table and puts the third plate down. She runs a hand through Evan's hair and caresses his scalp. He leans against her, taking all the affection she has to give him. "You must be hungry, big boy. Why don't you get the glasses for Myra? And I made your favorite cookies, but you have to eat all your dinner before your daddy will let you have a few."

"I want five," Evan says.

"Well, that's up to that man over there." Myra points at Colt. "But you have to be good." He turns and wraps his arms around her thick waist before he does as she says. She looks at me and winks.

Myra leaves a few minutes later, leaving us to enjoy the delicious roasted chicken she made. Evan is quiet while he eats, looking from me to his father. He's a big eater. He eats everything on his plate and drinks a full glass of milk.

"Your dad tells me you're going to kindergarten next school year," I say to Evan.

"Yeah," is all I get back. He puts his head down and stares down at his empty plate. "Can I have the cookies now, Dad?"

"Maybe after you answer Vickie."

"I said yeah." He rolls his eyes at his father. Colt purses his lips, but I put a hand on his arm before he can utter a word. He looks at me and I subtly shake my head.

"Cookies sound great," I announce. As soon as Colt nods at Evan, he jumps off his chair and runs to the kitchen island. He opens a jar and pulls out a stack of cookies. He's already shoved one in his mouth before he runs out of the kitchen and to the back of the apartment.

"I'm sorry," Colt says. He picks up my hand and kisses it. "I'll talk to him. I promise you he's a good kid. I raised him to be respectful and kind. I've never seen him act this way before."

I wave my hand in dismissal. "He's five. It's okay."

"It's not." Colt rises from his chair and stands. "I'll be back."

I make up my mind on my next move before Colt is out of sight. I stand from the table, walk to the counter and take out one of the cookies. One bite later, I spit it out in a napkin. It's obvious a sugar substitute was used. I close the jar and push it as far away as possible.

After meeting Colt at the club, I spent a few hours googling him, and one consistent thing was his rigid diet. Obviously, he makes sure his kid eats healthy too. I find my tote on the living room couch and take my phone out. I send a short text letting him know I'm leaving and walk out the front door. For all the reasons I have for not dating men with kids, the kid not liking me never made the list. That's never happened before. My reasons were always about me not wanting to share the man with his ex.

In this case, I can't blame the kid for his feelings. His daddy is the only parent he has, and he doesn't want to share him. I wouldn't either. I was Evan once upon a time. We didn't want to share our dad with Cheryl, but lucky for us, Cheryl never gave up on us.

I press the button for the elevator, but Colt's front door opens. He walks out with Evan under his arm like a football and approaches. He throws an arm across my shoulders and turns me away from the elevator.

"I don't think so. Come back inside." After taking a few steps, I stop in the middle of the hallway.

"I'm taking off. I don't want to intrude."

"You're not intruding if I want you here. Come back inside so we can watch a movie."

While I consider the best way to tell him no, Evan grumbles, "I'm sorry." He purses his little pink lips and looks down at the floor. "My dad says I have to be nice to you." Colt pulls me back inside his apartment.

"Apology accepted." I mess Evan's hair. He looks up and gives me a small but sincere smile. "As fun and as good as dinner was, I think you boys should enjoy some father son time."

"I thought the three of us could watch a movie." His arm drops from my shoulders and snakes around my waist. He lifts me off my feet and walks us back inside the apartment.

"Why don't you go find a movie," he says to Evan. "We'll be right there." The little boy runs off to do his father's bidding. Once he's out of sight, he turns his attention back to me. "I apologize in advance. I'm about ninety-nine-point nine percent sure he's going to choose *Annie*. You can thank his maternal grandma for that."

"I'm gonna go," I tell him, unwilling to intrude.

His smile drops, and he lowers his head. He runs his big hands over his curly hair and sighs. "Please, stay." He pokes his head down the hall and when he doesn't see Evan, he says, "Come with me." He takes my hand and pulls me in the opposite direction through a set of doors, leading to his bedroom. "It's my fault. What just happened. Please don't blame him."

"I would never blame a five-year-old for anything." He lets out a breath of relief at my words. "But what do you mean it's your fault?"

He gestures to the bed, which is unmade, and I sit. He sits next to me, but our bodies don't touch. "About a year ago, I was seein' someone for a few months and things between her and Evan did not go well."

I stand and look down at him. "What do you mean by did not go well?" I put a hand under his chin and force his face up to look at me.

"It does things to me when you get so protective over my kid." He takes my hand and puts it to his warm cheek. "She didn't take to him. We were supposed to go do somethin'. I can't even remember what exactly, but she very bluntly asked if we could leave Evan at home because he annoyed her. He overheard, and although he would not admit it, he was really hurt by it. So, this behavior of his is because of me. Because I brought the wrong person into his life." His shoulders hunch and I can sense the regret oozing off him. I take my seat on the bed and rub between his shoulder blades.

"I should punch you in the throat for bringing that woman around Evan." I think my words shock him. His head shoots up and his mouth opens. His shoulders start to shake, and he drops himself on the bed and laughs. His shirt rides up, revealing his taut stomach.

"What did you say, darlin'? Did you just threaten me?"

"I'll do more than threaten you if you bring some bitch around that boy again." And because he continues to laugh, I hit him in the stomach. He snatches my wrist and holds on to me. "Stop tickling me."

He pulls me on the bed next to him. "That night when we met at the club. You were so beautiful and sexy. Easily the sexiest woman I've ever seen. Darlin', you can't feed a stray cat and expect it to stay away. You stick up for my son, I'm stickin' around."

"How was I supposed to know that would turn you on?" He kisses the inside of my wrist. "You are like a stray cat. I can't get rid of you for nothing."

I lie beside him and enjoy his rough, calloused hand caressing the inside of my wrist. Every few seconds he brings it to his lips and kisses it. "I understand how he feels, but I will hurt you if you do that to him again." He lets out another loud cackle, stands, and pulls me into his arms. "And the next words out of your mouth better be that you showed that woman the door."

He nods and says, "I did. I've learned my lesson. I'm very selective now. Case in point, this woman in my arms.

Please, stay." He pulls me closer and kisses the side of my neck while I run my fingers through his hair.

The bedroom door bursts open, and I jump out of his arms. "I thought we were going to watch a movie." Evan walks over and takes Colt's hand. "Come on." I follow them out of the bedroom and back to the living room.

"What did you choose, Son?" Evan points to the television, and Colt mouths 'I told you' to me. "Why don't you two start it and I'll join you once I clean the kitchen." Evan looks at me and nods, but I can sense the uncertainty coming from him, so I smile. He doesn't smile back.

"I love Annie. I used to watch this with my siblings all the time." That gets his attention.

"Does Alan like *Annie*?" he asks in awe. I nod, giving him my most serious face.

"He does, and he knows all the songs. We all do."

"Me too. My grandma says *Annie* was my mom's favorite movie." He puffs out his chest in pride and understanding dawns. He has a special connection to this movie. "But Daddy doesn't know any of the songs. He says Annie's singing makes him want to get his shotgun and shoot the TV."

Colt cackles, but I don't share his amusement. "No guns. Ever," I tell him. "I mean it. You better not have one in this apartment."

He holds both hands up and says, "No guns, but you can't blame a man for wantin' to protect his sanity."

"Grandma says Daddy's singing is like six cats fighting in a sack."

"I hate to break it to you, Son, but you get your singin' skills from me." He rubs Evan's head and leaves us in the living room.

"You don't need to be able to sing well to enjoy a good

song. Come on." I gesture for him to join me on the couch. I take a seat at one end, and he sits at the other, but he jumps off the couch before he can start the movie.

"I want some popcorn. You can have some too if you want since Daddy told me to be nice to you." He stands there, probably unsure of what my reaction will be.

"I love popcorn."

He nods and runs out of the room. "Daddy, Vickie wants popcorn. She wants soda too." I hold my laugh at the little manipulator.

"Coke, if you have it," I yell out.

"I most certainly do not," Colt yells back. "But I have six types of water."

But Evan's not one to give up. "Can you go get her some?" he asks. "She looks thirsty."

"Not gonna happen."

TWENTY-FIVE

Colt

I toss the shirt in the corner of the room. She visibly winces right before her body stiffens. I walk over, pick it up, and fold it. Her body relaxes, and I make a mental note to be less of a slob when she's here, but it's my default. My mom cleaned up after me until I went to college, and by the time I was living on my own, I could afford to pay for someone to clean, cook, and do my laundry. The only chore Mama insisted I do was the dishes.

I walk to the bed and drop down face first on the pillow.

"I thought Evan was the worst singer I ever heard until you opened your mouth. And those high notes that Annie hits when she sings Tomorrow? Please, don't ever sing that song again. You and Evan were like two wolves howling at the moon. I'm traumatized, darlin'. Traumatized." I put my arm around her and pull her onto the bed next to me. "Make it up to me. Rub my shoulders."

When she makes no move, I say, "Evan's out cold. My shoulders are tense and it's all because of you two. The only thing worse than your singin' was your dance routines. God, I hate that movie."

She finally lets out a chuckle, takes off her shoes, and sits on my lower back. Her soft hands start to slowly rub my shoulders, and I sigh in contentment at the sensation.

"Why are you wearing all those clothes?"

"Because Cynthia is off duty and I'm pretty sure the Uber driver won't let me in the car if I'm naked. Did you get hit in the head with a basketball today?" She puts a hand in my hair and gently pulls.

"No more Ubers. You have a driver, and you can't leave, Queen Vee." I surprise her when I turn over and pull her down on top of me. "Even though I didn't miss you while I was gone and barely thought of you, I want you to stay with me tonight." I lift my head from the pillow and push hers at the same time. Our lips meet in the middle, and I deepen the kiss. She moans in my mouth, and my body wakes up.

I pull her shirt out of her jeans and break the kiss long enough to pull it over her head. Her bra goes next, and my lips find their way around a nipple. One of her hands ends up in my sweatpants and wraps around me. While I bite a nipple, I squeeze the other breast in my hand. She pulls my pants down, and I let go of that soft breast so I can undo the button and lower the zipper of her skinny jeans.

"Take off these pants." I lift her off my body, and when she's standing on two feet, I pull down the jeans. She kicks them off while I do the same to mine. When we're both naked, she shoves me, and when I fall on my back, she straddles me.

She leans down and kisses me as if I'm the very air that she breathes. My hand caresses her spine and goosebumps spread across her skin.

"Don't even think of making love to me right now," she says right before she sucks my bottom lip into her mouth.

"Too late."

"Hand me a condom." I reach into the drawer in my nightstand and grab the box I put there earlier, giving myself a mental high five for thinking ahead. I hand it to her, but when she reaches for it, I snatch it away.

"I don't think so. You promised." I look down at my crotch and look up at her full lips. "I've been thinking about those lips wrapped around me for ages." She leans in and kisses me deeply, running her soft hands over my bare chest. "Since I first saw you."

"You want these lips," she kisses me slowly, "on that dick." She reaches down and grabs it in her hands.

"Heck yeah."

She kisses me again, deep this time, opening her mouth wide. She leaves my mouth, kissing down my neck and down my body. She gives me no time. She doesn't tease. She doesn't lick the crown. She takes it all in her mouth, and I almost combust from the sensation of her hot mouth on me. "That feels good," I moan, barely able to catch my breath. She licks the crown before swallowing the entire thing. I close my eyes and grip the back of her head, wishing this moment would never, ever end. "Baby, if you don't—" I almost cry when her mouth leaves me.

She snatches the condom from me, opens it, and puts it on me within seconds. She aligns herself on top of me and slowly slides down. My hands grab her waist, and I guide her movements as she rides me. She puts a hand on my chest, and I pick it up, kiss her hand and lick her index finger. I trace that finger down her stomach, spread her lips apart and rub her clit.

"Fuck, Colt," she mutters. "I'm not ready to come yet," but she's already convulsing on top of me. She throws her head back and moans my name, prompting my own orgasm.

This time, it's me who rubs her soft skin, marveling at the smoothness of her back. She has a little heart-shaped tattoo right above her left buttock. I pay special attention by massaging and kissing her exposed skin. It's after midnight. After making love, I checked on Evan, who was sound asleep in his bed. Now, I'm in bed with my girlfriend. I push her hair to the side and kiss her exposed shoulder. I lie next to her and pull her naked body into my arms.

"Tonight's been amazin'," I confess. She rests on her elbows and looks down at me. "One of the best nights of my life."

She sighs and climbs on top of me. I wrap my arms around her and cover us with the bedspread.

"I have a hard time believing that you've been lonely." She runs a hand through my curly hair and runs it down my face, caressing me. "You're sweet when you're not being dramatic. Not to mention, you're handsome and rich. That's not a recipe for loneliness, Colt."

I caress the skin at the base of her spine and relish having her full breasts pressed on me.

"I married young and had a child. I never cheated on my wife. Not once. And before her, there were women, but you can have a different woman in your bed every night and still be lonely." opens her mouth to speak, but I put a finger to her lips. "Not that I had a different woman every night. Kelsey died, and one bad relationship later, I was lonely until I met you. Even though you made me chase you."

She remains quiet in my arms, but I can tell she's absorbing my words. She takes my hand and intertwines our fingers before she brings our joined hands to her lips. I sigh, happier than I've been in years.

"When I was at Duke, I met Jerry." I freeze at the mention of another man's name while we're in my bed. "He was a medical student, and the first serious boyfriend I had. We were together for two years before we broke up."

I wait for her to say more, and when she doesn't, I ask, "Is that before or after he called you an ice queen?"

She sighs at my question. "Before, during, and after. It was a theme with him. I ran into him a few weeks before we met. He's back in the city, it seems."

She slides off my body, but she cuddles to my side. She throws an arm across my torso and twines her legs with mine.

"I will have no problems beating that doctor's behind." She lets out a loud laugh, and I love the sound so much, I make a fist to show how serious I am.

"You don't have to worry about him. Were you in love with Kelsey?" she asks. She lowers her voice, and the previous lightheartedness is gone. The room almost turns cold at the mention of Kelsey. I want to tell Vickie that there's no room to talk about her here, but I know we need to have this conversation.

"I hate to say this because I love my son, but no. I didn't love her. We were high school sweethearts, but when I left for college, we broke up. She got married, had a child, and divorced young." I take a deep breath and continue. "When I first got here, it might as well had been another planet. Like any twenty-year-old kid with more money than brains, I went a little crazy with the women." I look away from her, but she grabs my chin, forcing me to look back at her.

"Nothing wrong with that," she says softly. "You were young, single, and free."

"When she got divorced, she got in touch with me. Mama had given her my number, and she was familiar. She came to visit, and we picked up where we left off. I missed Alabama and having her here was like having a piece of home in New York. It was nice. At least at first. She and her first husband never had much. I don't know if she'd changed or if the money I had changed her, but she got pregnant on purpose. We got married, and it wasn't good. I'm grateful she was a good mom, but she didn't love me, and I didn't love her. I was her ticket out of Alabama. That wasn't strong enough to sustain a marriage. She had some vices I didn't know about and died of a drug overdose."

She remains quiet, but she kisses my shoulder.

"Part of the reason I was reluctant about us was because I didn't want to compete with your dead wife. I assumed you had this great love and that there's no way I could ever come close to that."

I turn on my side so we can face each other. She does the same.

"You don't ever have to compete with anyone. I'm in this. You and me, Queen Vee, we're together, but I'm a package deal. I need you to understand that and know what it means. It means—"

She puts a finger to my lips. "Shh. I know. I come from a blended family. I know what it means. It means we'll spend a lot of time here, or the three of us will be going to the museum or the zoo. You won't ever have to worry about me not wanting Evan around."

"Thank you, darlin'." I pull her on top of me. "Even though you came into this relationship kickin' and screamin', I'm glad you're here now. Make love to your man."

TWENTY-SIX

Vickie

We spend the night wrapped around each other. When I wake up, the bed is empty, and his pillow is cold. There's a bag with a department store logo in his spot with my name scrawled across the bag. I rub the sleep from my eyes and pour the contents onto the bed. There's underwear, a bra, jeans, and three tops. There are also three jerseys with the Mischiefs logo and Colt's number. My phone says it's after nine, so I jump out of the bed and hop in the shower. When I get out, I notice the new toothbrush on the counter. After dressing and making the bed, I walk to the living room and to the sounds of laughter and the smell of breakfast.

Myra smiles and waves me over when she sees me. Colt has Evan on his back, and when they approach, he towers over me, leans down, and gives me a kiss on the lips. He holds me tight against him, uncaring about our audience.

"Hungry? Myra will make whatever you want." Myra grabs a mug, pours coffee, and hands it to me. She points to cream and sugar on the table, and I reach for the creamer.

I exhale at the first sip of the coffee. After my third sip, I look up to find Colt looking at me. He winks, grabs Evan, and tosses him in the air. The little boy lets out a big belly laugh, and Colt does it again.

"Um, nothing to eat for me, Myra," I tell her when I see her pull out a carton of eggs. "I'm going to go so I can get my writing done before the game tonight." I finish my coffee, but when I approach the sink to wash the mug, Myra takes it from me.

"You can write here. Evan's got a full day at camp, and I have practice soon. I'll nap afterwards, and the three of us can go to the game together tonight." With Evan now on his back, he walks over, puts an arm around me, and kisses my cheek. "How about some bacon and eggs." He pulls out a chair for me, and Myra pulls out a skillet.

He puts Evan down, and he runs to his room to get dressed.

"I know you brought your laptop, and it's pouring rain outside," he says. I finally look out one of the windows and notice the rain for the first time. "Stay. I like having you here, and if you need anything at home, Kendall will arrange to have someone pick it up for you." I hear a loud clap of thunder. The smell of the sizzling bacon finally hits my nose, and I nod.

"Another cup of coffee would be great." He gets it for me, and I add my own cream.

Colt soon leaves for the day, and while he's gone, I sit in the living room and lose myself in my story for the next three hours. Just as I finish my next chapter, the front door opens and Colt walks in. I pull the AirPods out of my ears and put them on the coffee table. He walks to me, pulls me to my feet, and kisses me with a hunger I've only ever seen in movies or read about in books.

"My queen, my liege," he whispers.

TAKEOFF

"How was practice?" I ask against his lips.

"Great. I didn't think about you at all." He picks me up bridal style and takes me to his bedroom. The apartment is quiet. Myra left about an hour ago after cooking several meals to last the entire day. A housekeeper came by to clean and do laundry.

When we get to his bedroom, he drops me on the bed and I bounce. We strip naked and he pulls me into his arms. His hand slides between my legs and two fingers find their way inside my wet pussy.

"I want to make love to you," he whispers. He pulls his fingers out, leaving me feeling empty without his touch. He puts those fingers to my lips, and I suck on them greedily. "Are you on birth control?"

When I nod, he continues, "Can I slide inside of you bare, Queen?"

"You did our first time, remember?" He rests his forehead on mine.

"You distracted me so much, and you felt so good. I really want to be inside of you without a barrier from now on." I can barely form a word. A nod and a whimper are all I can eek out.

Once I give him the okay, he flips us over and lands on top of me. He looms over me, looks directly into my eyes and slowly slides inside of me. I know it's been years for him, probably since his wife died, but it's been even longer for me. I sigh happily when he gets all the way inside of me.

∽

"You better win because I don't want to go to California. Just make sure you throw the ball into the round thing. Bend your knees or whatever. It's not that hard," I say to Colt when we arrive at the game together.

"Bend my knees or whatever," he repeats. "I never thought of that."

He goes with his team, and I take Evan to our seats. By the time we arrive, my sister and the rest of my family are there. Evan lets go of my hand and runs to Vincent.

This is the sixth game in the series, and the energy in the stadium is contagious. All of us sitting center court are wearing Colt's jersey. I'm so nervous, I wrap my arm around Tara's. If they lose, the team will fly to LA tonight, and I'll fly there tomorrow. The lights in the stadium dim and the noise of the crowd grows quiet. The other team is called, and a few get booed by the crowd. The stadium's noise level grows to deafening when the Mischiefs are called out. When Colt comes out, the crowd goes wild, including my sister who is busy yelling beside me.

"Did you do that to his hair?" she asks. Colt has his hair in neat cornrows.

"He was supposed to take it out before the game. He promised he would," I yell over the crowd.

"It looks good on him," she says.

His hair has gotten so long and curly, I threatened to braid it after waking up from our nap. He told me to go ahead, and an hour later, his hair was braided. We snapped a few selfies, and I told him to undo it, but I guess he never intended to.

Throughout the game, the jumbotron captures me several times. Each time I'm either talking to my sister, my dad, or Evan, who is less icy than before but not completely trusting yet.

The first half of the game is a blur, and Colt scores twenty-eight points. I forget all about hating the sport and follow him with my eyes. He seems to be weightless while he runs up and down the court. I don't think he's missed a shot. I'm in awe of his long arms and his ability to maneuver not just the ball but his body.

Despite the thousands of people in the stadium, I only see him. It's not until I feel a little hand tapping me on my thigh that I look away and stare into Evan's brown eyes.

"Hey, buddy," I yell so that he can hear. "You okay?" He's never sought me out before. He crooks his finger, asking me to come closer.

When I do, he whispers in my ear, "Can I have a soda?" He puts a finger to his lips, and I know he's asking me to keep it a secret between us. I flag the server assigned to our section and ask for two Cokes. He smiles and gives me a high-five. When the drinks arrive, I give them to the boys, ignoring the narrowing of Ethan's eyes.

The second quarter ends, leaving the Mischiefs ahead by twelve points. My eyes follow Colt as he leaves the court and retreats to the locker room with his teammates. The second half of the game flies by. When I watch at home with my dad, I always lament how unending the games are, but when you're watching in real time, everything goes by so fast. The other team closes the gap and gets ahead by two points, but that only lasts as long as it takes Colt to make a three-point shot.

When the other team fouls the Mischiefs, they pick up two more free throw points. By the time the fourth quarter ends, the Mischiefs win by six points, declaring them the winner, and advancing them into the NBA Finals. Confetti falls from the ceiling, and the teammates all huddle in the middle of the court in victory. Family members of the team join them. Colt finds me and gestures for me to come forward. When Evan and Vincent start to approach him, I follow the boys and my sister and Ethan to the floor. My father and stepmother get there before me, and I lag behind them.

Colt picks up his son and gives Vincent a high five. Once he puts Evan down, he wraps his arms around my waist, and kisses me in the middle of the court.

"I've wanted to do this since you came to my first game." I hug him back, for a moment, uncaring about the eyes watching us or the pictures being taken by onlookers. I wrap my arms around him and let him lift me off my feet.

"I have to do the press thing, but I want you in my bed tonight. I want the three of us to spend the day together tomorrow."

I look into his eyes and run my fingers along the bits of exposed scalp. "I'll get your dinner ready." His smile widens, and I realize what I just said. "Did those words just come out of my mouth?" I do a gagging sound and he tightens his arms around me.

"They did, my queen. They did."

I swat his chest. "And you were supposed to take your hair out."

"I like it. It's good luck." He gives me another lingering kiss. "I'll see you at home."

TWENTY-SEVEN

Colt

The house is dim and quiet when I walk through the front door. I walk into the kitchen and wrap my arms around Vickie's waist.

"My queen, my liege," I say against the shell of her ear. "You smell good. You feel even better." She turns in my arms, and I lift her off her feet. She wraps her legs around me, and I kiss her soft lips. She runs a hand through my hair, which I had to unbraid to wash after the game. "I'm starving, so hurry up and get my dinner ready like you promised." She pinches one of my nipples through my shirt, and I wiggle my brows at her. "Food first, then we can get frisky, but you should know something. I pinch back." I stick my head in the crook of her neck and bite down. I let her go without warning and slap her ass.

Like she does every time I have a home game, Myra has cooked a full meal. Vickie makes plates for us and sits with me, asking me questions about the game. I answer but make fun of her for asking such basic things. Once we're done with dinner, she massages my entire body using sweet smelling oil, and when I'm relaxed, she lets me into her body, bringing her to orgasm twice before I release inside of her.

"I was just at this stupid game. Why do I have to rewatch it ?" She cuddles into my side, stroking my naked skin while I watch tonight's game. She's no longer fighting me or us. She's here with me, happy and mine. She makes it halfway through the game before she falls asleep in my arms.

I text Myra and the housekeeper and tell them they can have tomorrow off. I plan on going to breakfast with Evan and Vickie and spending the day doing whatever they want. I have a few days until the Finals begin, and I'm relieved that the first two games will be in New York, so I won't have to travel for a while.

I check my phone for texts and missed calls. As expected, there are about a dozen from Mama.

Mama: I was praying so hard. I knew you'd win. Can't wait to see you next week.
Me: Can't wait either.

I add a heart because Mama likes those. Now, all I need to do is tell Vickie that she'll be meeting my mother next week, and not a month from now. I'll have to point out that I've already met all her family, and it's only fair that she meets another person from mine. But that can wait. Tomorrow will be our day to spend together, just the three of us.

∼

TAKEOFF

I HOLD EVAN'S HAND AND THROW MY FREE ARM ACROSS Vickie's. I pull her close and kiss her temple while we walk out of the restaurant and onto the sidewalk.

"Why is your car here?" she asks. Dante has the back door opened for us.

"I thought we would go to your place so you can get a few things. I want you to stay with us for the next few days." She looks down at Evan, who is busy looking up at the sky.

"Okay, but only one more night, and you have to promise not to distract me while I write."

"Whatever my queen desires." I want her to stay longer, but I'll leave it alone for now. Evan's still getting used to her, and he attached himself to me like glue during breakfast, but he wasn't dismissive of her like he was the first night. He didn't initiate conversation, but he wasn't rude when Vickie addressed him.

"Where are we going, Daddy? I thought we were going swimming?"

I ruffle his hair. "We are, but Vickie needs to pick up a few things at home first."

Evan looks at Vickie, and she smiles at him. He doesn't smile back. Vickie seems a little deflated, and her smile slips.

My driver opens the car door for us, and after we get situated, I reach behind his booster seat and rub her shoulders.

"Is she going to live with us now?" He sounds a little outraged, and his cheeks have turned red like they do when he's excited.

"No," Vickie answers before I can. "I'm just staying one more night." She looks out the window, and I wonder if her feelings are hurt by his reaction.

"Can we watch *Annie* again?" He lowers his head and talks low. "You know the songs better than my dad."

"Yeah, we can."

He smiles and sits up straight.

"Daddy always complains when we watch it, but my grandma says daddy has bad taste in movies."

Vickie snakes her fingers through his hair. She bends down and kisses the top of his head. He leans into her.

"Sure. We can watch it whenever you want. I love that movie, so I'll never complain. Your dad obviously has very basic taste when it comes to movies."

"Yeah," Evan agrees.

"I don't think that's it at all," I snort. I take Evan's hand in mine. We ride to Vickie's house in silence, but Vickie seems more at ease after her exchange with Evan.

Traffic is light, and we get to her place without any delay. I put Evan on my back and take Vickie's hand. I stop short when we get to her front door. There's a bouquet of red roses waiting for her. She squeals in delight when she sees it and kisses my cheek. As much as I love her kisses, I haven't earned this one. I step in front of her and pick up the large bouquet of red roses. She snatches it from me and swings the door open. Evan whines about needing the bathroom, and I tell him where it is. When he's out of sight, Vickie turns to the bouquet.

"How did you know roses are my favorite? Did Tara tell you?" She takes the card, and I take it from her.

"I didn't send these." My jaw clenches. "Says here they are from a Jerry. Your Jerry berry to be more specific." She snatches the card from me and reads it. "He says he misses you."

She sighs and puts the card down on the table.

"Oh," she says. "Well, I told you he's an ex."

"The a-hole who called you the ice queen."

"He's irrelevant. Let me go get a few things in my room." She walks past me, but I grasp her wrist, pull her to me and give her a rough and possessive kiss. She pats my chest and walks down the hall, leaving me alone in her living room.

I stare at the offending bouquet of flowers and tamp down my need to toss them out the window. I pick them up to put them outside her front door, but Evan comes running back.

"You want to see my room?" Vickie yells from down the hall. Evan runs to the sound of her voice. I pick up the bouquet and step outside the apartment. I take the stairs one flight down and leave them in front of a random door. By the time I return to Vickie's apartment, Evan's lying on his back on her bed and flipping through the TV channels. I sit next to him and take off his shoes. "I have some coloring books and crayons if you want to color." She goes into her closet and returns with a bag. Evan jumps off the bed and lies on the floor with the crayons scattered around him.

It takes her about thirty minutes to pack a bag. I have Evan on my back and Vickie's hand in mine when we step out of her building, but a man approaches right before we reach the car.

She comes to an abrupt stop before I hear her say, "Jerry, what are you doing here?"

I stand between them, but he tries to go around me. Dante, who is standing by the car with the back door open must sense the tension. He walks over and takes Evan back to the car.

"I was here yesterday, but you weren't home. Did you get my flowers?" He gives me the side eye and takes a step closer to Vickie. I step between them, towering over him.

"About that. I'm going to have to ask you not to send any more flowers to my lady."

Vickie bristles next to me and steps around me to face the uninvited guest.

"I was with Colt last night. Jerry, we've said all we've had to say, okay."

She takes my hand and we start to walk away, but I turn my head and stare at this man. He looks into my eyes, holding my glare, almost as if he's sizing me up. He's in good shape, but I'm an athlete in the prime of my life. He can't handle me, but that doesn't stop him from approaching my car.

"This guy, Vickie? Some uneducated hick from Alabama?"

"So, you do know who I am?" I inch closer to him, my fist itching to connect with his smug face. He steps closer to me too, but Vickie gets between us.

"Your son, Colt," she whispers to me before she turns her head to address him. "Jerry, stop it, and while you're at it, shut the hell up."

"I'm not going to stop. I still love you, Victoria. I haven't moved on, baby." Having had enough of him, I stand in front of Vickie and block his view. I know better than to order her inside the car, and that's not a fight I'm willing to have with her right now, but Jerry is a different story.

"I have a problem with you telling my lady that you still love her. Back off, Jerry." I say his name with a sneer. "Desperation doesn't look good on you, and I'm almost out of patience." We stare at each other until Dante approaches, opens the car door, and gestures for Vickie to get in.

She nods at him, but looks to Jerry and says, "Goodbye." She gets in, and I walk around to the other side of the car without giving him another glance.

"Who is that?" Evan asks.

Dante looks at us through the rearview mirror. I give him a nod, and he pulls away from the curb.

"Just an old friend of mine," Vickie says. "So, you boys are going swimming, huh?"

TWENTY-EIGHT

While Evan runs to his room, I go to Colt's to put my things away. Just as expected, he follows me.

"I'm just going to throw these clothes in your closet," I tell him. "I'm going to write while you guys go swimming."

I step inside the walk-in closet, only for him to follow behind me and close the door behind him. He wraps his arms around me and pulls me to him.

"You're mine, Queen Vee. I won't be so calm next time he decides to tell you that he's still in love with you. He's lucky Evan was there today."

"Jerry's an ex, and I have no feelings left for him. Don't start any of that macho bullshit, okay. I don't find it flattering. Just like you, I have a past. I don't know what else to tell you." I pull my hands away and head for the door, but he pulls me to him, putting my back to his firm chest.

"I'm a man, Victoria. And another man is trying to take you from me. I can only react as a man. I'm not interested in being any other way." He pushes my hair away from the side of my neck and bites me. Rough hands grab my hips.

"I swear, I don't know what century you're from sometimes. No one can take me. I'm here because I choose to be." He undoes the button of my jeans and unzips them. A hand slides inside my panties, pulling my pussy lips apart. He must not think that contact is enough. He pulls my pants and panties down, and I kick them off. My shirt goes over my head next, and I do the same to him,.

"He had his one chance, didn't he?" He spins me around. Before any words can leave my mouth, his lips are on mine. He's commanding and rough, kissing me with everything he has. I get on my toes, but that's not enough. He's much too tall. I jump in his arms and wrap my legs around him. He moans into my mouth, and I tug on his hair. "I have to make sure that you always choose me." He puts me back on my feet and pulls down his pants.

He spins me around, and I hold on to the built-in shelves in the closet. I toss my head back while he leaves hot kisses down my spine. A hand goes between my legs, and two long fingers find their way inside. My wetness coats his fingers. He pulls them out and slowly glides his wet digits up my stomach, between my breasts, up my neck before sliding them into my mouth.

While I suck, he bends me over, letting my ass stick out in the air. He slaps a butt cheek, jolting me, then gets on his knees, spreads my ass cheeks apart, and glides a hand through it, circling my asshole. I let out a loud yelp of surprise when the tip of his pinkie goes inside. As quickly as it happens, he pulls it out and eats my pussy from the back. He's savage, licking and sucking on my clit, bringing me to the edge of orgasm before he pulls his head back. He stands abruptly and aligns his dick at my entrance before he fills me with his thickness.

"Say my name, darlin',"

"Colt." It's a shameless moan. When he starts to pull

out, I cry out, "No." He slides back in, putting an arm around my waist to hold me upright.

"Tell me you want me," he says against my ear. "Tell me," he commands.

"I want you," I say. He removes the hand from around my waist and puts it on my lower back. When he's positioned me against the shelves, he grasps my hips with both hands and slides all the way inside. He takes total control of my body but gives me as much of himself as possible.

"I want you, too. I've wanted you since the night at the club, and now that I have you, I'm not going to lose you to someone who didn't value you." Once the words leave his mouth, he fucks me hard, claiming me and showing me who I now belong to. His fingers find their way to my clit, rubbing me until I combust and come all over his dick. He's not far behind. I think he only held on until my release. He convulses against me, calling my name while he releases inside of me.

We're still connected minutes later. His long body is on top of mine, and his face is in the side of my neck as he tries to regain control of his breathing. He finally gets up, kissing along my spine before he takes his pants all the way off, and spins me around into his naked body.

"I'm glad you're here," he says against my mouth. "And thank you for trying with Evan."

I wrap my arms around him and rest my head in the middle of his chest. "He's a good kid, and you're an amazing dad."

"I'm sure you would let me know if I wasn't," he teases.

"I sure would."

"Come to the pool with us." He lets me go, rummages through a drawer, and pulls out a pair of bright blue swim trunks and a matching top. "Evan picked these out. He has the same set."

The door to the bedroom opens, and Evan calls out for his dad. I shoo him out of the closet. He opens the door only wide enough for him to get out. By the time I dress and put myself back together, they're both still in the bedroom, lying in the middle of the bed, watching cartoons.

"What happened to swimming?" I ask. Colt extends his hand and gestures for me to come closer. When I do, he pulls me onto the bed next to him. Evan moves over to make room, and I cuddle into Colt's side.

"Do you want to come?" Evan asks.

I look at Colt, who shrugs and nods at me. "I can't, buddy. I don't have a bathing suit, but I'll hang out here while you guys go. I have some writing to do."

"Are you writing a story?"

"I am. It's about a girl who was given up for adoption and what happens to her when she finds her birth parents."

He sits up and straddles his father's stomach. "Will you read it to me?"

The question takes me by surprise, and it takes me a minute to think of a response. This is not the kind of story you read to a five-year-old. It's more of a Shakespearean tragedy than a fairy tale.

"It's not ready yet for an audience, and I think it might be a little too mature for you, but I'll read you any story you want, any time you want. Maybe you can show me your books later." He looks at his dad who nods at him.

"You'll really do that?" The question breaks my heart, and when I think of what Colt confessed to me about the previous woman in his life, I pinch his thigh hard.

"Ouch," he says as he moves his leg away. "What the heck?"

"I'll really do that, Evan. I want us to be friends. You know how Vincent and Tara are friends?" He nods. "Well, I hope we can be like that, but only cooler."

"Really?" he asks.

"Really." I mess his hair.

He looks up, giving me a shy, uncertain smile. I make it my mission in that moment to win him over.

TWENTY-NINE

Colt

The house is quiet and dark when we come back from the pool. Evan trembles next to me as his flip-flops make a squishing sound along the hardwood floor.

"Go get in the shower. I'll be right there," I tell him.

He runs down the hall, dripping water along the way.

"Queen Vee!" I yell in the apartment. She's not sitting at the kitchen table or on the living room couch. When I burst through my bedroom door, she's not in there either, but her things are still in my closet, so I know she hasn't left.

I grab my phone from the nightstand and send a text.

Me: Not that I miss you or want you here, but where are you?

It takes a few minutes until I see the three bubbles that indicate she's sending a text.

Queen Vee: Upstairs with Tara. Coming back now

Me: Door's unlocked. I'm going to wash Evan up

I add a kiss emoji and go find my son.

About half an hour later, I find her at the kitchen table with her laptop in front of her, typing away furiously. With Evan on my back, I approach and kiss the side of her neck.

"How was swimming?" she asks. "I'm sorry I missed it."

"We're getting you a bathing suit tomorrow. Swimming is our thing," I tell her.

She raises both eyebrows and says, "You have a lot to learn about being with a black woman, Chastain. So much to learn. Mama didn't prepare you for this." She picks up the wineglass I hadn't noticed before, raises it to me, and takes a sip. "Tara gave it to me," she says with a wide grin.

"The devil's milk in my home." I put a hand to my chest. "Why, I do declare."

"Yup. Go ahead and clutch your pearls." She hands me the now empty glass. "Pour me another."

"Can I have some?" Evan asks.

"No," we both say at once.

I walk to the fridge and return with a full glass of white wine and place it in front of her.

"I can get used to this." I stand behind her and rub her shoulders. "I say jump, and you say how high."

"I am but your lowly servant, Queen Vee." I bow with Evan still on my back. "But this is the perfect little segue into what I've been meaning to talk to you about."

TAKEOFF

Colt puts Evan down and tells him to go fix himself a snack. He takes the seat next to me and holds one of my hands. He puts it to his chest, then repositions himself in the chair, all the while sighing loudly. He shakes his head as if he's about to deliver bad news.

"You're being incredibly dramatic right now. Way more so than usual. Should I be worried?"

He kisses my hand, but he doesn't let it go. "Mama's coming to New York for the Finals. She's only going to the home games, though. She'll stay here with Evan when I travel. She'll be here in a few days."

I stare into his eyes, unsure of what I'm supposed to say. I blink twice and try to pull my hand from his. "Well, it's great that she's coming to support you." I shrug.

"I'm glad you feel that way." He makes a show of exhaling and wiping his brow.

"Has anyone ever told you that you can have a career as a soap opera actor if this basketball nonsense doesn't work out?"

"We'll pick her up and go to dinner unless she wants to cook for us all," he says, ignoring my dig about how dramatic he is.

I finally manage to pull my hand from his and stand. He does the same, almost as if he's preparing himself for a fight.

Evan's in the kitchen watching us as he tries to spread peanut butter on a piece of wheat bread. He puts so much pressure on the bread that it breaks in half. I walk to him, take the spoon and spread the peanut butter for him. He hands me grape jelly and I do the same on another piece of bread.

"Be gentle next time," I tell him while I cut the sandwich in half. He thanks me and sits at the kitchen island, watching me and his father the entire time.

"Or I can have Myra make something so that way we'll have more time to chat," Colt says.

"What?" I ask. I wipe the counter, making sure it's free of crumbs.

"Queen Vee, come on." He runs a hand over his face as if he's exasperated with me.

Evan's still watching us, so I grab Colt's hand and pull him down the hall into his bedroom. "I agreed that this would happen over the summer. You can't just blindside me. And how long have you known she'd be coming? You are so manipulative. This is just like that first basketball game when you—"

He crosses his arms and leans against the wall. "So, how would it all work?" he asks, interrupting me. "She's at my game. You're at my game and the two of you never talk? Come on, Victoria. We're two adults in a relationship. This is ridiculous."

I stare at him. He's absolutely correct, but I'm not ready to admit defeat yet. And meeting his mother would take this relationship to a whole other level. One I'm not so sure I'm ready for.

But you already agreed to meet her. And you knew how this man was when you agreed to be with him.

He pushes himself off the wall and approaches, wrapping me in his arms.

"It's only fair. I've met your mother, stepmother, father, brother, cousin, sister. Pretty much everyone in your family, and I'm only asking you to meet one person."

"Um, excuse me, but Ethan's the one who invited you over so he could suck up to Dad. But fine. You win. I'm being crazy," I finally admit. "Even though I am certain you've deliberately kept this from me until now."

"So, I'm right? Having you admit that is better than winning a championship."

I swat his chest, and he takes two dramatic steps back before he falls on the bed. "Savor it then because I'm not wrong often. You know, Colton, you chased after an independent woman. One who doesn't need the constraints of a modern relationship."

He jumps off the bed and presses his forehead to mine. I never realized how sexy and intimate that could be until Colt. "And you agreed to be with a man who believes in tradition. Go figure." He lifts me as if I weigh no more than a feather, and I wrap my legs around him. "Do you want to go out or have dinner here? And she gets here in two days."

I grab his messy head of hair and pull. "I'll leave the details up to you, but maybe we can go out. If it goes well, we can all have dinner together at my parents' house before she leaves." He smiles in appreciation, and I melt at the gesture.

"I don't know if you know it, but that's about the most traditional thing I've ever heard. Our parents meeting each other. What are you trying to do? Get me to propose?" I freeze at his words and look into his eyes right before he bursts into laughter. "That deer in the headlights look would scare away a lesser man, my queen, but challenge accepted. I'm taking home the championship when it comes to this relationship."

I wrap my hands around his throat and pretend to choke him. "I have no idea what that's supposed to mean, but that other thing you said..."

"About proposin'?" He wiggles his eyebrows.

"Don't even think about it, Chastain."

"Don't tell me what to do, woman. Victoria Renee Chastain sounds nice. Much better than Victoria Taylor."

"I would never, *ever* change my name," I say. He smirks, which is not the reaction I was expecting from him. He spins us around and pins me against the wall. Dizzy from the spinning, I lean down and kiss him. "And what are you smirking at?" I pull on his hair.

"You said you'd never change your name."

"Yeah? Why would a traditionalist caveman like yourself find that funny? I'm surprised you haven't clubbed me over the head yet."

"It's what you didn't say. I was expectin' a non-traditionalist to say she'd never get married. So, I guess you're not against marriage. You're against taking your husband's name. I'll just file that away for later." He steps back from the wall and drops me on the bed.

"For the record, I'm not against marriage. Far from it. My dad's married. Tara and Ethan will probably get married. I hope Alan does, but as for me—"

He puts a finger to my lips. "Stop pressurin' me."

"Let me save you some time. The answer is no."

"I'll ask when I'm ready." He winks. I reach for his hair again, but he anticipates my move and moves to the side, all the while laughing at me. His phone rings, and he says, "Behave, or I'll fight back." His smile widens when he looks at his phone. "Mama," he says. "I was just talkin' about you.

Hold on. I have another call." He checks his phone and types something. A few seconds later, there's a knock on the door. "That's for you, Queen. Get the door."

"Mama's boy," I whisper.

I jump off the bed and roll my eyes at him before I walk out and give him some privacy. When I open the front door, the doorman has a trolley with several bouquets of roses, all different colors. He rolls it in and sets out six bouquets on the dining room table and leaves.

I pluck out the card.

Queen Vee,
The only man who will get you roses is me, and my queen deserves all the roses her champion can provide.

I press the card to my lips, close my eyes, and will myself not to fall heads over heels for this man, but I'm afraid it might already be too late.

When I get to the kitchen, Evan has the fridge open and his head stuck in it.

"Still hungry?" I ask him. He looks at me and nods. I grab a paper towel, dampen it and wipe dry jelly from around his mouth. "How about I warm you up some of the leftovers in the fridge? Or I can make you a grilled ham and cheese. Those were my favorites growing up."

His eyes widen, and he says, "You'd make that for me? Did Alan like them too?"

"I will make it for you, and Alan still loves them."

He nods and jumps on one of the stools at the counter. I look around until I find a skillet and everything I need from the fridge.

"You don't have to." He looks down, and my heart breaks a little. "It's okay if you only like my dad. The last person didn't like me."

If Colt was here, I'd pinch him again. I walk to the kitchen island and sit next to him. I put a hand on his shoulder, and when he doesn't pull away, I inch closer. "I told you I want us to be friends, and I mean it. I like you." He finally looks up and gives me a shy smile. My heart breaks for this little boy who's lost so much in his short life. "We'll watch movies, go out and do things. And tell you what? You tell me something you want to do, and we'll do it together." I expect him to shrug and not give me an answer, but I'm surprised by what he says next.

"I want to learn to knit. Can you teach me?" I'm so shocked, I bite my lip to stop myself from laughing.

"I don't know how, but we can learn together. I'll find us a class. How does that sound?" He looks up at me in awe and slowly nods his head. I guess I should have asked Colt first, but I don't think he'll object.

"Okay. My grandma and Rosalie knit, but when they tried to teach me, I made a mess with the yarn, so they kicked me out, but I was only a baby then. I was four."

"We'll learn together. Deal?" I hold up my pinky and he wraps his around mine. I mess his hair and return to the stove.

"You must be excited about your grandma visiting," I say to him.

"She's nice, and Daddy says she spoils me." All shyness is gone from his voice now.

"She's your grandma. She's supposed to." That's one thing I missed out on growing up. My dad's mom died when he was a teenager, and he was never close to his father. I've only met my maternal grandmother once before she died a few years ago. Mother never talks about her.

"She lets me have soda and sweet tea, and she tells Daddy he has to deal with it. And my Uncle Charlie is nice too, but he got into a big fight with Daddy when we were there for Christmas." He lowers his voice and says, "Daddy punched him. I saw it. And the police took Uncle Charlie away. Grandma cried and ran to her room. After that, we went to Disney World. Daddy won't let me talk to Uncle Charlie anymore, but I miss him. He makes good brownies."

Holy dysfunctional family Christmas. I turn my back on Evan while I gather my thoughts. "Wow. Sounds a little wild, kiddo," I tell him. Tara did say Colt has a brother he doesn't get along with. I wonder what happened at Christmas, but I'm not about to pump a five-year-old for info on his family drama.

"Uncle Charlie would play baseball with me. He was teaching me to pitch. I want to play baseball when I'm big, not basketball." His little shoulders slump at the mention of his uncle. I flip his grilled cheese over and think of a way to change the subject.

I grab the last cookie left in the cookie jar and give it to him. "How about we make some chocolate chip cookies together. They will taste better than those, but don't tell Myra I said that." He shoves the last bit of cookie in his mouth. I plate the sandwich, cut it diagonally, and put it in front of him. I wash some grapes, slice strawberries, and put them in a bowl for him.

"What if Daddy says no to the cookies?"

I almost laugh at the thought. Just as the question leaves his mouth, Colt walks in and sits next to his son.

"I'll take whatever he's having," he says to me. "Please

and thank you." I walk to him, bend down and give him a soft, chaste kiss on the lips.

"Thank you," I tell him. "And my champion can get me all the flowers he wants."

"Good. Now, go make my sandwich." He winks at me.

"Watch this, kid," I say to Evan. "Colt, I'm going to make Evan some real cookies. Not the stuff with the sugar substitute. You're just going to have to deal with it."

His head snaps up, but I can see the amusement in his eyes.

"I know better than to argue with a woman, especially one who's going to make me a sandwich."

"Me and Vickie are going to learn to knit together," Evan announces to the kitchen.

"How long was I in the room?" Colt asks.

I roll my eyes at him and Evan giggles. "Hurry up so we can go to the store."

Evan shoves the rest of the sandwich in his mouth and runs off to get his shoes.

"You know," Colt says. "Shopping for groceries together is very traditional. Just so you're aware, there will be pictures taken of us together."

"Are we going or what? You talk too much, and I'm really in the mood for cookies."

He raises both hands up in surrender. "Yes, ma'am, but I want my food first. And this knitting thing." He pulls me close and looks into my eyes. "You don't strike me as the type of woman who knits. You seem more of the cashmere sweater buying type. Cute little hat with matching scarf type. And mittens. I'm picturing it now." He raises his eyebrows, and I shrug.

I get up and butter the whole wheat bread and put the

first slice in the skillet. "Whatever. I'm going to find us a class."

"Oh, a knitting class with Evan." I hear him stand and walk around the kitchen. He wraps his arms around my waist and pulls me into his body. "You," he says, brushing my hair off the side of my neck and kissing the exposed skin, "are the most amazing woman."

THIRTY

Colt

Pictures of us together are tweeted almost immediately. There's one with Evan on my shoulders while I hold Vickie's hand. There's another one of us at the checkout line where Vickie offers cash before I can put Evan down to take out my wallet. The absurd caption reads "Did Colt the Bolt Chastain find himself a sugar mama? "The third picture is when we step outside, and I put my arm across her shoulders to hold her close. This time, Evan is holding her hand.

It was a great evening. The two made cookies while I got a workout and stretch from my personal trainer. Whatever resistance Evan had regarding Vickie is gone. He talks nonstop in the store and at home. He runs around the kitchen, doing her bidding, practically bouncing off the walls in his excitement to bake.

When I emerge back into the kitchen, Tara, Vincent, and Ethan are there, eating cookies and talking. The kitchen smells great, and after the boys grab a few more cookies, they both leave for Evan's room.

"Tara brought more devil's milk into your house.

Whoops," Vickie says. She breaks a cookie in half and hands it to me. I stick the entire thing in my mouth and reach for another.

"I'm glad you two are here. I want to invite you to a little dinner party I'm throwing while my mother is here. Maybe after we win and before we leave for Alabama." I snake an arm around Vickie and pull her to me, surprising her. "Queen Vee has very graciously agreed to meet Mary Leigh Chastain. Watch out, you two," I say pointing at Ethan and Tara. "You're no longer the best-looking couple in Manhattan."

Tara laughs at me and says, "You guys can have Manhattan. We're taking the entire northeast."

"The world, baby," Ethan says.

THIRTY-ONE

Colt

Two days before

"You have to make sure you rest and make all your practices. Listen to Coach Walsh, and don't forget to pray. I've been prayin' all season. I think this will be your year, Son. Another year to bring a championship to Manhattan. And I love that it's one of our own from Alabama that's bringing them all these wins." I listen to Mama on FaceTime. She has her eyes closed tight when she mentions praying. I would hope the Lord has better things to worry about than my championship, but I don't dare tell her that. Her eyes pop open again, and something changes. I can tell she's going to talk about something I don't want to discuss.

"I was thinkin' I could bring your brother with me to New York. He's been killin' himself at the restaurant and—"

"No, Mama." My voice is firm but not hard. She stops and stares into my eyes. When I was younger, I'd always look away in shame when she would give me that look. It's a *combination of sadness mixed with disappointment. I'd apologize and agree to whatever she wants, but not now. Not this time.*

"Well," she says, shaking her head as if that would erase my refusal, "where would we all be if we weren't forgiven for our sins? Jesus died so that we could be saved." I run a hand over my face and bite my tongue. This is not an argument that I want to take on, so I let her rant. "Do you know how many times in this life I've messed up? Or how many times your father, may he rest in peace, messed up? It's only by His grace that we were able to move on."

"Well, Mama, maybe Charlie should ask the Lord for forgiveness. I'm fresh out." I get the look again, but I don't back down. "Can we talk about somethin' else?"

She lets out a deep sigh but nods. "I was going to wait until after the Finals, but I've been followin' you on the Twitter. I've noticed a young lady at your games that you've been kissin'."

That's it. The sentence ends, and I'm not sure if she's asking me a question, so I stay quiet. I was going to bring this up now since she's visiting soon, but I want to see what she says. "I notice she's uh..." She shuts up and looks up as if she's pondering her next words. "She's black."

"You noticed that, did you?" I smile at her, and she smiles back and shoos me with her hand. "What gave it away? I'm glad you brought it up because I want you to meet her when you get here. I was thinkin' we can pick you up at the airport and take you out to dinner."

My mother might be a country girl, but she also loves the noise and bright lights of New York City. And for someone who hardly ever ate out when we were growing up, she loves when I take her to fancy Manhattan restaurants.

She opens and closes her mouth several times. "So, it's

serious? I figured it was when your brother and I noticed she was at all the games recently." She goes quiet again. "Are you sure about this, Colton?"

I stare into her eyes, and this time, it's Mama who looks away. "You know I believe people should be able to be with whoever they want, regardless of color. Don't tell Reverend Richards, but I believe even same sex couples should be together. Who am I to judge?"

I've always known she feels this way, so I'm not surprised by her words. "Then what is the problem?"

"I had always hoped that you and Evan would come back home once you retired. Maybe you can get a coachin' job at Alabama, or one of those commentator jobs, but I always thought you'd be here with me and your brother."

I decide I'm going to ignore all comments about my brother.

"Mama, New York is all Evan's ever known, and I don't want to raise him back home. I like it here. You can always move here with us. Or you can live here part of the year. Whatever you want, but I'm not coming back. I want to talk to you about Vickie. I think you'll like her."

Her eyes soften and I can tell she's swallowed a lump in her throat.

"I really care about her."

"Your brother said her daddy owned a chain of toy stores and her sister is with that Ethan Bradford. They managed to get themselves two rich men." She arches her eyebrows, and for the first time in a long time, I'm losing patience with my mother.

"Yes, her father did. They are well off, and she doesn't want or need anything from me. I'm lucky she wants to be with me, not the other way around. It took some convincin' for her to give me a chance."

At that she bristles. "My son doesn't have to convince a woman to be with him. All the young women at the church are ready to meet you since you are so stubborn about Robin—"

"Mama! I'm in a relationship. Please stop talkin' about other women who are ready and willin'. And as for Robin, there was no chance I was going to get involved with Kelsey's sister. I don't know what you were thinkin'."

She closes her mouth and purses her lips. "You watch your tone, Colton. I'm still your mother." She sighs. "Your brother warned me you'd get defensive if I said anything, but I'm your mother and I have the right to speak my mind."

"I still don't understand what you're tryin' to say. Get to the point."

"I was sayin', I want you to come back home, but I guess you've made up your mind. And of course, I'll meet Victoria, but if I think she's wrong for you, I'm gonna let you know it." I open my mouth to give her a rebuke, but she holds her hand up. "And it will have nothin' to do with her being black, so calm down. I don't care about that. You lost your wife, may Kelsey rest in paradise. You deserve all the love and happiness in the world. And even though I don't get a vote in who you're with, I still want to have a good relationship with her. You, Charlie, and Evan are my world. I promise I won't alienate her, but you can't blame me for wantin' you home."

Relieved that she's finally gotten to the point, I nod at her. She knows she has no say in who I date. I made that clear about a year after Kelsey died when I told her to drop it about me and Robin. She gave up on that, but she invited an unsuspecting member of her church over for lunch. The woman was just as surprised and embarrassed as I was.

"Thank you, Mama. I appreciate that." And I bite my

tongue and don't tell her that I wish Charlie would stay out of my business.

"And is she good to my grandbaby?"

She's amazing with Evan, who didn't make it easy on her. "She is."

"You're a great father, Colton. You were meant to be a father, and I don't know why the Lord in his infinite wisdom took Kelsey from us, but I'm so glad Evan has you. I hope Victoria knows what a great man she has, and I hope she shows you. You deserve that." *Her eyes fill with tears, but they don't fall. She won't let them, at least not in front of me. The closest I saw her come to crying in front of me since my father's funeral was last Christmas after I punched Charlie in the face, but she ran to her room before I could see her tears.*

"Thank you, Mama. I think you'll like Vickie a lot. She's looking forward to meetin' you." *As much as someone looks forward to walking the plank, but Vickie is willing, and that's all I can hope for.*

After agreeing to let her cook for us on her first night here, we end the call, but only after she tells me she loves me about a dozen times.

"I never thought I'd see the day that Queen Vee would be nervous. And it's all for Mama." I put an arm around her waist and pull her closer. "You're still short, though," I tell her.

She does her best to push me away, but she can't. Evan is holding her free hand, and she's stuck to my body. To show her how powerless she is, I bend down and give her a lingering kiss on her cheek. "You look nice. You smell nice too." It took her hours to pick out an outfit. She decided on black pants and a hot pink top. I've never seen her in such a feminine color, but I like it on her. She even has her hair in tight curls, giving her a nineteen-fifties look. "I can't wait to have you naked in my bed tonight."

"Not happening," she whispers. She's been adamant about not spending the night with me while Mama's in town, but I'm adamant that she is.

"You're such a traditional woman, do you know that? Next, you'll want me to put a baby in your belly." I hold my laugh when she gives me an incredulous look and put my free hand on her belly. She subtly elbows me in the ribs. "Don't worry. It will be after we get married. Of course, I have to ask your daddy for your hand. I hope our kids inherit my height. And then—" She elbows me in the ribs hard. "Did you fall on your head today at practice? You're with the wrong woman if you want that." She looks down at Evan, who's not paying any attention to us. "And I swear to God, Colton, if you ask my dad for my hand or any other part of my anatomy, you will regret it. Now, shut up before I give you a black eye in front of Mama."

I run my nose along her cheek. There are a few people at baggage claim watching us, taking pictures and video, but I don't care. Vickie is still stiff in my arms, but she's going to have to learn to deal with the scrutiny.

"Mmhmm. You'd never do that in front of Evan but go ahead and threaten me all you want. I'm pretty sure I'll win if we ever get into a fist fight." To prove my point, I lift her off her feet using one arm with hardly any effort. "Yes, I will fight a girl." I kiss her cheek, and say, "There she is, so behave. Mama's got my back if you start anythang. You're outnumbered."

She's at the top of the escalator wearing my jersey. She's

still beautiful with her dirty blonde hair. She's a tall woman, at one inch over six feet but she's plump around the middle. She lets out a shriek when she sees us. Evan lets go of Vickie's hand and runs right into her arms. She picks him up, and they walk over to us. Vickie stands there with a fake smile plastered on her face. Mama smiles in my direction, but I can see her eyes darting back and forth to Vickie. I hand her the flowers I brought for her and kiss her cheek. When she puts Evan down, I take her in my arms and spin her around. She laughs, and so do I. Her cheeks are pink by the time I put her down.

"Mama, I'd like you to meet my Queen Vee, Victoria Taylor. Queen Vee, this is my mama, Mary Leigh Chastain."

Vickie offers my mother her hand, but Mama pulls her into a bone crushing hug. "My goodness, aren't you pretty." Mama pats both of Vickie's cheeks, and Vickie lets out a little shriek of surprise before taking a step back.

"It's nice to meet you, Mrs. Chastain," Vickie says.

"It's Mary Leigh. Mary Leigh. Never Mary." She shakes her index finger in disapproval, but she has a smile on her face. "Colton, honey, go get my bags while I get to know Vickie." Mama wraps an arm through Victoria's.

Minutes later, we're in the car, with Mama sitting in the front with Dante. She talks nonstop. "I'm so excited. I can't wait to cook in that kitchen of yours, Son. Vickie, I hope you're one of those girls who likes to eat because I like to cook."

"Vickie made me spaghetti and meatballs last night, Grandma," Evan says before I can answer. "And not the frozen meatballs. She called the evil one for the recipe. She let me help her, and she didn't get mad when I dropped an egg. But she got mad when Daddy started juggling the eggs and dropped all three. He had to clean up the mess."

"He's the worst juggler," Mama says.

Dante snorts from the driver's seat and I clear my throat. "I want you all to listen and listen good. You too, Dante."

"I'm listening, boss," Dante says.

"I cleaned up that mess because I wanted to, not because of Vickie. I'm not scared of her. Look at how short she is."

She looks at me and waves her fist.

"But she yelled at you, and you ran to get the mop," Evan insists. Vickie giggles and Dante smirks. "You said you were but her lowly servant in that weird voice, and you bowed."

"That's not a weird voice, that's my British accent, and you have a big mouth." I mess his hair.

"Grandma, me and Vickie are going to learn to knit together. Vickie says we'll be better than you and Rosalie in no time."

"You have no idea how competitive the Chastain's are," I whisper to Vickie.

"Bring it, Chastain. I'm a Taylor, and we never lose."

Mama twists around in her seat and looks at Vickie. I hold my breath and wait to hear what she's going to say. "The evil one? Do you have a direct line to the devil, Vickie? Tell him I rebuke him." She giggles and turns around. I never know how she's going to react to perceived jokes about the devil. "And I admire your confidence, but me and Rosalie can be sleep deprived, blindfolded with one hand tied behind our backs, and we'll still wipe the floor with you when it comes to knitting."

"The evil one is my stepmom," Vickie says. "It's a long

running joke." Vickie absentmindedly runs a hand through Evan's hair. "And challenge accepted, Mary Leigh. I'm a quick learner, and Evan is too."

"And the only one who'll be wiping the floor is the boss," Dante says, right before he bursts into laughter.

THIRTY-TWO

Vickie

I don't leave like I intended to the night before. His mother makes dinner, a very impressive seafood gumbo, fried chicken, and baked Alaskan sea bass. After dinner, I insist on leaving, especially since Evan was spending so much time with his grandmother. I tell Colt I would go so they can have some alone time together, but he asks me to stay. When Mary Leigh put on Annie for Evan, he pulls me into the bedroom with him and says his sanity can only be saved if I don't leave.

~

I sit in the middle of his bed and work on my novel while he lies next to me and watches his old games. Every few minutes one of his hands rubs my back and my shoulders.

"You have to handle the ball better," I say, looking up at the TV. "You missed that shot."

"Handle the ball better? Is that the same as bending my

knees or whatever? Do tell." He pauses the television and waits.

"You didn't hit it on the floor enough times."

"You mean bounce it?"

I sigh, close my laptop and stand. "Watch me," I tell him. He sits up on the bed and crosses his arms. "You have to beat the ball against the floor at least five times, and then throw it. Like this." *I mimic bouncing a basketball and throwing a shot.* "It's physics, Chastain. Did you ever go to class? Watch me again." *I pretend to bounce the ball between my legs.*

"What was that you just did? You looked like you were having a seizure."

"Am I going to have to teach you everything? Handle the ball better and do a better job of throwing it in that round thing. That's how you win. Duh." *I roll my eyes at him.*

He reaches for me and pulls me on his lap. I straddle him.

"Coach better watch out. I think you're after his job." *He tightens his arms around me.*

"You want a job done right, send a woman."

He lowers his voice and says, "I have a job for you. I have two balls you can handle right now, but you can't beat them against the floor."

Now, with my heart in my throat, I wait for the Mischiefs to come out for the first game of the Finals. His mother is beside me with Evan and Vincent next to her. I have Tara and Ethan next to me. My dad, Alan, and Cheryl are behind me. Despite how nice Colt's mother is, I'm still nervous to have the entire family together. I haven't done this since Gerald, and that didn't end well. Mother took to him like a fish to water and did everything to make Cheryl feel excluded. She was like a dog marking her territory that night.

I push Gerald out of my mind and think of the past day. Tara nudges my side and whispers, "I think you're more nervous than the players."

When Colt returned home from practice this afternoon, I gave him a massage. He got so relaxed he fell asleep while I was still rubbing his back. He was out cold, and I braided his hair in cornrows. This time, he didn't tell me he was going to take them out. The players get called out one by one, and we all cheer for Colt when he comes out, giving high-fives to all his teammates. When the announcer comments on his hair, he runs a hand over his head.

The first half is a blur, and the excitement in the stadium, filled with people wearing magenta and gold, is infectious. The opposing team from Milwaukee is playing well, not giving the Mischiefs room for much of a lead, despite Colt scoring twenty-three points in the first half. By halftime, the Mischiefs are only eight points ahead.

"I'm just gonna have to start prayin'," Mary Leigh whispers while she grabs my hand. Evan distracts her by whispering something in her ear. She's the epitome of what a grandmother should be. She spoils Evan, and when Colt balks, she tells him to hush and sit down. Evan loves it, and I love that he's so happy to have her around.

The only hiccup happened an hour after arriving at Colt's place.

I'M IN DESPERATE NEED OF A GLASS OF WINE, BUT OUT OF respect for his mother's wishes, I won't have any. I even go so

far as to hide the unopened bottles in Colt's closet. Mary Leigh picks up her phone and touches the screen. While the phone rings, she sets it down on the kitchen table, takes a seat, and plasters a wide smile on her face. It's so wide, it looks like her face might crack. I lean against the wall, curious to see what she does next. I can spot a manipulative mother from a mile away, and as nice as she is, she's as manipulative as they come.

"Hi, honey," she says. "Sorry to just be callin', but I was with Evan." Just as the words leave her mouth, Colt and Evan come walking back into the kitchen. "Evan, honey, come say hi to your Uncle Charlie." Evan runs over and sits on her lap. Colt freezes and stops mid step. I push off the wall and approach him. I massage his lower back and hope that my touch will give him some solace.

"Hi, Uncle Charlie." Evan waves frantically into the phone.

"I miss you, bud," Uncle Charlie says. "You take care of your grandma and your daddy, okay?" Evan nods.

"You want to meet Vickie?" Evan asks. He turns, and when he sees me, he jumps off his grandma and comes to take my hand. When I don't make any moves, Mary Leigh gets up and brings the phone to me, shoving it in my face so I can stare at a Colt lookalike. He has the same curly, black hair and dark eyes. The only difference is he has a full beard, and his hair is much shorter.

"This is Victoria Taylor, your brother's lady friend. The one we saw on the Twitter." She whispers the last part.

I wave at Charlie, who has a genuine smile on his face, making him look even more like Colt.

"Lovely to meet you," he says, his accent thick and rich. The words roll off his tongue like molasses.

"You as well," I tell him, reluctant to say more given what Evan's told me.

"Hi, Colty," he says. He lowers his voice and his eyes when he addresses his brother. Colt only gives him a curt nod before he walks away, pulling me along with him. He doesn't speak again until we get to the bedroom. He slams the door behind him, and for the first time since I've met him, he's angry. I didn't know he was capable of being angry, and it unsettles me.

He plops himself on the bed, and I sit on the edge before grabbing his hand in mine. He tugs me, and I sprawl on top of his chest as his large hands rub my back.

"Are you still mad about whatever happened at Christmas?"

His head snaps up in surprise. "How do you know about that?"

"Evan told me you got into a fight and punched his uncle." He flips us over, and suddenly he's on top. Warm lips search the side of my neck, and I feel my nipples harden. He kisses his way down, bites my shirt, and starts to tug. I playfully punch his arm.

"You are not a puppy," I tell him.

He growls and starts to bark like a little dog. "Let's get a dog. I bet you'll want one of those little poodles. Or worse, one of those tiny mutts that can fit in your purse." He distracts me by unbuttoning my pants. He unzips them, but I grab his hand before he can go any further.

"You wanted to do this relationship thing, so let's do it." I manage to roll out from underneath him and stand up.

"You wouldn't understand," he says. "You and your brother and sister are so close. It's not like that for me and Charlie, at least not anymore."

After zipping and buttoning my pants, I take his hand

and pull us to the couch in the corner of his bedroom. I sit next to him and wait for him to speak.

"No one's like me and my siblings. Others shouldn't even try." *I bump his shoulder with mine to lighten the mood, but he doesn't smile.* "Tell me." *I take his hand and hold it.* "Maybe I can help."

"We were close once. Out of the two of us, he's the more gifted athlete. He's two years older and got the same scholarship as me. He was all set to go off to college until he got drunk one night, climbed a tree, and fell. He fractured his femur and needed surgery. He lost his scholarship, and all his hopes and dreams were dashed. That was bad enough. When I got the same scholarship two years later, he became angry. Told me I wasn't good enough to make it, and all I was doing was followin' in his shadow. He criticized everythin' I did, but that's not the worst of it. He went into my email and replied that I was not acceptin' the scholarship." *I let out a surprised gasp.* "My high school coach found me the next day and almost ripped my head off because the school called him. I told him I had no idea what he was talking about. He dragged me to the office, and we called the school and cleared things up. I didn't want to admit it, but I knew Charlie was behind it. I didn't take it to Mama. I figured me and coach had fixed it, but Charlie only got angrier. He tried to hurt me next. Pushed me down the stairs at home. I called him out on it, and we started fightin' in the livin' room. Broke the coffee table, the television, and punched a hole through the wall. He's freakishly strong and had me on the floor. He tried to stomp me, but I got away and got the upper hand. I told Mama everythin' when she got home. She believed me but told me that my brother needed help and was not in his right mind. To her credit, she got him therapy, but he wouldn't go. I left a few weeks later, and he went down a deep spiral. He* *has a drinkin' problem and just finished his third stint in rehab a few months ago."*

He stops speaking, and I squeeze his hand for comfort. He picks it up and puts it to his lips. I rest my head on his chest, and he pulls me closer, almost as if he's absorbing some of my strength.

"Does this last stint in rehab have anything to do with what happened last Christmas?" I whisper.

"He got drunk. I guess he was still drunk when he woke up the mornin' after Christmas. Evan was up, and he decided he was going to get in a car with my son while he was still intoxicated because Evan wanted donuts. He got pulled over and was arrested. Mama got a call from the sheriff, telling us they had Evan. We were both still sleepin'. When I got there, I punched him and told him never to speak to me or my son again. Because this was his third DUI, he had to serve three months in jail, and when he got out, he went to rehab, promisin' our mother he would never drink again. He's supposedly openin' a restaurant."

He puts his head on my lap as if the confession has taken a lot out of him. I stroke his hair and try to make sense of his words. I've never felt any jealousy toward my siblings. I've only always wanted the best for them. Alan's the smartest, and Tara's the pretty one, but that's never bothered me. I can never imagine hating them for things that aren't their fault.

"I'm sorry," I whisper. "That's a lot. I understand why you'd be angry, especially after putting Evan in danger. Families are complicated, Colt. Even the ones who seem to have it together have their demons." I stroke his hair, tucking a piece behind his ear.

"Are you finally going to tell me about you and your mama now?"

"There isn't much of a story about my mother. She left

my dad when I was nine. We went to school, and when we came home, she was gone. We'd go months without seeing her sometimes. We still do. This is about you and your brother. I understand your anger, especially the part that involves Evan."

"And the other parts?"

I run my fingernails through his scalp. He sighs and closes his eyes.

"I understand how you feel about that too. I'm trying to put myself in your place, champion. I can't ever picture Alan or Tara doing that to me, but if they were not themselves and drinking, I don't know. If they came to me and begged for forgiveness, I'd think of all the good times we had versus the bad. I would forgive, but that's a decision I would make based on our shared history. These decisions are always personal. There's no wrong or right answer. Has Charlie asked for forgiveness?"

I let my hand fall away from his hair, but he picks it up and puts it back. I start stroking the nape of his neck.

"He has. Many, many times, and I feel guilty, Vickie. I think he keeps drinkin' because I won't forgive him."

"That's not on you. Don't put that in your head."

He's quiet, but I can tell he's thinking of what to say next. I continue to touch him, but Evan bursts through the door with Mary Leigh behind him. She's wringing her hands and taking slow steps toward Colt, whose head is still in my lap.

When I stop stroking his hair, he whispers, "Don't stop." So, I continue.

"I'm sorry, Son," she says. "You know I want you and your brother to make up, but you don't need any extra stress before the Finals. Forgive me, please." She stands over him,

looking down. He lifts his head from my lap, stands, and takes her into a hug.

"Nothing to forgive, Mama." She lets out a half laugh, half sob, and wraps her arms around him. Evan joins in and hugs his father's leg. I smile at the sweet scene. Colt offers me his hand, and when I take it, he pulls me up and wraps his arm around me too. His mother does the same, and the four of us hug.

~

Now

"I can't believe how mean you were to Ethan when he has his own personal luxury suite at Madison Square Garden." Tara makes a face. I'm almost positive she had no idea Ethan had this until very recently. She's as opposed to basketball as I am, maybe even more so. At least I'll watch with our dad, who is now sitting with the boys on either side of him while he explains the game.

Colt's mother texts on her phone, and I'm pretty sure she's texting Charlie. Every so often, she'll leave a voicemail for Colt, praising him for something he did before she forgets.

"Who is Mary Leigh texting?" Tara whispers.

"I think it's her other son, Charlie. You were right. Things are not good between him and Colt."

"God, she's so tense. I feel like adding rum to that coke the next time she looks away," Tara whispers. "If she had pearls, she'd be clutching them right now."

Right on cue, she puts the phone down and grabs the lapels of her shirt, pressing them around her neck.

"She's sweet. Very doting," I say to Tara in Mary Leigh's

defense. Her phone lights up again, she grabs it, stands, and goes to the side of the room to talk. She waves at me when our eyes catch, and I wave back.

"Look at you getting along well with your boyfriend's mother."

"I'm too old for a boyfriend. Every time someone says that, I feel like I'm back in the eighth grade."

"We weren't allowed to have boyfriends back then," Tara reminds me.

"Yeah, but we did anyway." She starts to giggle, and as if he can hear us, our dad looks up. We both burst into laughter.

Mary Leigh stays on the phone until the game resumes. The last half flies by, and the Mischiefs win with a nine-point lead.

It's late by the time we get back to Colt's apartment. Evan's fast asleep when the driver pulls to the front of the building, and I end up carrying him inside. His grandmother insists on getting him ready for bed, and I leave her to the fussy little boy.

Colt gets home at the same moment that I'm zipping my suitcase. I've been at his house for days, and I've decided tonight is the night I'll be spending in my own apartment.

He rolls his eyes to the ceiling when he sees me, but he walks in, cups my face and kisses me. "Please, stay," he whispers. Once I nod, he picks up the bag, and puts it in the back of the closet.

"Come on." We go to the kitchen, and he pulls out a plate from the microwave. His mother fixed it for him before we left for the game tonight. It's a chicken ziti dish that she made, and the smell makes my stomach growl.

I sit on his lap and he offers me a bite. "Oh my God," I

moan. I snatch the fork from him and eat some more before I hop off of him to get my own.

"So, Mama's going to stay here with Evan for the away games. She's not up for all that travelin'."

"Sounds good, but are you sure you wouldn't prefer alone time with her and Evan without me hovering around?"

He eats but watches me as he chews. He leaves the table and returns with two bottles of water.

"I want you to stay." He picks up my hand and intertwines our fingers. "I like havin' you here. I like having dinner with you after my games. It's comfortin'." He tugs my arm, and I end up on his lap. "I thought we were in this?" He stands with me in his arms and walks us back to the bedroom and locks the door.

He lifts the jersey over my head and tosses it to the corner. My pants and underwear come off next, followed by my bra. He lays me on the bed and spreads my legs. "I think I'm ready for dessert."

THE MISCHIEFS WIN THE SECOND GAME IN THE SERIES, and Colt flies to Milwaukee immediately after the game. I fly out the next afternoon alone. Alan won't arrive until the next day. I write during the entire two-hour flight on the private plane that Colt got for me. It's warm when I arrive, and it's still light out when my driver takes me to Colt's hotel. He's busy with the team, and I won't see him until evening.

He shows up in my room a few hours later, and we order room service. We have dinner with Evan and Mary

Leigh over FaceTime. Evan talks nonstop and gives his father advice on how to win the game.

Once dinner's over, I treat myself to a hot shower. A few minutes into the shower, while I have my eyes closed and my face under the strong spray, I feel the shower door open and large hands grab my hips. He pulls me into his naked body, and I sigh. He takes the washcloth from my hand and washes me, taking special care between my legs and my butt cheeks. Once he's done, he slaps my ass, and the sting takes me by surprise. When I try to hit him back, he grabs both my wrists and holds them with one hand. No matter how hard I try to pull out of his grasp, I can't. That doesn't stop me from trying. Each time he laughs, it makes me fight harder. He lifts me up by both wrists with one hand, hardly exerting any energy at all, and pins me against the shower wall. When I wrap my legs around him, his free hand travels down my back and between my ass cheeks. Like he's done before, he sticks his pinky finger in my rosebud, and he covers my mouth with his, swallowing my protest in the process.

"I'm going to eat your snatch," he says against my mouth. "And then I'm going to eat your ass." He lets me slide down his body. He steps back, his dick now hard and pointing straight at me as if it's a compass and I'm home. He approaches, gets on his knees, and sticks his head between my legs. His tongue hits my clit, almost bringing me to my knees. I throw a leg over his shoulder and grab his now tangled hair for support.

He ravages me, taking me to the brink of orgasm only to pull away before I can succumb. He spins me around to face the wall and spread my ass cheeks apart.

"Colt!" I say, but the rest of my words gets swallowed by the sounds of the shower when his tongue hits my most sacred place. I tense at first, not knowing what to do or expect since this has never happened to me before.

"Relax. Unclench those cheeks." He squeezes my ass, and I relax. I rest my forehead against the wall and give in to him. His tongue teases my hole, and he presses his entire face into my ass. A hand finds its way to my pussy and two fingers slide inside of me. I relax fully, giving in to the sensation. His tongue rims my ass, and I groan at having both holes filled at once.

"Oh, God," I mutter when I feel myself start to convulse. The feeling of euphoria takes over, stemming from the lower parts of me, and travels to the top. Just as I'm on the precipice of an epic orgasm, his face leaves my ass, and his fingers leave my pussy. He spins me around, lifts me, and pins me against the wall. The water falls on us. My shower cap has gone completely askew. He pulls it off with his free hand, and I yell in protest. He orders me to spread my legs. When I happily oblige, he sinks into me, filling me in one long thrust. He holds me up and fucks me against the shower wall. I come almost immediately, but Colt's nowhere done. He pummels me into the wall, shoving his long and thick dick inside of me. I call out his name, and he calls mine. I come again, this one taking me by such surprise, I think I might fall, but his strong arms would never let that happen. He roars close to my ear, convulsing against me when he finds his release. It seems like his orgasm goes on forever. By the time he sets me on my feet, my legs have turned to rubber, and he grabs my hips, preventing me from falling over. He pulls me into him and wraps his arms around me.

"I needed that, darlin'," he says with his warm lips against my temple.

HE'S LYING ON TOP OF THE BED, COMPLETELY NAKED. I stop and admire his taut body. He's so long, but his body is nothing but tight muscle. He's on his phone typing something, but he extends a hand to me without looking up from the phone. I slide in next to him and rest my head on his shoulder. He absentmindedly kisses my forehead while he texts with his mother. When he finishes, he tosses the phone across the room, and it lands on the chair. He grabs the remote, and his last basketball game comes on the screen.

"Ugh," I groan. "Do we have to? I already told you how to win these stupid games. Bend your knees and flick your wrists or whatever. And why did you toss your phone? What if your mom needs to contact you about Evan?" I get out of the bed and retrieve his phone.

When I try to slide back into bed, he opens my robe and takes it off my body.

"Skin on skin, Queen Vee. As much as I hate hotels, I like being able to be naked with you."

I slide my hand over his flat and rippled stomach. "It's not so bad."

"Face it, Queen, I'm the best thing to ever happen to you."

I sigh and drop my head on the pillow. "Shut up."

He pulls me up and puts me on his naked lap. I wrap my legs around him, grab his damp hair and kiss him.

"Don't tell me what to do," he says against my mouth. "I know what you're doin'." He kisses the side of my neck, biting me.

"What am I doin'?" I mimic his accent,

"It's not workin'." He moves away from the side of my

neck and looks into my eyes. I stare at him, eager to hear what nonsense is going to spew from his mouth. "I don't care how right you feel in my arms, or how good you smell. I'm not fallin' in love with you."

My heart skips a beat, and my mouth falls open. I look away, but he puts a finger underneath my chin and tilts my face back up. "Did you hear me?" he asks.

I swallow, unsure of how to respond. It's been years since I've said those words to a man. Looking back now, I didn't love Gerald. That's why it was so easy for me to walk away and refuse to go to Kentucky with him.

As much as I wasn't looking for a relationship when I met Colt, and as much as I tried to push him away, he's here. He's included me into his life, even the parts that I wanted nothing to do with. Now that I'm here with him, in every facet, there's nowhere else I want to be.

"Yeah, I heard you," I say to him. I square my shoulders and look into his clear brown eyes. "I'm not deaf, champion. Don't worry, I'm not falling in love with you either."

He smiles so wide that dimple makes an appearance.

"Good." He dramatically exhales. "I would hate for this thing to be one sided. So, just to be clear, I do not love you, Victoria Renee Chastain." When I stare at him, he laughs and shakes his head. "Oh, Jesus. What did I just say? I got hit in the head again earlier. A slip of the tongue. Let me rephrase." He loudly clears his throat. "I do not love you, Victoria Renee Taylor. I don't love how smart and selfless you are. I hate how patient you've been with Evan, and despite how reluctant you were to meet Mama"—I roll my eyes at the mention of his mother—"you've embraced her. I don't love how you know who you are and what you want. I don't love anything about you."

I stare at him with an eyebrow arched. "Are you done?"

When he nods, I say, "I don't love you either. There's nothing about you to love. I don't love that you're an awesome father to a great kid. I don't love how kind you are to everyone, and I don't love your ugly face. You annoy me. I'm only here for the free hotel room and the private plane. Oh, and the sex." He wraps his arms around me and takes me in a kiss. "You have a nice dick," I mumble against his mouth.

THIRTY-THREE

Colt

I don't have much time to spend with Victoria the day of the third game, and I'm once again grateful to have a woman who is not only smart and beautiful but independent. She has no problem kicking me out of the room in the morning with orders for me to win the next two games because she doesn't have time to keep traveling back and forth to my stupid games. That was after she reminded me to handle the ball better and to throw it right.

I spend the day at practice and then got a massage to loosen my tight muscles. I do leg extensions to relieve the pain in my knees from the fall I took at practice, and by the time I get back to my room, I'm ready for my nap. Once I close the curtains and the room is shrouded in darkness, I slide in between the sheets and grab my phone.

"My queen, my liege," I say when she answers. Wherever she is, it's loud. I hear a man's voice, and I remember that her brother would be arriving today, otherwise, I'd be heading to wherever she is.

"Hey, champ," she says. "Isn't it your naptime?"

"It is, but I wanted to check with my Queen Vee first. I take it Alan got in okay?"

He says something, and she playfully calls him an idiot. There's a part of me that wishes I had a better relationship with my brother. It's so easy with the Taylor siblings, and I remember when me and Charlie had something similar.

"Yeah, we're getting Mexican food. I never turn down a good margarita. I'll come to your room and braid your hair before the game."

"Come and get in bed with me when you get here. I don't miss you, and I definitely don't love you," I tell her.

"Good because I don't miss or love you either. You suck."

"You're the one who'll be sucking when you get here."

"Is that what you two are doing now?" Alan asks.

THIRTY-FOUR

Vickie

THE MISCHIEFS LOSE THE NEXT TWO GAMES BY THREE points each time. I get my first glance into moody Colt. The charming guy with the ready smile and quick wit disappears right before my eyes. There were no words of comfort that I could offer him. After the loss of game three, I go to his hotel room hours afterward, and he's in the middle of the bed watching the game. He holds me against him, but we don't talk much, and I fall asleep almost immediately.

I spend the next day with my brother, touring a beer garden in Milwaukee. There are only a few texts from Colt, but I get quite a few from his mother, sending pictures of Evan. She tells me that Colt can be his worst critic and for me to not let him fall into despair. I thought she was being dramatic, but she most definitely was not.

There are tweets about me being bad luck or that his hair must be braided too tight and messing with his game. Worse was when he limped off the court at halftime and sat on the bench for most of the third quarter. Even though I was several feet away, I could sense the disappointment oozing from him. When the game ends and I meet with him outside the locker room, he hardly speaks to me at all. He kisses my cheek and tells me he'll see me in New York the next day. The team gets on their private plane and flies back immediately after, but my flight back home doesn't leave until morning.

It's early afternoon when we land in New York City on Friday. Instead of going home, we meet Tara at Capital Grille on 51st Street. It's crowded but we're led to a small private room when we give them Tara's name. She's already there with Ethan. He stands, kisses my cheek, and offers Alan his hand.

"I hope you don't mind if I crash your lunch. I have to fly out of town for a work emergency and I wanted to spend a little more time with the lovely Tara Taylor," Ethan says. He wraps his hand around hers and kisses it.

She smiles and rubs her nose on his, and something inside of me melts. I pick up my phone and send a text.

Me: I don't miss you. I don't wish I was having lunch with you instead of my siblings and Ethan.

I know he's probably at home after his practice and massage, but I get excited when I see the three bubbles on my screen.

Colt: Who is this? Another crazy fangirl?
Me: If fangirls have your number, we have a big problem.

Colt: Queen Vee. My queen, my liege. I don't miss you either. Under no circumstances are you to hurry up and get here.

Someone tosses a piece of bread at me. When I look up, Tara's staring at me with a knowing smile on her face. Alan throws another piece of bread, but I catch it and eat it.

"Who was that?" Tara asks.

"Colt," Alan answers. "Keep this one, twin. The accommodations in Milwaukee were very accommodating.

"Yeah, I'll remember that, idiot. Oh, how was your date from a couple of weeks ago? You never told us."

Alan sighs. The waitress arrives and we order drinks. Still tired from my trip, I get water. Ethan orders a whiskey, and Alan orders the same. I catch Tara's eye, and she side eyes our brother.

"So, my date," Alan begins. Ethan finally puts his phone down, throws an arm across Tara's shoulder, and waits for Alan to continue. "She offers to cook me dinner, so I'm thinking I'm going to get to at least third base." I groan and throw a piece of bread at him this time. "I put on my good blazer. The navy blue one that makes my shoulders look wide. Anyway, I get there, and she has on this yellow sundress that makes her breasts look perfect." He holds both hands at his chest as if he's cupping something. When Ethan starts to cough, Alan turns to him and says, "I'm a breast man."

The waitress returns with our drinks. "Carry on," Ethan says once the waitress leaves.

"And it's not just the breasts that look good. The ass is so tight, I could bounce a quarter off it. She's also smelling good. She checked all of Alan's boxes. We're drinking wine, sharing appetizers, and laughing. Every time she leans over me or the table, I get an eyeful. She must be doing that on purpose, right?"

"Obviously," Ethan agrees. "Your sister does that to me too."

"Please, man. I don't need that in my head," Alan says.

"But we need to hear all about how you're lusting for this woman's body? And you haven't even told us her name," I tell him.

"She who shall not be named." He takes a sip of his whiskey and starts to cough, so I offer him my water. He coughs so hard, his glasses slide off his face. After finally catching his breath, he says, "About forty-five minutes after I get there, her brother arrives. Cool, right? Maybe he's just stopping by for a minute to make sure I'm not a serial killer. I'm all about the sibling love. She serves dinner, an incredible paella that she made herself. She sits across the table from me, giving me a clear view of the girls." He makes that cupping gesture again. "It's going well until her brother, who was sitting next to me, puts his hand on my lap."

The entire table pauses. I stare at Tara, who stares back at me until she turns and looks at Ethan. Then, all at once, everyone but Alan bursts into laughter. I laugh so hard, tears fall down my face.

"Are you guys done?" Alan asks a few minutes later. "Let me continue because I never want to talk about this again. I nearly jump to the ceiling when he squeezes my thigh. I had a semi from the view of the girls, but after the thigh squeeze, I shrivel up like a raisin."

"Ew," Tara says.

"You three really do tell each other everything, don't you?" Ethan asks.

"Taylor three," we all say at once.

"Turns out, she invited me there to fix me up with her

brother." We all burst into laughter again. "I thought it was going great. I was telling all my best math jokes, and she was laughing. But now that I think about it, she didn't laugh as hard as him." Alan lets out a sigh of defeat, sits back in the chair, and covers his face with his hands. "I blame you two for this." He straightens back up and points at us.

"How is it our fault someone tried to fix you up with a man?" Tara asks him.

"Because you two are always in my business. I spend too much time with two females, and you've tainted me. I don't want you in my business anymore."

"Boy, please." Tara waves him off.

"Oh, guess who I saw? Tilly." I tell everyone at the table about running into our former neighbor. "She's back in the house. She had the biggest crush on Alan," I tell Ethan.

Alan rolls his eyes and casually sips his drink. When he starts to cough again, I take the drink away.

"She followed him around like a puppy."

"She was twelve and I was sixteen. No. Just no," Alan says.

"She's all grown up now, Alan." He rolls his eyes and sips his drink again. He coughs so hard, he spills the drink on the table. I flag the waitress down and order him a piña colada.

COLT'S APARTMENT IS DARK AND QUIET WHEN I WALK through the front door. I take off my shoes and walk down the hall to his room. Slowly, I twist the knob and find him lying on top of his covers. He's completely naked. His long arm is hanging over the bed, and he's snoring softly. I approach and run my fingers through his hair. His hand shoots up, grabs my wrist, pulling me on top of him.

"My woman," he growls into the side of my neck. His hands land on my ass and he grinds into me. "Kiss me, you fool." And I do. I kiss him as if we hadn't been together in years. "I didn't miss you."

"I didn't miss you either."

"I don't love you. Not even a little bit." He looks into my eyes before he leaves slow, opened mouthed wet kisses on my lips and chin. He tightens his hands around me.

"Let me take off my clothes so I can show you how much I don't love you."

THIRTY-FIVE

Colt

"You should be napping," Vickie says half an hour later. She's naked in my arms, and I can't stop running my fingers on the side of her ribcage.

"I'm sorry, Queen Vee."

She runs her fingers through my hair and looks into my eyes. "For what, champion?"

"For shutting you out after we lost those games. I still want you to come to all my games from now on."

"Don't even think of dragging me to that nonsense. I have a life. Do you know there are eighty-two games in the regular season, and half of them are away games?" I pull her on top of my naked body and kiss her.

"No, Queen, I had no idea. Tell me more about my job." I squeeze my arms around her.

"Fine. Here's another tip for you. Bend your elbows better before you throw the ball into that round thing. I don't know how you ever won a game before I came into your life." She sighs dramatically and blows out a breath.

"I never thought of that. I'll keep that in mind."

"Please do."

"I like having you here. I like having you in my life, Vee." She goes stiff in my arms. "I know we play around a lot, but I don't want to play right now. Look at me." She slowly raises her head. A piece of hair falls and covers her face. I move it away so I can look into her eyes. "I don't like having you here."

She relaxes and laughs. She opens her mouth, but I put a finger to her lips. I know what she's going to say. She's going to tell me she doesn't like being here either, but that's not how I want to interact tonight.

"I love having you here. I love how you eat with me after the games, and how you include Evan. I never thought I'd find that. At best, I figured I'd find someone who tolerates him because they want to be with me, but you do things for him and with him, and you do them because you want to, not because of me. Thank you for that, but that's not why I love you." She goes stiff, and her smile disappears. She licks her lips while she waits for me to finish. "I love you because you're everything I've ever wanted in a woman. You're beautiful. You're strong. You're tough, but you're also sweet and funny and loving. I never had that before you, and now that I have it, I don't know how I can ever be without it. So, Queen Vee, I love you. I had to drag you into this relationship, but I'm going to do everything I can to keep you. I'm going to be the man you didn't know you needed. That's right, Queen. I want you to need me." I give her a gentle kiss on her soft, full lips.

"You want a lot, champion. Do I look like the type of girl who needs a man, huh?" She smiles at me, and it's like my entire world shifts its axis. My heart pounds and I feel the blood coursing through my veins. Victoria Taylor gives me more of a high than basketball.

"You don't, which will make it that much sweeter."

"You're greedy," she teases.

"I've never denied that. Especially when it comes to you."

"But I love you anyway." I finally relax and smile at the admission. "Because you're strong but gentle. You're an amazing father. You're handsome." She kisses me. "You're silly. That one took me by surprise because I didn't know I liked that, but I guess I do. And you're so polite. And the way you are with your fans." She puts a hand to her heart. "Kindness is definitely a turn on. Who knew?"

"I'd better be because you wouldn't settle for anything less."

"You got that right, but it's my turn to confess, so hush." She puts a finger to my lips, and I kiss it. "You're busy but attentive. Annoying but persistent. Dramatic but sincere. Very, very dramatic."

"I don't think you understand the assignment, teach."

"And I don't need a relationship to be happy, complete or fulfilled—"

I clear my throat and narrow my eyes at her. She laughs.

"Hush. You'll like this part. You've filled a void I didn't know I had, and I'm grateful to you for that. I do need you. I need this. I need us. You, me, and Evan."

"And don't forget Mama," I throw in just to mess with her. She does the usual eye roll, but what she says next surprises me.

"And Mary Leigh. I like her a lot, and I love her son even more."

"That wasn't so hard, was it, baby?" I kiss her cheek.

"Are you kidding?" She swats my chest. "It was like pulling teeth without Novocain. Like a colonoscopy with no lube. Like—" I squeeze her on top of me, and she screams before bursting into laughter. I laugh too, loving seeing her so happy and carefree.

"Okay. Enough. Tell me you love me again," I order. "Tell me now because I need to go back to sleep."

One dramatic eye roll later, she says, "I love you." Her mouth lands on mine and we seal her declaration with a kiss, but she ends it much too soon.

"Get on your stomach. I'm going to massage you to sleep because you are going to win tonight's game." I obey, and she hops off the bed. She rummages through her purse and pulls out a little bottle. She sits on my naked butt and pours a cool liquid between my shoulder blades. She rubs and kneads my aching muscles, and I surrender to the feel of her small hands on my body.

I sigh in contentment, happier in this relationship than I've ever been in my life. And to think I didn't want to go out that night I met her. My eyes become heavy, and I let out a small groan just as she gets up. I feel the comb in my hair, but I fall asleep before she can untangle the messy curls.

When I wake up hours later, I'm alone in the bed, but her pillow smells just like her. I put my head in it and inhale. When I walk into the bathroom, my hair is perfectly braided for tonight's game. I admire my reflection, feeling good enough to conquer the world. I make it to the living room, and Mama is in the kitchen with Victoria and Evan. Mama's stirring something on the stove while Vickie instructs Evan on how to make a proper Caesar salad.

"When you're done with Vickie, Evan, Grandma's gonna show you how to make proper sweet tea. It's part of your heritage." Evan nods at my mother, but he's focused on grating the hunk of cheese Vickie handed to him. He has his tongue sticking out on the side of his mouth while he slowly grates. She stands next to him, ready to take the grater if anything goes wrong.

I clear my throat and enter the room. Mama grins at me, and I kiss her cheek first. When I get to Vickie, I whisper in her ear, "If this isn't the most traditional scene this southern boy has ever seen. His woman cooking with his mama and son. I do declare, I love it here."

She discreetly pinches me, and I pretend to be hurt. "Since I'm being held hostage until your stupid games are over, I have to make the best of it. I hate it here." She whispers the last part in my ear while she kisses and bites the shell.

"Daddy, look at my salad." Evan picks up the wooden bowl, and I take a piece of lettuce. He runs off to makes sweet tea with his grandmother.

We sit together, and I have a big bowl of chicken Caesar salad while everyone else eats the pot roast and mashed potatoes Mama made.

"This is delicious, Mary Leigh," Vickie says. She offers me potatoes from her fork.

"Thanks, honey. When you guys come to Alabama, I'll show you how to make all of Colt's favorites. Kelsey, God rest her soul, couldn't boil an egg." I look at my mother and shake my head at her. "Oh, gosh, I'm sorry." She looks at Evan, but he's busy eating and not paying attention to us.

"It's okay," Vickie says. "It doesn't bother me to hear about Kelsey." She squeezes my lap.

"My Queen Vee is more horrified at having to cook my favorite meals than you talking about my deceased wife, Mama."

"You got that right." She winks at me. "Don't get any ideas." She makes a fist, and I cover it with my hand.

"Oh, well I don't mean it like that. He's just useless in

the kitchen, unlike my Charlie, who can cook like you wouldn't believe. We'll all visit his new restaurant when you come. And you'll meet Rosalie. She's like another mother to my boys. We do a girls' only brunch once a month." She whispers the part about the brunch as if it's a secret. "You'll have to come with us. No boys allowed."

THIRTY-SIX

Vickie

The Mischiefs win game five but lose game six. He flies back to New York with the team. Ethan has his private plane available for me and Alan, saving us from another night in a hotel. I arrive at Colt's apartment about an hour after him and slide into his bed. I hold him while he rewatches the game. We don't eat together. He ate on the plane, but despite the fake cheerfulness, he's distant and angry. They lost by one point because his teammate missed two free throws in the fourth quarter. I fall asleep before the game ends, and when I awake in the middle of the night, he's sitting on the couch, massaging his calf. I slide out of bed and take the spot next to him.

"You okay?" I tap my lap, and he puts his leg on top of me, but I don't miss the pinched look or the groan coming from him. When I rub his muscle, he flinches at my touch. "Why are you up? It's four o'clock in the morning?" He closes his eyes and rests his head on the couch.

"We should have won. We could have. If my damn calf wasn't hurtin'." His accent seems more pronounced tonight. He seems more stressed, almost as if the weight of the world is on his shoulders. I remain silent, giving him the time and the space to speak if he needs to while I rub his sore calf. Once I'm done, I stand and offer him my hand. We climb into his bed, and I cuddle to his side, taking as much comfort from him as I'm giving.

"Don't worry. You've got this, champion. You've been here before, and you've succeeded."

His hand grabs my chin, and he leans in for a kiss. "I want to make love to you, and then I want you to braid my hair tomorrow."

"Okay, but don't get any ideas. I still don't love you," I tell him. He climbs on top of me and pins me to the bed.

"I have never loved anyone less." He cradles my face, and stares into my eyes. I feel my heart rate accelerate at the gentle touch of his hands. "And when we win tomorrow, I'm not going to take you home and show everyone my beautiful woman."

"Good, because I wouldn't go."

He lifts my short silk nightgown to my waist and aligns himself at my entrance. I'm already wet and wanting for him. He slowly sinks into me. When he's totally ensconced, he says, "Tell me."

And because I can feel the pressure oozing off his body, and I can hear the need and seriousness of his tone, I tell him what he needs to hear.

"I love you." He slowly starts to move, and I wrap my legs around him, keeping him close to me. Tonight, I want to feel all of him. I want to smell his skin and feel him against me.

"You always give me exactly what I need. Thank you for loving me."

THIRTY-SEVEN

Vickie

I sleep in this morning. Colt is up and out for practice before I stir. By the time I go to the kitchen, Mary Leigh is there watching daytime TV and filing her fingernails.

"Hey, honey. Are you hungry? I'll heat you up some lunch."

I shake my head at her. "You relax. You've been cooking for us for over a week now." She sits at the island with a bottle of nail polish. I take the bottle from her and apply the lavender polish.

"You're really sweet," she says. "I see why my son loves you." My head snaps up, and I stare into her familiar eyes. Our declarations of love have always been between us, so I'm shocked by Mary Leigh's statement. "Oh, it's plain as day. Colt's always been easy to read. He doesn't know that I know he wasn't all that happy in his marriage, but we won't talk about that. That's his story to tell you. But, my point is, I like you. You're good for Colt and Evan." She pats my cheek, and I can't help but smile at her. "He's young and after Kelsey died, I figured he wouldn't stay single forever, but I worried about Evan. I worried the new woman wouldn't put in the effort with him. That's why I tried to find someone for him myself, but that was a mistake. My point is, I didn't want Evan to feel like an outsider in his own home, especially with Colt's busy schedule, but my worries disappeared the first night we met."

"My stepmother's been in my life since I was eleven, and I can't imagine life without her. I understand Colt's a package deal. And I like you, too," I confess.

She laughs and says, "I have a feeling that was unexpected."

I look away, but then I face her. "A little bit. I didn't think you would approve of me for your son."

She purses her lips, and I wonder if I've offended her. "Oh, honey, I love my boy, and as long as you love him and Evan, you're okay with me. He has no problem putting me in my place if I butt in too much. But, yeah, I like you. You have a good heart. I can tell."

She admires the polish and gives me her other hand. I ponder her words and admit that maybe Colt is not the mama's boy I thought he was.

"Thank you, Mary Leigh."

"You, me, and Rosalie will need to go to lunch." She stops talking and looks around the apartment. When it's clear of anyone else, she leans in and whispers, "Don't tell Colt, but when we go to brunch, I have an entire mimosa."

My eyebrows shoot up at the admission. I burst into laughter when I see the serious look on her face. "An entire mimosa, huh? You're scandalous, Mary Leigh."

She blows on her fingernails. "I sure am. My daddy was a drunk and so was my husband's daddy. He started drinkin' heavy when we first got married. Things were bad for a while, and I left him. When he came beggin' me to take him back, I made that my one condition. He could never drink again. He agreed, and we made it a rule in the house. Colt follows it, but my Charlie, he struggled for years with substance abuse issues. He's finally on the straight and narrow now, but that's where that rule came from. I want you to know I'm not a prude. I like to have fun." She puts both hands in front of her and does something that resembles dancing.

"You wild, wild girl. I think you and I are going to get along great. Come on." I grab the bottle of nail polish and twist it closed. "I'll finish your nails upstairs at my sister's place. While Colt's at practice, and Evan's at camp, we're going to have some girl time." She hops off the stool and goes for her sandals. "And she has the best wine. Or I can make you a mimosa. They have the best champagne too. They have the best of everything."

I wrap my arm around hers. "Don't we need to call first?" she asks.

"Nah. She's home today. Me and my siblings, we have zero boundaries."

"That's another thing I like about you. You understand the importance of family." She lowers her voice and says, "And the drinkin' part is our little secret, right?" She looks around the apartment again. "My boys can never know."

"Victoria Renee Taylor never, ever breaks girl code, Mary Leigh. That's the one and only rule." I stop walking, turn and stare solemnly into her face. "Can you follow it? If not, we can't go any further."

She stares at me, her lips pursed. She holds up a hand and sticks her pinky in the air, and I wrap mine around it.

Things are tense inside Ethan's private suite at Madison Square Garden. The crowd is getting restless, and so are Vincent and Evan. They're both running around chasing each other, neither one of them paying attention toor caring about the game. I wish I could be as carefree. My heart's been in my throat since Colt left us in the apartment a few hours ago. He left like a man off to war, not to a game. I didn't miss his slight limp when he walked away. I'm not sure if it's from fatigue from all the games, or if it's because of something else. I've been too afraid to ask, not sure I want to know the answer.

We're in the fourth quarter, and Milwaukee's team is up by two points with only four minutes left to go. In basketball, that's almost a lifetime, but I'd feel better if our team was the one in the lead.

"You want another orange juice?" I whisper in Mary Leigh's ear. I wink at her. Orange juice is our code for mimosa.

"I've had more today than I've ever had before. I think I need a clear head, but some water would be nice, honey." She pats my lap. A few seconds later, a server comes with three waters.

"I've never seen you so nervous," Tara whispers. "He's got this."

I ignore her, stand up, and approach the railing. I grab my binoculars and watch when Colt gets the ball. The stadium cheers when he passes to Wakowski, who scores, tying the game. I reach over and hug Tara, then turn and hug Mary Leigh, but our celebration was a little too premature. There's still three minutes to go, and in less than thirty seconds, the other team scores two baskets, giving them a four-point lead. One of the Mischiefs have the ball, and defense is surrounding him. He shoots and scores, but before we can cheer, someone bumps into Colt, sending him crashing to the floor.

The three of us stand there, frozen. This has happened before. This is a physical game, and this isn't the first time Colt's fallen or been bumped by another player, but he's always gotten right back up. He doesn't this time. Mary Leigh puts a hand to her bosom, and I hold my breath. The boys come running to us, and I put my hand in Evan's curly hair. He reminds me of his father, and right now I need to be surrounded by everyone close to Colt.

Two teammates help sit him up, and the team doctor approaches. I pull out my iPad and watch the instant replay while they figure out what's happening on the court. In slow motion, I watch as he lands hard and awkwardly on his left knee. He closes his eyes, and I can see him screaming from pain. Mary Leigh gasps from over my shoulder. I shut the iPad off and toss it on one of the chairs. Colt's escorted off the court, and Coach Walsh calls a timeout. This is when I wish I could pick up the phone, call him, and find out what's going on. Or go to him and figure it out myself. We all stand there, stock still, and wait with bated breath. Alan keeps the boys busy while we all wait. My phone vibrates, and it's my mother. I ignore her.

The next ten minutes feel like ten hours, but eventually, Colt walks back on the court. We all breathe a sigh of relief. I tune out the announcers as they speculate what happened and focus on Colt instead. I've become attuned to his body, and even though he's running around on the court, I can tell it's not with the same lightness as before. He's hurting, but he's going to push through the pain and bring home the championship for his team and for his city. This is the last game. Whoever wins tonight, wins. He's playing at home, giving his team the advantage. Someone hits him, and a foul is called. He gets two free throws, and he makes them both, tying the game with two minutes to go. A few seconds later, the Mischiefs score two baskets back-to-back, giving them a four point lead. Everyone in Ethan's private suite cheers. Alan picks up Evan and spins him around. I hug Mary Leigh and she squeezes me tight. A minute later, the other team scores a three pointer, shrinking the Mischief's lead to one point. A foul is called on the Mischiefs and the opposing team gets two free throws, which they make, giving them a one-point lead, and the stadium has gone deathly quiet.

The game resumes, and the clock starts to run down. Jarvis, a shooting guard on the team, has the ball, but he's unable to shoot. With only a few seconds left, he throws the ball to Colt, who attempts a three-point shot from down the court. The buzzer goes off immediately after he shoots the ball in the air, aiming for the basket. My life turns to slow motion, and I feel myself stand up and grab Mary Leigh's hand, certain that he's going to score and win the game for his team at the last possible second. It's like I'm floating outside my body as my eyes follow the ball. The next second seems like an hour, and I wish I knew then how wrong I was, and how one basketball game, a sport I never cared about before, was going to change my life.

The ball hits the rim, but never makes it inside. Colt stands in the middle of the court with his hands on his hips and his head down in defeat when he realizes The Mischiefs have lost the game by one point.

THIRTY-EIGHT

Colt

I don't think I've said a word since I left the stadium. I was on autopilot when I congratulated the other team and talked to the press. I made eye contact with no one. When Coach Walsh taps my shoulder, I shrug away from him.

"We're a team, Chastain. We lost as a team. Not one single player lost the game for us."

I nod, but I don't respond. Coach Aidan Walsh, the black sheep of his filthy rich family. The black sheep because he didn't want to go into the family business and chose to play basketball instead. When his career in the NBA ended after four short years, they expected him to take this rightful position, but he wasn't interested and took a job as an assistant coach instead, working his way into the head coach position for The Mischiefs. I read most of that online. Some of it was from Wakowski, who gossips more than an old church lady. But one time, I heard Coach on the phone with his sister, and he was refusing to attend a family function. When he hung up the phone, it looked like he had the weight of the world on his shoulders, and I was able to relate to that. For that split second before he wiped the defeated look off his face and turned back into the professional I've known for nine years.

The ride home is quiet. Dante looks at me through the mirror, but he doesn't utter a word. I don't make eye contact while I walk through the lobby and to the elevator. For the first time ever, I dread seeing the people inside my apartment.

I pause and rest my head on the door, unable to turn the knob and go inside. All I want to do is be alone right now in my failure. The idea of dealing with Mama and her fake enthusiasm and Vickie's words of encouragement are more than I can bear tonight. I know Evan's already asleep, and all I want is to slide into bed and watch the game, but I won't be able to do that right away. The pain in my knee continues to throb and shoot down my right leg. After a final deep breath, I turn the knob and walk inside. All the lights are on, and Vickie and Mama both fly into my arms. The best-case scenario happened when the two most important women in my life met. They genuinely like each other. I wrap my arms around them both for a split second before I step away.

"Come on. I've set the table so we can all eat together tonight." Vickie wraps her arm around my waist, but I hobble away, refusing to acknowledge the crestfallen look on her face. I'm sure I imagined it. She's not the type of girl who would be hurt by my actions.

"Not tonight. I'm going to bed." I leave them both standing in the middle of the hallway. I can feel their eyes boring into the back of my head, but I limp into my bedroom. Knowing Vickie will be right behind me, I limp to the bathroom and lock the door. I don't need a shower. I took one after the game, but right now I turn on the water to give myself more time alone. I've never regretted having Vickie here. I worked really hard to get us to where we are, but tonight, I only want to be by myself. My wants aren't granted. She's waiting for me on the bed, eagerly patting my side the minute I step out.

"Oh my God." She runs over and helps me limp to the bed. "Your knee is swollen. Maybe we should go to the emergency room." Once I'm seated, she runs out of the room and returns a few minutes later with an ice pack.

I hiss when the cold hits my skin, but I lean against the headboard and hold it in place.

"I thought I'd give you a massage and lull you to sleep. You played a great game, champion. You've had a great season." She reaches for my hair, and I flinch and pull back. I want to kick myself for hurting her, but all I want is space right now.

"I want to rewatch the game." I slowly position myself on the bed and grab the remote.

She reaches over me and tries to take it away, but I hold it straight up in the air. This is when I'd tease her about being short, but I don't have it in me tonight.

"Why don't you give it a few days before you watch it? I'll ice your knee and massage your back until you fall asleep. We can dissect the game another time." She smiles, but it doesn't reach her eyes.

"We? Basketball is my game. This is what I do after every game, whether we win or lose." I can feel her looking into my face, but I can't bring myself to look at her. This should be a night of celebration, but I not only failed the team, I also failed her.

"Okay. Let's watch." She sighs in resignation, turns off the light, and cuddles to my side. Normally, I'd put my arm around her and hold her close. Some nights, we'd share popcorn while she gives me nonsensical advice. Tonight won't be a night like that. She must sense it. She stays quiet until she falls asleep sometime in the third quarter.

Once her breathing has leveled, I move her away and rest her on the pillow. I pause the game and hop on my good leg to the bathroom. The ice hasn't helped my knee and the pain has doubled. Refusing to take any pain pills, I go back to bed and finish the game.

Vickie's not next to me when I wake up late the next morning. Evan's there, watching cartoons so loud that it wakes me up. The first thing I feel is the pounding in my knee, and I sigh in defeat. I grab my phone and text the team doctor, asking him to come to my place immediately.

"Hey, bud," I say to my son.

"Hi, Daddy." He's as happy as he's always been. He jumps on my stomach and straddles me. "Vickie says she found us a knitting class but it doesn't start until the fall, but she says we can watch videos on YouTube all summer and get a head start."

"I didn't know you were so serious about knitting." I ruffle his hair. I try to imagine Vickie knitting a hat or scarf but can't picture it. She's the type of girl who shops for those things, not make them herself, but it will be fun to watch.

"She says she can teach me whatever I want to learn, and if she doesn't know how, we can learn together." I can sense the enthusiasm in his voice. He's never had a woman, other than his grandmas, take an interest in him like this.

"You like Vickie, huh?"

"Yeah. She's nice and she never gets sick of me." The

guilt comes back from that one failed relationship. That was a defining moment in his life, and I'm the one who allowed this woman to hurt him. "They sent me here to get you. She made breakfast."

Fifteen minutes later, Evan holds my hand while I limp to the kitchen. I see the worry in Vickie's eyes when she sees me, and she rushes over and helps me to a chair. She returns seconds later with an icepack. While I ice my knee, she wraps her arms around me from behind and kisses my cheek several times.

"I so don't love you," she whispers in my ear.

"You better not. I don't love you at all. Not even a little bit," I say back. I turn my head and kiss her lips.

"That's so gross," Evan says.

"Where's Mama?"

Vickie does a dramatic eye roll. "Mama's boy."

"You knew that in the beginning, and you still let yourself fall in love with me."

She bites my cheek and I pretend to groan in pain.

"She's taking a shower."

"Evan said something about you making me breakfast. A woman cooking for her man. I can't think of anything more traditional. Were you by any chance barefoot while you were cooking?"

She swats me in the back of the head. "Bite your tongue." She leaves and returns minutes later with a delicious omelet.

I finish breakfast right as the doctor arrives, and from the pinched look on his face while he examines my knee, I know the news is not good. He presses on it. I howl and almost climb the wall in pain. When he tries to extend it, I almost curse.

"You'll need to come with me for an MRI. I'm pretty

sure you have a torn meniscus, but I want to be certain." Vickie covers her mouth with a hand at the news, and my stomach sinks to the ground. The food I just ate sits in my stomach like a bag of stones. Mama wrings her hands, but she knows what that can mean. She's been an involved mom of two athletes for close to twenty years now. "Don't worry. There are varying degrees, and with treatment and PT, you will most likely be okay."

Most likely. Those two words sit with me all the way to the hospital. I wouldn't let Mama and Vickie come, telling them that I need them to stay with Evan. Vickie argued with me, telling me there was no way in hell she was going to leave me to deal with this alone, but I was adamant. There are some things that a man must do alone, and this is one of them.

I'm a zombie with the doctor. In fact, I don't say much, I let the team doctor do most of the talking. Coach arrives, and he's as stoic as ever. He looks like an untamed lion with that long mane of hair, but I keep that to myself. He looks like I feel, like he hasn't slept all night.

"Where's the pretty woman who braids your hair?" Coach whispers to me once we have a moment alone. "She looks like the type who'd be here to hold your hand and fuss over you." That's the first time in almost a decade of knowing each other that he's ever asked me a personal question. I didn't even think he noticed. He often rolls his eyes at the younger players' antics, but he's never talked to me about anything that's not related to the job.

"I wanted to do this alone," is all I say.

"We already have Wakowski. We don't need two fools on our team. You can't decide you want to do it alone now when you've already made her a part of this." He looks like he wants to say more, maybe give me a cautionary tale, but the doctors return, and I get the bad news confirmed.

"I WAS THINKING THAT I CAN GO WITH YOU TOMORROW. I'll need to run home and pack, but as long as I have my laptop, I'll be okay. I can maybe spend time in Atlanta here and there. In fact, I can probably make my heroine from Birmingham and kill two birds with one stone." I've never seen her like this. She's in a nervous frenzy. "That way, I can help you. Drive you back and forth and—"

"Can you even drive?" I ask her.

"What kind of question is that? Of course, I can drive." She runs to the closet and pulls out a bag, stuffing her belongings into them without folding.

"I have a driver in Alabama, or Mama can drive me."

"Are you saying you don't want me to come?" she teases, but I can smell the apprehension on her. The answer to her question is no. No, I don't want her to come. No, I don't want her there if this is a career ending injury. In fact, I changed the date of our trip to ensure she can't come on such short notice. That means she had to cancel the dinner party her stepmother was planning for Mama.

The doctor said the dreaded word. Surgery. It's only a possibility, but if it turns into reality, I don't know how I'll be able to handle it. Even if I heal and return, I might not be the same, and this might be the beginning of the end of my career, and I'm not ready for that. I don't want her around me if I receive that news. The playful Colt she fell in love with might go away for a while. I'll need some time to come to terms with my career ending before she can be around me again. I was hoping for at least five more years.

"I won't be able to give you the time and attention you need while I deal with this."

"I'm not a pet. I don't need time and attention. I want to be there for you."

"Even if I don't need surgery, I'll have PT and other treatments. And I still have to do that commercial."

"I always knew about the commercial. I have my book to keep me busy, but you need me more right now." She smiles, the first genuine smile since the doctor gave me the bad news.

"I'm not going to have you rewrite important things in your book to accommodate me." I limp to her and grasp her hands. "I'm going to meet with my doctors—"

"And why are you going to doctors in Alabama when you can have a team here in New York?"

"Because I'm not from New York, I'm from Alabama. This isn't the center of the universe, Victoria!" She stops, and I immediately regret my harsh tone. "I'm sorry. I already have specialists at UAB ready for me. I'll feel more comfortable there." I want to get away from New York and the disappointed fans.

"Of course, you're right. It's your treatment, you should get to have it anywhere you choose."

The fact that she doesn't argue with me or try to put me in my place for snapping at her makes me angrier than I was before. She's handling me. She's not being herself because she feels sorry for me. Whether it's because we lost the game or because I'm hurt, I'm not sure, but neither one sits well with me.

"I'm going to go sit in the sauna," I say, turning around before she can sense my shift of mood. I leave the room and walk down the hall to my home gym before she can say another word or offer to come with me. Just as I lift my shirt over my head, the door opens and Mama walks in. From the set of her chin and the tight pursing of her lips I can tell she's not too happy with me.

"Colton." She steps in and slams the door behind her. "I know it hasn't been an easy thirty-six hours, but Son, you have to let that young woman in. Whether you want or need the help she's offering you, take it. You put a smile on your face, say please and thank you, and let her be there for you."

"Mama, enough." I toss my shirt to a far corner and wait for her to leave so I can remove my shorts.

"She's not the type of woman—"

"Mama, she's my woman. I know what type she is and what type she ain't!" I don't remember the last time I raised my voice at my mother, but I need some time alone, and she's not taking the hint.

"Boy, don't you even think of gettin' loud with me." She approaches and puts her finger in my face.

"I'm sorry for yellin', but I need some freakin' space," I hiss. I turn, give her my back and walk to the sauna.

"Son, you lost a game. It was an important one, but you lost. It is what it is. You lose some, you win some, but you're actin' like a child and pushin' everyone away."

I freeze at her words and her tone. I count to ten, rub my face with my hands, and count to ten again before facing her.

"It hasn't been two days yet. Am I not allowed to be disappointed? And what about my knee? At worst, this could end my career or be the beginning of the end. Am I allowed to be upset, or do I always have to put on a performance for everyone? Alabama's golden boy. Manhattan's star athlete. Mary Leigh's perfect son, the one who isn't a drunk. Evan's only parent, who is both mama and daddy. Vickie's perfect, southern gentleman? Can I be me for once? And the me right now is angry." I open the sauna and slam the door behind me. I can imagine the look on her face, but I don't want to see it.

THIRTY-NINE

Vickie

"I don't understand." I put the phone on the bed so I can fold clothes into a suitcase. "I'm almost done packing."

The phone goes quiet. I stuff three more shirts on top of the mountain of clothes I've already piled in and wonder how the hell I'm going to close this thing. I tamp down my alarm. This is Colt. This is the man who chased me and dragged me into a relationship kicking and screaming. He just suffered a major loss, and not only that, he's also worried about his knee. The media has not been kind. We haven't talked about it, but he's being blamed for the loss since he missed the last shot. There's also talk about trading him, which is just speculation. He just signed a new contract, and he hasn't uttered a word to me about trade, but I wonder what would happen to us if he had to transfer to a team in the Midwest or west coast. I push those thoughts away. First things first. We deal with the knee, and hopefully, the sting of losing will ebb in time.

I pick up the phone and stare into his face. His hair is just a curly mess, and he needs a haircut. He hasn't shaved in days and has the early beginnings of a beard. He looks a little gaunt, and his brown eyes have lost their shine, but he's still handsome.

"I don't love you," I tell him, hoping to pull him out of the pit he's in. He smiles, but his eyes don't light up like I'm used to.

"Good, because I don't love you either."

"So, I'll be ready by the time my driver comes back from eating lunch." I put the phone back down and resume my packing.

"Queen Vee." My hands freeze above the mountain of clothes on my bed. Whenever he calls me Queen Vee, there's always a playful lilt to his voice, but that's not there today. "You don't need to rush to Alabama. Meet us there in a few days. I'll have Kendall arrange a private plane for you. Give me some time to meet with the doctors and figure out what's goin' on. Please."

There's a doubt in the back of my mind. I might not have wanted a relationship, but I know how they work. I've seen it with my dad and stepmom. And even before my mother left, I saw it with her and Dad too. Relationships don't work well when one person is away.

"You don't want me there?" The air goes out of me, and I sit on the bed.

"Of course, I do."

"Then why are you telling me to wait a few days when I'm ready now?"

Relax, Victoria. You are not this man's wife.

"I just want to meet with the doctors first. When you get here, I want to give you all the attention you need."

Something tells me that's not the actual truth, but then I put myself in his shoes. He lost a championship and got hurt all in the same night. It's not wrong for him to need space to clear his head but knowing that doesn't make it hurt any less.

"I don't need attention. I'm not a child, but I understand if that's how you feel you need to deal with this."

This is what I've been trying to avoid. This feeling right here. The feeling of rejection and abandonment. One time was enough, and I've done everything in my life to not go through that again. I steel my spine, but I avoid his gaze for fear he'll be able to read my thoughts and find my weakness.

"Thank you, Queen. You are always my queen, my liege. I'll miss you."

He wouldn't have to miss me if we go together. I hate to admit this to myself, but I wanted to go with him to his appointments and ask my own questions. That's what the evil one does with Dad.

"Me too," I tell him. "Let me talk to Evan and Mary Leigh. I want to say goodbye."

∽

"It's been five days," I tell Tara the instant I sit down at the restaurant we're meeting for lunch. "He's been so distant, and it's like pulling teeth to get him to tell me anything. His doctors recommend minimally invasive surgery, followed by intense physical therapy. And he didn't tell me any of that. His mother did." I break off a piece of bread and spread butter on top.

"But you guys are still talking every day?" she asks.

"Yeah, but the calls are getting shorter and shorter."

"It's only been a week since they lost. Give him time and space." I nod at her, but the feeling of doom that I've had since he left for Alabama without me won't go away. We talked about celebrating the Fourth of July together, but now that it's only two weeks away, I don't know. I don't see it being very celebratory if things continue like this.

We're supposed to spend July and August traveling back and forth from Atlanta to Alabama, maybe take a little vacation to Mexico at an exclusive, family friendly resort I found, but I have a sick feeling that's not going to happen.

The fact that I've put myself in this vulnerable position starts to eat at me, but I remind myself that I love this man, and I'll give him the space he needs to work through his issues.

But aren't you supposed to work on it together? He's only shut you out. He begged you to be with him, and now he's gone and you're wringing your hands like a worried mother hen.

I change the subject from me and Colt to Tara and Ethan, who are planning a trip to Hong Kong and Bangkok in three weeks. It seems like all the Taylors except me will be out of the country for a while. Dad and the evil one are going to London for their anniversary, and Alan will be taking a trip to Istanbul with a few of his friends. We'll all celebrate Labor Day together as a family at our vacation home in The Outer Banks in North Carolina, and I was looking forward to having Colt, Evan, and Mary Leigh join us.

Tara heads back to work, and I return to my empty apartment. We've spent more time at Colt's place, but I keep seeing him everywhere. Those first few times we were together were here, and it's like his ghost is lurking around my apartment. The only good thing that's come from the separation is the attention I've given to my book. I've gotten a complete first draft. I can add the little details during the many rounds of edits that are still to come.

Five days turn into seven, which turn into ten. Our calls

have dwindled to about once per day, and each time, I'm given a different reason as to why I don't need to come yet. With his surgery scheduled in five days, he wants me to wait until it's done.

I close my laptop with a heavy sigh when my phone starts to vibrate, and assuming it's Colt, I pick it up without looking.

"Champion," I say. There's a pause, and I pull the phone away from my ear. It's not Colt. Colt has an Alabama phone number, and this is a New York area code.

"I go by Gerald. Doctor Prescott is good too. I'll let you call me doc since you're so cute." When I stay quiet, he says, "I'm calling to see if you want to have lunch with me tomorrow."

I close my eyes and rub the bridge of my nose, not having the bandwidth to deal with this bullshit right now. "Jerry, I'm in a relationship," is all I say.

"Oh, right. Well, why are you in New York when Chastain is living it up in Alabama." I resist the urge to roll my eyes. Why is he calling me about this?

"I'd hardly say he was living it up." He's getting treatment and taking care of a five-year-old, one I miss desperately, but I don't tell Jerry any of that

"Oh, really? I see you still have an aversion to social media. How can you be so smart and so clueless all at the same time, Vick? Call me when you're ready to talk. I know you. Chastain is not the type of man you will be with long term. I still love you, and I'll be here when you're ready." He ends the call, and I toss the phone down, wondering what the hell he's talking about.

After seeing a few articles after the finals, I haven't seen anything else, but I don't follow anything that has to do with sports. With a surge of curiosity, I grab the phone. It will only take a few seconds to check and see what Gerald is talking about, but the phone vibrates, and it's Colt.

It's not a FaceTime. He hasn't done much of those when he calls. I still do when I call him.

"Champion," I say, forcing a smile when I say his nickname.

"Hey." There's no joy or playfulness in his voice. "The surgery is scheduled for Friday. It's typically outpatient, but they're keeping me overnight. Physical therapy will start a week or so later. I was thinkin', there's no need for you to come out here since I'll be focused on gettin' better. Evan's at baseball camp, so he's gone all day, and Mama's got her charities and church. Maybe when I start to feel a little better, I'll come see you in Atlanta."

Maybe. All I hear is 'I don't want you here.'

"So, you don't want me to come at all? Is that what you're saying?" I ask.

"It's not that I don't want you here. It just doesn't make sense for you to come now."

"I thought the point was to be there for you, Colt. I don't need you to hold my hand and dote on me. I'm coming there for *you*. That's the fucking point," I yell, so frustrated by him that I don't know what else to do.

"Don't yell at me, Victoria. I'm already going through enough of my own shit." I arch an eyebrow. This is the first time I've ever heard him cuss. He clears his throat and says, "stuff. I'm going through my own stuff."

"I want to go through it with you," I tell him. "Let me help you. Why are you pushing me away?"

"Why are you making this about you? It's about me. It's my knee! It's my career, and I need to deal with it my way. I don't need you here feelin' sorry for me and givin' me those pitiful looks." I can feel the color on my cheeks, and for a second I second guess myself and wonder if I've made this entire thing about me. Then I realize, I haven't. Wanting to be there for someone you care about is not the same as making it about you.

"I've done no such thing," I snap. "All I want to do is be there for *you*."

"Well, I don't need that right now! I want to do this alone!" His accent gets thicker with each angry word. I pull the phone away from my ear and put it down. My eyes fill with tears, but I refuse to let them fall. Tears won't fix anything. I learned that when I was nine.

"This is the last fucking time you will yell at me. And if you don't want me there, fine. I've never needed to beg anyone to spend time with me, and I'm not going to force myself on you." I don't yell. I manage to calm my racing heart and speak clearly.

"Is that a threat, Victoria?"

"A threat? What the fuck are you talking about?" I raise my voice again. It's almost like he's goading me into losing my temper.

"And that's another thing. You have a foul mouth."

"Yup. I have a foul fucking mouth. What the fuck are you going to do about it?" I taunt.

"It's embarrassin'," he says. The words come out like a frustrated sigh.

"Well, don't worry about me embarrassing you, Colt. I'll keep my uncultured New York attitude as far away as possible." Stunned by the turn of events, I end the call. He calls right back, but I don't answer. I turn off the phone, leave it on the table and walk into my lonely bedroom. It's the middle of the day in the middle of the week. I climb into bed and close my eyes.

I wake up hours later, groggy and confused. The memories of the events that took place come back and I sigh and roll to my side. Minutes later, because my bladder demands it, I get up and use the bathroom. When I retrieve my phone from the table and turn it on, I have six voicemails, all from Colt.

"Darlin', I'm sorry—" I delete each voicemail without listening to them. I fix myself an early dinner of salmon and a small salad, but Jerry's taunts from earlier come to mind. I pick up the phone and open Twitter. I put #coltchastain in the search and my heart goes cold.

Right there on the screen is Colt and another woman. I know who she is. It's Robin Chase, Kelsey Chastain's sister. She's tall like Kelsey, with long dark hair that reaches the middle of her back. The picture is of their profiles, and it looks like she's looking into his eyes. It's the way he's looking down at her that has my heart constricting. He's smiling, and his eyes are soft and full of the mischief that I thought was reserved only for me. His hair is still a disaster of curls, and he has a full beard now, but his eyes are still the same. He's giving my look to another woman. A woman who probably still wants to take her sister's place in his life.

I scroll downward, and there are more. They're wearing different clothes, so it's not the same day. He has something wrapped around his knee, and in one picture, she has her arm wrapped around his. I leave the app and slam my phone down so hard, I'm afraid I break it.

It rings, and it's Colt. I don't answer, and I delete his voicemail instead of listening to it.

FORTY

Colt

"When is Vickie getting here?" Evan asks. "She was supposed to be here by now. And I want her to come to see me play baseball, and I want her to fight Jack." I type out another text apologizing and put down my phone.

"Why would she fight Jack?" I ask, confused.

"She said she would fight any kid who picks on me, and Jack is a jerk." He makes a face, and I hold back my laughter. That sounds like Vickie, always protecting those she cares about. My phone rings and my glimmer of hope is dashed. It's Coach.

I pick up and we talk for less than a minute about the surgery, PT, and the pre-season training schedule. I assure him I'll be ready to go, and I hope that's true. The swelling has lessened, but it's still there. And it hurts to the touch, but I don't care about that right now.

The fight I had with Victoria is the most pressing thing on my mind. I call her again, but the phone goes to voicemail. The words of apology get stuck in my throat and I end the call. The least she deserves is a FaceTime apology.

My knee is only part of the reason I don't want her here right now. I'm also dealing with Isabel who's frantic about Mia. Her father's threatening to take her and move out of state.

Charlie is the other reason. He's been calling and managed to find my new house. It's in a very exclusive gated community, but it's not far from the house he shares with Mama. He tried to come here a few times, and I've had to have security ask him to leave. That didn't sit well with our mother, who has been given me the silent treatment for days now.

Vickie's family, despite her parents being divorced, is one of the most functional I've ever been around. The bond she has with her brother and sister can make anyone jealous, especially me, who had a good relationship with his only sibling until things soured. I've told her some of it, but I don't want her to witness this. At least not right now when I'm in pain and my career is filled with uncertainty.

I hobble to the kitchen table at the back of the house. It's a spacious two-story house with cathedral ceilings. The back is filled with natural light from the wall of windows that takes up both floors.

I could have Kendall do this for me, but I need to find a bouquet of flowers that say 'I'm sorry, I was a jerk.'

As I'm looking at different arrangements, I hear rushed footsteps coming down the back stairwell. Mama's been staying here, hovering over me, and silently judging me for not having Vickie here with us.

"Everything okay, Mama?" I ask without looking up. The silent treatment is her preferred method of choice, so when she answers, I get alarmed.

"No, everything's not okay." She wrings her hands, and

I notice she has her purse slung over her shoulder. "Rosalie called. She got a call from Bastian who was at The Watering Hole." I finally look up at her. Bastian owns the bar in our old town. He's a nosy old man who knows everything that goes on, and there's only one reason why Mama would get a call about what was happening at The Watering Hole. "He's fine." She puts a hand to her chest. "Bastian wouldn't serve him, and when he couldn't get in touch with me, he called Rosalie. Charlie needs me, Colt. He's hurtin', and I know how you feel, and I understand, but I'm his mother, and I'm not goin' to lose him to alcohol again. I knew I shouldn't have left him alone this long."

I stare at her while I let the words soak into my brain. For a split second, I want to remind her that she's my mother too, and that I need her right now, but I'm not that selfish. I feel a twinge of guilt for not taking his calls and for sending him away. We're not close anymore, but I don't want him to resort to drinking again. Maybe if I had taken his calls things wouldn't have gone this far. Then I remind myself that Charlie is a thirty-one-year-old man who has made his choices.

Mama starts to cry in the middle of the kitchen, and I have no choice but to walk to her and take her in my arms.

"You can't drive like this," I tell her. "Let me call Sampson." She sniffles into my chest, and I feel my heart constrict at the thought of my mother being in pain. She's a strong woman, but she's gone through so much in her fifty-three years on this earth.

"Rosalie is bringing him here." I freeze at her words before pulling away to look into her eyes. "Don't worry," she says, disappointed. She lowers her gaze as if she's too ashamed to look at me any longer. "I'm going to drive us home." She runs a hand through her disheveled hair. "I didn't know what else to do. They were already on their way over here when she finally got a hold of me." She leaves my arms and walks around, frantically looking for things.

The landline rings, and she grabs it before I can get to it. She tells whoever's on the other line to let them through and practically runs out the front door, still holding a shoe in her hand. I step outside in time to see Rosalie's Hyundai Sonata pull into my driveway. She was our neighbor when I was growing up, and she lost her husband only a few years after Mama. The loss brought them closer together. Unlike Mama who still looks youthful though, Rosalie looks tired and worn. Her long stringy dark hair is mixed with gray.

She waves at me, and the passenger door to her car opens. Charlie steps out, and I can tell right away that he's sober. Despite his bloodshot eyes, he hasn't had a drop to drink. If he had, there's no way Rosalie would have been able to handle him long enough to drive him. I haven't seen him since last December, and since then he looks like he's lost weight. He looks gaunt and older than his thirty-one years.

"Hey, Colty." He sounds like a little boy who's about to be reprimanded. Mama stares at me, and when I don't respond to him, her shoulders sag before she runs into his arms and bursts into tears.

"I'm sorry, Mama. I'm okay." He kisses her forehead. "Please forgive me." It's like I'm floating above myself as I watch the scene. I'm unsure of what I'm supposed to do here. The only thing I know is that I'd rather be anywhere else.

Victoria. I need my Queen Vee, but I'm pretty sure I've got some groveling to do after our phone call today. I pull out my phone to call her, but another car pulls in behind Rosalie's and Evan jumps out.

"Uncle Charlie!" He runs to my brother, and Charlie lets Mama go just in time for Evan to jump into his arms. "Did you and my dad make up? He let me go to baseball camp. I'm going to show you all my moves." He kisses Charlie's cheek and hugs him tight. A sob escapes Charlie, and he tightens his arms around Evan. "Come on. I'll show you my room. Daddy, can I FaceTime Vincent so Uncle Charlie can talk to him?" He jumps from Charlie's arms, runs to me, and snatches the phone from my hand. "Come on, Uncle Charlie." Evan waves him inside the house but doesn't wait for him to follow. Mama, Charlie, and Rosalie all stare at me. It's like the three of them have stopped breathing while they wait to see what I'm going to do.

I can see the tears filling Mama's eyes from here, and the last thing I want to do is cause her more pain. I hold the front door open and gesture for everyone to get in. "Give yourself a tour, Rosalie," I tell her.

Mama squeezes my hand on her way in, but before Charlie can step over the threshold, I put a hand to his chest. "I don't want you alone with Evan, and under no circumstances is he to get in a car with you. Ever." He stares into my eyes and nods. I drop my hand, and he goes inside.

"I'm going to make a big dinner for everyone," Mama announces. "Rosalie, I'll show you around and then you can help me in the kitchen."

Evan returns and he goes outside with Charlie. I watch through the sliding glass door as Evan holds my phone in Charlie's face. After a few minutes, Evan puts the phone down and pitches the baseball to his uncle. Charlie helps him with his posture and demonstrates throwing. The two of them laugh the entire time. I finally step outside, grab my phone, and take a seat by the pool to watch. My phone buzzes, and it's Robin. I ignore the call. I've had enough of her already when we met up for ice cream with the kids. She tried her best to touch me at every opportunity until I told her to stop. Even though nothing happened, I feel guilty, and all I want is the one woman I pushed away.

FORTY-ONE

Vickie

"Queen Vee—" I delete it before I can hear anymore.

"Baby—" Delete.

"Vee, I'm sorry. The surgery is tomorrow, and I need—" Delete.

"I was a fool. Please come to Al—" I toss the phone away and zip my suitcase. I hate myself for even checking his voicemails, but he's left those over the past two days.

I hate myself for the feelings stirring inside of me. They are beyond anger. Anger I can deal with. I've dealt with it before, but the hurt isn't something I'm prepared for, which is why I'm leaving for Atlanta a week early. I have an early evening flight and my ride to the airport is due to arrive in under an hour. I won't be calling Cynthia for any more rides. As far as I'm concerned, I'm done with her as my personal driver. He had the surgery this morning, and he should be in his private room or home by now.

The resentment resurfaces, and I stuff it down, refusing to give in to the pain. My mind flashes to the conversation I had with Tara last night, our last night together for at least a month.

~

"I'm Victoria Taylor," I say over a very strong margarita. "I don't do relationships. I'm the one who walks away from men, not the other way around. I don't catch feelings, and one pretty smile and one dimple later, I'm in a relationship with a celebrity athlete, single father. From Alabama of all places. Who the hell does that? Not me!"

Tara reaches over and pushes my hair off my forehead.

"You're human and you're in love. Nothing wrong with that."

"And then," I continue as if I didn't hear her. "And then," I repeat for dramatic effect, "he ghosts me. After I get attached to his son. After all the work I did to get the kid to warm up to me. Not to mention, practically living there with his kid and mother during those stupid playoffs or whatever the fuck they're called. I had to watch my mouth around Mama." I mimic his southern accent. "Fuck him."

"Yes, fuck him," Tara says. "But," she pours each of us fresh drinks.

"But what?"

"Hear me out." I roll my eyes at her and cross my arms. "Promise me you'll hear me out." I shrug and gesture for her to proceed. "He lost the last game, and he probably feels responsible because he's the one who missed the last shot. And he hurt his knee and needs surgery. Maybe he didn't want you to see him like that. Maybe he's angry and scared and didn't want to take it out on you. I'm not saying it's right or that it makes sense but put yourself in his shoes for a second. I don't think we can ever understand. We're not *athletes. We can never understand having that much on our shoulders."* She grabs my hands. *"Be patient."*

"I have no patience left. He was with another woman, Tara. He didn't want me there, but there are pictures on the internet with him and another woman. They are out with the kids having fun while I was here pining and worrying about him. I had rearranged my plans to include him and then he cuts me out. No one cuts me out. No one walks out on me. Not anymore." *The last two words leave my mouth before I can think them through. Mother's abandonment is not something we talk about.*

"That's his dead wife's sister. She probably brought Evan's sister to spend time with him. I'm positive it's nothing. He loves you, Vick." I shake my head, refusing to heed her words.

∽

My phone buzzes, and it's a text from Gerald. I pick it up to delete, but the picture he just sent to me gets my attention. It's Colt, and it looks like he's in front of a medical center. His mother is there, along with an older woman with long, stringy hair. But right there is Robin, holding on to one of his hands. Another picture comes through showing her hugging him. He has his arms wrapped around her, hugging her back. She presses herself against his chest, and she's smiling.

Those are my arms that are wrapped around another woman. She's putting her head on the chest I've gotten used to. I'm the one who should be there wrapped around him and offering solace before his surgery, but I'm not because he abandoned me. He got on a plane with his mother and son and left me behind. He took the people he wanted and left the one he didn't. I put the phone down and return to my packing. Once I'm done and have my bags by the front door, I pick up my phone and forward the pictures to Colt. I search social media and find the pictures I saw a few days ago and forward those to him as well.

Me: Go to hell.

FORTY-TWO

Colt

I haven't uttered a single word since leaving my private floor of the hospital. I've only been gone thirty-six hours, but it might as well have been thirty-six million years. It doesn't help that Charlie is still in my house when I return. He's in the kitchen stirring something in a large pot. If I had any appetite, it would smell good.

Once I sit on the couch, Mama brings the ottoman and I extend my leg on a bed of pillows. The pain in my knee is a welcome relief to everything else I'm feeling right now. Evan fusses over me, but I tell him to go change for his swimming lesson. All I want to do is be alone and wallow in my own self-pity. I look at the phone again. I'd let out a string of expletives if Mama wasn't nearby. I can feel her eyes on me now. She's angry with me too but too worried to express it. At least for the moment.

"Do you need any pain pills?" She puts a pillow behind my back and pushes my hair off my forehead like she did when I was a kid. "You look flushed."

I shake my head at her and press Queen Vee on my phone. Just like before, it goes right to voicemail.

"Queen, can you please call me so we can talk? It's not what you think. I can explain those pictures. I know it looks bad, and I know you wanted to be there for me. I was stupid, Vee. I'm sorry. Can you –" The phone clicks and I hear a busy signal. I toss the phone and lean against the pillow behind me.

Mama looms over me with her lips pursed in disapproval.

"Charlie, what smells so good? Maybe you can bring some for your brother." She walks away. If she wasn't angry with me, she'd be sitting next to me, holding my hand, and saying everything in her power to make me feel better.

A few minutes later, Charlie approaches with a tray and a bowl with steam coming from the top. He puts it on my lap, and the smell hits, making my stomach growl. It looks like a type of bisque, and as hungry as I am, all I want to do is toss it against the wall. But I don't do that. Evan has a clear view of me from the pool, but since I can't take my anger out on the bowl, I take it out on Charlie.

"What are you still doing in my house, Charlie? You can have the run of the other house I bought our mother. I don't need you here. And I don't want this. Get it away." I try to lift the tray and it slips from my hand, crashing onto the tile floor. The bowl shatters and the liquid glides along the tile.

A sense of shame and embarrassment so strong takes me, I start to shake. I remember the words Vickie said to me the night she told me she loved me. She said my kindness was one of the things she loves about me, and right now, I'm not worthy of her love. I hang my head in disgust.

"Colton Chastain, I did not raise you to be unkind," Mama says from across the room. "I know you have—"

"It's okay, Mama," Charlie says. He bends down and picks up the broken porcelain. "I'll go if you don't want me here. I understand why you don't, but it's just that I don't do so well alone. I start thinkin' and—" He stands and shakes his head. "I'll clean this up and go."

I rub a hand over my face to hide from Mama's probing eyes. I'm sure she's as ashamed of me as I am of myself. Whatever issues we have, I don't want Charlie to spiral out of control. He can't be alone, or he'll fall into temptation.

"Charlie, wait. I didn't mean to snap at you. You can stay, but that doesn't mean I've forgotten anythang. And I meant what I said. I don't want you alone with Evan." He nods, and I can see the relief in his eyes. I stand on my good leg and grab my crutches.

"Mama, when the nurse gets here, can you please let me know. When Evan's done with his lesson, send him to my room so I can give him a bath." She runs over and offers me her body as support.

"I'll take care of Evan. You go rest. I'll keep an eye on him, so don't worry." I know Charlie would never willingly hurt Evan. I know this, but he's tried to hurt me so many times, I can't fully trust him.

Once I'm in bed, Mama puts pillows under my leg to keep it elevated. She kisses my temple and leaves.

I try to call Victoria three more times, but each time, I'm met with nothing but the sound of her voicemail. I miss her. I'd give anything to have her next to me right now, running her fingernails over my scalp. I haven't been able to cut my hair because I love when she braids it. I won't cut it until she agrees to let me do it.

I try her phone again, and it goes right to voice mail.

"Motherfocker!" I yell just as my door opens. It's Charlie, carrying another tray of food. I look away, unsure of what to say. He's like a puppy who keeps coming back after getting kicked.

"Mama insists you eat." He puts the tray across my lap, and it does smell incredible.

"Thanks," I manage to grumble. I expect him to leave, but he sits on the side of the bed. I pick up the spoon and taste it. It's chicken tortilla soup, and it tastes just like what Mama would make when either one of us were sick. I eat some more, hoping he'll leave me in peace.

"I know I've done some pretty awful stuff to you, Colty. And it was out of jealousy and spite." The spoon stops halfway to my mouth, and all I can think about is how much I don't need this right now. "I was an awful brother to you, and I'm sorry, but I would never hurt Evan. I didn't put him in the car." I look up, ready to punch him in the teeth. "I didn't. He asked for donuts, and I told him I would get him some, and I went to my room to change. When I came back, he was gone, so I thought he went back to bed, but he had snuck in my car. He popped out when I was down the street and yelled surprise. That's when I swerved and got pulled over."

"Are you kidding me?"

"No. I would never lie on him. I was still drunk, but not drunk enough to do that. You got so upset, and you've refused to speak with me, but I just want you to know. Now, the other stuff, that's all on me. I know I did those things to you, but I was so drunk, I don't remember doing them. I know that's no excuse, but I would never hurt you if I was sober. I was a jealous piece of crap, and I hope one day you'll forgive me." I put the spoon down, unsure of what to make of the revelation. I believe him. Part of my anger was because I felt betrayed. Betrayed because he put Evan in danger. For believing that he would never hurt my son despite our issues. I thought I had that wrong.

"Does Mama know?"

"No. If I told her, she would have told you, and I wanted it to come from me." I nod. "I didn't want it to be another situation where she would try to fix things between us. All that did was make things worse."

"I believe you about Evan, but that doesn't erase the other things you've done, Charlie." He hangs his head in shame. "It doesn't. I'm not here to make excuses, but I hope you can forgive me one day, Colty. I want you to know I appreciate everything you've done for me, even though I don't deserve any of it. I promise that I'll never drink again. That's behind me."

I finish the soup, and Charlie sits in the room the entire time, watching me. I remember what Queen Vee said to me weeks ago. She said she'd forgive because some bad behavior wouldn't erase all the good times. I've had a lot of good times with my older brother. I've looked up to him. We were friends until the future he thought he had was taken from him and handed to me.

"I don't know what to say, Charlie. I do know I'm tired of being angry at you." That's all I can offer him right now.

He nods, and I think I see a smile spread across his face. "I'll take whatever you can give me."

My phone vibrates, and I grab it, only to be disappointed. It's Robin. The source of my problems. I hit ignore and throw the phone down.

Charlie looks at the phone and then back at me.

"Robin." That's the only explanation I give him.

He shakes his head and says, "She's a piece of work, that one. She could barely keep her eyes off you at her own sister's funeral. But why isn't your pretty lady friend here? She's all Evan and Mama talk about. Is it because I'm here?"

I wish I drank because I could use a strong one right now. "She's not here because I'm an idiot and I mucked it up. She's not here because of me. It has nothing to do with you."

This is the longest conversation we've had in years, so he's going to prolong it as long as possible.

"Time to turn on the Chastain charm. If that doesn't work, send flowers. Or jewelry or maybe even a fur coat. Women love fur coats. Chocolates too."

"A fur coat, Charlie? Really? That's the stupidest thing I've ever heard." I shake my head at his stupidity. "That would only piss her off. I need to go to her, but this darn knee." I try to get up, but he puts a hand on my shoulder, keeping me in place.

"Maybe I can help," he offers.

"Can you build a time machine so I can go back in time and not be so stupid?" I reach for one of my crutches and toss it to the floor. It crashes, and I put my head in both hands. "I really screwed up. I hurt her. She's going to put up a wall higher and bigger than the first one I had to climb. And that's the best case scenario."

He makes a face, and I'd laugh if my situation wasn't so dire. The door to my bedroom crashes open, and Mama walks in.

"What is the meaning of this?" She shoves the phone in my face. It's a text exchange between her and Vickie, but it's the last thing Vickie texted that made my stomach drop to my feet. "She broke up with you. I told you pushing her away wasn't a good idea, but you never listen. You always think you know everythang." She walks out, slamming the door behind her.

When I try to get up, Charlie puts the tray down and holds me for support.

"You need to rest so you can heal. You have to be ready for physical therapy."

TAKEOFF

"I need to go to Vickie."

"Are you crazy? You can't go travelin' right now. Look, I'll go find her and bring her here, but you can't go." I let out a humorless laugh and shake my head.

"She'd kill you in two point five seconds."

FORTY-THREE

I shut down my computer for the final time today. It was another day where I got nothing done. Colt keeps calling, and I keep ignoring his calls, but I can't keep doing that. I need to tell him that we're over, especially since I received an email telling me I've been accepted to teach in Mexico for a year. Someone dropped out, and the position is open to me. They'll expedite my visa and give me a place to stay.

I've already accepted. This was something I've always wanted to do, and now is the perfect opportunity. Maybe this breakup between me and Colt happened for a reason. I don't know if I would have given this up.

He never would have asked you to. He would have made it work. He would have puffed his chest out in pride at your accomplishment.

That might be true, but I'm not going to let a man push me away whenever things aren't going perfectly in life. I might not have wanted to be in a relationship, but I know how a functional one works. I've seen it every day for years between my father and stepmother.

I've already been blindsided once, and I was a child who had zero control over anything. That's not the case now. So, when the phone rings and Colt's name flashes across the screen, I accept his FaceTime request.

The first thing I notice is how haggard he looks. His hair is a mess. The dark curls are full and now reach his ears. He hasn't shaved either. He smiles when he sees me. It's a smile full of happiness and relief, but I don't find it in me to smile back.

"Hey, beautiful." His eyes light up while he looks at me, and as much as I want to, I can't look away. "God, I've missed you so much, Queen Vee. I was an idiot. I'm sorry."

I almost want to laugh. Almost. The abandoner always thinks that one apology will erase all the damage they've caused. Gerald, even though I didn't love him, thought he could waltz back into my life with nothing but an "I'm sorry". Mother's never once bothered to so much as offer an explanation, never mind an apology.

Now, there's Colt. A man who chased after me, convinced me to be with him, promised me things I didn't even know I wanted, only to push me away when things got hard. Now, he's here, giving me a lame apology as if I'm supposed to be grateful.

"I'm glad you called, Colt," I begin. He sobers up, and the smile leaves his face.

"Well, I've been callin' and callin'. Listen, baby—"

"No, you listen. I got accepted to teach in Mexico. Someone pulled out at the last minute, and they've offered me his spot. I've accepted."

The room goes deathly quiet. His eyes nearly bug out of his head, and the tension in the kitchen becomes palpable.

"Without talkin' to me first, Victoria? You accept a job that takes you out of the country for an entire year."

I scoff at his audacity. "Yeah, I did. We're not married. I can do whatever the hell I want, just like you."

I think I see a little color in his cheeks. I see something flash through his eyes like I've never seen before. He's angry.

"For your sake, Colt, that flash of anger I just saw better not be directed at me."

"Who the hell else, Victoria? Who the hell else am I going to be angry at?"

"Be careful. You don't want Mama to come wash your mouth out with soap," I taunt. "And if you want to be angry at someone, look in the goddamn mirror."

He looks around the room, then he gets up and walks away. I hear a door open and close. He positions himself somewhere, and I see a mahogany headboard behind him.

"I do blame myself, but can you put yourself in my shoes for a minute? I lost us the game. I injured my knee. My entire career is hanging by a thread."

"Right. And you push me away. I was expendable. You go home with your mother and son, and you expect me to sit around, wringing my hands until you're ready for me. Well, fuck that. You picked the wrong woman if that's what you want. Maybe Robin will put up with that, but Victoria won't."

We stare at each other until he says, "Nothing happened between me and Robin. We took the kids out a few times. You know it's important that Evan spend time with his sister. I didn't ask her to come to the hospital. She showed up on her own, and I told her I didn't want her to stay."

All I can think about is that he had the people he wanted there. Maybe he didn't invite Robin, but she was still there when he shut me out.

"How did she know when and where?" I ask him. He looks down, but when he looks up again, I see something in his eyes I can't read.

"She asked me when we were with the kids. I thought it was just conversation."

I nod as I let the words sink in. "Well, Colt, it seems like you had the people you wanted there. You know who wasn't? Me. But that's okay. It's your surgery and you call the shots. And I swear, if you open your mouth and spout some macho crap about how you didn't want me to see you when you were down, I will fucking scream. Here's what I know about relationships. I've been around a pretty functional one for a long time now. You support each other. You lean on each other. You don't push the other one away on some bullshit. I have to go now. Whatever we had is over. See?" I point at myself. "I get to decide that. I don't wait around for anyone to decide where I'm going to fit in their life." And I end the call before he can utter a single word. He calls right back, but I ignore it, put the phone on vibrate, and toss it on the couch.

I sit at the table, my face in my hands, and let the reality of the situation hit. After several minutes, I realize I'm doing something I haven't done since I was a kid. I wipe away the tears, disgusted with myself at this sudden and unwanted burst of emotion.

I stand and go in the master bedroom. I lie on my back in the middle of the bed and stare at the ceiling. More tears fall, and I let them. I don't bother to wipe them away. For this moment, I'll allow myself to feel this pain, and then it will be time to move forward.

FORTY-FOUR

Colt

"Charlie," I burst into the first-floor bedroom Mama had made up for him. He's on his laptop, talking to a woman. He holds up a hand, and I shut up. He turns and looks at me, and he must sense my mood.

"Vanessa, thanks for talking with me, but it looks like my brother needs me. I'll check in with you in a few days." She waves at him and says something I can't hear since he has on headphones. He waves at the screen and closes the laptop.

"That was my sponsor," he explains. "What happened? Is Mama okay? Is it Evan?" He stands and rushes to me and helps me sit on the messy bed.

"They're fine. I need you to drive me to Atlanta. Right now." He eyes me. He knows Victoria is in Atlanta.

"That's over two hours away. You can't sit for that long this soon after your surgery."

"Charlie, if you don't take me, I'll drive myself. She's broken up with me. I can make her understand in person. We'll take the Suburban and I'll sit in the back and prop my leg on some pillows, but I'm going. Right now." He runs a hand over his face, but he nods. I take the keys out of my pocket and toss them to him. "I mucked it all up."

"We need a plan. Will she even let you in?" I stop short. He's right. She won't. I'll have to have him break down the door. "And I can't drive you. My license is still suspended, but I'll call Sampson."

While he types something on his phone, I say, "Evan. We'll pick him up early from camp." It's perfect since Mama is out with Rosalie and is not here to ask questions or to judge me for being stupid. "She'll be happy to see him. He's our ticket in." I should be ashamed for using my son, but these are desperate times.

It's not the job in Mexico that's an issue. That's only a plane ride away, and it's temporary. We can make that work. I don't want to lose her, and I won't.

FORTY-FIVE

The two-hour ride takes almost five. Evan whines about leaving baseball camp early until he falls asleep in the back. We stop every half hour so I can walk and stretch my leg. Charlie walks by my side for support.

We also go to the wrong place. Of course, she would have changed locations. She must have known I'd come find her.

How would she know that the way you abandoned her? After all the work you did to get her, stupid.

It took three tries until Ethan picked up the phone, and it took another ten minutes for him to figure out her exact location, but he did.

Now, Charlie's holding Evan's hand and walking beside me while I maneuver the crutches. It's six PM, and Evan's complaining about being hungry.

I hold my breath and knock on the front door. There's silence for about a full minute until I hear soft footsteps. I imagine she's barefoot and walking against tiled floors.

"Hurry up, Vickie, I have to go pee!" Evan yells, and the door flies open.

She takes him from Charlie and slams the door in our faces. Charlie turns the knob, and we walk through the front door. "Oh my God, I've missed you," she says. "You can use the bathroom right through there." She points to a door and Evan runs off.

Just like I thought. She's barefoot and in a yellow sundress. It's short, several inches above her knees. My eyes travel up, past her stomach to the apex of her breasts. Her dress has a long V-neck, and I look straight down and lick my lips at the sight of her brown skin.

Our eyes lock briefly, but she looks away before I can read her expression. She looks a little thinner, but she's still my Vickie. She's still the same woman I fell heads over heels in love with all those months ago. She'd be with me right now if I'd stopped wallowing in my own pity.

"Vickie—" I begin. She takes a step closer and puts her palm in my face without looking at me.

"I'll get to you in a second." She takes two more slow steps toward Charlie. He visibly swallows and takes a step back. "You," she points at him. He looks around the room as if he's expecting someone to come out and save him. "You think it's okay to go joyriding while drunk with a kid in the car? You think that's okay?" He raises both of his hands.

"That's not what happened," he tells her.

"Oh?" She closes the rest of the space between them and looks up at him. If the situation were different, I'd find this funny. He's almost twice her height, and in his day was a prime athlete. Even now, he might be on the thin side, but he's as strong as an ox and can probably body slam someone twice his weight. But now he looks like he's about to piss himself over a girl half his size. "How was it then? Enlighten me."

He opens his mouth to talk, but she talks over him. "You

have five seconds, and it better be good or you're gonna catch these hands." Charlie looks around, probably unsure of how to react to the angry woman in front of him.

"It wasn't like that, Queen Vee. Evan snuck inside Charlie's car. He had no idea he was in there until it was too late."

"I'm speaking to *him*," she says without turning to look at me. "Explain yourself, Charlie. Three seconds."

He takes a big step back. "I would never do that. What Colt said is true. I love that boy. I'd die before I'd put him in danger. I told Colt the truth about what happened."

She doesn't respond. She continues to look into his face as if she can read his mind. She must be satisfied with what she sees because she nods and turns away from him.

"Fine. You two can get the hell out of my house. Come and pick Evan up tomorrow." Evan runs out of the room and goes directly to Vickie.

My heart melts when she picks him up, hugs him tight, and rains kisses on his face. Evan giggles at her actions.

"Look, Vickie." He opens his mouth and points to his missing bottom tooth.

"You have got to stop growing up so fast."

Evan giggles and says, "I'm hungry. Daddy wouldn't let me have McDonald's on the way over here."

"Your daddy is the worst. You know what? That sounds really good. I'm going to take you, and you can get whatever you want." She puts him down and takes his hand. Evan bounces up and down in his excitement. "I need his booster seat," she says to no one in particular. She grabs her purse from a nearby chair.

"Can we make mac and cheese instead?" Evan asks. "I really want some."

Vickie drops her purse and nods. "I made some last

night and couldn't bring myself to eat it. Let's go warm it up."

They rush off to the kitchen, leaving me and Charlie standing in the middle of the hallway. "You can watch TV in my bedroom while it warms up in the oven. How does that sound? Let me go turn on the TV for you." She picks Evan up and carries him to the bedroom. She comes back a couple of minutes later.

"You can pick him up in the morning." She opens the front door and gestures for us to leave. "Drop off a change of clothes and leave it at the door. Goodbye."

Charlie lets out a cackle but sobers quickly under Vickie's stern glare.

"I came here to talk to you. To apologize." I lean my crutches against the wall and hobble to the living room. Charlie grabs the ottoman and helps me elevate my leg.

"You've already done that. I don't need to hear it again." She eyes my leg, and for a brief second, she softens. The Vickie I fell in love with returns and she runs a hand through her tightly coiled hair. I wish I could hear her thoughts. I know she's thinking of a way for me to be more comfortable, but she won't show it. "Can you two please leave before I lose my temper?"

My Queen Vee doesn't have a temper. She holds it all in and tries to show as little emotion as possible, but maybe that's what I need to do. I need to get her to explode and let it out.

Evan returns, complaining about being hungry and thirsty. They go into the kitchen, leaving me and Charlie in the living room.

"She's going to kill us both," Charlie whispers. "I've never been scared of a girl before today, but she still loves you. I can see it in her eyes. But seriously, Colty, why? She loves you. She loves Evan. I don't understand."

"It was a lot, Charlie. I was depressed about a lot of things, and I screwed up."

"I know all about that, but fix it and hold on to her. She's all Evan talks about. I'm telling you, a fur coat is the answer."

Before I can call him an idiot, we hear a ding in the kitchen and Evan's nonstop chatter. He tells her everything about baseball camp and his swimming lessons. He even invites her to come see him play. The smell of the food from the kitchen finally reaches us, and I hear Charlie's stomach growl.

"Damn, that smells good. Do you think she'll let me have some?" Charlie asks. He gets up and goes to the kitchen, abandoning me.

I sit there and wince at the throbbing pain in my knee. Charlie's right about one thing, stress is not helpful to the healing process. I'm supposed to start physical therapy next week, but the doctor won't allow it if I don't heal enough to sustain the therapy.

Minutes later, Charlie returns with a tray. I normally stay away from carb heavy meals, but it smells good, and I had some when Vickie made it with Evan before. It was just a few short weeks ago when we were happy and in love, then I mucked it all up. There's also a Caesar salad, diced fruit, and a bottle of water.

He leaves it on my lap and returns to the kitchen. My stomach growls, and I devour the food in front of me.

"I love the evil one's mac and cheese," I hear Evan say.

"Who is the evil one?" Charlie asks. I can tell he has his mouth full.

"That's Vickie's evil stepmother, but she's really nice."

"She can't be that evil if she makes food this good," Charlie mumbles.

I don't hear anymore. I know there's talk, but the pain in my knee has gotten so bad that I put my head back on the couch. I can feel sweat on my forehead, but I refuse to take a pain pill.

"Charlie," I manage to say. I can feel my heart beating fast. Charlie comes over and takes the tray. "I need an ice pack." I open my eyes, and Vickie is looking down at me. My heart drops when she walks away, but when she returns with an ice pack, I have a glimmer of hope for the first time since I got here. She positions it on my knee and leaves.

Charlie helps to turn me around on the couch. He puts pillows underneath my leg and one behind my head.

Evan runs to me, holding an ice cream sandwich. He grins, knowing full well I don't approve of sugary snacks.

"Hey, bud. Is there another one of those for me? Why don't I take you to that playground over there?" Charlie points to the sliding glass door. "That way, we won't make a mess. Go get one for Uncle Charlie." Evan runs back to the kitchen, and Charlie turns back to me. "We'll only be outside. You can see us through the door. I'd die before I'd hurt him." I can tell he's holding his breath while he waits for my answer. I nod at him, and he exhales.

"Come on, Uncle Charlie," Evan yells from the kitchen. Charlie leaves, and a few minutes later, they go outside, leaving me alone with Vickie for the first time in weeks.

FORTY-SIX

I don't care. I don't care. I don't care. I replay that mantra in my head but it's my heart that won't cooperate. There's a thin sheen of sweat on his forehead, and his breathing is shallow. He looks thinner than when I saw him last, but he's always been on the thin side.

I leave, get a damp washcloth, and put it to his forehead.

"Thank you, Queen," he says. I can tell he's uncomfortable, and I decide I'll treat him like I would any other human being who is in pain.

"You should take something for the pain." I know he won't take anything that's prescribed. No controlled substances because of the addiction problems that run in his family.

I grab a bottle of ibuprofen from my purse and take out two. "Here. This is over the counter. It might take the edge off. And you shouldn't have driven all the way over here a few days after your surgery. That was stupid." He takes the pills and I put his water bottle to his lips.

"I came because we need to talk." He winces and the bottle slips from his hand, splashing on the floor. I tell him to lie down and cover him with a throw I keep on the couch. While he's lying there, breathing hard, I grab a roll of paper towels and wipe the excess water from the floor.

"Vickie," he begins.

"Just shut up. I've said all I'm going to say. It's over, Colt. I gave you one chance. You don't walk away from me and waltz back in when you feel like it. You made your choice. You chose everyone but me."

"It wasn't like that. Let me—"

"I said shut up. You can stay here until you feel better, but after that, you've got to leave."

FORTY-SEVEN

Colt

I can hear her in the kitchen washing dishes in the sink. I exhale and relax on the couch. In too much pain and tired from the car ride, I let sleep take me under. When I wake up, it's gotten dark outside, and I groan at the sound of Evan and Vickie bellowing out "Tomorrow". Charlie joins in too. I wince and sit up. The pain in my knee has gotten better, and there's a fresh bottle of water on the coffee table. They hit a high note, and I swear the windows shake. The three laugh, and I yell for my brother. "Can you bring my crutches? I need to use the bathroom." He comes over and helps me up. Vickie follows, but Evan remains glued in front of the TV.

Charlie helps me to a half bathroom down the hall. The rest has not only helped my pain level, but I feel refreshed. Much more than I did when I first left New York, and I know it's because I'm near Vickie again.

I lean against the sink and hang my head, cursing my own stupidity for pushing away the only woman I've ever loved. There's a soft knock on the door, and Vickie walks in. She's holding another bottle of water for me.

"You slept for three hours. Are you feeling better? Your mom's worried sick. Maybe you and Charlie should get a hotel room for the night, and Evan can stay here with me. I've missed him, and if this is going to be the last time I spend time with him, I want to make it count."

I hang my head again and let out a deep sigh. She sounds so matter of fact, and despite being the cause, it hurts.

"I made a mistake, Victoria. Can you please forgive me so we can move forward?" I stand up straight and look into her face. She's as stoic as ever. I reach for her hand, but she jerks away and takes a step back, bumping into the door. I continue my approach and put both arms on either side of her, boxing her in. I make sure to put a hand on the doorknob so she can't get to it. "Can you put yourself in my shoes just for a minute?"

She juts out her chin. Her eyes darken. She's doing her best to hold in her anger, but I need her to unleash it so we can get this behind us.

"For a minute, Colt? I put myself in your shoes for weeks. Weeks while you were in Alabama, telling me in word and deed that you didn't need me. Weeks where you had ice cream dates with another woman. Weeks where—"

"Are you kidding me? Robin is not another woman. We had the kids together for ice cream. All I did was think of you the entire time. You and my darn knee and the fact that my career is hangin' on by a thread."

She crosses her arms and brushes my chest with her elbow. It's the most she's touched me in weeks, and I want more.

"Come back with us. I need you." I rest my forehead on hers, crowding her even more. She puts a hand on my chest to push me away, but I wrap my hand around her wrist. "I love you so much. You're the first and last woman I will ever love, Victoria. I love every little thing about you. Every last thing." She puts her free hand on mine, trying to get to the doorknob. "You came into my world and changed everything for the better. Despite not wanting a relationship at first, I love how you embraced it and fit so perfectly into my family. I love how smart and independent you are. And I know how much this teaching job in Mexico means to you. It won't change anything between us. It's only for a year. We'll visit often, and I'll fly you back and forth to New York. We can make it work. I just need you." I drop her wrist and wrap my arms around her. "You feel so good. I've missed this so much."

I kiss the side of her neck and bring her in closer, but she pushes me and manages to escape my arms.

"No. You had one chance." She holds up her index finger. "One. That's it. That's all anybody gets."

She grabs the doorknob, but I'm faster. I push her hand away.

"I didn't end things. I never ended things."

She lets out a humorless laugh. "Oh, really? Was I supposed to wait for the great Colt Chastain to dump *me*? That's not how it works, darlin'. No one walks away from me. Not anymore. Not since—" It looks like she's going to say more, but she catches herself and shakes her head. "Move," she orders.

"Don't dismiss me, Vickie. We need to have a conversation." I do my best to keep my voice calm because the stress is not good for me, but I can feel anger bubbling just underneath the surface. "I'm not your mama. I didn't leave you.

"Don't talk about my mother," she warns me. "It doesn't feel good to be dismissed, does it?" she grits out. "I waited around for you for weeks like a simpering idiot while you went on with your life and now—"

"While I went on with my life? Are you kidding me? Look at me." She turns her head away, but I cup her face so she has no choice but to look into my eyes. "I'm a mess. I'm in pain. My knee's not healin' like I was hopin', and you're actin' like a child right now. Do you know what it's like for me?" I find myself yelling out the last question. The TV gets louder, and I imagine Charlie is trying to drown out our arguing. "Do you know that basketball is the only thing I've ever had that made me feel special? It's the only thing I'm good at, and the idea of not having it anymore hurts, Vickie. It hurts a lot, and I pushed you away because I didn't want you to see me wallowing around. I didn't want to take my hurt and frustration out on you. I—"

She puts a palm to my face, but I put it down.

"Do you think I live in some fantasy world, Colt? Do you think I need everything to be perfect all the time? I agreed to a relationship, not some alternate universe where everything is always roses. You're supposed to wallow with me! You're supposed to show me your ugly sides. Snap at me if I hover over you too much. I'd tell you where to stick it, and then we'd figure out the rest. Together. Why am I the one telling you how a relationship is supposed to work? What you don't do is get on a plane and leave the woman you say you love."

I feel about two feet tall after her rant. That's exactly what Mama said to me too. Even Charlie gave me the side eye the entire five-hour drive here.

"I know that, baby. I know. I lost sight for a minute. Please understand that I have issues too. I was never a good student. I'm not smart like you. I never had a wealthy parent to fall back on. Everyone has always relied on me.

From my mother on down. I'm it. I'm the support, and that's a heavy burden. I know you don't understand that, but—"

"Don't tell me what I understand. Don't. Just shut up. How dare you say those things? Basketball is not all you have. Your mom is amazing, and so is your son. They are worth more than basketball any day. You also had me, Colt." She points at herself. "You had me, but I wasn't enough. I was a fool to believe everything you promised me. I understand how important basketball is to you. I would never belittle that, but you don't get to push me away when things in your life get rough and expect me to sit around until you get out of your funk. I'm a person with feelings, and abandonment—" She stops speaking and looks away.

"Abandonment is what? I didn't abandon you. I love you. I've told you that every day until you stopped taking my calls, which was crap."

She sighs and runs a hand over her face. "Look, I want your knee to heal. I really do. So, why don't you go sit down and elevate it? I think we've said enough."

I put a finger under her chin and force her eyes back on me.

"Tell me you don't love me anymore, Queen Vee. I dare you." Hope blooms in my chest when she can't utter the words. "You can't." I press myself to her and say, "I love you too." I cup her face and kiss her sweet lips for the first time in weeks. It's like I'm breathing for the first time. She tries to push away from me until she gives in and kisses me back. I lift her dress up and stick my hand between her legs. She moans in my mouth.

I spin her around and pull her panties down. She kicks them off. My basketball shorts and boxers are pushed down, and I stand tall and rigid. There's already a bead of pre-cum at my tip. It's been weeks without her. Without her warmth and sarcastic wit, or false detachment. I slide inside. I slide all the way home. She lets out a half moan, half cry. And because her carnal moans are only for me, I put my hand on her mouth to mute the sounds.

I take her rough and fast, giving her as much as my body will allow. I can feel the dull pain in my knee, but being inside of her, reminding her of everything that we are together is more important. She moans, and I stop my thrusts. I stay buried inside of her and let her feel me.

"This is for you, Victoria. For the rest of my life, I don't want to do this with anyone but you. You will always be my queen." I bite the side of her neck and suck on the soft skin. It doesn't take long for her to tremble against me, moaning in my hand. I soon follow behind her and flood her with my release. I rub her engorged clit with my fingers and she shudders. She's soaked, and our release coats her inner thighs. I pull out and pull my shorts and underwear back up and sit on the toilet to catch my breath.

Her breathing is still shallow while she pulls herself back together. She leans against the sink, head hung low. While she washes her hands and splashes water on her face, I approach and wrap my arms around her.

"Let's get married." The words leave my mouth before I can think them through. "We'll get married before you leave for Mexico." She stares into my eyes, mouth opened into an o while I speak. "It's only a year, and it will fly by. I know what it's like to have a career that's important to you. That's one of the things I love about you. I will always support you in that. But don't tell your dad I've already asked you. I'll call him tomorrow and ask his permission—"

She holds a hand up and says, "Stop talking right now, Colt. Just stop. This," she says, gesturing between us. "What just happened right now changes nothing." She pushes away from me and walks out of the bathroom before I can catch her.

I find her sitting on the couch staring at the television but not really watching it. Charlie eyes me, probably making sure I'm alright, before he turns back to the TV.

"Why don't I help you get washed up, Evan?" Charlie says when the movie is over. He throws Evan over his shoulder.

"You can use my bathroom." Vickie points to the master bedroom.

"Did you and your brother get a hotel?" Vickie asks. She jumps off the couch and starts to straighten up. She takes the empty popcorn bowl to the kitchen and starts to clear the counter. "I really would like Evan to stay with me for the night, but if you're not comfortable with that, I understand."

She's unprepared for me when I put both hands on her shoulders and press my chest into her back.

"I trust you with my son. I trust you with my life, but I'm not leaving this house, Victoria. Not unless you come with me." I slowly turn her around to face me. "What can I do, baby, to fix this mess that I caused? Tell me, and I'll do it." I kiss the side of her neck and try to snake an arm around her waist, but she moves away.

"Colt," she begins, and my heart sinks, "you had your one chance, and I don't do long distance relationships. We tried this and it didn't work." She walks away and heads for the master bedroom, but she must remember that Charlie and Evan are in there, so she goes through the sliding glass door.

I follow her to the deck and sit next to her. "I will never give up, Victoria, because you are everything I've always wanted. But you're also everything I've always needed. I didn't know I needed you until I found you, and I'm not giving that up for anything. I'll ask you to marry me every day until you say yes."

She shakes her head but won't look at me. I grasp her chin and turn her toward me. "I know I hurt you," I whisper. "I know I was selfish and only thought of myself. If I was thinkin' clearly, I would have realized you would see this as an abandonment. I know that's a—"

She shoves my hand away and stands. She puts both hands on her hips and takes two steps closer to me. When she gets to my face, she points a finger. "I would never give you the power to hurt me. The only people who can hurt me never would. But yeah, I let you in further than I've ever let anyone else, and that was obviously a mistake." She spins around, rests a hand on her forehead, and looks off into the distance. "I changed my plans around for you, Colt." She looks at me again. There's color in her cheeks, and the control she's been trying to hold onto breaks. "I got attached to your son. Your son, Colt! And your mother! And I let you climb my walls. I was traveling to your games, and I hate basketball. I did all of that for you and that was okay because I liked what we had. I loved it. I loved the playful guy, and the one who jumped in to save me without a thought to himself. The one who would puff his chest out in pride at my accomplishments." She wipes a stray tear. "But one tragedy and you ghost me. I'm not going to put myself in a position where that happens repeatedly. So, yeah. You hurt me. You did, and I'm not the girl who just forgives that type of thing. Face it. You didn't need me. You had everyone you needed around you, and I have the pictures to prove it. You can justify it any way you want, but when you left New York, you took everyone who mattered to you."

I stand and almost trip, but she runs and holds my hips

to steady me. "And I want you to heal so you can continue to play. A long-distance relationship won't work."

She helps me sit down, and I wince as the pain returns, harsher than it was before my nap.

"I've been in the league nine years. I figure I have five, maybe six years left. Do I want those years? Hell yes, but I want you more. I don't give a damn about my knee right now. I want you. I want us, and I'm going to show you every day how much I want you and how much I'm willing to fight for what we have. I've never had someone love me like you, and—"

My words are lost when Evan comes running out, wearing the blue pajamas we bought for him on the way here. He runs to Vickie. She picks him up and hugs him as if this is the last time she's ever going to hold him.

FORTY-EIGHT

Vickie

Two months later

My nerves finally calm once the plane reaches cruising altitude. I've never been more grateful for the extra room in first class as I am now. I was doomed to fail at my dream job the minute I stepped foot in Mexico.

I was there barely a day before the flowers started arriving. Every day like clockwork, I got roses or lilies or a large bouquet of exotic flowers. And that was the least of it. There was also food. Breakfast and dinner were delivered every day. There had been daily declarations of love, either in a private phone call or text or a public display on Twitter. True to his word, he's asked me to marry him every day.

There were daily, sometimes multiple, videos of him at rehab or speaking with his doctors.

"I know you can't be here, darlin'. I know I kept you away before, but I want you to know everything. PT is going well. It's kicking my butt, but it's going well. As soon as I'm cleared to travel, I'm getting on a plane and coming to you. I miss my Queen Vee." He would always be sweaty and disheveled in the video, spent from his physical therapy.

He sent jewelry. Beautiful and expensive pieces. Things I never would have picked out for myself, including a diamond tiara. All the card said was 'A Queen shouldn't be without her crown.' As crazy as the tiara is, it's not the craziest thing he sent me. The most ridiculous gift was a long, white mink coat. It's ostentatious and gorgeous at the same time. I don't know why he figured this was something I would like. It's not something I would ever buy for myself, but I love it. I walked around the small apartment wearing it and strutting like a supermodel on the runway. In fact, I couldn't bear to pack it up and ship it like I did the rest of my things. I found a special carrying case for it, and it's sitting in the overhead compartment right now.

I put thousands of miles between us and it's like I never left. He never stops calling, and I don't have it in me to block him. Those times I got to see Evan or talk to him were worth it. Besides, I speak to Mary Leigh regularly, who also keeps me up to date on Colt's day to day. She always puts Charlie on the phone too. It's hard to break up with a man when neither he nor the people around him will acknowledge that our relationship is over. He still believes we are together and has a calendar counting down the days until I return to New York for good. He has no idea I'll be landing in New York in a few hours and that I have no intentions of returning to Mexico. Not under these circumstances. A bout of nausea hits and I close my eyes and wait for it to pass. Luckily, it does and I'm able to fall asleep. When I open my eyes again, I've landed in Miami.

I could have talked to my sister, and her fiancé would have sent me his private plane, but no one knows I'm coming back to New York today. If they did, Colt would find out and he'd be waiting for me at the airport. He's been back in New York since school started and getting all his treatments there now.

"If things go well, I might not have to sit out any games, Queen Vee," he had said one day in a video he texted. I could see the relief in his face through the phone, and my heart was glad for him.

The first thing I see when I turn on my phone is a video from him working out with his physical therapist and with his personal trainer. He's at full weight bearing now. He still hasn't cut his hair, and it's a curly mess.

"I'm not cutting this until you get back to me. Maybe you can cut it for me. Or I'll keep it and you can braid it. Tell me what to do to get us back, Queen. I'll do anything." The look in his eyes is so haunting, I look away and move on to the next message.

It's a video from my sister. She's on Ethan's private plane with our parents, Alan and Ethan's sister.

Please, don't say you're going to Mexico.

My shoulders slump in relief when they tell me they are taking a spontaneous trip to Bermuda for the Columbus Day weekend. Even better. I can have three days to figure out what I'm going to do before my family comes back to town and bulldozes their way into my apartment with questions, concerns, and hugs.

The line at immigration is long, and once I clear customs, I only have an hour until my next flight. I'm hungry, but there's no way I can eat. My mouth has a sour taste, and the thought of food makes me ill. I settle for a lemonade, and a few sips later, I toss it in the trash, grossed out by the sweetness.

The three-hour flight from Miami to New York seems to take forever. By the time I land and take a cab home, I'm exhausted. The apartment is still spotless. I had the cleaning service I sometimes use come and do a thorough cleaning. After a bowl of chicken broth and a piping hot shower, I climb into bed without a stitch of clothes on and pass out. I wake up hours later, groggy and disoriented. I run from the bed and reach the toilet just in time for all my stomach contents to come up.

FORTY-NINE

Colt

I RUB MY HAND OVER MY FACE AND EYES, CERTAIN THAT what I'm seeing is wrong. If this is correct, Victoria Taylor is back in New York City, and she didn't tell me she was coming. The last time I checked her location, she was in Mexico City, but I couldn't track her for most of yesterday. Now, she's currently at her old apartment.

"Are we done here?" I ask Kathy, one of my physical therapists. She takes my leg and bends it. I wince. The pain is not nearly as bad as it was, but it's sore. My mind has already shut down. I'm done with PT. Kathy just doesn't know it yet. I text my personal trainer and cancel my session for today. "I'm done, Kathy." I pull my leg away when she reaches for it again.

She sighs and nods. I'm already pulling my shirt over my head and heading to my room to shower. It's only nine o'clock in the morning, and I can be at her place in under an hour if traffic behaves. I text my driver and tell him to be ready. It only takes me ten minutes to shower and dress. Less than an hour later, I'm at her building, going inside behind another resident. According to her phone, she's still there, but five minutes later, she still has not come to the door. I jiggle the doorknob, prepared to knock the door open with my shoulder when it swings open.

It's like I'm breathing for the first time in months. I cup her face and kiss her mouth without a word. I push us inside and slam the door closed with my good leg. She smells of sleep, but her mouth tastes minty, and I never want to stop kissing her.

She pushes me away and takes a step back, but she's breathless. I close the space between us. It's been months without her, and I pull her into my arms and hold her tight.

"Why didn't you tell me you were comin'? I would have sent a plane for you." I pull back and cup her cheeks. "God, you're beautiful, darlin'. So beautiful." I kiss her again, but she steps away.

"Colt, stop. I can't deal with you and your drama right now, okay." She takes her robe and tightens the sash around her. She's beautiful, but she's a disaster. Her hair is a frizzy mess. Her eyes are sunken in and dark underneath. She appears thinner too. Maybe she's been just as miserable without me as I've been without her.

"Are you sick, darlin'?" I check her glands and put a palm to her forehead. She feels fine. "I can get a doctor for you. Let's go home." I grab her hand and start to pull her toward the door.

"Colt! Stop."

"I'm sorry. Get dressed and we'll go."

"Just stop. I can't deal with your drama today. Can you please just leave me alone?" She spins on her heels and returns to her room. She slams the door behind her. I follow, unwilling to let her out of my sight for another minute.

I walk into the bedroom to find her rummaging through her suitcase. She takes clothes out and tosses them on the floor. She finally finds something and rushes out of the room, slamming the door behind her. I sit on the bed and wait. She's not pushing me away. Not now and not ever. After ten minutes, she still doesn't come back. I walk to the bathroom and knock on the door. She doesn't answer, but I hear her moving around in there.

"Queen Vee, I'm going to order us some breakfast and we'll talk. I need you to listen to me, baby. However long you're here, we're going to spend it together. I'll order you eggs and French toast. I know how much you love—"

The door swings open before I can finish my sentence. She's cleaned herself up. Her hair is in a tight bun, giving her a regal look. She's added light makeup, but something about her still looks off. She doesn't have her usual healthy glow, and I put my palm on her forehead again. No fever.

"No food." She winces as if the thought of food is off putting.

"Did you catch some sort of bug over there? Let me take you to see my doctor."

"Colt, I have my own god damn doctor, alright. I don't need you here trying to fix things when you're the one who —" She stops and catches herself. She shakes her head and walks past me. "Leave," she says when I step into her bedroom.

"What's the matter?" I take both of her hands in mine and pull her against me. I wrap my arms around her and hold her close. She lets out a strange sound and bursts into tears. Something cold grips my heart. I feel like the ground I'm standing on is starting to crumble.

"What is it? Are you sick? Did you get a bad diagnosis?" I'm already thinking of specialists when she shakes her head no. Relieved, I pull her to me and wrap my arms around her. "Then whatever it is, we can deal with it. You can tell me. We're a team." She lets me hold her and her cries turn into quiet sobs.

Her phone rings and she pulls away.

"Hey, Tara." She's doing her best to sound cheerful, but she doesn't pull it off. Not even close. There's no way her sister will buy her fake enthusiasm. "Wait! What did you say?" The alarm in her voice puts me on high alert. "When? Oh my God." She looks around the room like someone who's just had her world altered. She runs to the closet and shoves her feet into a pair of sneakers. "I'm in New York. I'll explain later, but I'm on my way. I'll see you when you get here. Love you guys too."

She walks away without giving me another look or an explanation. She snatches a jacket out of her closet, grabs her purse, and runs out. I follow behind her, and when we get outside, I steer her to my car.

"Leave me the hell alone," she says.

"What's the matter? And where are you going? I'll take you." She stares at me, and I guess I must be her best option because she nods.

"My mother's in the hospital. She was in an accident." She bursts into tears for the second time this morning.

FIFTY

Colt

She pulls her hand away when I try to hold it, but when I put that same hand on her lap, she doesn't push me away. Maybe it's because she needs me, or maybe it's because she's afraid and tired of fighting. Whichever one it is, I'll take it. In the harsh light of day, she looks awful. She's still beautiful, but she looks haggard and worn out. Maybe Mexico just didn't agree with her. Maybe she was sick before she was able to travel back, but I know she's talked to my mother. She talks to Evan on a regular basis. They are taking an online knitting class together every Thursday night. Evan's recruited Vincent and Tara too, and the four of them log into the class every week. It warms my heart that she's kept her promise to him.

I check out her profile, and her skin looks sallow. It looks like she's holding her breath, and she has a look of discomfort on her face. I touch her forehead and feel her glands again. She doesn't fight me, and that worries me. We arrive at First Presbyterian half an hour later. She makes a mad dash for the front door before my driver comes to a full stop, and I follow behind her, but she's fast.

I've never been this happy to have access to the world's best medical care than I am at this moment. Maybe she has a healing effect, but my knee feels great and I'm able to follow her with ease through the hospital emergency department.

I reach her in time to hear her say, "Alicia Taylor. My sister got a call that she's here." The nurse behind the desk tells her to hold on while she looks at her computer screen.

"And you are?" she asks without bothering to look up.

"I'm her daughter, Victoria Taylor." The nurse writes something on a piece of paper and hands it to her, all without looking up. "This is her room number."

The nurse looks at us for the first time. "Aren't you Colt Chastain? Oh my God! You're Victoria Taylor. Are you two back together? Girl, you just fell off the face of the earth and we haven't—"

Vickie turns her back on the talking woman and walks away. I nod at her and follow Vickie to a set of elevators.

"Thank you for the ride, Colt. I've got it from here." The polite detachment ticks me off, but I rein in my irritation and follow her into the elevator and all the way to the intensive care unit. She's told to wait, and I take a seat next to her. Her knee bounces uncontrollably and I put my hand on it to calm her down. It works. I throw an arm over her shoulder and pull her closer. She stiffens but doesn't try to pull away. We sit like that until a heavyset nurse with red hair and a nervous facial tick approach.

Victoria stands. I can feel the tension oozing off her while she waits to hear the news. "Ms. Taylor?" She nods, and I hold my breath. I inch closer and take her hand in mine, intertwining our fingers. She squeezes my hand, and I squeeze it back. "I'm Beth. Your mother was hit by a car. When she fell, she hit her head and was out for about twelve hours." Vickie lets out a sharp sound and I pull her close.

"How long has she been here?" she asks, holding on tight to my hand.

"About twenty-four hours."

"Twenty-four hours?" Vickie runs a hand over her face. "Why did it take so long for someone to call us? I could have been here." Tears fill her eyes and roll down her face. I take her in my arms and cradle her to my chest. "I should have been here," she sobs. "She's been all alone."

I kiss the top of her head, but I remain silent. I don't think there are any words in any language that would make her feel better. Now, she needs strength and the feel of another human being, one who loves her.

"She had no identification on her when she got here. We had to wait for her to wake up."

"Can I see her?" She chokes on the question and bursts into tears. The nurse's left cheek twitches. A door opens, and I hear footsteps.

"Vickie." I know that voice. I remember it from a few months ago. Vickie moves out of my arms and turns to that idiot, Dr. Gerald Prescott. The man who is in love with the woman I also happen to be in love with.

He's in blue scrubs. He stands in front of us and watches her. I know that look in his eyes. He wants her. So, I pull her closer and wrap my arm around her, pressing her into my body.

"Hey, Vickie." She sobs, flies out of my arms and into his. He pulls her into his body and rests his forehead on top of her head. It's an intimate gesture. One that makes my stomach drop. He looks directly into my eyes and smiles in triumph.

"Jerry, are you working on my mother? Please tell me

she's going to be okay." She cries against him, wiping her face on his scrubs. Something inside of me snaps. Her tears are my responsibility to wipe, not his or any other man's. I take her arm and pull her away from him. I stand between them and tower over him.

I've never used my size to intimidate, but I've never had to before. He smirks, and I remain stoic, ready to pounce if necessary.

"She's a little groggy and has a dislocated shoulder. We can't get her blood pressure down, but given the stress she's been under, that's to be expected."

Vickie exhales in relief. I put an arm around her waist and pull her back where she belongs.

"You can go and see her. Beth will take you." Vickie extricates herself from me and follows Beth down the hall and out of my sight.

Dr. Prescott doesn't leave, so I take a few steps back, lean against the wall, and wait to hear the nonsense he's about to spew.

"You know, for a second, I thought you were a threat," he says. I pull out my phone and send a text to the nanny with instructions for after school. I put my phone in the back pocket of my jeans and give him a disinterested stare, but the truth is, I'd love nothing more than to punch this guy's teeth in. "But all I had to do was wait for you to fuck it all up. Didn't take long." He inches closer to me. "Your problem is you don't understand her. I made the same mistake, so don't feel bad. I know her now, and I'm going to pick up where you left off."

He makes the mistake of tapping me on the shoulder. My hands whip up. I grab his shoulders, spin us around and pin him hard against the wall. He winces and tries to push me away, but I press against him, making it impossible for him to move.

"Stay away from her," I warn.

"See? You think you own her. Mistake number one. The second mistake you made, you left her. You guys aren't a good fit anyway. You might have a little money now, but you'll always be a hillbilly. Did you really think you were long term material with a woman like that?" He chuckles at his own joke. I drop my hands and he stumbles, but he laughs all the way down the hall.

FIFTY-ONE

Vickie

Her hands are warm, but her grip is faint. She smiles but winces.

"Stop moving, Mother. Are you in pain? Let me call the nurse. She can give you something to make you more comfortable." She tries to sit up, but I shake my head disapprovingly at her. She winces but tries to mask her pain with a smirk.

"And I thought Tara was the mother hen," she moans.

"Don't try to talk. Jesus, you need to watch where you're going. You know the drivers in this city are crazy. It could have been a lot worse. I'm so sorry no one was here." I lay my head on the bed and sob quietly, then pull myself together because this isn't about me, and I need to be strong for someone else.

When I feel her hand in my hair, I sob louder. Guilt washes over me in waves. Each time she's called, I've hit ignore. Each voicemail message I've deleted, and each attempt of getting together I've rebuffed play in my mind like a loop. I didn't tell her about Mexico until the day before I left. I sent her a one sentence text, and when she called me, I didn't pick up.

"I'm so sorry," I sob. "I'm so sorry." I lose all attempts of trying to be strong and break down in the hospital room. "We could have lost you," I say. "And you've been here all alone and all I was doing was feeling sorry for myself."

She caresses the top of my head, just like she used to when I was little and upset. Her hands were always a source of comfort.

"I'm a little banged up, but I'll be fine. It's okay, French fry." For the first time ever, I love the sound of my nickname. "Look at me."

I wipe my nose on the blanket and do as she says. God, she looks like Tara and Alan. And me too. We all have her eyes, and I know I have her smile. There's no denying she's our mother.

"I'm glad you're here."

I do a half laugh, half sob.

"I bet you're shocked that I am. I haven't always been—"

"Shh. You've always been perfect to me. You've always been true to yourself, and I admire that. I've been a shitty mom. I acknowledge that too." She coughs and winces again. I stand, fluff her pillows and offer her water.

"We're not going to talk about that," I tell her. "We have to watch out for your blood pressure—"

"Let me say it. I don't know when I'll get another opportunity." I sit. I could argue with her, but I know what she means. It's almost impossible for her to pin me down. I've made sure of it.

"You weren't always, though, Mom. I think it would have been easier if you were. It would have at least made more sense. The nine-year-old Vickie didn't understand why you left her father. He's perfect to me. But adult Vickie understands relationships aren't always easy, and that only the two people involved know what's really going on. What I'll never understand is why you left us too. We'd go months without seeing you. You'd make plans and bail. I felt like you didn't want to be around us, and that we were a nuisance to you. I still feel that way. I don't understand how the mother who took such good care of us just walked out." The words come rushing out of me. I've held onto those feelings for almost twenty years and having them come out was like a weight being lifted off my shoulders. A weight I didn't know I was carrying.

The room goes deathly quiet after my speech. Beth comes in, checks Mom's temperature and blood pressure. "It's gone down a little bit, but it's still high. Dr. Prescott will be back soon."

Once Beth leaves, Mom grabs my hand in hers. "I was selfish, Victoria. I can't make excuses."

"We don't have to talk about this now." I rest my forehead on the back of her hand. "You need to rest."

"Let me say something." She clears her throat. I hand her the cup of water, and she sips, but her hand shakes the entire time. "This might not be pleasant for you to hear, but I fell out of love with your father." Affronted, I sit up, ready to eviscerate her for daring to speak ill of my father. The man who has always been there, unlike her, but she squeezes my hand and I swallow my sharp rebuke. "It was nothing that he did. It was me. He was a good husband, but he was busy building the business and I was building my own career. Then my career stalled and his took off. The ugly side of me was jealous, and instead of being happy about his success, which was good for all of us, I became bitter. I blamed him for the lack of progress in my own career. I wanted to be a news anchor, and it never worked out, but things for your father were great. And it all became too much. I blamed you kids too." I look up, shocked by that admission, but she holds a hand up. "We both had careers, but I was the one who had to handle almost everything at home. It was like I was working two full time jobs, and I was burned out. I left. I figured everything would be perfect for me if I could make my own life without the shackles of marriage and children. All I thought about was me."

A coughing fit hits her and when the nurse returns moments later, I'm ordered out of the room while she's examined. On the way to the waiting area, I slip into a bathroom and throw up. I haven't eaten yet today, so I dry heave until there's nothing left, and my chest starts to hurt. I sit on the floor for several minutes and gather my thoughts. I've always known Mother was selfish, and this story is no great revelation. It just confirms what I've always suspected, but the idea of her blaming us for her floundering career is something I've never considered. I'm not surprised she blamed Dad.

I stand, and since I've spent the last two weeks throwing up, I pull out the little bottle of mouthwash I keep in my purse. Once I rinse my mouth and my face, I return to the waiting room.

Colt rushes to me when he sees me, but I push against his chest and move away. He sits next to me and grabs my hand.

"She's okay." He's been here with me. He has a right to know her progress. "We talked, but she started coughing so the nurse told me to leave. You can go. Thank you for bringing me here, but you don't need to stay." I stand and start to pace the small room. It's going to be hours until my family gets here, but I plan on staying in the building until their arrival.

"I'm not leaving."

"We're not in a relationship anymore, Colt. You did your good deed." I stare out the window and into the overcast city.

FIFTY-TWO

Colt

I APPROACH BUT I DON'T TOUCH HER. I STAND AS CLOSE to her back as possible without our bodies making contact. I'd give anything to pull her into me and wrap my arms around her right now, but I know she'll fight me, and she's already under enough stress.

"I'm not going anywhere. You're not pushing me away."

She scoffs and shakes her head. She steps away and stands on the other side of the room.

"Right. I pushed you away. Of course, you'd blame me because I'm the one who went to another state and forgot you existed. You know what, Colt? Go to hell. In case you haven't noticed, my mother is in a hospital bed. This isn't about you."

She sits and we both remain quiet. She's right. This isn't about me, and we'll have plenty of time to talk about our relationship, but now's not the time. I take the seat next to her and remain quiet.

About an hour later, her cousin Bernie comes into the room. Vickie runs into the woman's arms and they hold each other. I've met Bernie a few times, but right now I envy the fact that she's consoling my woman and I can't. She should be in my arms getting comfort from me.

"Your mama's going to be okay," Bernie says. "She's a tough old bitch." Vickie nods her head in agreement. "But I'm surprised to see you here." Bernie cups Vickie's cheeks and stares into her eyes. "Oh," she says as if everything makes sense. "I see." She looks over at me but doesn't offer me a smile. She's always flirted with me, but today, her eyes are dark and practically shooting fire at me.

For the next three hours, we wait. Vickie excuses herself to use the bathroom four times, and each time she wrings her hands before she goes. When I get a text from the nanny, I tell her where to meet us. A few minutes later, she walks in with Evan.

"Vickie!" Evan yells. He runs and jumps into her arms. "You're back! Daddy said we were going to Mexico for Thanksgiving and Christmas. Does this mean we're not going anymore? I'm playing soccer now that baseball season is over. Will you come to my game on Saturday?" He talks nonstop, telling Vickie about everything she's missed since she's been gone. She holds him the entire time, nodding and answering all his questions.

My heart swells at the sight of her and my son. As much as I've missed her, I know Evan has too. I'd give anything to take them both home tonight.

"Well, I'm not going back to Mexico," she tells Evan. My ears perk up at that. I'll have to find out the reason later. "And I've missed you too, so yes, I will come to all your games. How about we go to the cafeteria and get you a snack? If you eat it all, I'll get you ice cream." She brushes his hair off his forehead. Evan nods, and they start to walk out without asking me if it's okay.

"I'll call you if anything happens," Bernie says to

their retreating backs. I dismiss the nanny, but instead of taking my seat, I walk around the room to stretch my legs.

"You know, I liked you," Bernie says to me.

"Liked? I thought we were friends, Bernie." I give her my best smile, but she doesn't return it.

"I love Vickie and her siblings like they're my own. Anyone who hurts them goes on my shit list. That's an automatic." I stop my pacing and face her.

"I understand. I'm glad she has someone like you. You should know that I love her, and I'm doing everything in my power to get her back." It's the truth and I'll keep saying it until everyone believes me.

"Mmhmm, good luck with that." Her phone rings and she turns away, leaving me alone. Evan and Vickie return about an hour later with Evan still chatting nonstop and making plans that include Vickie. In his mind, we're going to pick up right where we left off, and he's right. There are no other options.

While she ignores me from across the room, I text her.

Me: I love you

I add a string of hearts.

Me: I've missed you so much
Me: I hate that you're so close to me but feel so far away
Me: I'm sorry for hurting you. I'll never do that again.

While Evan talks, she pulls out her phone. She reads

the texts and puts the phone away. She doesn't look up at me or respond.

Two hours later, the rest of her family finally arrive. She runs into her stepmother's arms, and her father wraps his arms around them. Tara and Alan join in, and the family holds each other.

Dr. A-hole returns and gives an update.

"She's doing better, but her blood pressure is still higher than we'd like. We're going to keep her in the ICU tonight, but she should be in a regular room by tomorrow. I'm going to ask that she only have a couple more visitors today." Alan and Tara decide to go, but they can only go one at a time for a few minutes. Alan goes first.

Tara drags Vickie into a corner, and they talk in hushed voices. I step closer, doing my best to hear them, but Vickie pulls Tara out of the waiting room. Once outside, Tara grabs Vickie's face and Vickie says something I can't make out. Tara takes her in a hug. Whatever it is, I'm sure it's not about their mother. There's a look in Vickie's eyes that wasn't there before. She's afraid, but there's more than that.

"Did you know Vickie was coming back to the U.S.?" I ask Ethan.

"No one knew."

"Something's going on with her." I watch through the glass as the sisters hug. Alan returns and Tara goes. She comes back ten minutes later.

The family decides to go home since Alicia is not allowed any more visitors tonight. Tara invites everyone to dinner at her penthouse, and I tag along so the boys can see each other, but when I get there, Tara and Vickie are gone.

Me: Where are you, Queen Vee?

I get no response, but I know she's read the message.

"Where's your sister?" I ask Alan, but he shrugs and walks away, which is unlike him.

"You want to come watch some practices?" I make sure to ask loud enough for his father to hear. They look at each other, and I can tell they are wavering. "What? We can't be friends anymore?" I ask when they don't answer.

"You upset my daughter," John says. "Ask Bradford what happened last time someone upset one of my kids."

Ethan smirks. "He punched me in the eye."

"Look, I love Victoria. More than I've ever loved anyone, and I messed up. I pushed her away, but I'm never going to give up on her or us. Come on, Taylors." I put an arm around John and Alan's shoulders. "I love you guys too."

Cheryl approaches and gently pats my face. She smiles sweetly, and I know I've got at least one Taylor in my corner. "Talk to him, John," Cheryl says. "Make him understand." John eyes me, but he does what his wife says. He gestures for me to follow him into Ethan's office. Once I get there, I close the door behind us.

"What you did? The way you left, that was the worst thing you can do to someone who already has abandonment issues. I don't know if Vickie told you anything about her mother, but Alicia left us. Just left while the kids were in school, and I was at work. They were devastated. She was a good mom until then. Vickie has never quite healed from that. She puts everyone but me, her siblings, and Cheryl at arm's length, but she let you in."

"And then I abandoned her." I sit in a chair and hang my head.

"Look, I know you were dealing with a lot. Losing a championship and getting injured, but all you had to do was let her be there for you. You promised her this amazing summer, and you took off and left her here. She took that as a rejection. She's done everything in her life not to be rejected by another person. She only trusts a few people, and she let her guard down with you. It's going to take work on your part, Colt. She's got her walls up ten miles high."

Those words stay with me while I wait for her to return. She comes into the apartment an hour later, looking downright frantic. She runs away from me before I can get to her.

"Leave her alone," Tara tells me. "Just give her a little space."

"What is going on with her? I know it's more than just your mother."

"That's for Vickie to tell you, not me." She nudges her head toward Alan, and the two of them go upstairs after their sister.

FIFTY-THREE

Colt

She never comes back downstairs. Tara fixes her a tray and takes dinner to her, but I'm not allowed upstairs. I reluctantly leave after a few hours. After giving Evan a bath, I read him a book. He falls asleep halfway through the story, and I tiptoe out of his room. The apartment has never looked so empty. She's so far away, but she belongs here with us. John's words stay with me for the next few hours. If I was a drinker, I'd be imbibing right now.

I fall into a restless sleep, tossing and turning the entire night. It's Saturday, and I'm grateful that Evan doesn't have school today. There's no way I can fake it and pretend to make polite conversation with the other parents. I roll to my side, too depressed to get out of bed, and hope Evan sleeps in. It's raining, and there's a text message canceling today's soccer game.

My phone vibrates, but I ignore it. It becomes alive with messages. Hoping it's Vickie trying to get in touch with me, I pick it up. There are several missed calls from my mother and Charlie but none from Victoria. Just as I'm about to toss my phone down, a Twitter alert about me comes through.

I almost don't open it, but something tells me to. There are several pictures of Vickie and Tara. I know they're from yesterday. I remember what Vickie was wearing. There's a picture of them in a drugstore, but the next picture zooms in on something Vickie is holding. I almost drop the phone when I see a home pregnancy test. The next picture shows the two sisters walking into the bathroom inside the same drugstore. The next few shows them walking toward the door. Vickie is noticeably upset. I enlarge the picture and zoom in on her face. She's crying. There are several pictures of them in the street showing Tara hugging a distraught Vickie.

I can't believe I've been so stupid. Of course, that's why she's looked so haggard and worn. How could I not put it together before this? All the signs have been there all along. She's clearly having a rough first trimester. It was the same way with Kelsey, but unlike Vickie, Kelsey couldn't wait for me to know. In fact, she went to Mama first and the two of them told me together. It's like she knew Mama had a hold over me and she would want us to be married. It didn't hurt that Kelsey cried and said all she wanted was for us to be a family.

It worked for Kelsey. She got what she wanted, but Vickie is completely different. Vickie had to come into this relationship kicking and screaming, and she doesn't need to trap a man with a baby. No, I bet she thinks she's the one who is trapped now. Victoria Taylor believing she's trapped will gnaw her own arm off to get free.

Maybe she was never going to tell me. Maybe she has no intentions of having my baby. That thought is like an icy hand around my heart. I don't think. I jump out of the bed, and I track her phone to this building. She's still upstairs.

I open Evan's door, and he's still in a deep sleep, and I

realize I can't leave him here by himself. My phone vibrates and it's Mama. Another call comes in from Charlie, but I ignore them both. I know they've seen it.

As I think of a plan, my front door opens.

"Mr. Colt," Myra says. "Did you get my texts? I left my wallet here yesterday. At least I hope I did," she prattles. She limps into the kitchen, and I've never been so happy to see her. I approach her and kiss both her cheeks, surprising her. She giggles like a schoolgirl and waves me away.

"Myra, can you stay here until I get back in case Evan wakes up. I won't be long."

She nods absentmindedly as she looks around. She finds her wallet on the counter and waves it around before opening the pantry and wrapping her apron around herself. "Take your time. I'll wait out the rain." Relieved, I run back to my room and brush my teeth. I don't bother changing out of the shorts and t-shirt I slept in.

Me: Can I come up?

Ethan texts back a few seconds later with a thumbs up. I'm in his penthouse less than five minutes later.

"Victoria!" I yell, walking past Ethan. "Victoria." I take the stairs two at a time even though I have no idea where she is.

"Colt," Ethan says from behind me. "I thought you were bringing Evan up for breakfast. Listen—"

"Victoria! Where are you?" I yell again. "How could you not tell me you're pregnant with my baby? That's my baby too, and if you think—"

I open the doors along the way, too frantic to think straight.

"Colt," Ethan yells behind me. "I think you need to stop and—"

A door opens and John and Cheryl step out.

"What the hell did you just say, Colt?" John steps in front of me, preventing me from going any further. "Did you just announce that you got my daughter pregnant?" If I was thinking, I'd have kept my mouth shut. I never would have barged in here. I would have waited and found her at home. I would have hugged her and told her how happy I am, and how much I want us to be a family, but that Colt isn't here.

This is a man who's messed up the best thing that's ever happened to him. This is a man who knows that baby inside of her was conceived in love, and given half the chance I will win her back. This is my chance.

I walk past John, almost knocking him over in the process. I open the door next door to his bedroom and almost collide with Vickie. She looks worse than she did yesterday. Her coloring is off and she's holding the robe over her body as if to shield herself from me.

"What the hell is going on here?" She ties the sash around her. "Colt, not now, okay. Just don't." She turns her back on me, but I grasp her shoulders and spin her around.

"Get your hands off my sister." Alan rushes in and pushes me away. I can easily grab him and force him out of the room, but even in my frantic state, I know putting my hands on Vickie's twin would be a horrible mistake. I step back and hold both hands up.

"I have no problems with you, Alan, but this is between me and your sister. I only want to talk to Vickie." I take a step around him and address the woman I love. "I know, Victoria." Her mouth opens in surprise. She looks around like a trapped animal. Her father approaches us, crosses his arms, and waits.

"Shut up, Colt," she whispers. "This is not the time. Please."

"You heard her. Leave," Alan says, but I ignore him and take a step closer to her.

"Not the time? You're pregnant with my baby and didn't tell me. You don't get to say that this isn't the right time. I was with you for hours yesterday. God, I feel like such an idiot. You were green and obviously pukin', and I kept checkin' your temperature like a fool." She walks around me, out of the room and I follow behind her. She steps into a bathroom and slams the door in my face, but I push it open before she can lock it.

"What's all the yelling?" Tara comes running down the hall. She quickly reads the room and steps between me and her sister while the rest of the family looks on.

"Vickie, is that true? Are you pregnant?" John asks.

Vickie flares her nostrils and looks around the room. I can hear her shallow breaths. She's not done fighting me yet. "Colt, for once in your life, will you shut the hell up and leave? I'm not ready to talk about this right now. And where the hell is Evan? You know better than to leave him alone so you can come up here and harass me over stuff that's none of your damn business."

"That's my baby. That's my business." I point at her belly to make myself clear.

She takes a deep breath and says, "It's okay, Tara." Tara steps from between us but she doesn't leave. The entire family stands and watches.

Vickie takes a few slow steps and gets in my face. "Are you done?" She points a finger and glares at me. "Are you done giving me orders on what to do with *my* body? Are you done announcing to the entire world that I'm pregnant? Something I've only just confirmed yesterday, by the way, but thanks for taking it upon yourself to tell my family. Was it too much for you to treat me like a human being and give me some time to get used to it before you bulldozed your way in here? Maybe I wanted to be the one to tell my parents, but you had to come and take that from me, didn't you?" I open my mouth to defend myself, but she puts her palm to my face. "Shut the hell up."

It's my turn to look around like a crazed animal while everyone looks on. Her father narrows his eyes at me, walks to Vickie's side and puts a protective arm around her.

"I think you better leave," John says to me.

"I'm not going anywhere—" I begin.

"The hell you're not," he says.

"Not yet, Dad." Vickie extricates herself from him and steps forward. "I don't want to see you. I don't want to talk to you. I'll have my lawyer contact you. You give her the name of your attorney, and we'll work out a custody agreement. I don't want any contact with you again until this baby is born. You will be notified when that happens, but until then, I call the show. I run this," I say, gesturing to my body. "If you have something to say, relay it to your attorney." She walks past me, out of the bathroom, and disappears down the hall.

"Evan is always welcome here, but you're not," Tara says. She shakes her head in disgust. "Ethan, can you please get him out of here? Otherwise, I won't be responsible for my actions."

FIFTY-FOUR

Vickie

Eight hours later, I still haven't calmed down. I had to stuff down my anger at Colt. I didn't have time to be angry this morning. When Ethan took him away, I threw up for a full twenty minutes. Over ginger tea and dry toast, I confirmed what Colt so rudely announced to my family. Everyone was quiet around the breakfast table. Everyone but Vincent, who had no idea what was going on. He was only interested in talking to Alan. After breakfast, we all went back to the hospital to visit mother. She's out of the ICU and in a private room until she's discharged tomorrow. Dad and the evil one wanted me to spend the night with them after our day in the hospital, but I want space and time to think without everyone hovering over me.

Colt's calls and texts so much, I turn my phone off. This is the first time I've been alone since yesterday, and all I want is a hot shower before I crawl into my bed and sleep for the next twelve hours. Or at least until I wake to throw up. But I did plenty of that today already. Hopefully this little nugget will give me a break until morning.

"Do you promise to let me sleep?" I ask my stomach as I

rub it. "You're going to keep me on my toes, aren't you, nugget?"

I had suspected I was pregnant for the past month. I had a period once since I left for Mexico, and that was just spotting. Looking back, it wasn't a period at all. It wasn't hard to get out of my contract. I was teaching at a religious, private school. It would not be a good look to have a pregnant, unmarried teacher, so they happily let me go when I implied I was pregnant. I was still in denial and hoped it was just stress, but when the vomiting started, I knew what it was, even though I didn't confirm it until I had my sister with me.

After a steaming hot shower, I decide I'm going to put Colt out of my mind for now. Tomorrow, I'll find a good family lawyer so that we can do everything by the book. Right now, I'm not ready to deal with the emotional side of everything. I'm not ready to think about this morning's ugly scene and how betrayed I feel by his actions.

If he knew me at all, he'd have known that was the worst way he could have approached this. He would have known that was something we needed to discuss in private, but maybe he doesn't care about me. He only cares about what he needs, but whatever he thinks, I'm the one who is pregnant. He's going to have to do this my way, but that's a fight for another day. Right now, all I want is to sleep.

I CLOSE MY EYES AND WILL MYSELF BACK TO SLEEP, BUT the pounding on the door gets louder.

"Victoria!" Boom! Boom! Boom! "Let me in."

If I had a gun, I would shoot Colt Chastain in the face and bury his body in Central Park, kidnap Evan and raise him as my own. He bangs on the door again, and I pull the covers off. It's barely eight o'clock in the morning, which means I slept all night. I grab my robe and walk briskly to the door. I yank it open, ready to confront him, but my stomach does something funny and bile rises to my throat. I turn and run to the bathroom, tripping and almost falling along the way.

I kneel and my stomach contents go into the toilet. Most of them anyway. Some hit the toilet seat and slide down to the floor. I haven't eaten much at all in the past week. I can't stand the sight of food and most smells upset me, but the little broth I had last night comes back up, and the bile burns the back of my throat.

I hear his footsteps into the bathroom, and I wave my hand behind me. "Out!" I yell. For once, he does as he's told and closes the door behind him. It takes twenty minutes for me to stop heaving. I hop in the shower after and spend extra time brushing my teeth. Even the peppermint in the toothpaste makes me nauseous, but I manage to keep the rest of my stomach contents inside.

He's standing outside the bathroom and leaning against the wall when I step out. I ignore him, go to my room and lock the door behind me. After putting on a pair of yoga pants and a plain long-sleeved t-shirt, I take a deep breath, steel my spine, and leave my room. If Colt Chastain wants a fight, he's about to get one. He might also get a punch in the face, so I hope he's ready for that.

I find him in the bathroom, mopping my mess. That angers me even more, but I walk to the kitchen and put on water for tea. He finds me a few minutes later.

"What are you doing here?" I ask. I cross my arms for fear I'll hit him. "Didn't I tell you yesterday that I don't want to see you? You know what? You can go fuck yourself,

Colton. Get the hell out of here. I don't need you to clean up after me." The kettle starts to whistle, but when I look inside my pantry, I realize I have no tea. "Fuck!" I slam the pantry shut and walk away.

"Where are you going?" I'm putting my shoes on as he approaches. "Come sit down so we can talk."

"I don't want to talk to you ever again. Didn't I tell you to have your lawyer call my lawyer?" As of yet, I have no lawyer. I've never needed one, but I'm sure I can find one quickly. A jaded female lawyer who's been divorced three times and hates men. I stand up straight and the room starts to spin. He catches me before I fall and carries me bridal style back to bed.

He sets me down gently and says, "I'm going to get you a doctor." He texts something on his phone, puts it down, and lifts a hand to my forehead to check my temperature. I swat his hand away, and he leans down to kiss my forehead. The tender movement shocks me, but I'm too nauseous to fight him right now.

"Can you get my phone? I'll just text my dad. You can go." He sighs loudly, puts his hands on his hips, and looks down at me.

"I'm here. I'm going to take care of you." He sits next to me and gently takes my hands. "It's only fair since I'm the one who did this to you." I look away from him, but when he tries to put my hands to his face, I pull them away. "Your hands are ice cold, Queen Vee." I will myself to not admit how much I've missed hearing that nickname. "And don't take this the wrong way because you're the most beautiful woman on earth, but you look awful. I'm worried about you."

I bristle at his words and finally look at his face. He probably looks worse than me. He hasn't shaved, his hair is a disaster of tangled curls. It's gotten so long, it reaches past his ears now.

"You're not worried about me. Not beyond me being an incubator for your baby, right?"

"Do you know how much I love you? If you did, you wouldn't say that."

I yank the covers off and hop off the bed but fall into his arms when the room starts to spin. He lifts me back onto the bed and sits next to me. "Please, don't try to get up again."

"Where's Evan? You should be with him," I tell him.

"Mama and Charlie got here last night. They are with him." My eyes narrow at him. I can see the worry and concern on his face, and I know it's for me, but I'm not ready to admit that yet.

"Why are they here?"

"They know. They saw the same social media posts I did, and they wanted to be here for me. For us. Look, I'm sorry about yesterday. I saw the posts and I reacted without thinkin' and confronted you. I should—"

"You should have approached me like a human being, Colt."

"I thought you were going to make certain decisions without me," he admits.

"Yeah, like what decisions?" I press. I know what he was thinking, but I want to hear him say the words. When he doesn't, I say, "So you thought you'd take that choice away from me by telling my entire family. If you think you can try to control me, you don't know me."

He stands and sighs, probably doing his best to gather his thoughts. "I would never try and control you or tell you what to do. I fell in love with you the way you are. You're perfect to me, Queen Vee. Perfect. All I want is to have you back in my life. I want things to go back to how they were before that last game. You can add yesterday to a long list of things I want to fix, but I'm only human." He sits next to me and takes my hands. "Give me a chance to prove myself to you."

I open my mouth to tell him that I already did that, and he failed miserably, but he puts a hand to my lips. "I know. One chance. I had my one chance, but I'm begging for another. We're having a baby, Queen." One of his hands finds its way to my stomach. "A baby. We made him or her together." He caresses me. "We created this baby in love, and I want us to raise it together. As a family." His phone vibrates, and he picks it up, walks over to the window, and carries on a conversation.

There's never been a part of me that's wanted to be a single mother. I didn't even know if I wanted to be a parent until I suspected I was pregnant. All I wanted to do was come home and go through the pregnancy here, but that still didn't stop me from freaking out once it was confirmed. I spent that night thinking of ways I was going to tell Colt, yet social media took that away from me.

"Okay. I'll get her there." He ends the call and says, "Our team doctor is married to an OBGYN. She's going to meet us at her office so she can examine you." I start to sit up to argue, but he puts a hand up. "Look, you're not well, and I'm worried about you. About you both. Please." Another wave of nausea hits and I run to the bathroom. He doesn't stay out this time. He leans down and strokes my back while I dry heave. Once I'm done and I rinse my mouth, he picks me up and helps me with my coat. I can barely put on my sneakers, and he helps me with that too before he carries me to his waiting car that drives us to the doctor's office across the street from New York Presbyterian.

FIFTY-FIVE

Colt

SHE IS ADMITTED TO THE HOSPITAL. SHE CAN'T KEEP any food down. Dante has to pull over twice so she can throw up. Once she is examined, she is diagnosed with hyperemesis gravidarum which the doctor explains is extreme nausea and vomiting during the first trimester. I spend the next two days in the hospital with Vickie. Her family is in and out, often visiting her and her mother. Alicia is discharged the day after Vickie is admitted, and instead of going home, she spends the day with her daughter.

Between me, her family, and mine, she is never alone. She's told to eat small meals and is prescribed anti-nausea medication. We don't have any more fights, and she doesn't ask me to leave. Not one single time. She let me listen in when the doctors come to examine her. She let Mama visit with her, and even allows Charlie into the room. We get our first ultrasound picture, and the entire family cheers when I show it to them. Tara forgets she's mad at me and hugs me but quickly pulls away. This baby is probably the size of a pea, but he or she has so much love already.

Everyone is gone now. It's just us. Her coloring is back to normal as is her breathing. She hasn't thrown up in hours, and she's in pajamas Tara brought for her. She looks away when I walk in, but I sit next to her.

"You should go home to Evan." Always thinking about my son. Even the first night we met, she wanted to know why I was out and not at home with him.

"He's so busy getting spoiled by Mama and Charlie, I'm probably the last person he wants home right now. I might tell him no." I sit on the edge of the bed. It's in a private room in a part of the hospital few know exists.

I reach over and take her hand. It's warm. Unable to help myself, I lift it and put it to my cheek. She leaves it there, but only for a split second, before putting it down.

"Well, I'm tired," she says, clearing her throat.

"I want you to come home with me when you get discharged. I want to take care of you. I want us to get back what we had before I screwed it up. I want you at my games when the season starts. I want to be at all your doctor's appointments. I want to be the man you need, and in return, I will never, ever abandon you again. No matter what. No matter what happens, you will always be my queen. I'm sorry that I let you down before. I was selfish. I was only thinking of myself." She looks down at me, and our eyes lock, but she looks away. I don't say more. I don't expect an answer tonight, but I want to show her that I'm not going anywhere. I sit on the sofa next to her bed. It's a pullout, but I know I'm much too tall for it.

"You don't have to stay. I told you, I'm feeling better."

"I'm not leaving this hospital until you do. We're walking out together, and every single day I'm going to be the man you fell in love with."

She shakes her head and looks away, but I take her not

telling me to leave as a victory. I'd give anything to lie next to her and hold her in my arms, but she needs the bed, and we're not there yet.

"I still don't love you," I say and hope and pray she will say it back.

"Don't." My heart breaks at the rejection, but I don't let that stop me.

"I don't. I don't think about you either. I don't want to lie next to you in that hospital bed and hold you." I hold her hands and wait.

She sighs like a woman with the weight of the world on her shoulders. A weight I put there. "I'm not ready for that yet, Colt." She didn't say the words back, but I still sigh in relief.

"Yet? I can wait, Queen Vee. As long as you don't tell me you don't love me anymore."

She continues to stare ahead. A lone tear rolls down her cheeks, and I swipe it away with my thumb. "If only I could turn my feelings off. Loving you is not something I can control at will. As much as I wish I could, I can't."

FIFTY-SIX

Colt

"Can I talk to y'all for a minute?" I ask John, Cheryl, Alicia, Alan, and Tara.

"Yes. I believe we have some things we want to say to you too," Cheryl says. Her soft brown eyes turn on me, and she gives me a sad smile and a subtle nod.

"We sure do," Tara says with a lot more hostility.

I haven't left the hospital since Vickie was admitted, and I won't until she's discharged, which will be sometime today according to her doctor. I gesture for them to follow me, and we go into a small room a few feet down the hall. The five of them lean against the wall and cross their arms. I don't know if they're aware of how hostile they look. Maybe I should have Mama and Charlie here for backup. I lean against the opposite wall while I gather my thoughts. The speech I've practiced in my head disappears. I must have practiced it one hundred times last night while Vickie slept, but now I can't remember a word of it.

"I'm sorry about how you found out. I shouldn't have confronted Vickie like that in front of everyone. I want you to know that I love her and intend to make things right. Obviously, we still have some things to work on, but I'm—"

"You're damn right you shouldn't have confronted her that way," Tara says. She crosses the room and points a manicured finger in my face. "You're probably why she's in the hospital right now with your caveman attitude and your assumption that it's your right to tell her what to do. Let me tell you something—"

John takes Tara's hand and says, "Let the man talk, Tara. He's trying to apologize."

"He can take his apology and shove it." Tara crosses her arms and walks as far away from me as possible.

"You hurt my twin," Alan says. "She's tough, but she's human, Chastain. She let you in and you disappointed her. And if you think you can control her, you're an idiot."

I hold my hands up and say, "I don't want to control Victoria, not that I ever could. I'm not that man, but I'm human too, and I make mistakes just like everyone else. Give me a chance to fix them."

"So, fix them," Alan practically yells. "Why do you need to talk to us about it?" He looks at his watch and says, "I need to see my sister before my flight to Boston. Get on with this, Chastain."

"Okay, I'll make this quick. I'm asking you guys not to offer her to come home with you." I look at John, Cheryl, and Tara when I say that. I know there's no way Vickie would go home with Alicia. She's not a source of comfort. Their expressions go from not friendly to hostile, but I speak before they can lay into me. "I want her to come home with *me*. She's pregnant with my baby, and I want to be the one to take care of her. Please."

They look around at each other and seem to have a conversation with just their eyes. It's amazing how close and in sync the Taylors are with each other, especially the siblings.

"It's not unreasonable, darlings," Cheryl says. Always the voice of reason. I smile at her, and she smiles back. "We're all human here," she reminds everyone.

"I won't tell her no if she asks," John says. "That's the best I can do."

"Neither will I," Tara replies, still as hostile as ever.

"Fair enough," I tell them.

Alan doesn't say another word to me, but he goes to see Vickie before he leaves for the airport. Alicia follows behind her son, but she gives me a look full of loathing before she leaves.

After about an hour, eager to see Vickie, I go to her room. Alicia is still there so I lean against the door and watch.

"I hope this baby is ready for three grandmothers," Alicia says. She's sitting on the edge of the bed and runs a hand through Vickie's hair. "I thought Tara would be the first to have a baby, but life is full of surprises, huh?" She lets out a carefree laugh and rubs Vickie's stomach.

John, Cheryl, and Tara follow behind me into the room.

"Mother, you should go home and rest. I'll be okay, and I'm looking forward to leaving this hospital bed. I'll go home with Dad and the evil one." The room goes deathly quiet, and the Taylors all look around.

"Queen Vee, I want you to come home with me, baby, please. Let me take care of you."

"It's not a bad idea, darling," Cheryl says. She sits on the side of the bed and takes one of Vickie's hands. "Sometimes in life, we have to open our hearts and give someone a second chance." She presses the hand to her face. "Especially when they own up to their mistakes and want to do everything to make things right." She leans in and whispers something in Vickie's ear that I can't hear.

She looks around the room and looks into my eyes. She holds my stare, and for this moment, I'd give up my entire fortune to be able to read her mind. I mouth please.

Alicia whispers something in Vickie's other ear, and whatever she says makes her tear up, but she nods and says, "Okay." That one word is all I need. This is my chance, and I'm not going to let it slip away.

"I'm going to call Mama and see what she has going on for dinner. Everyone is welcome." I excuse myself and walk down the hall to call home. I give her a list of things that Vickie can't eat or smell, and she tells me out of the two of us, she's the only one who's been pregnant and that she has it under control.

I step into the bathroom and check my reflection in the mirror. I don't think I've slept five hours in the past three days, but I haven't felt this good in months. Vickie is coming home with me, and we're having a baby. That's something we didn't plan, but when the woman you're in love with is pregnant with your child, there's no better feeling in this world.

After splashing cold water on my face, I leave the bathroom with a pep in my step that wasn't there before. I know my physical therapy will be rough tomorrow, but now my career is not the only thing I won't be losing. I'm so eager to get to my woman that I don't question why her family is in the hallway and not the room. Tara looks around wildly when she sees me, and I know instantly that something is wrong.

"What happened?" I ask. "Are they okay?" I turn to run into the room, but Cheryl puts a hand on my wrist.

"They're fine. Gerald is there, and Vickie asked us to leave so they can talk alone."

It takes a few seconds for her words to sink in. When they do, I snatch my wrist away and sprint down the hall. I get in there in time to hear him say, "I'm not raising another man's baby, Victoria. Terminate it and I'll forget this ever happened." I grab him by the back of his scrubs and push him against the wall, ready to beat him within an inch of his life.

"Colt, no!" Vickie yells, and I step back. The last thing I want to do is upset her more than I already have. "Gerald, leave. You were never in any danger of raising another man's baby. He or she already has a father. Get the hell out of here."

"Yes, leave." Alicia steps in and approaches Gerald. "Right now."

I pull him by his collar and drag him out of the room and down the hall. He tries to pull away, but he's no match for me. I push him inside an empty bathroom and close the door. Before he can utter a single word, I punch him in the stomach. He doubles over and falls to his knees. "I hope I never have to see you again, but if I do, I will not hesitate to beat you within an inch of your pathetic life." I leave him gasping for air and walk back to Victoria.

FIFTY-SEVEN

Vickie

Colt's apartment smells like a combination of fresh bread and vanilla. I don't know what Mary Leigh is cooking, but it smells great and doesn't upset my stomach. It still feels unsettled, but the intense nausea and aversion to smells have diminished. I'm barely through the door when she engulfs me in a hug, squeezing me to her bosom. When she lets me go, Evan jumps into my arms, and I stumble back at the sudden assault.

"Vickie, Uncle Charlie wants to watch Annie, but he said we had to wait for you." Colt takes him from me and messes his hair. Charlie hugs me next, but our bodies never fully make contact. He taps my back with his hand, almost as if he's afraid I'll break.

"She's not made of glass, Charlie. Come sit down, honey. I made some ginger tea that will help your tummy." She hugs me again and says, "I'm so glad we're all together."

She made three different soups and homemade bread. I had bone broth and chicken noodle. Colt hovered and buttered my bread, never once taking his eyes off me. After dinner, while he cleans, I watch Annie with Evan and

Charlie. I let them do the singing and dancing this time, but it's nice to have normalcy after months of uncertainty. Despite the very loud and very bad singing, my eyes get heavy. Strong arms carry me and gently lay me down on the bed. I sigh when I feel the soft down comforter covering me.

I wake up hours later in Colt's dark bedroom. He's not in the bed next to me. He's on the couch, reading a book. I chuckle when I see the title.

"You're reading a cookbook?" I ask.

He rushes over to the bed. "Are you okay? Do you need to throw up?" He touches my forehead. "Let me carry you."

I shake my head and he steps back. I get up on my own and use the bathroom. He's standing right behind the door when I step back out. He helps me in bed and climbs in next to me. I usually cuddle to his side or let him spoon me. Despite our extreme height difference, we've always been a perfect fit. Now I don't know what to do, so I make sure our bodies don't touch.

"I'm glad you're here," he whispers. "I know you haven't agreed for us to be together, but you have to know that's what I want." I roll my eyes in the dark room. I do know that. He's made that clear to me every day for months. "When I went to Alabama, I—"

"When you went to Alabama without me," I correct him.

"When I went to Alabama without you, it wasn't meant to hurt you. I was in a bad place. I didn't know if I'd have a career, and I was miserable to be around. And frankly, I was embarrassed. I'm used to winnin'. I'm sorry for pushin' you away. I really am. All I can do is promise that will never happen again."

I don't speak while I try to digest his words. He sounds sincere. The truth is, I've not only missed Colt, but I missed

Evan too. I even missed Mary Leigh and looked forward to her calls.

"But you don't win every single time. You haven't won every game you've ever played. Truth is, you pushed me away repeatedly. We talked every day, and every day you put me off. Every day was another rejection, and I don't do well with rejection or abandonment. I don't forgive that easily." Then I sigh and say, "But I don't want to raise this baby alone."

He turns to his side, and I do the same.

"Please, Queen, don't say you'll give me another chance only because you're pregnant. I want you to come back because you want me. Because you love me."

"I do love you, and I do want you. If there was no baby, I would still take you back." I can feel him exhale in relief next to me. "But now I don't trust you. Not with my heart. Remember in the beginning you told me you never had what we had? I didn't either because I never allowed myself to open up enough to have that. I did with you."

I can see him thinking about the weight of my words by the moonlight seeping through the blinds.

"And I let you down," he says, and I nod.

"And I know you're sorry," I say quickly. "I don't need you to apologize again. I believe you when you say you're sorry. I believe you were in a bad place, but I wanted to be there with you. Truth is, I love what we had, and I miss it."

"Will you give me a chance to earn back your trust?" He grabs both my hands and brings them to his cheeks. "Please."

I nod and he inches closer. Before he can kiss me, I say, "But I don't want a relationship in the public eye. If we're going to try again, I want it to stay between us. At least for a while. I have this pregnancy to deal with, and I don't need anyone else breathing down our necks. I'll tell my family in my own time."

"Okay, but I can't control the media. I can't control pictures being taken of us, but everything else, we'll do it your way. Thank goodness for Wakowski and his scandal."

Two days after the pictures of me came out, three pregnant women went public claiming Wakowski is the father of their baby. Everyone forgot about me and focused on him.

Colt caresses my cheek, moves closer, and says, "Just promise me you'll give this a real chance."

For the first time in weeks, I smile. The smile turns into a low chuckle.

"Remember what I told you. Vickie does what Vickie wants. If I wasn't going to give you a real chance, I wouldn't be here. We also need to be sensitive to Evan's feelings."

He nods and closes the sliver of space between us. "We'll go at your pace. Whatever pace you want, as long as it leads you here permanently, and Evan will be thrilled to have a little brother or sister." He caresses my cheek. "I'm sorry for chasin' you away." He leans so close, our lips almost touch. "And I'm sorry for the scene I made when I found out. I was so afraid of losin' you." He caresses my stomach. "Please, forgive me for that too."

"I forgive you, but don't ever do that again. You have to trust me too. I spent that entire night thinking of ways to tell you."

He leans in and gives me a tender kiss, and I realize how much I've missed being with him this way. "I don't understand how you can want to kiss me after seeing me at my worst these past few days."

"Easy, Queen Vee. That's because I love you."

FIFTY-EIGHT

Vickie

"So, you're not back together?" Tara asks.

It's been two weeks since I was discharged from the hospital. I'm still nauseous and throw up at least once a day, but the medication helps and I'm able to function. I'm even working again at the school. One of the other English teachers is going through cancer treatment, and I was asked to step in. Colt was concerned, but the doctor had no objections, and I was bored out of my mind.

"But you're living with him," Alan reminds me. He's been coming to New York every weekend it seems. He says as long as he doesn't need to be in a classroom, he can work from anywhere.

"I'm not living with him. I spent the night at my place just last night?" I don't tell them that Colt came home with me. Evan stayed home with Mary Leigh and we had a night to ourselves. "Okay, we're trying, but not labeling anything right now. I've agreed to give him another chance, but we're keeping it private. This stays here."

It's hard to be with someone who is famous. I love my privacy and being with Colt kind of takes that away from me, but for the past two weeks, there haven't been any pictures of us, mainly because we've been either at his place or mine.

"Dad's gonna be thrilled. He asked me last night if he had to stop liking Colt forever," Alan says. "He said he didn't want to but would pick you if he had to." I pretend to be offended, but part of me is happy that my father likes Colt so much.

"And what about you guys?" I look at my siblings and best friends. I don't need them to like Colt, but I want them to. I don't want a relationship to come between us.

"Relationships are work, and he was lost when you were gone and frantic when you were in the hospital. I believe he loves you, so if you're willing to forgive him, so can I," Tara says.

"And you?" I ask my twin.

"As long as you're happy, I'm happy. Otherwise, I'm gonna kick his ass."

I look at Tara and we both smirk. "Boy, please. You know you can't fight," I remind him. I reach over and take their hands. "Thank you," I say to them.

Tara's housekeeper comes and clears the plates away, and I check my watch and sigh. "I really don't want to do this, but I'm working on being more forgiving. It's supposed to help me heal," I say with an eye roll.

It's our first session of therapy with our mother. She had her doctor call me, and she strongly suggested we all come for a group session. I agreed. I could have lost my mother. Despite everything, I love her and I want no regrets.

"I'm fucking sick and tired of therapy," Tara says. "I already go with Ethan and his ex-wife, and now our mother. I don't know if I'll have the patience for our mother if she cries."

FIFTY-NINE

Colt

While Vickie meets with her siblings and mother, I leave physical therapy and head to her family home in Sugar Hill. I can only hope that she doesn't come over here after her appointment with Alicia. I know she went in with an open mind, but I also know it's not something she was looking forward to, but her absence freed me to do this. Dante lets me out, and I tell him I'll text him when I'm ready. They're expecting me, and the door swings open before I get a chance to knock.

After turning down Cheryl's offer for food, the three of us sit at the kitchen table. Between Mama and Myra, there's more than enough to eat at home. Before Charlie left, he was cooking too, but he had to get back to work on the restaurant. Rosalie has agreed to stay with him until Mama returns.

"I just want to apologize again for my behavior after the last game and for what happened after I found out Vickie was pregnant. I'm goin' to do everything to make sure she has a healthy and safe pregnancy." I clear my throat, wanting to say so much more but can't. Victoria wants to keep our relationship quiet for now without family members breathing down our throats.

I want to do things her way, but I'm also dying for the entire world to know that we're back together.

"What are your intentions with my daughter, Colton? I thought you said you loved her, but she's pregnant and I have no idea what your plans are."

"I assure you that I do." Cheryl puts a hand on his arm, and his hostility wanes but only slightly. "But I'm doing this on her terms. She knows I'm ready to pick up where we left off, but I know she wants me to prove myself first. I'm willin' to do that."

I think I've done a good job of answering his questions. He stares at me, and I don't shrink or look away. "And then what?" he asks.

And then I put a ring on her finger, and you walk her down the aisle. We buy a bigger house and fill it with more children, but I can't tell anyone that right now.

"Let them find their way, John," Cheryl says, saving me. "If Vickie wants him to prove himself, that's what he needs to do. At least she's giving him the chance to do that." Cheryl reaches over and rests a hand on mine. I lift it and put it to my lips. After Vickie, she's definitely my favorite Taylor.

"Thank you, Cheryl," I whisper.

"Fine, but you need to prove yourself quick or you and I are going to have a serious problem," John says.

THE REST OF THE CONVERSATION WITH JOHN AND Cheryl was a lot less combative. The discussion turned from me and Vickie to my knee and my plans to play this season which is set to begin in less than two weeks. My knee feels good, and I've been performing well at practice, so my doctors and physical therapists have cleared me to play.

Me: Where are you?

I see the three bubbles show up and her message pops up.

Queen Vee: Headed home

My heart sinks. We didn't talk about her coming back here. I assumed she would since we spent the night at her place yesterday. It's Friday, and Evan has a birthday party tomorrow that I promised I would take him to, so we need to be here, otherwise, we'd go to her.

Me:How was therapy?
Queen Vee:Good. I'll tell you about it when I get there. Going to get clothes. Cynthia just pulled up.

I fist pump the air.

Me: Are you feeling okay?

The nausea is controlled with medication, but she gets sick at least once per day.

Queen Vee: Was sick earlier, but fine now. Let me pack so I can see you soon.

It takes two hours until I hear my door open. I practically tackle her, lifting her off her feet and kissing her senseless.

"I didn't miss you," I tell her.

"Me neither, but guess what?" I take her bag and her hand and walk into the bedroom. I try to contain my happiness when she puts her clothes in my closet. "I'm actually hungry."

I approach and rest my hands on her stomach. There's not much of a difference, but I'm familiar enough with her body to know the slight change. "That hasn't happened in a while." Eating has become a chore for her. She does it because she has to, but she hasn't enjoyed food in a long time. "Do you want to go out?" I pull out my phone, ready to make a reservation wherever she wants.

"Um, let's stay in." I sigh, disappointed. "I'll probably get sick again, and I'd rather stay here if that happens. And you know I like your place." She wraps her arms around me, gets on her toes, and I meet her halfway to kiss her. "I'd like to spend this Friday night with my guys. Where's Evan?"

"He's at a pizza party with the soccer team, so you're stuck with me for now. Come here." I pull her into my arms and feel her against me. "I love you," I whisper in her ear.

She pulls back and runs a hand through my hair.

"I love you too. And you need a haircut." Her fingers get tangled in my curls.

We walk to the kitchen, and while she warms up whatever Myra left in the fridge, I set the table in the kitchen. I go so far as to dim the lights, light candles, and pour sparkling apple cider in wine glasses.

"Myra is a saint," Vickie says. "She made me lemon chicken soup with dumplings, and yucky fish for you." She puts the perfectly plated food on the table. "Are you excited about playing again?" she asks. She smells the soup before putting a little in her mouth. She must find it acceptable because she takes another spoonful.

"I am." I take her hand and intertwine our fingers. "I'm looking forward to eating with you after each game. And I promise I won't shut you out when we lose." I put her hand to my lips and kiss it. "And whenever you can get to an away game, I'd love that too." I drop her hand and lay my free one on her stomach. "At least until you're too far along to travel."

She puts the spoon down and looks away as if deep in thought. My stomach drops and I put down my own fork.

"I want to talk to you about something," she says. I stop breathing and wait. "If the baby is a boy, I want to name him after my dad, John Phillip Taylor."

I'm so relieved, I let out a loud laugh at the table. "Darlin', any boy would be lucky to have that name, but it will be John Phillip Taylor Chastain." I rub her stomach. "And if it's a girl, I want to name her after Mama."

She rolls her eyes at me but grins. "We'll see. It's moot because it's a boy." She sticks her tongue out at me.

"When are we going to go public, Queen? I love our little bubble, but I want the world to know we're a family. And I want to marry you." I put my hand on her stomach again. I can't stop touching it. Knowing that a life we created together is in there does things to me.

"You are so demanding, Chastain. You know I'm not the marrying type."

It's me who rolls my eyes this time. "It's fine if you come into the marriage kickin' and screamin'. I'm used to it."

"Things are good. We're happy. We know we're together. Let's wait a little longer. I still get sick, and I don't want pictures taken of me yet. I want to enjoy our private life a little bit more."

"Okay." I lift her hand and kiss it. "I did agree to do this your way." She runs her fingers through my hair. "Though, you're going to give us away when you braid my hair for the first game."

"You're getting a haircut tomorrow but forget about that for now. How long until Evan comes home."

"A couple of hours."

She pushes her half-eaten bowl of soup away. "I feel really good right now, Chastain." She gets up and surprises me by sitting on my lap. Her hand goes inside my sweatpants next. "Do you know what I mean?"

I stand with her in my arms and run to the bedroom.

SIXTY

Vickie

He's lying between my legs, kissing the top of my breasts while we enjoy the afterglow of our lovemaking. I've been so sick that this is the first time since Atlanta that we've made love. That's probably when we conceived the baby, and as much of a surprise as it was, I wouldn't change it. I've loved it since I first suspected I was pregnant. I run my hand down Colt's sweaty back, enjoying the feel of him.

"How was therapy?" he asks as he kisses his way up before taking the spot next to me and pulling me closer.

We turn to face each other, and I intertwine our naked legs under the blanket. I shrug and say, "Meh."

He waits for me to say more, and when I don't, he says, "Can you expand on that, darlin'?"

I sigh as I gather my thoughts. "Mother cried the entire time. Tara lost her patience and yelled at her, threatening never to return if she can't get her shit together and speak. Alan held her hand and tried to make her feel better, and I stayed detached. The highlight was when she said she felt not only trapped being a wife and mother, but she was bored to death by it. And then she burst into tears."

He let out a long whistle into the bedroom. I inch closer to his naked body, ready to leave the unpleasant conversation behind. The room is dark and warm, and since I'm feeling so good now, all I want to do is be close to him.

"Next time will be better," he says.

"I don't want to go back. It was awful. This is to make her feel better, but I'll go. I've figured out that I've been punishing her all this time, and I built this wall around myself because I never want to be hurt like that again, but —" I run my hand across his chest.

"But?"

"If I continue to do that, I might miss out on this. And what we have is too good. I love you. I love Evan, and I love this baby too."

He grabs me and puts me on top of him. "That is everything I've always wanted to hear."

"I INVITED TILLY," I WHISPER TO TARA. WE BOTH LOOK over at Alan, but he's busy with the boys. He has Evan on his back and Vincent wrapped around one of his legs. "I didn't tell Alan, so shh." I put my finger to my lips. She winks back at me, but Ethan walks behind her, wraps an arm around her waist, and hands her a drink.

"Rat poison for my lady love." It's a purple liquid, which they've claimed as their signature drink.

"What? That's not fair," I hear Evan complain. He slides down Alan's back and runs to me. "Vickie, Alan says when Tara marries Vincent's dad, Alan's going to be his uncle. Can you marry my dad so Alan can be my uncle too?"

I look around the room at a loss for words. Tara lets out

a chuckle. Ethan crosses his arms and waits, and Vincent takes Evan's place on Alan's back.

"You both can call me Uncle Alan now," Alan says, and I elbow him in the ribs.

"But mine won't be real. Dad!" Evan waves Colt over. My dad overhears and joins us in the kitchen.

Tonight is Tara's birthday, and the penthouse is filled with family and friends. I'm reminded of how happy I am to be home. While I was in Mexico, my sister got engaged, and I wasn't there. The pregnancy brought me back, and it was exactly what I needed.

Things have finally leveled off. The nausea continues to be controlled if I take my medication. Colt and I are still in our bubble. I spend every night with him when he's home, continuing our tradition of eating together after his home games. I miss him when he's gone, and I even went to one of his away games, though I stayed in the hotel and watched him on television. We ate takeout together when he got back.

He hasn't missed a game, something I know he was concerned about, but his knee appears to be in great shape.

"What's goin' on?" he asks. He lifts Evan into his arms.

"Can you marry Vickie so Alan can be my uncle too?"

"Of all the reasons, I never considered Alan," Colt says.

"That's where you went wrong," Alan responds.

Colt does his best to hide his amusement but fails. He whispers something in Evan's ear then puts a finger to his own lips. "It's a secret," he whispers.

Whatever he says satisfies Evan, who jumps out of his father's arms and approaches Alan and Vincent. My phone vibrates with a text from Tilly. I ask Tara to follow me to the elevator, and a few seconds later, it opens. A server takes her coat, and I pull her into a group hug. She's in a dress with a red and black skirt, white top with black polka dots. She's wearing big glasses with black polka dots on the frame.

"I haven't seen you since you were twelve," Tara says and wraps her arms around Tilly's. "Let me introduce to you to everyone."

They nearly collide into Alan, who is running around chasing Evan and Vincent.

"Alan," Tara says. She catches my eye and we both smirk. "You remember Tilly, right?" Alan's eyes nearly bug out when he sees her, staring directly at her chest that is barely restrained in her top.

"Tilly?" he mutters. "Hello." He clears his throat. "Wow."

"Why is Alan looking at her like that? And why is his mouth hanging open?" Vincent asks. Alan abruptly shuts it. Cheryl comes and pulls Tilly away in her excitement to see her.

I give Tara a high-five and spot Colt. His Adam's apple bobs as he approaches, but my dad intercepts him, grabbing his attention. I narrow my eyes at him as one of the servers walks by and hands me a non-alcoholic drink. I sip it slowly while holding his stare. I take the cherry out the drink and bite on it slowly. He continues to watch me while he talks to my father. My breasts have almost doubled in size in the past month, and he can't keep his hands or eyes off them. He's been patient about keeping our relationship quiet, but I know he's getting restless. He wants us out in the public eye, and I know my days of privacy are numbered.

"Your father is about to faint," Cheryl says. "Colt invited him to watch the team practice tomorrow. As if the season tickets aren't enough."

Colt catches my eye again and winks.

"Lame," I say and walk away. I approach one of the food stations Ethan has set up in the kitchen. I'm still only eating small portions, and certain smells still set me off.

"Let me get you something," Mother says. "How about some soup." I nod at her and take a seat. Things with us have improved. I no longer avoid her calls, and we've had a couple of more sessions of therapy. She brings me a bowl of minestrone. She takes a seat next to me and rubs my stomach. There's only a small bump.

"I was thinking I want a Christmas picture with you kids this year. I mentioned it to Tara, and Vincent overheard. He's excited. He's so adorable." All I can think of is if Ethan and Vincent are included, Colt and Evan will be crushed if they're not. "Maybe you and Colt can work things out." She nudges my shoulder with hers. "I'm sorry about the Gerald thing. I thought that if I helped you guys get back together, I'd finally do something right by you. Believe it or not, I only wanted to help. But after what he said in the hospital, forget him."

I enjoy the soup, and for the first time in a long time, I enjoy my mother's company too. She rests her head on my shoulder and says, "I'm proud of you." The spoon stops halfway to my mouth. Unsure of what to do or say, I remain frozen. She's never said those words to me before. I don't think she's said it to any of us. "You always remain true to yourself. You stand up for what you believe in, and you love with your whole heart. Don't ever change." She runs a hand down my back, and I put my spoon down.

"Thank you, Mother." She kisses my cheek and gets up but returns moments later with a bottle of water.

With the party in full swing, I slip out of the penthouse and head down to Colt's apartment. He comes in right behind me, pins me to the wall, and kisses me.

"This top," he says, "has driven me crazy all night. Each time that bartender checked these out, I wanted to punch him." He rips the blouse in half, tossing the ripped pieces to the floor.

"You brute," I tell him. I jump into his arms and wrap my legs around him.

"I'll show you brute."

∼

Hours later, we sneak back into the penthouse. It's quiet and back to its pristine order.

"Go home," I say to him. "And I don't appreciate you ripping my blouse, you brute."

"I'm not ready to let you go yet. I'll get up and leave before anyone wakes up." When I don't agree, he raises both hands and says, "I promise."

I'm pretty sure my dad and Cheryl know we're together. They're probably waiting for me to tell them.

"What about my blouse?" I ask.

"I'm a possessive man, Victoria. These," Colt says, putting both hands on my breasts, "are mine."

"No part of this belongs to you," I say, gesturing at my body. I try to shove his hands away, but I'm no match for Colt. He snakes an arm around my waist, pulls my body against his, and savagely attacks my mouth.

He carries me upstairs into the guestroom where I take off my skirt and slide into bed wearing nothing but Colt's jersey. He strips down to his boxers and pulls me into his arms.

"I love you," he says against my temple.

"I love you too."

SIXTY-ONE

I TIGHTEN MY ARMS AROUND HER AND SPREAD MY PALM on her growing belly. It feels bigger than it did just yesterday. She mumbles something in her sleep, pokes out her butt, and presses it against me. I could slide inside of her. She's getting her sexual appetite back, and lately, it's been like a sex buffet. On the nights that I'm home, as soon as Evan goes to bed, she'll drag me to the bedroom and have her way with me. The second trimester is turning out to be my favorite one.

I hear a loud throat clearing, look up, and almost fall off the bed.

Cheryl Taylor and her husband are staring down at me. She's smiling, but he's scowling. I almost laugh. What more can I do? I've already gotten her pregnant.

"When you two are done pretending not to be together, come downstairs for breakfast. Everyone's awake," John says. Cheryl waves and drags her husband out.

"What happened?" Vickie mumbles. She sits up and rubs the sleep out of her eyes.

"We've been outed. Your dad and Cheryl have ordered

us to breakfast." I hop out of bed and send a text to my housekeeper, asking her to bring me a change of clothes.

"You were supposed to leave before everyone woke up." She stands and stretches, exposing her lower belly. It's definitely starting to show.

"My queen, my liege. Alas, I fell asleep with you in my arms." I do an exaggerated bow. "Our bubble has burst. There is nothing we can do about it. Let's shower and eat," I tell her, having had enough of keeping our relationship and our baby a secret. "It's time, baby."

She groans and says, "Fine. I'm too nauseous to fight with you right now." She takes my hand and drags me to the bathroom, where we share a shower.

When we emerge, my bag of clothes is on the bed waiting for me. "I was thinking," I say while I rummage through it, "I want you at my game tomorrow." I take out a shirt and a pair of jeans and after putting them on, I walk to Vickie and pull the towel from her body. She's definitely starting to show.

"Fine, I'll be there." She rolls her eyes and playfully shoves me away.

I wrap my arms around her from behind and cup her belly. "I want to marry you. Soon." I turn her around to face me. "Very soon. Next week soon."

She pulls my hands off and huffs. "You can never have enough, can you, champion? Your rogue sperm attaches itself to my egg, and now you want to club me over the head and drag me down the aisle."

I grab her chin and force her eyes on me. "I'm serious, Queen. I know we're already a family, but I want to make it official and legal."

She stares at me while she ponders my words. "Hear me out," she says, and I brace myself for a fight. She grabs her bra and covers her breasts. "I've been thinking about it."

"Oh, really?"

"Yes, really." She puts on a pair of jeans and a black V-neck sweater.

"And?"

"And if we're going to get married, I want to do it right. I want to feel good, and right now, I feel sick quite a lot. I also want to look good." She takes my hand. "I swear, I will deny it if you tell anyone, but I want to put on a wedding dress so beautiful and sexy, that you fall on your ass. I want to drink champagne and dance with you. I want to cringe at whatever stupid joke Alan tells when he makes a speech. I want to take Mary Leigh shopping for her mother of the groom dress. I want to recite my own wedding vows, and then I want us to go to a family friendly resort for our honeymoon because I'm not leaving Evan and this baby behind."

I shake my ear and pretend to knock debris out of it. I pull her in my arms and lift her off her feet. "And this dress, what color is it going to be? White?"

"Whatever damn color I choose," she huffs. "And there's one more thing." She gets serious again. She gestures to the bed and we both sit. "If you say no, my feelings won't be hurt. In fact, I'll never mention it again, okay?" I lift her hand and kiss it and wait. "Maybe, we can consider—" She stops and looks down as if she's gathering her thoughts. She's never been nervous to speak her mind before, so that unsettles me.

"What is it? You know I'd never deny you anything."

"How would you feel about the possibility of me, down the line, maybe talking to Evan about me adopting him? If you say no, I'll drop it. If *he* says no, I'll never bring it up again." She stops and stares into my eyes. This is the first time she's ever been nervous about a reaction from me. I lean down and rest my forehead on hers.

"The most traditional woman on earth. I knew it the moment I saw you." I cup her cheeks and stare into the most beautiful eyes I've ever seen. "Yes. I would love nothing more than for you to be his mother." She rests her head on my shoulder.

"Of course, I don't want to replace her. I'll honor her memory in every way."

"I know you will. I was not worried about it."

"But let's give him some time to get used to me and a new sibling."

"Deal. Now, there's one thing I want. What you talked about earlier is a wedding. We'll have whatever wedding you want when the baby is born, but I want a marriage. Right now."

NO ONE IS SURPRISED WHEN WE WALK INTO THE kitchen together holding hands. In fact, John says, "It's about time. I was tired of pretending I didn't know. Colt, get my daughter some breakfast."

"Yes, sir. Whatever my queen wants." I turn to Victoria and say, "I am but your lowly servant." I bow, and she throws a napkin at me. I pull a chair out for her and ask the chef for oatmeal and fresh berries, a favorite of hers. I sit next to her, intertwine our fingers, and bring her hand to my lips, relieved to finally be able to do that with the family.

Family. This is my family now. I never could have predicted this a year ago, or even months ago when I went to the Taylor family home for the first time.

The boys come running into the kitchen with Alan chasing behind them.

"Well?" her dad says to us.

Alicia and Cheryl both look on, anxiously waiting.

"Since when is this family so old fashioned?" Vickie asks.

"Since always. So, now what?" her dad insists.

"Now, I ask you for your daughter's hand in marriage." The words are barely out of my mouth when Vickie elbows me hard in the ribs.

"Chastain, I warned you about asking my father for any part of my anatomy."

"Permission granted," her father says.

Her eyes widen in shock when I drop to one knee and pull the ring out of my jeans pocket.

"Yes, I've been walking around with this thing since you went to Mexico." I clear my throat and begin my speech. "Victoria, my queen. Since the day I laid eyes on you—"

"Oh my God, enough with the drama! Yes!" she screams. "Give me my ring!" She holds out her ring finger, and I slide the ring on. The instant I do, I stand and she jumps into my arms, tears streaming down her face. The entire kitchen cheers, and the women pull her away from me to admire the new jewelry. It's a five-carat yellow solitaire diamond. It's beautiful and rare just like her.

"We're still planning Tara's wedding, so I want to wait until after I have the baby for a big wedding, but Colt wants to get married now," she tells everyone.

"I've always liked Colt," John says.

I give him a fist bump.

"Let me and Cheryl plan something," Alicia says.

"Yes. Please," Cheryl insists.

"Okay, but you have to include Colt's mom. How soon? Just family."

"Give us a couple of weeks," Alicia says.

"Colt, call Mama," Vickie says, and my heart almost bursts.

She smiles and shrugs.

"I'm so going to marry you," I whisper in her ear.

"Whatever. I don't love you," Vickie whispers back.

"I don't love you either. Not even a little bit."

SIXTY-TWO

Colt

THREE WEEKS. THAT'S HOW LONG IT TAKES FOR OUR mothers to plan our wedding. We told them we wanted a justice of the peace and the immediate family. I don't know what they heard, but that's not what we got. Ethan is letting us use one of his family homes in Sand's Point. Home is an understatement. It's a palatial estate that sits on acres of land and overlooks the ocean. It's the middle of December, in frigid temperatures, and it just snowed this morning, giving the place added beauty.

I'm not sure if our moms tricked us into having a wedding instead of a civil ceremony but I'm happy. Instead of just close family, our moms invited the entire team and about two dozen people from Alabama, even though Mama's hinting that we have a huge wedding next year there also. I actually love the idea, and since they were inviting everyone, I made sure Myra received an invitation too. Our moms didn't want a justice of the peace, so Mama flew in Reverend Richards, and Cheryl got their pastor from their church. Both men are waiting at the makeshift altar under the heated tent in the back of the mansion, surrounded by white roses and blanketed in soft lighting.

Now, Myra sees me and limps over. She's in a frilly, red dress with a wide collar. She even has a flower in her hair.

"Myra, I've never seen you look prettier," I tell her.

She blushes and takes my hands. "You look so handsome. I'm so happy for you, Mr. Colt. So happy." She looks around and waves over a young woman who is sitting in the last row. She stands, but I can tell she'd rather be anywhere but here. She's dressed in all black, more appropriate for a funeral than a wedding. "This is my daughter, Jeannie. Jeannie, this is Mr. Colt." Jeannie offers me her hand.

"Congratulations on your wedding," she says, looking unimpressed, but she does give me a genuine smile. She's a younger, prettier version of Myra with clear brown skin and big eyes.

"Thank you, Jeannie. Welcome." She walks to the back and takes a seat. From the corner of my eye, I see her pull out a book. There are about a dozen NBA players here and she couldn't care less. Good for her.

I guess Vickie's friend Tamron has that covered. She's in the corner between three of my teammates talking and laughing.

"You ready?" Charlie asks. "Mama's been frettin' like a mother hen all darn week. She's cried about five times today."

It's supposed to be casual, but Mama insists I wear a dark gray suit and tie. She also orders Charlie to stand next to me at the altar. I know what she's doing, but I'm too happy to fight with her today. I'm getting married, and nothing can go wrong.

I take my position at the altar as the room fills and everyone takes a seat. Coach Walsh sits in the back. He stares at Jeannie, who has yet to look up from her book. Whatever she's reading must be engrossing.

Cheryl and Alicia are escorted to their seats by Alan, and Mama by Evan. Tara and Ethan are next as they hold Vincent's hand. The room goes silent when John escorts Vickie down the aisle and I almost fall over when I see what she's wearing. It's the white mink that I sent to her in Mexico. She also has the tiara on top of her curly hair. Maybe it's the coat or the tiara. Or maybe it's the healthy glow of her pregnancy, but she's never been more beautiful. I don't realize I'm crying until Charlie hands me a handkerchief.

The mink is so long, it almost brushes the floor. The coat is open, revealing a curve hugging white dress with a long slit in the side. The dress also nearly brushes the ground, but I still catch a peek of her stilettos covered in rhinestones. She looks regal, just like my queen should.

"Did you get her that coat?" Charlie whispers in my ear. I nod, unable to take my eyes off her. "See? I told you."

When she gets to me, Tara takes the coat from her sister, and my knees nearly buckle at her beauty. I grab her hands and the ceremony is a blur. We kept the vows traditional, promising to recite our own at the next wedding. Minutes later, we're pronounced man and wife and I take her in a kiss.

"Alan's my uncle now," I hear Evan shout.

"I don't love you," I whisper against her mouth.

"I've never loved you less."

"Look at Mama dancing with Wakowski," Vickie whispers. "He can barely keep up with her. He's not acting like a man who needs to take three paternity tests soon." I look away from that scene. Wakowski is dancing way too close to my mother.

Dinner's been served and everyone is either dancing or drinking. Even Charlie is having fun talking with Alicia and Myra. Alan watches Tilly from across the room, practically drooling. Unfortunately for him, she brought a date.

After dinner and cake, the boys go upstairs with their nannies to watch movies, and the adults are left to enjoy the party.

"Everyone is having fun except for two people," Vickie whispers. "Call Coach over." I gesture for him to come over, and he leaves his spot against the wall. His hair is down as usual, making him look a bit like a Viking.

He shakes my hand and hugs Vickie. "Congrats again, guys. It's a nice party." He hasn't cracked a smile all night. I'd hate to see his face if it was a bad party.

"Let's get a drink." Vickie wraps an arm around his and practically drags him away. She's up to something, so I follow. On the way to the bar, she stops at Jeannie's table. She's all alone, still reading her book.

"Hey, Jeannie," Vickie says, with a big smile. Jeannie slams the book shut and stuffs it in her purse before I can read the title. She stands, looking a little embarrassed. "Have you met Colt's coach, Aidan?"

Jeannie seems surprised by the question but offers him her hand. He takes it, practically drowning it in his much larger one. He lifts it and kisses her knuckles. She clears her throat loudly and yanks her hand away.

"So, you ah, coach football?" Jeannie asks.

Vickie giggles and I cackle.

"Basketball," Coach corrects.

"Are you sure?" Jeannie asks. "My mom said you're a football player," she says to me.

Vickie tries to hide her laugh but fails.

"I'm going to have a talk with Myra," I say with a smile.

"Yeah, and I'm pretty sure I coach basketball and not football," Aidan says to her.

"Oh." Jeannie waves her hand in dismissal. "I don't watch either," she says and starts to walk away.

"More of a reader, I see," Coach responds. "What book has you so engrossed?"

Her eyes dart to her purse. I'm pretty sure she's double checking to make sure that the book is hidden. "Nothing you would find particularly interesting." She clears her throat, but she holds Coach's stare

"Try me," he says. She takes a step toward the table, grabs her purse, and shoves it underneath her chair. Vickie lets out a little snicker.

"I know what it is," Vickie says. "It's Jeannie's copy of the women's guidebook on how to take over the world and kick the men out."

Jeannie smiles for the first time in hours. She puts a finger to her lips and says, "Shh. That's supposed to be a secret."

"Should we be worried?" Coach asks, smiling so wide I barely recognize him.

"Very," Jeannie says.

"Why don't you two get a drink or more dessert? Coach, escort the lady," Vickie suggests. "And ask her to dance."

"Oh, that's not necessary. I've had enough and—" Jeannie starts to stammer, but Coach offers her his arm, and she stands like a deer in headlights. She finally takes it, and they walk away.

"He's been staring at her all night. I had to do something," Vickie says.

I take my wife's hands and pull her into my arms. "Mrs. Chastain," I whisper.

"The name's still Taylor."

"You are playing matchmaker at your wedding to a celebrity athlete who was also a single dad. I told you I was taking home the championship in this relationship, Queen."

Her mouth flies open. "Is that what you meant by that? You knew you wanted to marry me then?"

"I'll tell you a secret," I whisper close to her ear. "I knew I wanted to marry you way before that."

"When?"

"That's for me to know."

Hours later, in the honeymoon suite at The Plaza, I sit on the chair like she orders. She's been in the bathroom for ten minutes, and I'm so ready to slide inside of her, I could burst. Our non-wedding turned into a full reception of cake, toasts, food, and dancing. I've never seen Vickie so happy, and when Tara talked about the night we met, Vickie laughed so hard, I thought she was going to fall out of her chair.

"Mrs. Chastain! Hurry up! Your husband is horny."

"Classy! And the name's still Taylor!" she yells back. She's already agreed to change it, but she tells me she'll get around to it when she feels like it. I'll make sure she's ready by Monday. That's about the longest I'm willing to wait.

The door to the bathroom opens and music starts to play. She comes out wrapped in the fur coat. She slowly unties the sash, all the while swaying to the sound of the music. She opens the coat, and I nearly pass out. She's in a white lace teddy that shows more skin than it covers. She lifts her leg to show me that it's crotchless. I lick my lips at her and gesture at my erection.

She straddles me, and my hands cover her ass. She's put on weight in all the right places. Her belly is finally starting to stick out, and I can't stop touching it.

"You like?" she whispers above my lips.

"I love. Where did you get this thing?" The top is a tight corset, and it pushes her breasts together. The entire thing is like a wet dream.

"Mama," she whispers.

I can feel my eyes widen in shock. "Mama? Whose mama? Not mine."

"Yours. She has a wild side and I'm going to get it out of her."

"As much as I love how you two love each other, can we not talk about her now?" She grinds on top of me and gives me a slow, deep kiss.

"I'm going to fuck my husband while wearing this coat."

"I see you like this thing, huh. I had no idea. I was just desperate."

"I love it."

"I'll get it for you in black too." She kisses me

"Yes, please. You know what else I love?"

"Me?"

"I guess." She rolls her eyes, and I squeeze one of her butt cheeks. "I was talking about our wedding. I loved it, and all we had to do was show up. Tara even picked out my clothes. We don't need another wedding."

I kiss her deep, making her moan in my mouth. I can feel her pebbled nipples on my bare chest, and all I want to do is slide inside of her.

"Oh, darlin'. Mama already has her heart set on a big wedding in Alabama, but if you can tell her no, go ahead."

"Will you back me up?"

"No, absolutely not. I never say no to my mama."

"Mama's boy. And I see how it's going to be." I put my hand over her stomach and caress it, marveling at the life that we created together.

"It's Mama first around here. Always. Now, call me your husband again." I lift her and let her slide down, ensconcing me in her velvet walls.

"Kiss your wife, husband," she whispers.

"Whatever my wife wants."

"Who can possibly be calling us right now?" she moans while she rests on top of me. She bites the chocolate covered strawberry and offers me the rest. We've been in bed since last night. We ordered room service for breakfast because I couldn't bear for her to put on clothes. Her teddy is long gone, ripped to shreds in my need to have her. It's lunchtime, and I promised her we'd go out, but neither one of us are in a hurry. She reaches for her phone.

"Why are you calling me?" she asks, then she bursts into giggles. "I'm going to put you on speaker."

"What are you doing?" Tara asks. "I miss you guys."

"I'm eating chocolate off my husband's chest," Vickie says. "I've found his weakness. He's eaten about six chocolate covered strawberries today."

"Hardly a secret," I say. "And this is the second best chocolate I've eaten today." I take another strawberry and savagely bite it. She looks at me in shock, then we both burst into laughter.

"I really didn't need to hear that," Tara says.

"That's the risk you take when you interrupt our honeymoon. We only get two days since he has that stupid game tomorrow." It's an away game, and I fly out tonight. I was going to miss it, but she insists I go, but she's coming with me, so it's not too bad.

"I'll let you go. Love you both," Tara says, and Vickie ends the call. It rings again almost immediately.

"Are you kidding me?" I groan.

"It's Mama," she says. "Maybe it's Evan." I snort. It's definitely not Evan. It's just our nosy family. "Hey, Mama," she says. "Everything okay?"

"Everything's great. Just checking on you two. You feelin' okay with the morning sickness?" It's never gone away, but it's manageable. "You have to make sure you eat regularly." She's right, otherwise she gets sick.

"We're good," I tell her. "Just about to leave for lunch." I cup my wife's bare butt and Vickie mouths 'liar.' We're both stark naked. We won't be going anywhere until we shower and wash the smell of sex off our bodies.

"Don't worry about a thing. Everything is fine here. We'll see you in a couple of days."

"Thanks for calling us to say nothing's wrong, Mama." Vickie bites my chest, but I still hear her muffled giggles.

"You're welcome, honey," Mama says, completely oblivious to my sarcastic tone.

"Forget going out," Vickie says after ending the call and tossing the phone to the floor. "Room service will have to suffice, but I'm having dessert first." She slides down my body and takes me into her mouth.

THE END

EPILOGUE

"It won't be the same this year without you at all my away games for the playoffs," I complain to my wife. I play Boston tomorrow, and we arrived late last night. I reach over and cover her protruding belly with my hand. She's seven and a half months pregnant now, and I can't stop touching her. Our son or daughter rewards me with a kick. This is the last time she'll be traveling with me until the baby is born.

"Ugh! The things you've done to me, Chastain. Either I'm going to your dumb games or I'm incubating your baby." She tries to playfully shove my hand away, but I pull her closer and plant a loud kiss on her cheek.

"My traditional wife, supporting her husband." I grasp her chin, and she tilts her face up for a kiss.

"Am not. Bite your tongue. I'm a rebel. Remember that."

"The pregnant mother of my children." I press my forehead on hers. "I always knew it would be like this."

"Caveman."

She comes to all my home games, but she stays home

with Evan when I'm away. She's only with me now because it's spring break, and Evan is spending time with Tara, Ethan, and Vincent.

My driver pulls up to a brownstone. It's bigger than I thought, but this is Ethan. He's always going to have the best. I step out first and help her out of the car. The door of the house swings open and Evan runs down the steps. I pick him up and spin him around. I put him near Vickie's face, and he kisses her cheek.

"Come inside," he says, once I set him down. "Vincent's new uncle is here and he's teaching us to fight. He got us boxing gloves."

I take Vickie's hand in mine, and we follow Evan up the steps. Once we're in, I help her with her coat. The television is on, but I hear talking and laughter from the back of the house.

"Surprise!" Alan takes his sister into a hug, but Tara pushes him away and hugs Vickie. She then leans down and kisses her belly. Ethan follows behind, along with his sister, Elizabeth who has her arm wrapped around a guy who's an exact replica of Ethan, only younger. He's holding the hand of a woman.

"Colt, Vickie," Tara begins, "this is Adam Flynn and his wife Melanie. As you've heard, Adam is Ethan and Elizabeth's little brother."

He might be younger, but he's not little. He's taller than Ethan, and he looks like a trained athlete. He gives us a firm handshake.

"The prodigal brother," Vickie says. "Welcome to the family. I'm Vickie Chastain, and this is my husband, Colt."

"You know what it does to me when you call yourself Vickie Chastain," I whisper in her ear.

"Tone it down, Neanderthal," she whispers back.

"And my daddy," Evan says. "Can we go fight now?" My son and Vincent are both holding boxing gloves.

"Adam's teaching the boys to box," Ethan says. "Go ahead, guys. There's a makeshift gym downstairs with a new punching bag."

"Come on, Uncle Adam." Vincent snatches Adam's hand from Melanie and starts to pull him.

Alan clears his throat and says, "I guess old Uncle Alan will just wait here." Vickie rolls her eyes at her brother. "With the women."

"Do you want to come?" Adam asks Alan.

"I mean, I guess." Alan shrugs in disinterest. "Are these lessons just for the kids?"

"Do you need to learn?" Adam asks.

"I already know almost everything about boxing, but it will be nice to get someone else's perspective."

Vickie and Tara both snicker.

"Sure you do, twin," Vickie says.

"Come on then," Adam says. He walks away with the boys, and Alan follows.

"Who can't fight now?" Alan says to his sisters.

"Just remember when you make a fist that the thumb goes on the outside," Tara yells at him. Alan gives her the middle finger and leaves."

The rest of us follow Tara into the kitchen while she prepares lunch. Melanie volunteers to help, and I pull out a chair for my wife.

"When's the baby due?" Melanie asks.

"Six weeks," I announce.

"How long have you been married?" she asks.

"Less time than I've been pregnant," Vickie answers. "His sperm attached itself to my egg. Didn't bother to ask permission."

"Rude," Melanie says.

"Sorry, not sorry," I say.

"I know. I like you." Vickie stands and approaches Melanie. "We're going to be good friends."

That afternoon, in the privacy of our hotel room, my wife braids my hair for the game and massages my shoulders until I fall asleep. That's our tradition whenever she's with me before a game. I don't know how I ever played before this.

∼

Six Weeks Later

She leans over the bed, and I put my hand on her lower back. She shoves it away.

"You're not going to make it out of this hospital alive, Chastain." Oh, boy. I bite my bottom lip to stifle my amusement. Another contraction hits and she cries out in pain. I rub her lower back and whisper soothing words in her ear. "You're dead. Dead Chastain walking. How dare you do this to me, and you stand there in all your male glory while I endure this pain. Before I kill you, I'm going to rip your balls off so you can feel just a fraction of the pain I'm feeling."

The nurse lets out a chuckle, and I offer no words in my defense. The contractions started two hours ago, and she was already eight centimeters dilated when we arrived, making it too late for an epidural.

"Let's get you in bed, Mrs. Chastain. The doctor is going to see if you're ready to push." Her eyes go wide as if the very idea is ridiculous. She grabs my collar.

"No. Don't let them do this to me, Colt. I'll let you live

if you make them go away. I can't do this. I can't. I'll just walk around with this baby inside of me until he's old enough to go to college." She blows a breath upward. "Why did your sperm have to go rogue? This is all your fault, and I'm going to make you pay. My uterus was on ice!" She looks around the room like a crazed lunatic.

I remove her hands from my collar and take one in mine. I bring it to my lips and kiss it.

"The baby's coming, Queen. I'll be with you the entire time. You can do this." She shoves me away.

"You do it, then. You push it out. I have nothing left in me." She spouts more nonsense while I help the nurse get her into bed.

"All our family is out there waiting on you to give them another child to spoil. You can do this, Queen Vee." She's in the bed, looking around wildly. Dr. Jenkins steps in, smiling as if Victoria's reaction is nothing new. She covers her legs, puts on her gloves, and checks her cervix.

"Time to push, Vickie. This baby is ready for the world. Colt, take her hand."

"I'm not ready, Dr. Jenkins. I need another week or two. A month at the most."

"You have about fifteen minutes until you meet your baby. On the count of three, push."

Ten minutes later, our baby boy comes out screaming louder than the beautiful woman who pushed him out.

"Why does he look just like you?" Vickie asks from the bed. Our son, John Philip Taylor Chastain, came out weighing exactly nine pounds. He's currently being cradled by Grandma Alicia, who snatched him from

Grandma Cheryl. Everyone is playing musical baby with our son, and I've barely gotten to hold him. Mama already says she's next, even though she held him for about an hour earlier.

"Because he's my boy," I say with pride.

"I did all the work. And he peed on me earlier when I changed his diaper. He should look more like me."

"He has your nose." He doesn't. He's my spitting image, but I tell my wife that to appease her. "And your lungs." She swats my chest. "I've never heard a baby wail so loud before in my life."

"You're lucky I let you live."

"I am always at the mercy of my queen," I say.

The baby starts to fuss in Alicia's arms.

"Can I hold him next, Mom? The grandmas have been hogging him," Evan says. Each time he calls her mom, I want to cry. We brought up the idea of Vickie adopting him after we got back from Boston. We both wanted to give him time to adjust—not just to her, but to having a sibling. We were so nervous about his reaction. Vickie was expecting him to say no, or to ask more questions, but the conversation didn't go as we thought it would.

HE LOOKS FROM ME TO VICKI AFTER SHE TELLS HIM SHE *wants to adopt him.*

"It doesn't mean you have to forget your mother. In fact, we'll make sure that you don't. We will talk about her whenever you want, and you know you can always call your other grandma too. She loves you as much as we do." Isabel is the only one who has a problem with Vickie adopting Evan. She

hung up the phone on me when I told her and has refused to speak of it again.

Evan stays quiet, and I can tell Vickie is bracing herself for his rejection.

"Can I call you mom?" I look at her, and she's just as surprised as I am by his response.

"Of course, you can. I'll be your mother."

"You'll be my mom just like you'll be the baby's mom?" He's excited about having a sibling and has been since we told him.

"Just like that," Vickie says. "You'll both be my kids."

"Because Jack says his stepmom only likes her new baby and not him. I don't want that. I want a real mom. Like when you took care of me when I was sick. I liked that. I like how you come to all my games and how you get me ready for school in the morning. I don't want that to change." I inch away from Vickie so she won't pinch me, but my heart breaks for my son.

She moves closer to Evan and puts an arm over his shoulder. She pulls him close and kisses his hair.

"Those things will never change. I love you as much as your little brother or sister. I'm always going to take care of you. In every way. We're going to still do things together, just me and you. I'm already your mom, but adoption will make it legal. Nothing else will change between us."

"You promise?" I can hear the hope in his voice.

"I promise."

We both hold our breath while we wait to hear what he says next.

"Do I have to wait until you adopt me to call you mom? Alan let me call him uncle before you married my dad."

"You can call me mom whenever you want."

He shrugs and says, "Can you take me to the park to ride

my bike, Mom?" He wraps his arms around her, and she squeezes him tight. I see the tears pool in her eyes.

"Let's go, Son," she croaks. "You coming, Daddy?"

~

"Can I have him? I want to try to nurse again." Vickie opens her arms and Alicia gently puts the baby down.

"Watch his head," she says.

"That's our cue to leave," Alan says. "Let's go, men. Evan, let's go get a snack."

"Fine, but I'm holding my namesake when I get back," Vickie's dad says before all the guys but me leave the room. Vickie puts the baby to her breast, and when he latches on, she sighs in relief.

"I so don't love you," I whisper.

"I've never loved anyone less," she whispers back.

THE END

Can't get enough of Vickie and Colt? Sign up for my newsletter and get this bonus epilogue.

https://dl.bookfunnel.com/rirug0bx4n

Want to learn more about Tara and Ethan? Check out their story here.

amzn.to/3tobGay

ACKNOWLEDGMENTS

I have a confession to make. When I first wrote Takeover, I was so nervous to release it. A couple of times, I considered just shelving it. Who would have thought I'd be here now with two of Takeover's side characters? I knew who Vickie was going into this book, but Colt was a different story.

He started to speak to me over time. I asked myself, what kind of man would make Vickie want to run screaming in the opposite direction. The answer came to me. A southern boy who lives his life in the spotlight. On paper, they are complete opposites, but as the story unfolded, I hope you recognized that they are not all that different.

I grew to love these two, and as always, it's been incredibly hard to let them go. Hopefully, we'll see them again in future books as supporting characters. 😊

I want to take a minute and thank my group of supporters.

To my good friends, Amy, KC, Sheree, Kiki, Erin, Unique, Simone, Suzan and Lanie. Thank you so much for reading, listening, and providing feedback. You're invaluable.

To all the readers who keep coming back for more, THANK YOU SO MUCH! There are not enough words to express how much I appreciate every single last one of you. Stay tuned.

ABOUT THE AUTHOR

A Boston native, wife, mother, and wine enthusiast. If she's not writing, thinking about writing, you will find Evelyn with a book in her hands. While a new publisher, she's been writing for years, and she will continue to write for many years to come.

Evelyn is obsessed with assertive and confident men who will stop at nothing to get their woman. Her stories are filled with love, passion and humor.

She currently lives in Chicago, IL with her husband and two daughters.

CONNECT WITH EVELYN

Let's stay in touch!! You can find me here:

Readers' Group - Evelyn's Entourage - Evelyn's Entourage | Facebook

IG - Evelyn Sola (@evelynwriteseveryday) is on Instagram

Amazon - Evelyn Sola

TikTok - Evelyn (@authorevelynsola) TikTok | Watch Evelyn's Newest TikTok Videos

ALSO BY EVELYN SOLA

The Clark Family Series:

Crave

Cherish

Crash

Unwrapped - A holiday romance

Broken - A second chance romance

Takeover - An enemies to lovers, single dad romance

Make Me - A small town, single mom romance

Takedown - An accidental marriage romance

Coming soon:

Downfall - An age gap, office romance

Printed in Great Britain
by Amazon